DAVID PALIN

THE SCORPION ARCHIPELAGO

A CHILLING THRILLER OF LOST CIVILISATIONS AND BURIED TRUTHS

The Scorpion Archipelago
Published in 2026 by
Matthew James Publishing
(an imprint of Andrews UK Limited)
West Wing Studios
Unit 166, The Mall,
Luton, LU1 2TL

www.matthewjamespublishing.com

My heartfelt thanks, as ever,
to my publisher for their support.

Also to Sarah, my partner, for her patience
as I indulge my love of writing instead of gardening!

CHAPTER ONE

The cigarette perched between Pete's lips scrawled the surreal, smoky shapes of his words in the air as he spoke.

"So, what is the old... chap up to then?"

Ash dropped onto his shirt cuff and he cursed, flicking it away in irritation then scrutinising the material for any hint of a stain.

"He's not up to anything," Jane bridled in the en-suite bathroom where she was applying mascara. "This dinner party's been on the cards for a long time." She could have volunteered a little more information, remembering her father's words when the original invitation had been mooted, but didn't feel inclined. The two men just couldn't seem to get along. As she was the reason they needed to interact on very rare occasions, she tended towards a mixture of guilt and defensiveness when either of them was at all critical of the other, coming down on the side of the absent party most of the time. The flaw in that tactic was the impossibility of choosing a side at family gatherings, which made things awkward in the extreme, leaving her feeling like a United Nations peacekeeper. However, though both men were proud, only one of them was arrogant, which simplified matters in her head if nothing else.

"Damned inconvenient, sweetheart." The term of endearment was perfunctory at best; at worst, condescending.

In the mirror Jane saw Pete struggling with his bow tie and couldn't deny her distaste at the way he squinted through the cigarette smoke. The circles in which he aspired to move meant he would never have dreamed of wearing a clip-on, though he always had problems tying the real McCoy, but it seemed he gave no thought to what his would-be peers might think of him smoking as he dressed. Still, she was past commenting.

"A long time," she re-emphasised, returning to the theme of dinner. "It has priority over your poker night. By the way, don't forget your toiletries. Remember, we might be staying over. Don't know how late – or drunk – it will get."

"Mmmm." He stopped what he was doing and gave the tie an abrupt jerk, ripping it from round his neck. Seemed he'd decided it wasn't worth the effort after all, just for dinner at her father's. "Never can do these damn things."

"Well, you don't have to. No-one said it was a James Bond themed party."

The dagger in his look just about stayed sheathed. "I'm going to get a bourbon. You want one?"

"No, one of us had better stay sober – at least for the drive there." She didn't know whether he heard the reply, as he was already halfway down the stairs, though the second part of her response had been in an ironic whisper. It looked like she was driving again. "Shouldn't you be drinking a Martini instead; shaken, not shtirred?" she muttered, grinning at her attempted Sean Connery accent. *He* would always be Bond for her; her husband's blonde, ripped looks might do it for some women, but it would never do for 007.

Jane stepped out of the bathroom, caught sight of herself in the full-length mirror and got a surprise. It was like looking at a stranger.

"Not bad for forty," she whispered, "though I say it myself." Then she experienced a frisson of regret. She straightened up and moved across to stand in front of the mirror. "Who knows how things might have been, old girl..." The impromptu discussion with her reflection stopped for a moment as she heard Peter's epithet pass her lips. Then, with a sigh, she continued anyway. "What if you'd allowed yourself to be something other than that geeky, studious girl; had let your hair down a bit – what there is of it?" She ran her fingers through it, noting with a twinge of sadness the practical shortness. Peering at herself again, she smiled at the irony of having a reflective moment in front of a mirror. Jane put her fingertips to her face. Her skin was, to her mind, over-tanned, though not by choice, and prone to dryness; the result of spending most of her life al fresco in hot climates – but she didn't scrub up too badly, in her self-critical opinion.

She pressed her lips together in momentary annoyance; this self-evaluation was out of character, so why now? Not even when she'd passed forty a few weeks before had she bothered to wallow in self-pity; her first concern that particular morning had been for a rare Coptic manuscript, not her ancient self. Her interest in the past tended to exclude her own – she wasn't someone given to backward glances in her story, just history – but as she heard the clink of ice dropping into a glass downstairs, she wondered if that was because she didn't dare to look.

Whatever her motivation it seemed, right now, she needed to take stock of what faced her: accentuate the positives and, just for once, see what today offered, instead of yesterday.

Appraising her strong, slender figure – the plus side of an active life – she gave it a curt nod of approval. There were no regrets about the lack of children in her marriage but, glancing towards the stairs, she knew that decision had not been reached for all the right reasons.

She shook her head. Damn it all, she'd reached the top of her chosen field. One couldn't excel at everything.

Perhaps she would have a drink after all. Sighing, she smoothed the front of her outfit, taking some pleasure from the flatness of her stomach, and then headed downstairs to the lounge.

"If the offer's still open..."

Pete turned from the French windows and went over to the drinks cabinet.

There was no denying that Pete and she did have at least one thing in common – a curiosity about that evening's dinner. Jane didn't want an atmosphere to spoil things, so she settled on the sofa and took the proffered drink with grace.

"Really, I know nothing about this evening other than Father's making good on a promise. I'm as much in the dark as you." Pete grunted, unconvinced. "Ever since he confirmed the invitation, he's shrouded the event in secrecy."

"Does this mean he'll be making one of his 'announcements'?" Pete drew exaggerated inverted commas in the air. The sarcasm was unmistakable, but despite herself Jane smiled.

"You mean, waiting until the break between dessert and coffee, tapping his glass and cracking some poor joke before getting round to the business in hand."

In that sense her father was predictable – and that was cool by her. Mariners of old needed mooring posts as much as they needed the stars. It wasn't good when the only certainty was unpredictability.

Both she and Pete laughed at the image of her father's harmless showmanship, but the effect of that rare moment of togetherness was immediate and awkward. All that was missing from the ensuing silence – as Pete resumed his stance by the window and Jane examined the contents of her glass – was the desolate howl of the freezing Antarctic wind.

Her roving mind moved on, though it would return to that same spot of darkness soon enough. Her irritation with Pete was an ongoing thing – she lived with it like backache – but in recent times she had sensed something lurking just out of the light, some presence, and she couldn't shake the feeling it was creeping up on her again. She remembered seeing the mist of its breath a couple of months before, as she had studied that amphora, trying to decipher its code. She had looked over her shoulder, wondering... well, she wasn't sure now exactly what she *had* been wondering.

She glanced at Pete, still standing by the window. At what point in a relationship did a cigarette dangling with studied carelessness from the lips stop looking raffish and insouciant, and become coarse, taking you from East of Eden to the East End? Likewise, she pondered which parent had passed on the proud gene that had prevented her from admitting it was so.

CHAPTER TWO

"What do ye see, Cap'n?"

"I see a ship full of scared men, Mr Perkins, trying to outrun us..." Captain Henry Black chuckled in jovial triumph, revealing teeth of surprising whiteness as he continued squinting down the telescope, before adding: "at last."

"What do ye mean 'at last'?" On occasion Perkins forgot to use Black's title; they had long ago swapped the naval ensign for the skull and crossbones. He always remembered when in earshot of the crew, but they had shared too much – adventures, booty, women, even diseases – for their friendship to be affected by his minor disrespect.

Black clapped the old salt on the shoulder. "I mean that after almost a month at sea they've finally realised they can't outfox Captain Henry Black. We've got 'em."

Perkins rasped a hand across his stubbled cheeks and frowned. "But they're 'eading north, Cap'n. Thought ye said 'ome was likely somewhere in the south."

Black peered again into his telescope. "They're desperate, so they're running before the wind, no matter the direction. They've just made their second mistake."

"What was the first?"

"Letting me see that fine cargo they're carrying."

Perkins continued to look puzzled, which had the peculiar effect of turning his lazy right eye even further off beam. "Cap'n, I can't believe we've been trackin' back and for'ds across the devil's own sea, like a flea in Neptune's beard, for the contents of their 'old." He looked sidelong at Black, who lowered the telescope, winked, and in doing so sparked into life the fading handsomeness of his saturnine features.

"Well, ye know me, my friend." He gazed towards the distant ship across the broiling ocean – perhaps the most furious waters known to man. "I'm curious, Mr Perkins, about that strange ship, about its crew and about where in God's name they're going. I want to know why they've led us this merry jig. It vexes me, Mr Perkins. Why risk being caught out here, far from sanctuary, rather than head back home? They must know we wouldn't risk sailing into their waters."

"Yer orders, Cap'n?"

"Full and by, Mr Perkins. Let these coves feel our breath on the backs of their necks."

As *The Black Wolf* turned, the crew met the full spite of the wind that scours the Southern Ocean. It was a monster roaring in their ears; beating salt-soaked wings as it swooped past, blowing the breath of icy death in their faces. But Black's men were spawn of that same beast. In many ways they lived for it as much as they died by its hands. Skilled sailors, they hauled and climbed and cursed, all the while clinging with tenacity to the tail of their sleek black quarry, which appeared to be labouring. More than once, the Captain had been unable to resist the joke of 'one Black ship chasing another'.

"They're not versed in the art of sailing close-hauled." Black continued watching his prey through the telescope as he spoke. "At least not with the grinning teeth of this corsair's cutwater at their backs. Old shellbacks like thee 'n' me can tell when a man's sailing scared."

On they went, giving more hours of their lives to the ocean. Then, all of a sudden, the sea-leathered lines around Black's eyes unfolded and widened. "Man overboard," he whispered, not wanting to panic his own crew by mistake.

A loose barrel on the deck of the other ship had rolled and knocked a deckhand over the rail. Black watched, his features turning grim and his voice angry. It was one thing to make your captives walk the plank, or keelhaul your men for indiscipline, but not returning for a fellow crewman in distress...? He raged. "They're not throwing him a line. God's blood, they're not turning 'er round, nor even 'eaving to, to save their shipmate!"

Back in Zanzibar, where Black had first spotted that mysterious vessel being loaded, a man standing on the deck had caught his attention; an imposing, muscular figure, but clearly not the captain, being clad quite unlike any mariner, in a kilt made of what looked for all the world like finest samite, interwoven with silver and gold. He seemed impervious to the coolness of the breeze, and his handsome but cruel face was framed by a burnished, horned helmet, from beneath which dark, hooded eyes had watched Black, making him nervous. Now, through his eyeglass, the pirate saw how that same man, whom he had taken to be a shaman of some sort, seemed to urge his terrified skipper to even greater speed, abandoning the flailing figure in the water to his doom.

Black felt his mouth go dry; this was against all the codes of sailing. As *The Black Wolf* approached the place where the man had gone overboard, the unfortunate wretch had already been taken by the unforgiving sea – also a creature of no conscience.

Now Perkins, who had run to the rail to look for the lost sailor, came hurtling back, shouting, but grinning, his few remaining teeth a testament to scurvy and syphilis, and his prominent eyes almost ready to pop out and roll across the deck.

"We're gaining fast, Cap'n!"

"Aye, Mr Perkins, *The Black Wolf* has never been outrun. And they're low in the water with all that cargo."

The wind and spray added to the rush of excitement; old salts never lost that fever and Black felt its presence pass through the men; a ghost walking amongst them, raising the hairs on their arms.

"Shall we prepare for boarding?"

Black pulled at his beard and considered. It wasn't the smooth lines of the other ship – unlike any he'd seen before – which had kept it from his clutches; he was curious about so many things that he was tempted just to continue following. *"What are you hiding,"* he asked in silence, *"and who are you, with your obscure tongue and your ancient, weary eyes?"* No-one in Zanzibar had known, or rather, they had refused to discuss it, just shrugging shoulders and casting nervous glances in the direction of the strangers, whose taut, lean-muscled bodies seemed to bear no signs of weary months at sea and contradicted the fatigue in their eyes.

But at that moment, the decision of whether to board or not was taken out of his hands as their prey decided to turn south again.

"They're testing us!" shouted Black to the crew. "Coming around and sailing close to the wind. Helm-a-starboard, lads, and haul 'em in! Show 'em you have skill and courage. I think they're trying to run for home."

The merchant ship was soon within their grasp again; the last, frantic ploy had failed. But *The Black Wolf* was in uncharted waters and from the crow's nest came words that froze the blood of Captain Henry Black:

"WHIRLPOOL! WHIRLPOOL! STRAIGHT AHEAD!"

Great currents had conjoined to form a seething maelstrom. Black bellowed the only orders he could as the universal roar of creation the primeval song of the Southern Ocean - was replaced by something altogether more demonic and carnivorous.

"TURN INTO THE WIND!"

In irons – the point at which a ship lost all momentum as it turned through a headwind – was usually the last place a sailor wanted to be, but for Black it was his only hope of stopping before the gaping maw of that whirling monster consumed them. In the face of the devil, the crew fought as best they could. They might have been tempted to think their fate was out of their hands, but those hands were weathered and tenacious, the ship held fast and they were able to set a new course, while all of them shouted oath-filled prayers to whichever demon protected *The Black Wolf.*

Once the ship was safe, despite the frenzy and the fear, Black gave other orders:

"Turn, men. Like all good mariners we must bare our heads – aye, even Captain Henry Black – and watch, out of respect for them as share our perils."

Black had lied with such vigour in his life that few who listened believed what he had to say in the years to come, but he swore that the crew of the doomed ship had sheeted out their sails rather than in.

"Aye," he would say with typical bombastic eloquence in some den of iniquity, warming to his theme as another brandy warmed *him*, "either they sailed that great black ship with purpose to its doom to protect their secrets, or they returned to the netherworld whence they came, for I looked through my telescope and saw the last man to sink beneath the waves raise his hand towards us in a sailor's farewell."

CHAPTER THREE

Because everyone knew something was afoot, for Jane the conversation over dinner was like the supporting act at a concert; pleasant enough, but not something in which one could lose oneself – except... there was also the conjecture about the missing guest, which did add a little to their anticipation. 'They' being her and her mother, Candice. Pete kept his opinion to himself. Whether he had one was a mystery, but not something on which Jane wasted time speculating. Her father, of course, chose to play his cards close to his chest, enjoying their frustration and taking apparent pleasure in the power of knowledge. His thick but tidy white beard and the reflection of the candlelight in his glasses provided a degree of mask-like cover, but she knew his features so well, despite the months they spent apart, and could tell that, for some reason, he was rather pleased with himself. However, even he could not hide his concern for the whereabouts of the missing guest.

At last, the doorbell rang and Candice left the table. Her voice was counterpointed by a deeper one, which was nevertheless pitched higher than usual due to the latecomer's embarrassment.

And then in he came, the man whom Jane knew – somehow just *knew* – she should have waited for and married. Beneath mousy, bed-head hair, which spoke of someone who eschewed mirrors, or at least was not prone to her latest insecurities, the face was familiar; had she seen it either in magazines, or on the TV? He was somewhat windswept and also a little hot and flustered; both descriptions which she was sure matched hers at that moment. She glanced to her left and saw this hadn't gone unnoticed by at least one pair of eyes at the table, maybe others too.

"Hello, everybody, I am *so* sorry." He extended his hand towards her father. "Professor Sutch, please accept my apologies."

"That's always been your problem, James. Need a man to be in the wrong place at the right time... never an issue. But turning up punctually for something prosaic like a meal – forget it." The late arrival opened his mouth to protest, but the Professor had been smiling as he spoke and pre-empted the response. "Everyone, this is James – well, Jim..." he looked at the guest who nodded his preference for the less formal approach, "... Bolton."

There was a sharp intake of breath from Jane. "I've seen your work. Yes, of course! Very impressive." Both of them blushed a little deeper. She realised they must have looked like two ascetics who had discovered a shared, subsumed passion for silk.

"Jim, this is my daughter Jane."

Jim shook her hand. "And I've seen *your* work. Incredible. I just frame a snapshot of the present; you give it context."

"Nonsense," protested Jane. "What you do opens up the here-and-now to the world. I like to feel I open up the past, but when it comes down to it—"

"Indeed," interrupted her father. Jane saw her own embarrassment reflected in Jim's features. "This is Jane's husband, Pete." The Professor may have had little time for his son-in-law, but manners were manners.

Jim shook hands with Pete. "Hi, nice to meet you."

There was a short silence. Then Candice gestured, first to the empty seat for Jim to take his place, then to the dishes. "Just tuck in."

Pete reached into his pocket and produced a packet of cigarettes, but after Jane returned his just-short-of-a-dagger glance from earlier, he put them away again. "So," he looked at everybody in turn, "is anybody going to tell me what the late Mr Bolton does?"

"I'd have thought the previous comments would have made it obvious." The Professor struggled to conceal his impatience.

"Sorry, I wasn't really paying attention. Painting or something, wasn't it?"

"Well, Peter," Sutch, put his elbows on the table and folded his hands under his chin with the air of a man who knew revenge was best served cold, "perhaps we can let the man himself do the honours."

Jim's fork stopped halfway to his mouth. "What... uh, oh, yes, I'm a photographer." The fork continued its journey.

"He's a photographer." Sutch gave a wry grin. "Yes - weddings, christenings, not to mention Pulitzer Prizes, the odd lucky snap in National Geographic, or Time magazine or equivalent."

"I see." Pete looked at Jane, "That explains a lot."

She frowned and returned his gaze. "What's that supposed to mean?"

"Why you've seen his work." Pete gestured with upturned palms and faux innocence in his eyes, to which his wolfish smile hadn't quite tuned in. He had her there. "I guess for every archaeologist digging up a small wall there's a photographer snapping it."

Jane felt herself getting hot; part embarrassment at her over-reaction and part anger. "You don't win Pulitzer Prizes just for photographing small walls, even supposing that's what archaeology is all about. And you don't win them as a Brit unless you're bloody good." She directed an apologetic glance at her father. "And you do for capturing the horrors of genocide in Rwanda." She paused. "For example."

"Oh, okay." As a needling response to his wife's apparent defensiveness the understated reply was effective. Pete turned to Jim. "Do you do any sport or leisure photography, powerboating or stock car racing? For example."

Jim shook his head, warming to his theme with winning naivety, seeming unaware of the moment's undercurrent. "No, there are guys who do a fantastic job of that sort of thing." He turned to Candice and gestured towards the plate. "This really is excellent." Now he returned to Pete. "For me, capturing the wilder spirit of nature or man is more important than any sporting or other staged drama – I use 'drama' in the loosest sense of course; that is, the sense in which it's overused by commentators and journalists."

Jane smiled to herself; so, the young man wasn't as gauche as he seemed and was more than capable of a put-down or two.

Jim continued. "Apart from anything else, you can't stage the things I go for. They're unique. You miss them, you might never get another chance." His green eyes grew distant and clouded for a moment. "Sometimes you wish you'd never had the chance, when you capture the lost and wounded eyes of a Tutsi woman who's been left for dead and lain there helpless as the militiamen murder and mutilate her family with their *pangas*, or another who's been raped and infected with HIV by a Hutu soldier." He put down his knife and fork and took a sip of wine, while his hair flopped forward, drawing a curtain across his emotions.

There was the faint but audible buzz of a mobile phone on 'discreet'. Jane shook her head.

Pete removed the mobile from his jacket pocket, glanced at it and frowned. "I'm just going to pop outside for a cigarette." He stood, before the ensuing pause could become a meaningful silence.

"Don't forget to come in again before coffee," said Sutch.

Don't bother to come back – Jane read the unspoken thought in her father's eyes and echoed the sentiments, but she knew he'd held back for her sake in front of the visitor. Then she stifled a grin of self-congratulation – the mention of coffee meant her father's timetable was running with the precision of the German railway network. Now she looked at Jim and allowed a full-blown smile to break out. He winked at her, which was the last thing Pete saw as he left the room.

CHAPTER FOUR

When Pete returned, still frowning, the cafetière was on the table and the conversation in a flow that didn't break as he took his place.

"Amazing!" It was obvious the Professor meant it. "I didn't realise you did underwater photography."

"Oh yes, it's just that my calling has been in other directions so far. But the El Jacinto Pat caves, well, they were a special challenge, and you know me and challenges, Professor."

"Indeed, indeed, Jim. And please call me Edward."

Pete's frown deepened.

Now Sutch took a breath, as if he was about to say something, but Jim interjected.

"Look, enough about me. What do you do then, Pete, apart from the powerboating, stock car racing and..." he grinned, "... I assume they are two of your pursuits."

So, he had the savoir faire to bring Pete in from the cold, noted Jane, who felt like she was held in a vice, not developing a simple crush.

"I have my own business."

"Really?"

"I import fine ceramics, mainly from Europe – Spain and Portugal in particular – and sell them in the UK and the States."

"Excellent. It's obviously doing well if you can afford to powerboat. Nice little bit of cash that must eat up."

Jane glanced at her father's face and read his thoughts again. It was cash that should have been securing a future for her. Instead, the inversion saw Jane as the successful breadwinner while her husband, aside from some rather precarious investments, indulged his whims for extreme sports. More recently, the gambling tables of the world had become his venture portfolios, in particular those on the Formula 1 circuit such as Estoril and Monaco, where it had proved oh-so-

13

convenient that purchasing trips coincided with the Grand Prix weekend.

"I make a living," Pete's grin needled Jane in its smugness, "enough to keep me in debt." The joke went unacknowledged. "A powerboat doesn't have to be all that expensive; ten thousand a year keeps you in the game."

"All that high-adrenaline stuff," Jim shook his head, "that wouldn't be for me."

"Yes, well of course, diving into the claustrophobic El Jacinto Pat caves, spying on machete-wielding Hutu militiamen - they're like church outings really."

Jim's mouth turned down, accompanied by a nod of acknowledgement. "Touché."

For Jane this was a unique moment. Her arrogant, emotionally indolent other half was not in the habit of caring where she was or what she was doing, but she could see something in his eyes. Was it a spark of green to match those of his perceived rival? Jim couldn't have needled Pete more if he'd turned up in an Aston Martin wearing a tuxedo. But her usual instinct for self-deprecation kicked in. Who was she to assume jealousy or rivalry anyway? Even if Jim were competing for her attention in some way – she felt a blush rising at the thought – wasn't Pete's reaction just like a dog's over a bone? Still, it was flattering if it were so.

Again, she wondered what was wrong with her tonight. First there had been the assessment of her body and looks, and now she had developed an instantaneous need for a man a few years younger than her. More than once since Jim's arrival she had caught her mind wandering, imagining things that had caused her to tingle in places which felt as if they were last visited long before some of the tombs she'd unearthed.

Jim's voice broke her reverie as he continued: "It's a fair point you make, but then again, that's why I prefer something a bit more sedate in my free time." Now he turned to Jane. "And as for you, Jane, I doubt free time is something you know too well. One of the world's most respected archaeologists, a director at the British Museum and, perhaps the greatest accolade, a member of the Supreme Council of Antiquities in Egypt."

Jane felt her now permanent blush deepening. "How do you...?"

"I might give the impression of not knowing my ars—" Jim stopped, looking shamefaced in the direction of his hosts. "My apologies. I may look disorganised, but I make a point of never going anywhere without having done my research."

The ringing tap of knife on wine glass interrupted words and thoughts. Jane cringed at this use of a sledgehammer to crack a nut, as if her father needed to cut through the chatter of a hundred guests. Despite being in his own home, in the bosom of his family, Jane thought he looked nervous as the guests fell silent.

"Well, as some of you have doubtless worked out—"

"Some of the multitude," interrupted Pete, a sarcastic smile playing on his lips.

Sutch's eyes had lost none of their expressiveness with age and they narrowed, but he ignored his son-in-law. "I have a bit of an announcement to make." He looked towards Candice, whose serene features registered unusual concern. "Don't worry, my darling, it's nothing to do with my health... or the existence of a love child." Two of the guests laughed. "But, like that wonderful old character Bilbo Baggins at his eleventy-first birthday party, I am announcing that I'm about to go on a journey."

Candice and Jane sat up in awkward anticipation.

"Darling," said Candice, "you're approaching eighty and—"

"... am therefore too old to learn any new tricks, and too obstinate to listen."

Candice knew that well enough and backed down without further ado. "But through all the years I *have* kept one secret." The men remained impassive, but the women fidgeted. "To cut to the chase; dearest Jane, you remember when I told you that you would be invited to dinner if your work with my amphora led anywhere? Well, it has." Now Jane sat forward, concern giving way to curiosity. "What none of you knew was – the amphora was sent to me forty years after I first set eyes on it." The Professor ploughed on to avoid interruption. "During that time, as the result of a discussion I had with the original owner, I have been seeking a previously unheard-of civilisation." Now he paused, for effect and in anticipation of a response.

"What?" Jim's incredulous smile didn't quite stray across into disbelief for the moment.

"Yes, not only a land that time forgot, but one it never knew about, if we take the admittedly arrogant view that recorded history is time as we know it. Your efforts, Jane, took me part of the way, and my own research the rest of it. I know it sounds like an oxymoron, but this has been an occasional obsession of mine for four decades." Here he looked in apology at Candice, who remained inscrutable. "And now, given that I am eighty, there literally isn't any time to lose. I leave tomorrow."

There was a reaction from three of the four listeners:

15

"Tomorrow?"

"Darling?"

"Dad!"

The Professor raised his hands. "It's not simply impatience, it's also practicality. Firstly, Jim, as you can tell by the very fact you're here, the Royal Geographical Society is partly funding this and will hope for a swift return on its investment. Secondly, in the part of the world I'm heading to, it's now summer. I don't want preparations dragging on into the more inclement weather. Thirdly," he looked around and then grinned like a gleeful child, "I just can't wait."

"Dad," Jane saw her father's grin ease off a little at her tone, "Mum has a point. You're eighty and I know you're in great shape for your age, but you can't head off to wherever it is – and hopefully you're going to tell us – on your own."

"Yes, I am going to tell you... once we're on the way. You see, I'm not going on my own, unless you make me. I want you there; and you, Jim. I haven't said anything before because I don't want news leaking out. I'm a selfish and proud enough old man to want to find this place myself."

Jim sat forward emphatically. "Well, you know I'm game, even if I weren't being paid. Your reputation as a scientist and a man precedes you, Professor."

Sutch grinned. "Unfortunately, I'm an oceanographer, not an explorer."

"Well, what's the ocean if not the greatest unexplored area on earth..." Jim grinned and looked to the ceiling, "... or does that just prove your point?"

"QED." They laughed and it eased some of the tension, though it didn't disperse. Jane saw the look her parents exchanged – the blue of her mother's eyes was no longer that of a clear sky but of its reflection in a glacier - and the way her father now turned to her for sanctuary. "And you, my girl? This could be the find of finds, though I'm promising nothing."

"Daddy, if you think you have some evidence you know I'm with you. But even if you don't," here she looked at her mother, "I think my presence is required. I'll just have to nip home and pack some things." Now her gaze turned to Pete, who said nothing; his body language evinced an overstated lack of interest.

"There's no need. The bulk of this mini expedition is already prepared and waiting for us at our departure port. There's ample travel clothing here to kit everyone out – I've been around the world so many times that I've built up quite a collection of spares – as poor Candice knows."

There was silence from the other end of the table, so he continued. "Your beloved field notebooks and journals are still here from when you stayed over to examine the amphora." When there was no further response, Sutch couldn't help but clap his hands together. "Excellent, so that's settled then."

"Um, just a minute." It was Pete. As Jane suspected, he'd been taking it all in. She looked across and saw that her father had feared this moment. "If you think I'm allowing my wife to head off at the last minute to heaven knows where, you're mistaken."

Jane gave him a sharp look. "Pete, I am going. Don't worry about me; you don't usually."

"Darling." Pete spread his hands as if offended by the accusation.

"How many times have I been away for weeks or months on digs and assignments? I'm absent more than I'm home, and for all I know so are you."

Pete put his hand on her cheek. She knew her discomfort - her indecision about how to react to his touch - must have been obvious to him; the same look that had been in her eyes some weeks before when, after a few drinks, she'd allowed him to make love to her for the first time in months and halfway through had started to regret the decision. It had taken all her willpower not to ask him to stop. Now she felt as if they were doing it again, only this time in front of Jim and her parents. Though she fought hard to suppress the shudder, she knew Pete felt it through his fingertips. He smiled at her and only *she* saw what was in his expression. He seemed to gain strength from her unease and looked past her towards the Professor while continuing to address her. "Yes, well that's not really the point. I don't know where you're going, neither do you and, let's face it, none of you know what you're going to find there, by the sound of it."

"Don't worry," the Professor nodded, "I foresaw this, and you have every right to be concerned. In... well, let's just call it base camp, there's enough clothing and kit for you to join us." The Professor looked at Jane. She knew from his reaction that there was a mixture of gratitude and disappointment in her eyes. The bottom line was, he had indeed foreseen Pete's objections, but knew they would be all about his ego; a sense of aggrievement at being excluded. Taking him with was the line of least resistance. At the end of the day, what could the Professor say? They were married.

The same mix of emotions showing on Jane's face was not to be seen on her mother's. It was a parchment, the tale it told still waiting to be translated. She carried an expression that seemed as old as the sea to Jane, who knew she would say nothing now; her father would have to answer in due course and his next words made that inevitable, as they were not designed to put anyone's mind at rest. Though they were addressed to everyone, Jane believed the discouraging tone was for Pete's benefit.

"It's only fair to warn you all what we'll be up against: dense forest, which, if my estimates are correct, has grown without human interference for at least three hundred years; rough seas; a hostile coastline; and, at the end of it all, the possibility that we may find nothing."

"Excellent!" Pete, as if fully aware of the reason behind the speech seemed determined to defy his father-in-law. "I've been looking for a new extreme sport. Besides, you might need a pilot." There was a short, pregnant silence. Everyone ignored the obvious one-upmanship, though there was no denying the potential usefulness of that qualification.

"A *spare* pilot," corrected Sutch. "Dirk Munter's waiting for us at base camp. Okay, that's settled then." He continued, with a singular failure to sound impressed or to hide his vexation. "And remember, if you're in, you're in. Stuck. You won't be able to borrow some transport and get out of there. This preliminary trip is a secret – a hell of a secret – and that's how I intend it to stay, which is why – with apologies to my wife – I've told no-one where we're going yet."

Another uncomfortable silence – the definition of which had become a lack of words from Candice – meant Sutch pushed on again. "Well then, Jim, I'm sorry you've been hauled all the way down here just to have to repeat the trip. I guess you'll be wanting to go and pack equipment."

"No, Professor, I usually have everything I need in the boot of my car. You never know when opportunity beckons."

"Just like a boy scout." Pete grinned.

Jim ignored him. "Camera gear and spare threads are all there, and it sounds like you've taken care of the rest."

"In that case," Sutch placed both palms on the table, "there are spare rooms available and we'll be starting early."

Jane spread her hands. "So that's it?" was her laconic response.

"For the moment, my girl, for the moment. Just trust me." Jane issued herself a silent rebuke. She had been a bit slow there. Trust, or rather lack of it, was an issue for certain, when there was an entrepreneur around with an eye for a fast buck and a few hours to cash the chips with the press. "And now, I'm sure the three of you all have things to do to prepare. We'll leave at four a.m."

A 'hmm' from Pete was the only sound uttered. For the others early starts were nothing out of the ordinary. While her husband was no stranger to four a.m., Jane knew it was only at the top end of a few hours' sleep thanks to his new-found love of a night at the casino.

Now she managed to pop her head over the parapet of her own little castle of selfishness. Not everyone wanted to be away from their married partner. While for Jane there was the prospect of taking an active part in this adventure, her mother, who had remained silent, would once more be left alone. That took a different strength; a type Jane didn't possess. It was time to give her parents some space. She rose from her seat. "C'mon guys, let's get ourselves straight."

When the room had emptied, Edward Sutch felt the searchlights roaming across his face and looked at his wife, returning her frank gaze. "Candice, I... I should have told you."

"Edward darling, you know that this is not an accusatory stare. If that's the only secret you've kept from me in fifty years of marriage, which I believe to be the case, then I am blessed." She rose and came around the table to stand in front of him. "No, this is something you haven't seen before; this is my scared face."

He touched her cheek with tenderness "Why, Candice? I've been away before."

"But you've always been in your element – literally, the sea. And I've always known where you would be." She took his hand from her cheek and held it. "I don't mind you having kept this as a secret, my darling. What I don't understand is why."

"Candice, it was always my intention to tell you on this night, though I never knew when this night would be. But I couldn't afford for this to slip out, even accidentally, and have others beat me to the fulfilment of my dream." He saw the look in her eyes and raised a hand in acknowledgement. "Yes, I know that's selfish, but that's often the nature of dreams. I mean, if I'd met you when you were hitched to another man, my dream would have been to have you to myself." She squeezed his hand. "But the main reason was, if you'd known, you might just have taken me for a fool – an ageing one – and there's nothing worse than an old fool. Even a mad fool has an excuse."

She put her arms around him. "Never." They enjoyed the familiar warmth of each other's embrace for the last time, in silence. Then she leaned back from him and looked him full in the eyes: "Okay, tell me all about it."

"What are you looking at?" asked Jane as she slipped under the duvet.

Pete was standing at the window, hands in pockets, staring out into the night. "Just checking whether there's a phone box for Jim to change in tomorrow."

"Don't be ridiculous."

"Well, I'm not taken in by his Clark Kent act. He's such a bloody boy scout. And I think I know what he'd be prepared for as well."

"What do you mean?" She saw Pete looking at her reflection in the darkened window and knew her blush wouldn't show, but she busied herself with some night cream to hide her awkwardness, which intensified when, instead of answering, he started to undress.

Jane found these moments difficult, the more so since their sexual relationship had juddered to an apathetic halt. Her mind raced back to the drunken fumble of a few weeks before. There was a slight difference tonight, however, an added edge to the problem. Namely, she was aroused and even wondering, incredible though it was, whether, with the lights off, he could be Jim for a while. As Pete peeled the shirt from his broad back, she noted his physique, honed by years of free-form climbing, water-skiing, martial arts and any other extreme sport one cared to mention. Would it feel so bad in the darkness? He was attractive, his slightly-too-long hair and permanent stubble giving him a piratical edge, though blonde looks were not her preference, which made her choice of husband all the more puzzling. *What it was, to be twenty-eight and still feeling gratitude for the attention of the opposite sex, failing to notice that you'd developed at last into someone desirable to them.*

He was naked now, the way he always slept, and she saw enough in the window's reflection to cause her hips to stir. Before he turned around, she switched off the light and there was a simultaneous flick of another switch in her mind. She heard the man cross the room and felt his weight settle next to hers. But what was happening? He was saying something.

"I guess we'd better get some sleep before our early start."

It had been a surprising evening for Pete. First there'd been the jealousy he'd felt at the obvious attraction between Jane and Jim. Okay, he was realistic and could explain away his response as possessiveness. Then the phone call. Next, there was his decision to accompany the expedition, but again that could be put down to a combination of jealousy, the need to rain on his father-in-law's parade – be the party pooper – and an undeniable sense of intrigue. The biggest surprise of all, however, was the movement behind him now as he turned on his side to sleep; the finger placed on his lips to silence him as he made to speak, before it traced its way down his body, and the mouth that whispered a filthy promise in his ear before moving to join the hand.

For a hedonistic hour, husband and wife were lost in their own very personal dark thoughts, though each would have been surprised by the similarity of those imaginings.

***

TIME, UNKNOWN; PLACE, DARKNESS

Panic had set in when daylight vanished, a primeval fear against which mankind would never find a defence; not even a king or a great warrior, both of which he had ceased to be the moment he had realised he was lost in the dark. He cursed the pride and stubbornness which had seen him take up this challenge, knowing he might be walking into a trap.

The light from the entrance to the temple had soon disappeared and there had been not a glimmer of it since. The soul of the labyrinth was blacker and more complex than the heart of a woman, and just as unforgiving. For the sake of his sanity, he had to hope this she-devil would tire of him and release him from her embrace, allowing him to return to the sound of the sea and the cool breeze, which had become distant memories.

Like all men, he had betrayed himself by his weakness. It would be easy to blame the one who stalked him now – he hesitated to call him a man – and whose malevolent presence filled these tunnels, but in truth his own arrogance, allied to a desire to possess a mythical prize, had led him to take up the priest's challenge. So here he was – the gods only knew how many wrong turns and lost days further on – barely able to see his hand in front of his face.

Would he ever walk free? Pride and prize were nothing now; he just wanted to see the sky again. Or would this sword he clutched, now more of a reminder of the world he had known than a weapon, be the only way that he would ever bring an end to this, one way or the other?

21

He wept – as he would again and again – then found once more the part of himself that was still a king and continued on his way, hunter and hunted.

***

THE CALM... PORTSMOUTH, 10.30 P.M. OCTOBER 24TH 1997

"Okay, tell me all about it."

So, he had. Or rather, he had tried. But those six little words from Candice had made too great a demand of him. There was so much to tell, yet so little he could say. He described the box, not the contents. By the time he had finished recounting what he could, Edward Sutch was almost proud that he had maintained his record of having never lied to his wife, just kept things from her.

Now that Candice had gone to bed, seeming satisfied with what she had heard and respecting, as ever, her husband's need for some time alone with his thoughts, he poured himself a large malt whisky and sat at the desk in his study, staring across its scratched surface. Devoid of all clutter now – everything was packed in readiness – it enabled him to order his thoughts and think back on the sequence of events which had led him to this night. More than a night, the eve of something – his greatest adventure, his biggest discovery, but perhaps also, his worst misjudgement?

As he sipped the whisky, he noticed that his hand shook. Was it because of what lay ahead or what he had been through to find a way? He rested his head on the fingertips of the other hand and allowed himself to remember for a while.

CHAPTER FIVE

PORTSMOUTH, ONE MONTH BEFORE

As one of the world's pre-eminent oceanographers, Sutch knew that discovery can, but does not always, lead the way into darkness, trailing a thread for death to follow. As a man of science, he couldn't have lived with that precept. Of course, Robert Oppenheimer's dubious achievement with the A-bomb, and his response to it, had been examples of exploration taking man to places he should perhaps have left undisturbed. However, the culmination of a lifetime's search or obsession was not usually marked by an explosion that ends one world and breeds another, or by the stark recognition that 'I am become Death'. More often, all that was left was the emptiness that follows the excitement and mayhem of the launch of a great ship.

Professor Sutch would have enjoyed that image more if he hadn't been in a state of shock – he would have approved of the maritime analogy – but right now, the scientist in him was in denial; unable quite to comprehend that, after searching for forty years, he had at last found an answer in what he, and the other few academics who had bothered to read the journal, had always dismissed as the drunken ramblings of an old, egotistical sea-dog from the sixteenth century.

But when you have yearned for something to breathe, you accept whatever brings it to life. So, the Professor knew there was just a chance he might not have heard the door to hell creak open on its hinges; missed, like so many before him, the tiptoeing entry of Death as it hid behind him for the moment in the shadows of achievement.

It had been a long journey, but the last few days had been the most exhausting as he wandered through a strobe-lit world; moments of black disorientation followed by flashes of illumination, which had confused him more than they had enlightened. But it looked as if the way was lit at last. He had got over the road and hoped that he wasn't like the proverbial chicken, having crossed just to get to the other side.

Despite his dislike of such egotism, Edward Sutch could not suppress all feelings of self-congratulation. He gave the journal's ancient page an almost loving stroke, and then looking across, reached out and placed his aged hand on the rough roundedness of the amphora, caressing it like the breast of a virgin bride.

"You knew it, Eddie old boy, you knew it!" Yet he'd had to keep it to himself all these years. He hoped that would not preclude Candice being pleased for him when he revealed all. As a scientist he knew this was still a theory till he had the physical proof, and though he was bursting to tell someone, he would have to keep his own counsel a while longer. He would need to pick his team with care as well. Apart from anything else, there were too many cowboy adventurers out there, always ready to saddle up at the prospect of fame and glory. Such baubles were meaningless to him, and not just because of his age. Something far more fundamental had kept his inner flame flickering all these years.

All these years.

He paused for a moment's reflection but then shook his head and tried to dismiss some of the nonsense he had heard along the way. More important now was hard evidence. He wanted to put a huge QED sign at the bottom of this conundrum of four decades.

Now that *did* bring him up short. There was no escaping it. Forty years had been half his life, but just the blink of an eye for this amphora. Still, this moment, this tiny sliver of time on 21st September 1997, belonged to him alone. He was thrilled beyond words by the probability that he might be about to take a literal and metaphorical step where no-one alive today had been – assuming, as he had to, that the giver of this gift was now dead.

Sorrow caught him off guard. He looked away from the amphora and out of his study window towards the clouds. Tariq had known everything, of course; had known for a very long time, if his story were to be believed. Again, Sutch shook his head. Could he really allow himself to accept that part of it? After all, Tariq had lied about certain things, perhaps fearing ridicule, but possibly to whet the Professor's appetite. Well, in the latter he had succeeded.

Now Sutch smiled and caressed the amphora once more. "Just like Tariq you are – full of both secrets and revelations."

***

He had fallen for her, his rounded virgin bride, the moment he saw her in that market stall in Mogadishu. It turned out she wasn't for sale, and the merchant wouldn't even part with her for the equivalent of the king's ransom that he was offered.

CHAPTER SIX

MOGADISHU, 1957

"She's beautiful though, isn't she?"

"Yes." Sutch had to agree, trying to hide his frustration. He had not seen the like of it before in his already extensive travels. "An unusual motif. It's not Greek or Roman, Etruscan or Egyptian. I'm not familiar with it."

"No, no-one is." The merchant gestured towards him with an upturned palm. "Your Arabic is excellent. We can also speak English," he continued, switching, as if trying to throw the Professor off balance. "But whatever language you choose cannot do justice to the unique qualities of this piece."

"No, you're right." Sutch raised one eyebrow and continued to study the perfect proportions of the vessel's neck.

"Like some ancient, exotic whore; not beautiful, a bit battered, but alluring and still in one piece."

That allusion made him laugh. It hadn't come to the Cambridge-educated Professor's mind, and he had to admit it seemed apt, but for one detail. "Except she's not for sale at any price and has doubtless become more valuable the older she's grown." He turned his attention to the merchant, who smiled at the riposte. "But now it is my turn to commend your English."

And it was the merchant's turn to raise one eyebrow. "When you have been around as long as me, you get to see many places, learn many things." A slight flush seemed to warm his swarthy skin. "But look at us, talking like two old men, both in our mid-thirties at most."

"Ah, thank you, but I'm afraid I've nearly reached that age where they say life begins." Sutch smiled. "Apart from her strange beauty, is there any other reason you won't sell her?" The last words were spoken in the direction of the amphora, which he was still scrutinising.

"You may not think of her as a whore, but you do speak of her as a lady." The merchant gave a wry smile. "And, as you have implied, that is appropriate. To return to your question: she is not for sale because she belongs to me."

"Ah." Sutch swallowed his disappointment and tried to concentrate on the piece – *why did he want her so?* "What do the etchings represent?"

Instead of answering, the merchant pointed. "That café; I will meet you there in five minutes."

***

The evening hung over the lively confusion of the bazaar in a haze of dust and sweat, which the café's roof fan seemed only to stir into a sludge, rather like the coffee that the Professor was about to drink when he noticed the merchant coming over to join him. He wouldn't have recognised him with his djellaba pulled close to keep out the dust, except much to Sutch's surprise he was clutching the amphora. He entertained a moment's hope that the merchant had reconsidered and was prepared to sell it, before chastising himself for the greed inherent in that thought. His guest joined him, threw back his cowl, sat down and planted the object of Sutch's affection with solid yet delicate deliberateness between his feet. Sutch thought he heard the sound of liquid swilling inside it.

"You're not worried about anything else being taken from your stall?" asked the Professor.

"We're not thieves here." The Arab must have seen the look of shame that crossed Sutch's face and smiled. "At least not all of us. But this is all that matters." He tapped the stopper of the vessel with a finger.

Their ensuing silence hung in the thick, noisy air while another coffee arrived, and the two men took sips of the scalding liquid.

At last, Sutch had to ask – after all, it was why he had been invited here. "So, what's the story?" He gestured with his head towards the amphora.

"One you won't believe."

"Then why are you about to tell me?"

The merchant turned his mouth down and shrugged his shoulders. "Because I get a feeling that perhaps you will listen. And because it needs to be told."

"Two good reasons, I would say. Well, I'm all ears..." he paused, then extended his hand across the table, "... forgive my manners, I don't know your name."

"Tariq." The proffered hand was taken.

"Professor Edward Sutch. You'd make a good raconteur, Tariq. You've built up the expectation nicely."

"This..." he gestured towards the amphora, "... gift was given to me by a remarkable man; just a humble fisherman, but remarkable because he came from a place unknown to any man outside his own race, and because when I met him, he was possibly the last surviving member of that race."

The Professor leaned forward and smiled. "Well, you've certainly got me now."

"Still, I hear some scepticism." Sutch moved to protest, while at the same time marvelling at his guest's command of English. Tariq raised his hand to stop him. "I don't blame you. I would not believe me. Certainly, I did not believe him, until... but I get ahead of myself." Tariq looked around, and then, once convinced nobody could overhear them in the hubbub of the café, he continued. "This man said that he lived in an island kingdom far from here, in the vast southern seas. I think you know a thing or two about uncharted waters."

The Professor narrowed his eyes, feeling uncomfortable all of a sudden. His project was funded by a major shipping company and supposed to be shrouded in secrecy. "How do you know?"

"I've seen your boats in the harbour, your team, your equipment. You are mapping the waters of the western Indian Ocean, it seems to me."

"You see a lot, Tariq."

"So, if waters with such heavy traffic still need mapping, you would believe that there are parts of the great oceans where a civilisation could have existed about which we know nothing?"

The Professor took another sip of his coffee and thought for a moment. "There, in this day and age, I would be more sceptical."

"I agree."

"You agree?"

Sutch thought Tariq looked ill at ease for a moment. The merchant hesitated and did not give a direct answer. "I tell you only the fisherman's tale. One day, returning home from a long fishing trip, he saw, to his horror, his homeland being destroyed. Everywhere rivers of fire were consuming the land, and it looked as if a huge wave had swept across the kingdom. We both know the Southern Ocean is angry, feared and respected by the most experienced of sailors, but this force of water must have been way beyond the usual, carrying away people and their possessions. He wept as he told me of his country disappearing into the sea and of the family that he would never see again."

"This sounds like a volcano, or perhaps an underwater earthquake. I don't know if we're talking Krakatoa here."

"No, not Krakatoa."

"I meant in magnitude obviously. After all, that was in 1883."

"Of course." Tariq took a sip of his coffee and remained enigmatic.

"Nowadays there would be detailed records of something of that scale."

"You are right." The merchant's words had a peculiar inflection. "Unable to return to his home, the fisherman sailed the seas for many moons before he landed, bereft of hope, in this very port. I befriended him; took him into my home."

"Tariq, as an oceanographer for the past fifteen years, much of that time holding the seat of the Oceanography Department at Southampton University, I would know of an event like this, even from the furthest reaches of the oceans. I don't mean this to sound condescending in any way, but did you speak the fisherman's language? Can you be sure you understood exactly what he said?"

"The language was indeed a peculiar hybrid. What do you know of the Mayan culture?"

"About as much as the next man. I take an interest. Are you saying there were similarities to Mayan in the language?" Tariq gave the briefest of nods. "So, you think it's possible these people originated from there?"

"Perhaps. It was not unknown for primitive man to have undertaken long voyages by sea to escape from all manner of things, or simply to explore, to find a new home. But I see from your face you are doubtful."

The Professor looked long at him. "Actually Tariq, I was wondering how a merchant with a stall in a market in Mogadishu speaks so many languages."

"A merchant must travel to acquire the things he sells."

"And why does he settle in arid Somalia?"

"Who says I have settled?" That stopped Sutch in his tracks for a moment's reflection, and Tariq was swift in moving on. "I made of his words what I could, and he supported his story with drawings. He told me they were a trading nation."

"So how did they trade? You've said already that no foreigner ever visited their shores." Sutch frowned. There were too many discrepancies in this story and he was beginning to doubt the merchant's grasp of facts. Perhaps he was just someone who liked to spin a yarn over a coffee. "This sounds like the polar opposite of the so-called prophecies of Nostradamus. It's as easy to say that something has happened, when it cannot be proved, as it is to say it will happen."

Tariq seemed to absorb the cynicism, but continued: "It was a wealthy kingdom, but not self-sufficient. The fisherman told me of forests and rocks, of soil from which one could barely scrape a harvest. The seas were bountiful, but man cannot live by fish alone." He smiled. "So, they would sail to other lands, make long, hazardous sea voyages, to trade."

"Trade what? Timber?"

"They had another more valuable harvest. The mines on the island proved to be veritable chests of treasures; enough to buy these people whatever they wanted on whatever scale." The Professor didn't ask what these treasures might be. He had already figured that Tariq would tell the tale to its conclusion in his own way and time. But it was all sounding a bit too much like King Solomon's mines for his taste. He knew that his eyes reflected his disbelief, and that Tariq could see this, though it appeared not to faze him. "From other mines on the islands came stones, white like your famous Portland Stone, to build a citadel of much beauty; a walled city with parapets."

"I don't understand – what or who did they fear when their kingdom remained a secret?"

Tariq hesitated. "A good question. These people were expert seafarers and if they suspected they were being followed from foreign trading ports they set courses of great cunning to throw off any pursuit. Perhaps the walls were built for that inevitable day when someone of equal determination refused to be shaken off."

"But Tariq," Sutch leaned forward, "that they remained undiscovered into the twentieth century seems to me—"

Tariq stopped him in his tracks. "Let me tell all."

Sutch pursed his lips and leaned back again. "Okay. I have to admit it's an unusual story," he smiled, "and well told."

"There was something else; you asked also *what* they feared. A shadow hung over these people, something the fisherman could not – perhaps would not – describe, at least not in words that I could understand. He seemed unable even to draw it." Tariq leaned forward for emphasis. "He said that he would long ago have fled from the nameless threat of that place with his family, but for a gift bestowed by the island that held the people in its thrall, despite their fears." Edward Sutch fought off the indulgent smile that was tugging at his mouth. To appear patronising would have been anathema to him. But still, this tale of a forbidden, magical kingdom of fabulous wealth had taken on the air of some fantastical bedtime story, like an amalgam of every adventure he had read as a child.

His attempt to hide his feelings ended in miserable failure, because Tariq laughed. The mixture of humour and benevolence, which Sutch was relieved to hear, had the strangest effect, humbling him with its unexpectedness and making him feel he was the fool for being a disbeliever. "I understand your feelings, Professor. It would be my reaction too. You are a scientist; you need to see things for yourself. I am not, but I have seen the things you should." The peculiar intensity and belief in Tariq's eyes killed the beginnings of any smile on the Professor's face. "I am prepared to believe you are a man I can trust; the only man of whom I have believed this in a long time."

Sutch considered, then nodded. "Trust is a wonderful blessing to bestow on someone. Forgive me, and please continue."

Tariq's nod was almost imperceptible. "According to the fisherman there was a spring in a cave on the island, the waters of which possessed and imparted energies we cannot understand; the fisherman certainly couldn't. He himself was a young man in body, a fine specimen, but his eyes gave him away. He was old. Ancient. I read between the lines of his tale. From what he told me, there were priests – shamans – who built their temple near the spring and controlled it, becoming more powerful even than the king." Tariq gave a cynical smile. "Was that not always so in the history of the world? I believe they claimed the power of the water was a blessing of their own making.

"With a supply of that water on board ship, a man could sail the seven seas, never tiring, never ageing – though still he would need to eat, or else living would be nothing more than a walking death. So, you see, my dear Professor, the water was the reason they returned always to their homeland, why these people of youth and health and strength never spread and built themselves a far-flung empire. And why they guarded the location of their home so jealously – theirs was a gift they did not wish to share." Tariq sat back. "Eternal life must be a mixed blessing. Your mind cannot stay young; it can only become tired and more cynical by the day. The time will come when you have seen everything. And if death does come, the end must be terrible, as indeed it was to behold."

"What?" Sutch sat up; an involuntary action.

"Yes, I watched the fisherman die, and while I sensed it was almost a relief for him, especially having lost his family, it must have been torture beyond words to age countless centuries in one day. I wonder if all the pain you should have endured during your life comes to wrack

31

your body at the end. It seemed so to me, as I watched his death throes. Then at last I saw the sheet that covered his poor frame sink and settle between his bones like snow melting around the roots of a tree." Tariq squeezed his eyes shut and Sutch saw a single tear fall from the corner of one of them, tracing down a cheek as hot and dust-dry as the country in which they sat.

Sutch was moved, as well as caught by the desire that holds all men fast at some time or another. "You mean..." he hesitated, "... you said countless centuries?"

Tariq opened his eyes. "Yes, Professor, the reason none of your instruments have measured the cataclysmic destruction of the island is that it happened two hundred and fifty years ago, and the victims killed that day had settled there about twelve hundred years before that."

"You're joking!"

"I have never been more serious. See it in my eyes. They do not forget the sight of a man ageing many centuries in a few hours. And, if you are still doubtful, there is always the amphora." He tapped it once again. "By your own words, you have never seen its like. I do not know if any others exist. The fisherman gave it to me as a 'thank you' for my friendship; I think just for having listened, perhaps for giving him somewhere comfortable to lay his head after endless sailing of the oceans. And with it he gave more than you can imagine." Tariq smiled. "Unfortunately, I cannot extend you that courtesy." The smile became enigmatic. "At least not yet."

***

"At least not yet." Those words had taunted the Professor for forty years; irritating flies that had buzzed around him while he tried, without success, to ignore them and get on with his life during those four decades.

That he had the perfect excuse, as a widely respected oceanographer, to head off to sea in search of the mythical kingdom only added to his frustrations. He would have risked the ridicule of his peers – it would be like announcing you were off to find Brigadoon or Atlantis. If Tariq was to be believed – that was a big 'if' – the island had lain somewhere in the vast waters that comprised the southern Pacific and Indian Oceans and the Southern Ocean itself. That was a hell of a lot of water! The floor of the Pacific Ocean was immense; deep and alive with evidence of volcanic activity, past and present, above and below the waves. It would not have been like searching for a needle in a haystack, so much as for a particular piece of hay.

So, the hunt for the island kingdom had been relegated to a sort of hobby for him – though such things have a habit of becoming obsessions. There were half-clues – old, handed-down tales of strong waves rocking boats in Hobart, The Kerguelen Islands and the Mozambique Channel, pieces of driftwood in the middle of the ocean and South Sea superstitions – but presenting these as hard evidence would have been like claiming to have proof of ghosts or a piece of the True Cross. The one thread to which the Professor clung in hope during those years was a recurring theme in some of the stories he heard – passed down by word-of-mouth through the generations in some of the bigger ports such as Aden, Karachi, Muscat, neighbouring Matrah, Port Elizabeth – anywhere Sutch got the chance to chat with the locals. In these tales, merchants would arrive in great black ships, trading jewels for corn and cloth. One thread stuck with him, not because of any dramatic event, but because legend had it that everyone in the harbour was spooked by the appearance of the merchants. If Sutch had made a correct translation of the colloquial dialect, their bodies were young and strong, but their eyes told a very different story, one of weariness and discontent, as if they had sailed the seas for too many years. As usual, no-one knew the ship's heading when it left and, as the port in question was East London, right down in the Cape Province near the southern tip of Africa, it left the Professor with nowhere – or rather, too many places – to go.

As the years passed, Professor Sutch, who was the diametric opposite of the people he sought, being old in body but still young in mind, was forced to devote less and less time to his hobby.

Until a month before, when the ghosts had rattled their chains.

CHAPTER SEVEN

"A parcel for me? What is it?"

"If I had the power of second sight," said the Rottweiler, "I wouldn't be sitting here in Reception."

Fair, if unnecessary and sharp, he decided, but then again that just about summed her up.

A taped-up box, addressed to him c/o The Royal Geographical Society, sat at the front desk, placed just out of his reach behind it, as if to demonstrate the Rottweiler's power over life and death. He had not ordered anything and if he had, would not have requested that it be delivered *here*, unless it was a surprise present for his wife.

When it was handed to him at last, and he had taken it from between the long, manicured fingers, he decided he did not want to open it yet, and not just to frustrate the receptionist. So, it sat on the passenger seat alongside him all the way down to Southampton University where he still held an office as Emeritus Professor of Oceanography.

During the journey he ran his hand over the box. From certain peculiarities of the calligraphy, he guessed the address had been written by a foreign hand, but there was no postmark. By the time he reached University Road he was desperate to get to his office and open the parcel.

His jaw would not have fallen further open if the box had revealed the Holy Grail. He reached inside and removed the amphora with tender, delicate movements. "Tariq." It was an awestruck whisper. Then, placing the object with reverential care on his desk, petrified that it would slip from his sweating palms, he got up and locked the office door. This was a moment to be shared with no-one.

He walked around the desk, examining the piece as if it were a museum exhibit, eyes widening with wonder then narrowing as they

34

scrutinised. He wanted to pick it up again, but worried that it might not be robust enough to handle. "Stupid old man," he muttered at last under his breath, "this might have survived at least two centuries – longer, I suspect – much of that time on board ship."

The amphora had been packed with evident care and Sutch rooted around in the dense straw and wood-shaving filling to see if there was any letter or note, but there was nothing. That was disturbing, because it meant the bestowing of this gift – for what else could it be? – might remain an enigmatic gesture.

As he turned the piece over with exaggerated care to see whether there were any markings on the base, he both felt and heard movement inside. When he righted it again there was no doubt. Putting a finger gently down the neck of the vessel, he was thrilled when the tip brushed against what felt like a rolled-up piece of paper. Turning the amphora over once more, he used gravity to help him remove the document.

It was more than age that caused the Professor's hands to shake as he untied the parchment and started to read. The waft of spices and dust from the paper brought back a thousand memories, till he could almost see Tariq.

'My dear Professor, I trust this piece has reached you safely and I trust you to use it well. I know you will treasure it, and I would have given it to no-one else from the day I met you. It helped me to find what I thought I was looking for and now, with a little help from me, I hope it will do the same for you.

Why have I not left it to my sons or family, I hear you ask; why to this passing stranger? Well, I have a feeling about you and even had I not outlived my sons and their sons – and their sons! – I would have bequeathed this to you because, when a man has lived as long as me, his feelings, his instincts, are normally true. No-one else had ever commented on the amphora's strange allure and beauty – not even my family – and that, for me, was the acid test, so I knew you were someone unique, that it had found a place in your heart and you a place in its story.

Now I hear you ask why I have waited so long before passing this gift to you. Well, you will find out that this is a gift not lightly given away; one that can only belong to someone with an undying need to know its secrets. And forty years is a long time to hold on to a dream as you will have done, even if it marks but a blink of history's eye. So, you see, I need your forgiveness on two counts. Firstly, for not being able to let go of my prize before now; a mixed blessing is still a blessing and having seen, in the final terrible throes of the fisherman, what awaited me, I was too much of a coward to rush towards death. I put it off for as long as possible.

The second count is that I lied to you.'

The Professor's frown was deepening by the sentence, in part through the riddles in which Tariq wrote, but also because this letter seemed to be a harbinger of the merchant's death. There were other things too, more disturbing to him as a scientist. He read on.

'You see, the reason you must believe the fisherman's tale is because I fled our homeland with him two and a half centuries ago.'

Suddenly, Sutch needed to sit. His legs and hands appeared to have contracted an ague and trembled. He read on.

'It is true that he gave me the amphora, once he decided that a long life without his loved ones was not worth the living, but that was when we first made land after the destruction of our kingdom. And the water it contained helped me continue a life that would have run out along with my own supply of water at least a century ago. A tiny sip each day has given me one hundred years more. It does not turn back the hands of the clock; I was thirty-five years old in body when I fled with him; as I was when my people first settled our country; as I was when our paths crossed, you and I. But finally, the well of life has run dry. I am dying, Professor, but I have checked each year and know that you still live. So, I hope this amphora can now give one more gift. I hope it can help you achieve your dream – it is never too late for dreams, eh? Do you seek it still? I have heard tales of the learned Englishman who listens keenly, at every port, to stories of the southern seas, pursuing myths and legends. You see I, too, have travelled much. A man who never ages cannot stay in one place, especially those that are rife with superstition. He must move on, perhaps returning when he has passed beyond the memory of a generation or so, even that of his own sons. It was me who sailed the oceans for too long, not the fisherman. The weariness I described to you was mine, not his.

Forgive my writing for becoming shaky, but even today, as I parcel this treasure for you, I feel myself growing weaker, though it will be a few days still before the effects of the water of life wear off. Do not worry; I welcome the approach of death, if not its manner. It is time to stop moving.

Let me help you on your way. What you see as etchings and designs on the amphora are actually words and numbers. As you know, my people guarded the ways to our homeland jealously, so much so that we kept no maps on board ship for others to find. The information was hidden as decoration on our water containers. In keeping with the spirit of my people I will not give more information freely, but I feel sure your inquisitive mind will appreciate the challenge. To each man his desserts.

Professor – Edward, if I may call you that – I am dying and glad to do so. My parting words for you are of friendly warning: wondering is often better than knowing. Drinking too deeply of life leaves that vessel empty. Bon voyage.'

They sat together in silence for a long time, the Professor and the amphora, one trying to come to terms with what he had just read, the other perhaps having forgotten a thousand things more wondrous. "If only you could speak." Sutch stared at the keeper of secrets. Should he believe Tariq? For some reason he did, almost without question, which bothered him as it went against all the principles of science. Why would the old merchant have gone to the lengths, forty years later, of embellishing his already fantastical tale? And perhaps the Professor had known all along, from the moment he set eyes on the amphora, that it was not of the world he knew and upon which he relied. He felt an onrush of giddiness and excitement. He might not have opened the door to the chamber of knowledge, but at least he had located the lock.

He needed help and would have to choose with both care and detachment. To be entrusted with this secret was an honour, but perhaps also something that he had earned, and he was not about to beat a path for the hunters to follow, the adventurers and gold-diggers. He had an idea already of the people to whom he would turn. It was pointless asking the Royal Geographical Society to fund a major expedition yet, but they might stretch to supporting a preliminary field operation. He would have to take a sabbatical, which was ironic considering he was already well past retirement age, though that would raise few eyebrows.

But he was putting the cart before the horse. First, he needed an expert lock picker, and he had one very close to home; or rather, she would be in a few days.

CHAPTER EIGHT

PORTSMOUTH, AUGUST 29TH 1997

"What?"

"Nothing, just smiling."

Jane directed a look of mock-impatience at her father. "I can see that, but at what?"

"I don't know. It doesn't have a label."

"Well then it can't be worth knowing about."

"How can you say that?"

"I label every tiny fragment of bone and pottery I find on my digs. Something must be truly worthless to have no label."

Her little smile was blotted out again by a frown of concentration as she turned her attention back to the amphora. As she leaned on the table and stretched her neck forwards the Professor noticed how the lines around it were pale compared with the sun-blasted brown of the rest of its still-graceful length.

Unlike many students, *digs* had meant something different to Jane! After completing her studies at Alexandria University, Giza and the Bahira Oasis were just two of many places where she had spent years. He could smell the patchouli-scented moisturiser with which she attempted to stave off the effects of so much time working in heat and dust. It was one of her few concessions to femininity. Make-up was for high days and holidays.

With her short hair, jeans and checked shirts she might have been the son he never had, were it not for the softness of her blue eyes – a blessing from her mother and an oasis in themselves.

"You know, my dear," he placed a gentle hand on her shoulder, "for someone who's spent so much time underground you've caught the sun rather a lot. You should take more care."

38

She didn't look at him as she replied: "Just like you have, Father?"

He rubbed his hand with a rasp across his weather-beaten face. "I have to give you that one, I suppose, although in men it's seen as character."

"Besides, like life in general, it's only at the end we go underground, remember?"

"What, even in Alexandria? The whole ancient city lies beneath the modern one. People are forever falling into it. What do you need to dig for?"

She shook her head and continued scrutinising the amphora, though her little smile told him she was pretending to ignore his wind-up. "Where did you say you got this?"

"From a market stall in Mogadishu. Well, I didn't get it from there; that was where I first saw it. The merchant has sent it to me." He took off his glasses and rubbed his eyes. "Amazing really. Fort... a while back I spotted it. Now it arrives all boxed up, addressed to me at the RGS. He says he's dying and he wants it to have a worthy home."

Jane looked at him. "That *is* strange. You must have made quite an impression."

Careful, you old fool, he chastised himself, *when were you last in Mogadishu?* He pointed to divert attention from himself. "What I assumed were simply designs, here, he insists are characters or runes from some ancient language. I've already had it carbon-dated and the data confirms it's at least sixteen hundred years old."

Jane's mouth turned down as her eyebrows rose in semi-acknowledgement. "He could be right – about the characters. I've seen similar lettering in southern Mexico and Central America." She didn't see her father's sharp little glance in her direction.

"That *is* interesting." He paused, noting how his intonation sometimes matched hers – or was it vice versa? "I'd like you to do me a very big favour." She looked at him. "Translate it. I'd be as much use as a... what do they say these days... chocolate fireguard? But we still need to work on it together – and in secret." He tapped his nose for emphasis.

Her hand on his cheek was cool. "I'm sure you'd be of great assistance to me." A pause. "Father?"

Sutch knew from her reaction that his excitement showed despite his best efforts. He had to let her in on part of the secret at least. "I can't tell you much more for now, but it's my belief that the text on this piece contains information about tides and ocean currents, longitudinal and latitudinal readings."

"Who told you that?"

"The old merchant."

She put her hands on her hips, and then dropped them straight away, as if regretting that stereotypical female gesture of annoyance. "So, he's already translated it."

"No, but what he knows about the provenance of... this pot leads him to that conclusion."

Jane sat down on the edge of the desk with one of her bold, rather unfeminine movements. The amphora rocked in a gentle but threatening way and the Professor reached for it in a panic. "Sorry, Father, I've spent too many years in macho company to be delicate; in too many hot, dusty places and male-dominated societies."

Sutch puffed out his cheeks. "Yes, but I'd have thought moving around amongst the works of antiquity would have made you a tiny bit cautious. Anyway, back to the matter literally in hand," he held up the amphora, "we need to work quickly."

"Why the hurry? I thought this was an unexpected visitor in need of a home."

"I have my reasons."

She narrowed her eyes and gave a tight-lipped grin. "Hmmm, getting secretive in our old age. Okay, I'll take it away tonight and—"

"No!" She looked taken aback and he raised a hand in apology. "Pardon my abruptness." He dropped the raised hand and patted her on the leg. "What are your plans for the next couple of days?"

"Well, I'm due back at the Fitzwilliam Museum tomorrow, but I can get back from Cambridge to here in perhaps three hours if I leave early. Then I have to attend the Supreme Council of Antiquities in Egypt, but not for another week."

"Tell the Fitzwilliam you're indisposed."

"I'm never ill."

"Time you were then. Come and stay with us for a couple of days."

"Father?" she protested.

"It's important." He pointed to the amphora. "If this is what I believe it to be, you will be telling the Supreme Council that you're not going to be joining them for some time."

She, too, pointed to the amphora. "I hope this jug here is easier to decipher than you. But look, I can't just stay away from home for two days. Pete—"

"... can look after himself." Again, he knew his face gave him away as he felt the darkness fall. He glanced up to see Jane frowning at him, her pale eyes glinting.

"That's something he can't do."

"Only because you don't let him when you're there. What are you trying to prove? I mean, what does he do when you're *not* there?" The Professor had his own answers to that question, but that would be a step too far. "He's big and ugly enough—"

"Father, don't be like that."

The Professor's eyes widened and he opened his hands, knowing the gesture looked as unconvincing as it felt. "What? It's just a turn of phrase."

"That's disingenuous of you." She stood up, walked across the study to the old-fashioned globe in the corner, which she gave a spin just on the frustrated side of angry.

Sutch watched her and, as ever, felt a keen regret. But she was proud, fierce, highly intelligent and found it difficult to accept that there was an element of her life where, just perhaps, she might have made a mistake, or indeed lost control. He sighed. "My darling Jane, if you will help me with this, believe it or not, you might be unlocking a door for me that I've longed to open for years."

She turned and frowned. "I don't understand. You've never mentioned anything before. I thought you said you'd just received this."

Sutch was thrown for an instant but soon gathered his wits. "Janey, how often do our paths cross, where we can sit down and have a good old chat about our lives? And besides, believe me, if I were to tell you, now, the nature of this..." he hesitated, "... obsession of mine, you would consider me an old fool, though I was quite a bit younger when it first took hold of me."

His head dropped slightly. She came and sat on his lap, no longer the world-renowned archaeologist, just his little girl. "That's something I could never think." She paused. "Look, I'll clear it with Pete and come over for a couple of days."

He smiled and put an arm around her. "And I'll tell you what *I'll* do. If you can help me with this, and if I, as a result, can unlock my door, I'll invite you and Pete to dinner to hear what's behind it."

She put her arms around his neck and leaned back the better to look at him. "Deal." A kiss on the cheek and she stood. "All of which means that I must nip home to Hampstead to collect some things, and I'll be with you tonight." She was nearly at the door when she turned again. "Father, please don't be so hard on Pete. He's not a bad man. But, as the other one in my life, I guess he feels he has a lot to measure up to."

She blew him a kiss and was gone.

"None so blind," muttered Sutch under his breath. If he had his way he would slam his open door in that wastrel's face. His Janey would be better off for it. But somehow he knew that chancer would still barge his way through. He smelt trouble brewing, but for the moment there was nothing he could do.

CHAPTER NINE

PORTSMOUTH, SEPTEMBER 21ST 1997

Three weeks later, Edward Sutch leaned back in his chair and puffed out his cheeks. That promise of dinner still stood, having been an open invitation for nearly a month. But dear Candice was several steps nearer to receiving a shame-faced request to put on her apron because, thanks to that afternoon's research, three interlocking puzzle-pieces now sat on his desk.

He eyed them from left to right, laid out like an equation: the amphora, the piece of paper containing the fruits of the labours of several long evenings spent with his daughter and, finally, the diary of Henry Black. None of them meant much on its own, but put them together and 'x' became less of a variable, even if it did not yet mark the spot.

So, why was he delaying? Was it the final stand of a man of science; the pragmatist who didn't believe in buried treasure? Strange for someone who had spent most of his life afloat on that great repository of sunken secrets, the ocean. Perhaps it was his fear that everything spread before him might add up to nothing, and his dream would fade. What had Tariq said, wondering was often better than knowing?

Or maybe he was just savouring this moment of fulfilment and everything that had led him here.

He picked up Jane's work; the scent of her patchouli moisturiser was to those sheets of paper what the spices of the East had been to Tariq's letter, so he could almost hear her voice:

"What? You're not happy with it, are you?" He senses her bridling, but the frustration he knows must be showing on his face is not directed at her.

"No, no, no, Janey," he protests, "on the contrary, you've done wonderfully to make any sense of it."

She's still unsure; irritated. "If it's not good enough, perhaps you could have given me a bit more help, like you said you would."

He pats her shoulder. "In the end, I left you alone on purpose. I didn't want to influence you, except for helping with the odd bit of technical jargon. Sometimes these things are clearer to the less myopic outsider."

Defused a touch by his humour, her tone becomes milder. "Well actually, it makes no sense to me at all."

"But it does to me," he reassures her, "from a navigational point of view, allowing for a certain amount of superstitious clap-trap and deliberate obfuscation in the language." He sits down next to her and points to the sheets of paper. "See here; this describes a technique that was in practice for more than a thousand years. Ancient sailors couldn't read longitude, so most mariners of that time measured their journey from home against the stars using a knotted rope. All the distances are here." He leans back and sighs, releasing his frustration with caution. "Unfortunately for us it doesn't tell us the starting point of the journey, which might have been any port in the southern hemisphere." He assumes it was the main port of the still-mythical island kingdom. Even though he and Jane have taken an educated guess at the modern names of the stars and constellations, it has still left them with a lock they can't pick.

Sutch had almost smashed the amphora in frustration at the absence of that one so telling detail – the port of departure – on the night they finished their work together. He had so wanted to be able to share his secret with Jane as a reward. Then, some days later, in a moment of either genius or desperation, as if fate, in which of course he didn't believe, had nudged him, he had remembered the writings – assumed to be ravings – of Captain Henry Black.

Plenty had been written *about* Black, not much of it agreeing with his own opinion of himself. From what Sutch could tell, he had been an adventurer, a mercenary and privateer like his great friends Sir Francis Drake and Sir Martin Frobisher, heroes of the defeat of the Spanish Armada in 1588. He claimed to have taken part in that epic event, though there was no record of him, but given some of his acts of piracy on the high seas he may simply have wished to remain anonymous. Drake and Frobisher would have understood. Many of their deeds were given an undeserved gloss by Elizabethan historians and they had gone on to lead wealthy and esteemed lives. The same could not be said of Black, though what he did seem to have in common with them was his brilliance as a sailor, his command of the tides and the loyalty of his men.

Mad, or drunk, or both, he'd been jettisoned by Drake, who had abandoned him in Lisbon as a man might scrape shit from his shoe. Black had responded by leaving his post and plying his trade of piracy full-time. From time to time, he would heave to in some port, to replenish his supplies of drink and venereal diseases, the effects of both apparent in some of the writings in his bombastic journal; or at least that had always been the assumption of the cognoscenti. Black had considered his book enough of a contribution to posterity to have some copies made. The whereabouts of three of them were known, and Professor Sutch, a keen collector of rare maritime artefacts, was the proud, yet perhaps embarrassed owner of one, which he had pulled that evening from its hiding-place on one of the higher bookshelves in his study.

Like everyone else, he had disregarded it as part fact, part fantasy, and had dismissed it as the product of a fevered mind... until now. What if the chapter dealing with Black's pursuit of a sleek, black trading ship that arrived laden with an undisclosed precious cargo at the port of Zanzibar, were true? Sutch could have kicked himself from Portsmouth to the Barbary Coast for not having made the connection before between that ship and the ones he had heard described in tales during his own wanderings.

When Black described the eyes of the crew, Sutch had shivered in recognition:

'I am not easily unmanned and know not if the gesture still affords me protection after the life I have led, but I crossed myself, for young and old alike carried something ancient and, dare I say, eldritch within them that peered forth from the windows of their souls.'

Even more than Black's diary, it had been the look in Tariq's eyes, benevolent though his features were, that had started to convince the Professor, perhaps only in his subconscious mind, of the truth of the old merchant's story. The memory of those eyes now took on a more sinister aspect in the dying light of a late September evening, as branches tapped bony fingers against the study window in a breeze that brought autumn's rumour whispering by.

As a man who had seen the hold of a strange ship being filled to the gunnels with traded goods, Black had been unable to resist the urge to follow when it weighed anchor and left Zanzibar, setting out across the Indian Ocean.

Drunk or mad he may have been, but Black was an experienced mariner, and he had still kept a detailed log of his ship's course in his journal, alongside the pages of prose. It had become apparent to him, and to Sutch as he read the notes, that the course set by the other ship was designed to confuse. That the traders had spotted Black pursuing them was beyond doubt.

Having re-read the piece, the Professor removed his glasses, rubbed his eyes and at last made his shaky way across to his beloved collection of maps and atlases.

"Where are you? Where are you?" he mumbled to himself as he shoved documents and dusty tomes to one side. "Aha!"

He pulled down his favourite chart of the southern seas, brought it back to the desk and weighted down the corners with whatever other desktop objects were to hand.

So, if Henry Black's journal was correct, there could be little doubt that the search would take place in the Indian and Southern Oceans. That much Sutch had always assumed, not only because of Tariq's account, but also because all other seas were well enough charted – on the surface at least – to leave little room for hidden, island-based civilisations; no *mare incognitum* as such, though of course all seas deserved that title, with less than three per cent of the ocean floor explored. But south from Zanzibar still left a lot of sea to cover, much of it wild.

The link was the whirlpool, because it was mentioned right at the end of Jane's translation. If he was right, it marked a key reference point in the navigation records of the lost people, and a cunning one, because the great eddying mass of water was only there at certain times of the day, when particular currents converged. From that point, it was possible the islanders set varied courses to the ports at which they traded; perhaps these were etched onto other amphorae. But working backwards from the location of the whirlpool – using it as his starting point – he now believed he could find their kingdom.

"I can find your kingdom."

He felt compelled to say the words out loud, to see whether the dream of glass shattered at the sound of them.

What had seemed, on first reading many years before, to be the fantasies of a syphilitic madman made sudden sense. Had those sailors, whether willing or commanded, sacrificed themselves rather than give up their secrets?

The thought made him break off from his chart for just a moment's reflection. The water of life referred to by Tariq had to be a metaphor. Sutch couldn't allow himself to believe that bedtime story. But what of the nameless threat that the fisherman and all his people had feared?

Many ancient civilisations were known for the brutality of their religious practices. Perhaps the sailors that Black pursued had chosen the mercy of the sea instead of whatever awaited them at the hands of the shamans if they brought invaders in their wake. Indeed, it sounded as if one had been on board with them and he would have protected their secrets with all of their lives. In Sutch's experience, if it was worth protecting with your life, then it was worth discovering.

And then it hit him. It – the lost land, the quest, the very idea of it – had already claimed half his life, and if all that was left now was a lump of rock on the ocean bed it was worth finding, if only to claim back a part of his stolen years. To feel vindicated. To drink from his own amphora.

Sutch followed the readings from Black's journal to the letter, or number. They zigzagged from Zanzibar across the oceans, as if the islanders' vessel had been tacking against a wind sent by the universe to defy them. It took Sutch almost an hour to plot the course, but what was that mere blink of the eye compared with four decades of frustrated obsession? At last, he reached the point where Black had abandoned his quest and turned back in the face of the mighty whirlpool. Now he took the instructions from Jane's translation and, ancient though they were, plotted them on the map.

He sank down on his chair, open mouthed.

The Scorpion Archipelago!

He removed his glasses again, rubbed the heels of his palms into his eyes and stared into the pool of light that shone like a search lamp in the settling gloom of his study. It illuminated the new centre of his world.

"The Scorpion Archipelago!" he whispered in awe, moved once more to speak, as if his ageing body could not contain the excitement. Or perhaps he was trying once again to turn the dream of a myth into the reality of words. He bent close to the map, talking to the ghosts, waving his glasses and gesturing to his imaginary audience:

"Unbelievable, and yet now so plausible. A thousand miles from anywhere, never mapped by land-based cartography, only by satellite."

He had seen those images from space once. They showed a curving line of islands just to the west of the Southeast Indian Ridge; granite mountains that fell away sharply as cliffs to the north, their southern slopes covered by thick forest and surrounded by deep, dark, often raging seas. Sutch looked into the distance for a moment and thought of Santorini, where the continental shelf fell away into an abrupt abyss as a result of volcanic activity, making the island one of the prime contenders for the location of Atlantis. Its coastal waters were black and cold, like those of the archipelago. Then, looking back at the chart, which bore the scribblings of many of his findings and theories he muttered:

"The waters in the latitude of the archipelago are known for high levels of plankton and the nutrients needed to sustain marine life, which might have made them suitable for fishing. Yes, yes, that much, at least, is consistent with the ancient fisherman's tale, and if part of the land has indeed fallen away like Santorini as a result of a cataclysmic earthquake or volcanic eruption, that could explain the aftermath of destruction he witnessed."

In the midst of his excitement, a finger of doubt gave a light tap on the old man's shoulder, but he pushed it away. Edward Sutch's thoughts and words had distilled to a tiny point on a map, and he sat transfixed by that group of inconsequential islands, supposed uninhabitable and unattractive by modern man – till now. He could not be sure that they had never been visited, but knew of no reports or exploratory expeditions, and though it was not his specific field, as a member of the Royal Geographical Society for fifty years he believed he would have known. Of course, there was always the chance that someone had indeed explored the archipelago, only to find there was nothing worth reporting. There was no comfort in that thought and he tried to close his mind to the possibility – a unique action that went against every tenet on which he had based his life as a scientist.

That tapping finger wouldn't go away. What if this was a wild goose chase after all? What if there had been an undiscovered race of people, but every fibre of proof of their existence had been consumed by the sea or the earth's crust?

He looked at the amphora for reassurance. Its solid clay, maybe the last remaining evidence of an island nation, stood solid and irrefutable on the desk. As swift as the cloud of panic had been to cross the sun, it blew away again. The warmth that followed was a peculiar sensation – alien to his substantive, academic mind, but perhaps a symptom of his ageing bones; it was faith. A smile crossed his lips, and he pointed to the amphora, wagging his finger: "I knew there was something about you, from the moment I found you – or you found me. I knew you were more than you seemed. And that..." here he prodded the air with that same finger, "... is why this is meant to be. Mine might be just one of countless parallel worlds, and I found my way into yours – or vice versa. Even eighty is not too old to meet your destiny in an unexpected way."

There was another tap, this time at the study door. He did not bother answering, knowing she would come in anyway. In fifty years they never had any secrets from each other. Well, that was not strictly true, of course. For forty of those fifty years there had been the little matter of the amphora, but hadn't the act of hiding that from Candice really been about refusing to believe in ghosts – the same ones which had comprised his audience just now?

She wore a slight frown as she looked around the room. "Are you okay?"

"Yes, my darling." He gave a little grin. "You should be used to me talking to myself by now." He motioned for her to come nearer, knowing that a woman's curiosity is a part of her beauty which will neither wither nor fade. She crossed the room, her hips imparting, as ever, that graceful sway to her long skirt, and he placed his welcoming arm around her waist. She knew – and he knew that she knew – that his study was his sanctuary and he never entertained outsiders there. With his free hand he gestured palm upward towards the artefacts on the desk. "I do believe I have solved something."

She pursed her lips. "I thought I recognised that gleefulness in your eye. I hope this doesn't mean—"

"That I will rush off on some hair-brained quest? Oh, Candice, you know me."

"Mmmm." Her lips were still pursed, but ironic humour lit her eyes. Then she took his face in her hands and kissed it. "Were our Jane's efforts of any use to you, whatever it was you had her doing?"

"Absolutely."

Candice looked at the objects spread before her. Sutch watched her crane her neck. The profile was clearly from the same gene pool, but the movement was imbued with more elegance than Jane's when she had first seen the amphora. Candice was a throwback, a woman who believed she was indeed made for needlepoint and gentle pursuits. She did not have the ruddy complexion of a life spent outdoors in hot climes; seventy-five English summers spent beneath wide-brimmed sunhats had nurtured the bloom on her cheek, and only the whiteness of her shoulder-length hair suggested that quite so many summers had indeed passed. She had shared Sutch's hopes and enthusiasm, but not the miles he had chosen to travel through his work, yet he loved her all the more for the absences. Seeing traces of her in his daughter some weeks before had brought the smile to his face and did so again now.

With a knowing look she turned to him. "And what now?"

He pondered, biting his bottom lip, and then a light shone in his eyes. "I have a plane to catch and then dinner to organise."

She didn't ask. Sometimes it was better not to.

CHAPTER TEN

"Impossible. The board can't postpone the programme at this stage."

"But I just need a holiday."

"The trouble with you, Edward, is you've never been a good liar. Even complete strangers know when you're not telling the truth. Since I've known you forty-five years, you haven't a hope in hell. So, what have you got up your sleeve?"

The Professor's attempt at an ingenuous expression was thwarted by the smile that was tugging at the corners of his mouth. So, rather than spreading his hands in an 'I don't know what you mean' gesture, he nodded in acknowledgement: "Something. I just can't tell you what. Not yet. But more than as a director to a director, as one very old good friend to another, I tell you the Royal Geographical Society will be the first to know." He picked up his coffee mug again from Sir Arthur Tennyson's desk. "Indeed, I'll be approaching you for funding."

"Funding for what?" Tennyson's eyebrows required more of his hairdresser's time these days than his balding head; they flew so low they were almost performing aerobatics when he spoke. Yet they could not disguise the gleam in his eyes as he probed his sometime bridge partner.

Sutch put down the mug again, pulled his chair closer to the desk and leaned forward on his leather-patched elbows. Then, all the jollity in his expression slid into sudden, unexpected earnestness. "Arthur, I would tell you if I could, but I fear that even you, my dearest old friend, would be hard-pushed not to think me a fool and a dreamer. But I believe I am on the verge of discovering something unique and, in the process, fulfilling a dream of forty years." He leaned back again. "Look, I don't want to waste the Society's time or funds – heaven knows the days are tough enough – but I repeat, you will be the first to know. If I find what I'm looking for,

I'll want the best man with me to photograph it – capture it for the glory of the Royal Geographical Society and its archives."

"You mean young Bolton. He won't come cheap."

"Believe me, if my little jaunt goes well, he'll be paying me for the privilege of taking photographs. I'll need him to sign a confidentiality agreement."

"He's freelance; that's not something I think we can insist on if we want him on board."

Sutch waved a dismissive hand as if shooing away a fly. "Oh, come on, Arthur, use your clout."

The director leaned back and sighed. "I'll do what I can, but it's one thing keeping one person quiet. This sabbatical you're taking – God knows you could just take a holiday and disappear – will make people suspicious, particularly the press."

Sutch paled. "The press!"

"Edward, you always did underestimate your standing in the scientific establishment."

Sutch rubbed his face. "Oh dear. You're probably right. It's an old-fashioned sense of duty that makes me follow the right procedure. Okay, I'll just slip away. Arthur, I really need you to keep any hounds off my scent. It's one of the reasons I'm having to be so Machiavellian with you, my oldest friend. It's called plausible deniability."

"You set up the Shoals of Capricorn Programme, for heaven's sake. The Mascarene Ridge has been on our agenda a long time. You know how important it is."

"That's why I don't like just disappearing. But it's not important compared with this." Sutch slapped his hand on the arm of the chair. "Every member of that team is more than qualified to start without me."

Sir Arthur Tennyson knew that if Professor Edward Sutch was starting to lose his temper – or what passed for his version of it – then the matter in hand was of enormous importance to the academic world. He had never known his colleague and friend to display anything more than pique – with the honourable exception of his opinions about his daughter's marriage – but he could fulminate with the best when discussing the impact of overfishing. This 'matter' had to be of significance for the scientific community. He'd not seen Edward slap the arm of a chair in a long time. "Very well, in the face of such passion," he grinned, "or should I say, Sutch's passion, I'll do what I can, but it won't be easy. As you say, members of the Society will start sniffing around. If they catch a whiff of you behaving out of the ordinary, it will be as if they've seen someone standing with a theodolite in some virgin part of the Valley of the Kings. You know what they're like. And that means the press will come running."

"Arthur, I repeat, I need you to keep them off my back."

"I will, Edward, I will." Tennyson gave the side of his nose a theatrical tap. "I don't know who our mole is, but someone around here does more digging than your daughter. How is she by the way? Haven't seen her in a while. Is she back in the land of the living?"

One look at his friend's black expression, and Sir Arthur cursed himself, knowing he had touched on the old wound of the son-in-law again, even before Sutch responded with: "To adapt an old saying, 'there is a great deal to be said for being among the dead.'"

Time to move on, thought the director. "Can't you give me anything to work on? I mean, for all I know you've discovered the head of the Colossus of Rhodes. You don't think holiday-makers would perhaps notice your flotilla?"

Sutch came out from under his cloud again. "That's the point, Arthur. This is just a recce I'm doing; confirmation, some notes, a few photos – it'll be like an SAS operation; lowest possible profile. Once it's done, I'll approach you and the other members of the Society to organise the heavy artillery."

Sir Arthur smiled. "This must be big news, old friend."

"Possibly; possibly not. I'm hoping to find out."

As Edward Sutch prepared to leave the director's office, Sir Arthur put a hand on his shoulder. "I don't know what you're getting yourself into, Edward, but at your age many men are reflecting on the colour of their whisky in the firelight."

"And I was, Arthur, I was. And maybe it looked a bit too much like fossilised amber." He looked thoughtful and then turned to his friend. "You know, as a man of science I never thought I'd be saying this, but I guess fate took a hand."

CHAPTER ELEVEN

SOMEWHERE OVER THE SOUTHERN INDIAN OCEAN, SEPTEMBER 30TH 1997

"Big bitch, ain't she?" The Antipodean voice crackled through the headphones.

"I assume you mean the ocean, not the plane." Sutch tried to show wit in adversity. He had sailed, swum and dived in most of the seven seas, but flying thousands of feet above them had always made him uneasy, even in huge commercial airliners, never mind the Airfix kit in which he was now trapped, his hands gripping the edge of the seat between his knees.

Dirk looked across at him and laughed, his bluff Aussie features folding up into myriad sun-baked lines: "Aww, this is a smooth one for down in these latitudes."

"Really?" Sutch was seeking reassurance, but when Dirk then turned serious for a moment, he wished he hadn't.

The Aussie gestured out of the window. "She makes me nervous too, the sea. Been flying tourists into the Outback for a few years now; this is the furthest I've flown over water for a long time, perhaps ever. Forgotten how anxious it can make you on a grey day like this; snarling waters below you. The Indian Ocean, eh? Wonder how many tourists know it can look like this. There ain't much solid between here and the Antarctic. I tell ya, Prof, even with the extra long-range and wing-tip tanks, and the stainless-steel auxiliary ferry tanks I put in where the back seats used to be, this baby will be close to the limit of its juice by the time we get refuelled."

Sutch had been forcing his fingers loose from the seat edge, but that last word sent them into further lockdown. "Refuelled?" He tried his best to sound calm. "You didn't mention anything about running out of fuel. Where exactly are we supposed to find—"

Dirk waved his hand in the general direction of the horizon. "Aww, somewhere in the French Southern and Antarctic Territories."

"Somewhere? Is this a wind-up, Dirk?"

The Aussie winked at his passenger. "Don't worry, Prof, this isn't somewhere I'd wanna ditch." He patted the steering column. "And this is a Cessna C206. She's a strong bird. You can let some blood back in those knuckles." He laughed, and once he had relaxed a bit, Sutch could not help but join in.

After a few minutes silence and more stomach lurching, Dirk chipped in again: "Okay, Prof, I'm very flattered that you sought me out for this trip and curious as to why you offered double the usual fee. You gonna enlighten me?"

Sutch paused; felt awkward. "It really is very hush-hush, Dirk."

"Aw, c'mon Doc, I can keep a secret. You've known me long enough to know that. Besides, where I'm usually working, the only ones listening would be black and white and woolly."

Sutch took a deep breath. "Well, let's just SAY...!" The last word was shouted in accompaniment to another sudden drop in altitude. "Are you doing this deliberately to frighten an answer out of me?"

"Aw, it's a little windy up here."

Sutch came to a decision. "Okay Dirk, you really must keep this to yourself, I can't emphasise that enough."

"You got my word, Prof."

He looked at the pilot. "Well, that's always been good enough for me. Satellite images suggest that there may well be drilling opportunities near the Scorpion Archipelago."

I'm lying already. You found the right man, Tariq.

"You're shitting me!" Now Dirk looked embarrassed. There was something olde worlde about the Professor and he did not like swearing in front of his venerable passenger. "Sorry. You mean, out there, in the middle of some of the loneliest waters in the world?"

"Needs must, Dirk. The world's current oil reserves won't last forever."

"Yeah, but how...?"

"Precisely – I'm taking the first step towards finding out. Don't forget, the archipelago was possibly once a much larger landmass and the area may be unsuitable from a geothermal point of view. But I'm an oceanographer, not a geologist. I'm just having a preliminary look at the suitability of the area from a logistical point of view. When I return, I'll be checking to see whether there could be adverse effects on marine life. Of course, they'd have to use floating platforms, and they also want to know if I think it's feasible." He looked across at Dirk. "Personally, I think our planet's been exploited and plundered almost beyond the point of sustainability. I see this as a jolly good chance to stick two fingers up at the oil companies; firstly, by taking their obscenely high pay-out for doing the work," he patted his co-conspirator on the shoulder, "and then telling them there isn't a snowball's chance in hell."

"Good on yer, Prof." Dirk nodded in the direction of the horizon. "Much as the vastness of the sea frightens me sometimes, I wouldn't want to see signs of a permanent human presence out here." He didn't see the change of expression in Sutch's eyes, though he would have struggled to interpret it. Likewise, it was lucky he missed the previous look of shame in those same eyes; as Sir Arthur Tennyson had said, everyone knew when Edward Sutch was lying. Dirk grinned. "I could've lied for you." Sutch felt himself redden. "You could've just paid me the money, stayed in Perth for a couple of days and I'd've told them we made the flight."

Sutch laughed, relieved. "A nice thought. I know an excellent bar there, though thanks to your hollow legs I'm not sure I would remember how to find it. But I have to provide reports and some photographs. I also need to check the feasibility of landing a float plane like this near enough to get equipment onto the islands, and if any of them are suitable staging posts for an oil operation."

Already Sutch knew that, if he were to go ahead with a preliminary covert expedition, he would not want planes moored up in full view of satellites. Small boats could at least be hidden in coves. But a boat trip, even from the Kerguelen Islands, would eat into valuable time, as well as being risky as hell in those changeable waters, so he might yet have to turn to Dirk. But the big Aussie was a man he could trust. Of course, his son-in-law knew how to fly – an essential pre-requisite for the would-be playboy – and he would have a job arguing the need for an additional pilot past Jane. She was nothing if not practical. Plus, there was the remote chance she might see it as another snub; a lack of trust.

Dirk frowned. "Remember what I told you back in Oz? If we have to land this little girl today, we're gonna be eating up a lot of fuel. But hey, what am I worrying about? If we do have to bring it down short of the refuelling points we've got a radio."

Sutch grimaced, and not simply at the thought of this rattling Cessna coming down and tossing around on the ocean. He really did not want anyone knowing his whereabouts. But there was no choice. It seemed they would have to refuel. Then he decided that he was being a bit paranoid and perhaps even arrogant. He doubted anyone outside his field of expertise had ever heard of him.

"We'll see, Dirk. If we can get away without a landing and you can bring her in low enough that I can take a couple of decent photographs, that might do."

"I think we'll find out soon enough."

Dirk gestured ahead and Sutch followed his gaze to the horizon.

Ahead, still small in the distance, probably about half a nautical mile apart, were two jagged towers of rock, which looked as if the land between them had been sliced away like a loaf of bread. Far older than humanity, but outriders of a civilisation nonetheless. The gateway to the Scorpion Archipelago.

Sutch didn't know this area well; in the latter part of his career his work had been based in busier parts of the high seas, charting waters where shipping lines often still relied on marine charts from over a hundred years ago. Through financial necessity he had indeed, from time to time, worked with the oil companies. As a man of science he had a practical mind, which recognised that security for his family had to share an uncomfortable bed with altruism. But now, he was heading towards some of the most isolated and pitiless latitudes on the planet, with very few commercial shipping lanes and flight-paths. This was a tribal priestess of a sea; wild, beautiful and untouched.

Still, he knew enough about the region to slap his forehead now in exasperation. Of course! He should have put two and two together and remembered these twin spires, fangs of rock thrust up from the Southeast Indian Ridge by some primeval volcanic activity. Hell's Gate they may have been to many, but not to a sailor for whom they were a signpost home. Jane's translation had spoken of a door. Sutch cursed his myopia.

The true size of the stone towers could be gauged by how long it took to draw near. At last, the Cessna buzzed past one of them, reduced to insignificance by its bulk; a mosquito next to a dinosaur. What had been a mere jag on the horizon had grown to a massive hunk of granite that would dwarf a cathedral and, despite the battering of the seas, would probably outlast Christianity. The plane juddered a touch as warmer air reflecting from the vast, flat side of the slab caused a thermal.

"Well, that wouldn't make much of a staging post for even the craziest expedition," quipped Dirk, but the humour in his voice was strained. The size of the rock had unnerved both men, making them feel inconsequential and transient, which of course they were.

On they flew, knowing there would be no further physical landmarks till they saw the coastline of the archipelago. Sutch's palms were still sweating, only now it wasn't through fear of flying.

***

The islands themselves were almost lost in the grey swell and swirl of the horizon. Distant white flecks first caught the eye. Just being able to see those breakers from that distance told both men how big the waves were and how steep the land against which they crashed. These were waves hitting a landmass at full speed and height, unbroken by any continental shelf. There would be no landing place, for plane or ship, on such waters. But the Cessna's easterly approach meant they could tell that the waves were only on one side of the island chain, the south. To the north the waters were calmer.

The two men were so mesmerised by the islands that they became disorientated. As if staring at and through a colour-blind chart, there was a sudden realisation that they could make out details. They were almost there. The glance they exchanged was full of significance.

"This is not a good place, Professor."

"No." It took a lot for Sutch to admit that about his first sighting of the promised land.

"It's like someone's broken off a little piece of Cape Horn and dropped it here."

He could be more right than he knows, thought Sutch. What if these were the remains of something much bigger that had simply fallen away, taking anything of significance with it and leaving a now with no past? 'Discouraged' didn't do justice to how he felt at that moment, as he contemplated the logistics and questioned the sense.

The Scorpion Archipelago consisted of nine islands forming a narrowing crescent that curved in on itself at the end, like a scorpion's tail. Nature held sway now and it was hard to imagine it had ever been otherwise; that she had ever relinquished her hold. Only time would tell. 'Archipelago' was perhaps a rather grand term for this crescent, which covered an area of about thirty miles in length, the smallest island being the sting in the scorpion's tail. Nevertheless, it was an impressive, fearful sight, the more so for being dwarfed by the unending sea; a last stand made by a disappearing landmass against overwhelming odds. The southern sides of each island were vertiginous cliff-faces, slicing down to the thrashing and thundering waters of the Southern Ocean, which tried to reclaim its birth-right, hammering in anger at these stubborn survivors. The northern faces of the mountains sloped down more gently, smothered by forest. The canopy of trees made it almost impossible to discern anything below. Only at the fringes of the islands did the hostile environment appear less secretive, with shelves and lips of shingle or black sand. Here the sea was gentler, but through the calmer waters jagged rocks were visible, stretching out into the ocean. The two men looked at these with resignation.

Dirk pointed downwards. "Don't think we're gonna be landing anything here. Are these crazy sons of bitches you call paymasters seriously contemplating drilling out here?"

"Well, you know, Dirk, as I said, my recommendation will be no, but the oil companies are getting more reckless."

"Looks to me like these islands would only be bases for supplies at best. There wouldn't be any great inducement to spend R & R time here. Think the only way you'd get ashore here is with inflatables through some of those clear channels down there."

Sutch went silent, finding it hard to come to terms with his disappointment. This was an even more hostile world than he had imagined. The islands weren't that big, but still, looking for any evidence of a long-gone civilisation would mean... well, he was already tired of the haystack analogy. The forest seemed thick and impenetrable. But then again, one had only to look at Machu Picchu to see just how effectively nature could hide unrecorded history once mankind finished strutting and fretting its hour. Below them now was the natural balance, which humanity so often saw as chaos.

To Sutch, it seemed inevitable that he would need to bring a big team after all. He could not imagine coming here in secret with a small group, not the one he had in mind anyway, and sweeping all nine islands. Even completing a thorough search of just one would be an achievement in the time he had projected, given the apparent density of the forest and the lay of the land.

This moment had turned into something of a paradox. Part of the Professor argued that he should be seeking gentler pursuits at the grand old age of eighty, while another sprite within him, one he knew he would never subdue, insisted that, as he was nearing the end of his broadcast, why not try to sign off the transmission in style. And after all, if he found even one fragment of a broken pot or a human bone it would be a big deal for archaeologists, historians and anthropologists everywhere, not to mention OAPs.

And it was in these last thoughts that he recognised how this bleak place had already managed to eat its way under his skin like a parasite, infecting his logical thought processes. He had a sickness. How else could he explain his certainty that he would return?

The need for some inspired guesswork about where to start looking was given added urgency by Dirk's voice crackling in the headphones: "I tell ya, Doc, we've got enough fuel if you land now, but that's about it. Unless you want to become a permanent addition to the landscape here."

The islands at the sting end of the scorpion's tail were precipitous on both sides and possibly too small to be of any importance. A people seeking a new home would need the biggest area available. Also, the waters around the largest of the islands seemed deep and black. Might the land have fallen away to the most dramatic effect there, perhaps taking those very people and their civilisation with it?

"Let's think big, Dirk. We'll go for those great lumps over there."

"The sea's too rough for a landing on this side, Professor, and I reckon a hundred yards out is about the closest I'd get on the other side. What d'ya mean 'go for' anyway?"

Sutch shook his head. "I don't want you to land, Dirk, just make a couple of passes so I can take some pictures. You know, for the record? And if they do decide on bases out here, I need to show them the best possibilities." That he was looking for somewhere to base his own small team remained his secret for the moment. He wondered how Dirk would feel about being part of that.

"Hope you've got a steady hand with that camera of yours then, Doc; it's gonna be a bit bumpy."

Sutch held up what looked like a palm-sized camcorder and pointed to it. "This little chap is gyroscopically controlled. It's military technology. It doesn't matter how bumpy the ride, the picture will be good enough." The Cessna lurched suddenly and Sutch almost dropped the camera. He looked at Dirk and tutted in frustration, mixed with a lot of trepidation. "The camera will be good enough; the question is, will the pilot?"

"Sorry Doc, the shape of these islands is playing a few tricks with the air currents. Okay, I'm taking her in."

They flew past the implacable cliff-face of the largest island. It was black and threatening, creviced and seeming close enough to touch. The Professor flicked on the camera, and it started to beep.

"'Sit supposed to do that?" Dirk looked across when he got no answer, to see Sutch looking rather sheepish.

"Oh dear. I think I might have forgotten to charge it."

"You what!"

He looked at Dirk in apology. "It's okay, we should have enough time left on it."

Dirk twisted his mouth. "And you had the nerve to criticise the pilot."

As they passed the end of the cliff-face the plane gave a violent lurch once more, a plaything of the prevailing wind. Dirk looped around, banked the Cessna and then came in at no more than fifty feet above the rocky waters on the northern side.

The forest would have been impenetrable to the eye even if they weren't flying past it in a blur. Sutch knew already that it didn't matter what pictures he took; his irrational decision to return had been made and the choppy waters below him were those of his own personal Rubicon, though he could not be sure on which bank he stood. He was hoping it didn't prove to be the River Styx instead.

Still, something caught his attention and caused him to squint as they approached the second island, which was about a mile and a half from the first.

"My God!"

"What is it?" Dirk didn't look at his passenger as he was concentrating on keeping a steady height above the waves, some of which were getting pretty big even on this calmer side. He'd seen air-sea rescue crews mistime leaps out of helicopters, expecting to drop a hundred feet into stormy seas and having the wind knocked out of them as giant waves climbed to within a few feet of the machine. His question was greeted by silence. "Professor?"

"In a moment, Dirk, in a moment." They flew past the island and Sutch was sure: he was going to film that with maximum zoom on the next sweep. And it would certainly not be the plane causing his hands to shake. He turned to Dirk and put a hand on his shoulder. "Sorry for being abrupt, Dirk."

"No worries."

"I want you to make that pass of the second island again. But before we do there's something I need to tell you as concisely as I can."

***

The Aussie's mouth had opened with incredulity and remained that way for most of the Professor's brief exposition. When it moved, it was to say: "You're shittin' me! Sorry, you're kiddin'."

"No, I'm not, and I want you to know, Dirk, that it is a sign of the tremendous trust I have in you that I am telling you this. It's also a sign that I want you to come back with me. I'm sorry I lied before, but you must understand, I thought you'd think I was losing it." Sutch turned from looking at the Aussie's shocked face towards the window. "Talking of coming back, shouldn't you be turning the plane?"

Dirk realised that in his amazement he had lost track of what he was doing. He started to bring the Cessna around, and then looked, full of doubts, at Sutch. "Come back. To this place?"

"Yes. Not an inviting prospect, is it?"

"'Bout as inviting as spending a night in a sleeping bag on the banks of the Mara River." Sutch remembered Dirk's story about a close encounter with a Nile crocodile, but he hoped that saying *no* was not an option for a man for whom flying tourists across the Outback had provided a good living, but never replaced the excitement of supporting expeditions and humanitarian teams. However, it seemed he was wrong. "Aw, dunno, Prof. The here-and-now's more my thing. No disrespect, but I've never understood that need to..." he sought the right words, "... commune with the dead; literally or metaphorically digging them up. I guess I just think mankind's priority should be to help those who, through no fault of their own, seemed about to join them."

"Well anyway," continued Sutch, "we mustn't get ahead of ourselves. But what I saw back there has got me very excited. Bring her in from a bit further out this time, so I can explain what I think we're looking at." They dropped to fifty feet. The Professor pointed. "There! You see that bay?"

"You mean that cove there?"

"Precisely. It looks a bit like Lulworth Cove, on the south coast of England. You remember? Where we had that stunning rhubarb crumble that time." Dirk grinned. The Professor had that old school way of making people feel like they were down home in the most unlikely of circumstances. "Except the geology and oceanography here are all wrong. It's the currents, they wouldn't wear the rocks in that way. Nor would those rocks erode in that pattern. To me this looks man-made."

"No fu— no way. Surely."

"Someone has built this up; turned it into a harbour."

"Well, we're coming up on it quickly, so you'd better get that camera ready."

Sutch switched it on again, having left it off to save the remaining power. As they made the second pass and he peered through the zoom lens, something else made the hairs stand up on the back of his neck.

... BEFORE THE STORM; PORTSMOUTH 10.58 P.M. OCTOBER 24TH 1997

He became aware that his eyes were squeezed shut; also, that the room had grown cold, as if the history of the Southern Ocean lived on for this one night far away in the north.

It had been important to remember, but now the excitement was tinged with dread; a fear of what they might find; of what they might not.

Sutch got to his feet. The chill seemed to have invaded his bones. He thought of Candice lying warm in bed and couldn't wait to join her.

"What are you doing, you foolish old man?" he asked himself out loud as he thought of dragging his eighty-year-old body from that bed in a few hours' time and hauling it across two hemispheres. Pursuing a dream? It seemed the unlikeliest of answers at this late hour.

The clock in the hallway struck eleven. To Edward Sutch it seemed suddenly that he had heard the chimes at midnight.

***

MID-OCTOBER 1997

The old man struggled to breathe as he fought his way up the slope. In the oppressive humidity beneath the canopy of trees it would have been a tough climb for a younger man, never mind one in his condition.

He had not expected this but perhaps should have foreseen it. In panic he glanced back and through an opening in the trees; saw them disembarking from their boats far below. He was not scared of them and what they might do to him – it was too late for that – but he needed to find a sanctuary nonetheless, somewhere he could buy himself enough time to scribble a warning – add it to his journal – and hopefully where he could lie undisturbed until the note was found by its intended recipients. He needed to find that sanctuary soon. This was a race against time. After all, he was dying.

CHAPTER TWELVE

NORTH OF THE SCORPION ARCHIPELAGO, OCTOBER 28TH 1997

"Jesus, it's the fucking Lost World, isn't it? With any luck we'll find that dinosaurs still rule and we'll have big game hunting with a difference."

Jane's knuckles were clenched white, in part through the ostentatious and unnecessary crude language from Pete, which showed disrespect for her father as well as underlining the ever-present simmering tension between the two men. Worse though was that, in his Rabelaisian way, he had a point. She knew it would be wrong to underestimate his perceptiveness. After all, he had sensed well enough that her lust of a couple of nights before was not coincidental; had recognised, in her need for silence, other desires being satisfied. How else could she explain his mocking words after she had thrashed her way, *sotto voce*, to a voracious climax: "Was that good for you too, Lois?" Perhaps her anger now was for herself at some subliminal level.

Looking from the window of the plane, she realised that part of her knuckle-clenching was because she, too, didn't know how to react and had to wonder what the hell might be down there. Even from a distance the islands were unwelcoming, exuding the latent violence of a sleeping monster. The cloak of trees that softened the contours of the looming mountains was a dust-sheet thrown over the contents of a long-abandoned room; what ancient secrets or horrors might be concealed? Would anyone, even a people fleeing from deprivation or tyranny, really choose to settle here?

She prayed her father had not been spun a yarn, and if he had, why? Sure, it had made for unusual in-flight entertainment on the way from Perth as he told them the tale of Tariq and the amphora. Jane could understand why he had waited till they were enroute before telling it. She knew everyone had been mulling it over since; a returning fisherman flees from his homeland, a place unknown to civilised man, when he sees it has been consumed by fire and lava. One of his few possessions, an amphora, is passed to a merchant friend, who, knowing he is dying childless, then gives it to an outsider, the Professor, along with the revelation that the engravings on it hold directions to that long-lost kingdom. There is a secret that will only be revealed if the recipient of the amphora finds the kingdom, if indeed it still exists; a place of fabulous wealth, where the people mined precious stones that bought them all they might ever need.

On its own, it might have been an enchanting tale, as long as it didn't turn out to belong to the Arabian Nights, which were not the basis for heavy funding of exploratory expeditions. Jane had not tried to read the expressions on anyone's face, and didn't intend to, in case she saw respect for her father replaced by incredulity or indulgence. But what right had she to hope for unquestioning belief when she, herself, didn't know how she felt? Of course, Pete had simply snorted, not bothering to hide his disbelief, but he was here now, and her father's comment that this was a one-way ticket could prove to be double-edged; they were stuck with him.

There was no real mystery to her growing contempt for her husband. In the early days she had mistaken his cavalier approach to life as charming and debonair, instead of the spendthrift, raffish reality. Her family was well respected, and that had opened doors for him. Once marriage had bound them together, the tie had turned out to be a rope, at one end of which she tried to forge ahead, conquering the steepest slopes, blazing a trail, only to be held back by a pull on the line – the need for assistance.

And then, one evening, over the ridge of the summit, Jim had appeared. Nothing had prepared her for the way time stopped when he walked through the door; or rather the clock had started afresh, with her wanting him; wanting to be possessed by him. Parts of her body tingled right now as she remembered how she had come time and again at the thought of him inside her, her husband's body a mere tool – she had to smirk like a schoolgirl at that pun – to fulfil the desires her imagination had sent into overdrive. What the hell was all that about? She was Jane Sutch – she had never taken Pete's name – known for her affinity with the past and the dead. Yet she recognised that one smile of greeting from Jim had represented the drawing of a blade that could cut the rope, severing her from everything that had held her back.

She sneaked a sidelong glance at him. Perhaps five years her junior, but that didn't matter; she was like a hormonal teenager and, compared with the things he had seen and done, her achievements were a pass grade in domestic science. She remembered his discussion about Rwanda at that first dinner:

"It was a privilege to be invited back by the transitional government to present my record of the horrors of the genocide. They wanted to use that as a forum for reconciliation. Do you know, some of the perpetrators are now helping willingly to rebuild the homes of their victims? Amazing!"

Jim had stated it all as facts, without bombast or arrogance. He was someone aligned towards the future. That seemed appropriate to Jane. She loved her work, but needed a private life away from the past, with its dust and death. He wasn't striking or handsome in a classic way, but had open, honest features and sleepy green eyes. She nurtured the desperate hope that he didn't feel he was here under false pretences, chasing ancient heirlooms and the ghosts of folklore, or that her father had allowed his pursuit of a dream to cloud his judgement. But Jim was being funded by the Society, doubtless earning top dollar for this jaunt. And after all, the rugged scenery approaching from the south would surely provide some fantastic photo opportunities, irrespective of whether they did find evidence of the fabled island kingdom.

She gazed just a few seconds longer than appropriate at Jim's profile, unaware that she was the focus of similar attention.

The scene unfolding before them became the gradual focus of everyone's thoughts. The general mood dipped as they flew past the two oppressive fangs of rock. The Professor turned in his seat, looked at Jane and pointed:

"Hell's Gate," he mouthed, and she felt her spine shimmy as she remembered the translation.

They were homing in on the slender, lumpy scar of the archipelago in the middle of that featureless sea. Flecks of white below became waves that had travelled unhindered across hundreds of miles of cold, unforgiving ocean. To a man or woman, the chill they felt was down to more than the utilitarian nature of the plane's interior. The buffeting the Cessna was receiving in the strengthening wind was not helping their spirits.

That the mood overall had remained buoyant during the flight was thanks, in great part, to the presence of the three students, though to two of them in particular. All were hardy souls who had been only too willing to join the expedition without knowing where they were heading. They alone had seemed to accept things at face value as they had listened with deference to the Professor's tale. For them, two guys and a girl, this had the makings of a big adventure; in fact, it *was* already. They were young and, as far as Jane remembered, bad things don't really happen to you then – above all, not when you are led by a luminary like her father. He had earmarked them after asking some loaded questions in their respective departments at their university, and holding a disingenuous discussion with Jane, who also lectured there, at Kings College, Cambridge. Later he had explained how, having told each of them that he would be calling them that day, he phoned them all a little before his dinner party and checked their availability, leaving no time for them to rush off and tell anyone. Given the types of people they were, their acceptance of a place on the team had been almost a foregone conclusion – their types being enthusiastic, trusting and, on the whole, skint. Jane listened in on them, curious as to how they were dealing with all this, but also to get to know them a bit more than the little she knew from the college. Without arrogance, she knew they were too in awe of their older companions to dare talk to them yet, which made it all the more ironic that the muscular presence of the two guys was reassuring.

"Man," Cobus shivered, "it looks freezing down there. And I thought the waters off the Cape were bad."

"Four minutes." Robbie's response was elliptical.

"Four minutes what? You bloody Scots are tight with your words as well." The Afrikaner gave Robbie a playful thump on the shoulder that might have injured a lighter man.

"Till ye die. Without a survival suit that's how long it would take. We had a guy go overboard just south of the Arctic Circle on naval manoeuvres. Had him out the water in two minutes and his body temperature was already critical." He grinned. "Mind you, that's par fae the course for most Scottish kids who grew up with holidays on the coast."

"Ja, why did you leave the Navy, man? I mean, it's not like you have a designated period of National Service, like we do in SA."

Jane saw Robbie's brown eyes grow darker as he focussed into the distance for a moment. She knew from the discussion with her father on the flight from London that Robbie had been travelling the world after his stint in the Royal Navy, fallen in love with and married a Polish girl, then brought her back to the UK whereupon she'd finished with him, having achieved her aim of UK citizenship. Heartbroken, he had been unable to settle in a job and became a mature student in her father's Oceanography department.

"I realised that I loved the sea, but not the discipline." He turned to Cobus. "How 'bout you? You were in the army; didn't fancy staying on?"

Robbie took some of the Afrikaner's long blond hair in his fingertips. "The sodomy get ye down – as in, not enough of it?"

"Hey, you poes!" Cobus cracked him on the back of the head, and then looked around in haste just in case anyone knew enough Afrikaans to understand his strong language. Part of the diaspora of white South Africans following the end of apartheid, he joked that he was a real rock-spider – both a proud, rugby-playing Afrikaner, but also never as happy as when enthusing about rock strata, hence his chosen study path of Geology. "Don't go accusing us Southern Hemisphere forwards of the same behaviour as you poncey Northern Hemisphere backs. We're not the rugby world champions for nothing, man."

Robbie rubbed his head. "Yeah, well, we all know you guys win by resorting to violence." He looked past Cobus. "And by keeping Argentina out of the Tri-Nations tournament, eh Cat?"

The raven-haired girl sitting in the row behind broke off from gazing out of the window, though the oppressiveness of what she had seen there still lingered in her pale eyes. "Sorry? What did you say?"

Her Australian accent was a touch incongruous issuing from the dark Latin beauty of that face; looks which had not gone unnoticed by any of the men – much to Jane's chagrin, who had just about stopped herself from linking a protective arm through Jim's, except her jealouscope had picked up that the girl was not casting any sort of interested glances in his direction.

"No good asking her, mate, she's a Roo." Cobus wasn't done.

"Australian by birth, but Argentine by blood." Catalina's feistiness seemed somehow appropriate to her origins.

"So, your folks swapped a vast empty southern landmass for... another vast empty southern landmass."

"But I'll always be a Puma." Her response referred to her beloved Argentine national rugby team. With a dismissive shake of the head, she turned back to the window, while her two tormentors exchanged glances of mock penitence and schoolboyish giggles. "Call yourselves mature students." Her muttering was nevertheless accompanied by a fledgling grin.

Jane could not help wondering about Catalina. To be fair, she seemed unaware of the reaction she caused and earlier in the flight had been holding an animated conversation with her fellow students. Yet there had followed a gradual breaking off from the general discussions, and as the plane drew further away from twentieth century civilisation, some dampening of spirit had clouded her expression. It was puzzling in a girl who had spent weeks of her holidays on trails in the Australian Outback with only herself for company, and with a thirst for knowledge which had first drawn her to Jane's attention. She had been the star student in the Botany faculty, though she managed to combine her studiousness with a touch of feistiness. When she had quit Botany at the end of her first year, after a long talk with Jane, to study Archaeology, Jane had been delighted. This was someone she would be only too happy to mentor; the girl had real potential.

However, right now, the usual gleam in her eye had dulled, as if the battery of a liquid crystal display were running low, and Jane could only attribute that to the view from the window.

Someone else had withdrawn into himself, Jane realised. She looked at her father sitting hunched by his window. He needed her support at what was a major life moment, even for someone as revered in his field and, well, as old as Edward Sutch. Jane moved over to sit by him and adopted a positive tone that in no way reflected her mind-set.

"Well, Father," she patted him on the leg, "it's ironic, isn't it; a hotchpotch of itinerant people gathered on a small island that once ruled an empire on which the sun never set, and headed off in search of a kingdom on which it might never have risen – all because of the reputation of one man: you."

As soon as he looked at her, indeed even as the words left her mouth, she thought: *mistake.*

"Yes," there was soft anxiety in his voice, "and I'm feeling the weight of that responsibility."

"I know." She rubbed his arm and said nothing for the moment, just cursed herself in silence.

He looked back out of the window. "What felt like adventure, when I solved the conundrum in my study, feels much more like foolhardiness when faced by the threat of the landscape and the enormity of the Southern Ocean, even for me."

She squeezed his arm now. "It'll be fine. It's just a short trip. Don't lose it, Father; you're a sailor at heart – and the figurehead of this expedition – so your gut feelings will be taken as omens by others, and if our hired hands suspect for one moment that you're beset by doubts—"

But who was she kidding? The thought of it was eating at her already and the deepening silence in the plane told its own story about the reality of adventures.

Perhaps Dirk had noticed the torpor – they had spoken last night about his first reconnaissance flight a few weeks before. But he, at least, had concrete matters to attend to – his concern now was the landing. Maybe as much for his own sake as for the others, he tried to lighten the mood. "Hey, everyone, this is your captain speaking. Please return your stomachs to the upright position. Sorry if it's getting a bit rough back there, but this is nothing, eh Professor?" He looked at Sutch and gave a thumbs-up signal. "The Doc and me, we were in a Cessna C206 when we came down here last. This here's a C208 Grand Caravan, a much sturdier bird. I hope the smokers among you appreciated that when I had to choose between making the plane non-smoking or non-toilet I chose the latter." There was laughter, in the main through gratitude for the comic relief. They had all made use of the facilities provided in the form of some empty plastic bottles and a curtain. "Ladies, I hope you'll understand if I don't shake hands. After all, it's been a rough flight." More laughter. "I hope you've all jettisoned your handiwork – don't want that flying around when we land. Gives a new meaning to a drop in the ocean, don't it?"

Jane decided to help the keep the dialogue rolling. "Yes, why did we have to throw that all out?"

"Well, while it's a very rugged floatplane with plenty of room for equipment, especially as some of it is stored in the underbelly luggage pods, the extra fuel tanks added weight, so any additional ballast has to be offloaded. I'd have had to throw any passengers out who hadn't had a pee... or whatever!"

Having also reduced some of the weight of gloom, Dirk continued: "And now let me show you all where we're not attempting to land."

The archipelago was almost upon them and the details were looming larger. They could see just how dense the forest was; how in many places it came right down to the water's edge. The Professor leaned across to Jane. He had been quiet for so much of the journey that his whisper startled her. "That," he nodded towards the window, "is why I brought three fit, enthusiastic young people with us. It's going to be hard work, even though I have an idea already where we should start."

"Believe me, Father, enthusiasm soon wears off when you're confronted with hacking your way through dense forest. And who knows what lives in there."

"Oh, very little I'd have thought." He didn't sound that convinced. "This is an isolated piece of land."

"Yes, pristine forest, untouched by human hand, its ecosystem completely intact. I'm sure there's nothing creepy or crawly in there."

He ignored her sarcasm. "My feeling is, most wildlife would have been destroyed by whatever natural disaster the returning fisherman saw. And some species would have died out through being cut off from any major landmass."

"Either that, or the strongest, fittest and fiercest have survived, just like in Oz. We might find things no man – with the possible exception of a long-dead race – has ever seen."

They were right over the islands now, crossing the largest one. Rain clouds clung to the treetops like enormous dusty cobwebs.

"Okay good people," Dirk shouted over his shoulder, "just so you don't feel too bad about things, here, as promised, is a quick look at what you'll be missing – so look on the bright side. And hang on to yer hats, the air currents get a bit jiggly and temperamental... right about now."

It didn't matter what any of them had been through in their lives to that point – they all gasped.

CHAPTER THIRTEEN

The ground beneath the plane fell away to a sheer cliff decorated by what looked like lacy frills hundreds of feet below, which they could see were ferocious breakers, and above which wheeled gulls and other birds that might have been cormorants. Jane looked away, her head wheeling like those gulls, while her stomach dropping down that dark cliff-face.

"Wow!" Robbie's exclamation was a mixture of excitement and fear, "I hav'nae seen anything like that since I scrambled up Buchaille Etive Mòr."

"Would you mind repeating that in English, man?" Cobus responded in his broad Free State accent.

"You can talk. And aye, I would – I'm Scottish." Robbie's playful disdain marked much of the conversation between the two men. "But as ye've clearly not been tae God's ain country," he was laying the accent on thick now, "it's a mountain on the eastern approach to Glencoe. At the front it's a sheer climb, but ye can get up from the back and then, when ye stand on the summit ye've nothing but a two-thousand-foot drop between you and Rannoch Moor below. It helps ye understand what vertigo's all about."

Dirk arced the plane round again, then continued to shout over his shoulder. "Okay everybody, now listen up. We're landing round on the other side, not of this island, but the next one. It'll be a bit choppy. We're quite far out, but I can't take a chance with the rocks. Then we'll get out the inflatable boats and hopefully, if I've got it right, there should be a nice channel for the boats to get through to the shore."

Jane was about to say something but decided against it. However, Catalina spoke up and betrayed her increasing nerves, while at the same time voicing the exact concerns her mentor had swallowed in an attempt to keep the mood calm. "'Hopefully... if you've got it right... inflatable boats... rocks.' Does anyone else feel less than reassured by that?" She looked around, but before anyone could answer Dirk chipped in again, his voice full of humour, for which, whether it was forced or not, everyone was grateful.

"Strewth, Sheila, I'm ashamed a fellow Roo is whingeing. I'd've expected it from one of the Poms, but I was told you were made of strong stuff."

Catalina tried to smile as the others laughed, but her concerns surfaced in sarcasm. "I just don't think rocks and inflatable boats go all that well together. Besides, the sea is rough. How are we supposed to row a dinghy out there?"

"Relax Sheila—"

"Please don't call me Sheila."

Mocking noises followed from Robbie and Cobus. They were playful, but the girl looked upset. This didn't bode well for the coming days and Jane felt responsible. Catalina had been her unknowing recommendation and she did not want that to turn out to be a misjudgement. She looked in Pete's direction, wondering whether he would join in the general mickey-taking, but he was just relaxed in his seat taking in the view outside, a hand resting over the arm of his seat, an unlit cigarette balanced between his fingers. The pose looked almost studied, but for a moment Jane saw the man she had once believed she loved.

Dirk spoke again. "These inflatables are not dinghies as you know them. They're like mini inshore lifeboats, twelve feet long and six feet wide."

"It's called a six feet beam," said Pete without looking away from the window.

"Yeah, whatever." Dirk ignored the pedantic correction. "Anyway, they're powered by a thirty horsepower Mariner outboard motor and can do fifteen knots. I've got 'em ready to go in the back there, complete with twelve gallons of fuel in the flexible tanks, so they should be good for three hours."

Something was nagging at Jane during this conversation; something she had overlooked perhaps? She couldn't put her finger on it.

"I'm impressed." The Professor's comment almost served as a reminder to everyone that he was still there. Just the way he uttered those two words, alert and humorous, gave Jane hope. Perhaps now that the waiting was over and the time for action was here, he felt better.

"And I've had 'em adapted so that you can deflate them once you're ashore. Well, they are orange, and I know you didn't want to be noticed from the air, Prof."

"So those damned paparazzi won't get their scoop then." Pete's dry throwaway line landed in silence. He looked around at them all and grinned. Behind him Dirk made a repetitive, universally recognisable gesture with his hand, which caused suppressed smiles – even from Catalina, Jane noticed – and all seemed well in the world again. The irony of that gesture didn't escape Jane. She blushed once more as she remembered how she had started proceedings with Pete two nights before, and certainly not in fresh air! It distracted her from her continued attempt to overcome her mental block, the feeling that there was a point she needed to make.

"The boats inflate using the same principle as the airbag in a car, so they'll be ready for use again in the blink of an eye."

"Thank you, Dirk." Sutch grinned. "What would I do without you?"

"Swim." There was laughter all round. A crisis appeared to have been averted – for the moment at least.

"Now, unless you want that last part to come true, be ready for a swift disembarkation. I'm gonna bring the old girl down now, so please all get belted up. As soon as we're stationary I'd like you to open the doors and drop the boats, but keep a bloody good hold on the ropes. You can see now why you're all togged out in the dry suits. And put on the crash helmets. Oh, and at the risk of sounding like a cabin crew demonstration, don't forget to inflate your lifejackets. We'll be rocking and rolling down there."

Jane voiced a nagging doubt, which had been getting louder. "What about the gear?" How the hell are we going to get all of that into the boats? Does this thing have an anchor?"

"The water's rough, but it's not deep at the point where I'll be stopping. You've got most of the stuff you'll need personally in the rucksacks; I'm a good packer, so they're light. All of you – yes, you too girls – have got disposable razors in there, loo paper, survival bags, waterproof matches and malaria tablets, to name but a few things. I've put the camp kit in those flight boxes there." He pointed to three large yellow cubes. "They're adapted to float, so you can tow them in."

Now it hit Jane, but before she could say anything Dirk turned the plane once more and started the approach. She thought it better not to distract him while their lives were in his hands.

"Will this tub make it?" It was Pete again.

Dirk raised his eyebrows. "If you'd had time in the air you'd know this is a very rugged, reliable floatplane. I'd appreciate it if yer didn't call her a tub."

Pete sucked on his cigarette then put it back in a studied manner into the packet. He had kept it out to wind up Dirk, who made it clear he hated the habit. "Actually, I do have plenty of hours. Used to fly a DeHaviland Turbo Otter, taking people out for fishing trips into the wilds in Canada. Compared to that machine, which was inspected rigorously, this *is* a tub."

Dirk glanced at Jane and raised his eyebrows. Then she saw some concern flit across his features and, following his gaze, she noticed that Catalina had a face like thunder. What the hell was going on there?

Whatever it was, she could tell Dirk assumed it was some concern regarding the plane, because he tried to assuage her fears, as only Dirk could: "Don't you worry Sheil... sweetheart. She's a sturdy bird. I like a sturdy bird."

Nevertheless, it was a white-knuckle ride of a landing. There wasn't much to line up with, but it could have been worse. At least there was plenty of room. Dirk had brought planes down on improvised landing strips while under gunfire.

They opened the doors. A maelstrom of noise, spray and disorientation greeted them. The next moments were spent in a confusion of backpacks and flying limbs as first the inflatables exploded like aggressive orange flowers, then the struggling passengers sought to disembark from the pitching plane into the rolling boats. The sea was calm by the standards of the Southern Ocean, but its surging power surprised everyone except the Professor, who had spent most of his life in its embrace. The plane had all the grace and stability of a new-born giraffe.

"Shit!" Jim staggered and banged his head on the plane's doorframe. "Anybody'd think this craft was made for the air, not the sea."

The throwaway nature of the comment was lost in the general melee, which turned to panic for a moment when Cobus stepped into one of the boats, lost his balance and went over the side. But he was quick to bob up again. The dry suit earned its corn and got himself back on board. It said much about him that he was able to joke: "Don't worry, it's only a Martini moment – I'm shaken, but not stirred. And let me tell you, it's too cold in there for any Great Whites."

At last, they were all aboard the inflatables, with the flight boxes attached by plastic straps.

Professor Sutch pointed ahead: "Okay, let's head straight for the bay over there."

"What about Dirk?" Catalina's question caught everyone's attention.

"He's not coming with us." It was Jane. She had sussed it out in the end. Everything Dirk had been saying had the air of someone who was not going to be hanging around.

Robbie turned to the plane, but Dirk had disappeared inside under some pretext. It seemed like avoidance of the moment. "Professor, why not?"

This was a blow. The rugged, experienced Aussie was a man whose air of confidence rubbed off on others. His departure was not the best start to the trip, but it also made a lot of sense. "He's going back to Perth, Robbie." Sutch's response was tinged with a certain embarrassment.

"Why?" asked five voices in unison.

"There isn't a safe anchorage for the plane. Besides, Dirk's a pilot. By his own admission he'd just be cooling his heels here during that time. He'll come back for us in five days."

"But we could use the extra muscle power." Jim spoke for all of them.

"We've enough for our purposes." Sutch's glance at Jane evinced a silent request not to contradict him. "There is another minor reason as well. Satellites would spot a plane sitting out on the water and I'm paranoid enough not to want us noticed. Anyway, this is a preliminary visit. At some point, all being well, we'll come back, properly equipped to deal with whatever we find this time."

Now Pete chipped in. "I'm sorry, Edward, but that statement suggests we're not properly equipped now for whatever lies ahead."

It seemed Sutch hid his annoyance, not wanting internecine warfare breaking out in front of strangers. And, of course, there was the little matter of it being a perfectly valid observation. "Look, let's get moving. Once we're ashore I'll deal with everyone's concerns, but I'm sure you'll see that we're more than adequately kitted out for this initial foray."

Jane and Cobus started up the respective motors and everyone turned towards the plane as they prepared to set off. Dirk was nowhere to be seen.

"It's a superstition of his," said the Professor. "The last time he waved someone off they never came back."

As they headed through the channel picked out by Dirk, the water seemed to grow quieter. Soon the boats and boxes grounded on the shingle. The team disembarked and dragged them a few yards further in, to a point they could see the tide didn't reach. As Sutch's feet crunched on the black sand he turned to the others. "Well, there's definitely been volcanic activity here."

Having waited till they were safe ashore, the plane now set off, picking up speed and pulling out of the water. Some of the party waved, not knowing whether the Aussie saw them or not, but then they had their own situation to think of. Sutch walked across to one of the yellow boxes. He opened it and removed a flight case, which had joined their journey courtesy of Dirk at the very last moment. He took a set of keys from his trouser pocket, opened it and the top folded out in two directions to reveal customised compartments filled with rifles and pistols.

"Now that's what I'm talking about." Wearing a broad grin, Pete reached towards the case, but Sutch nudged it and the spring-loaded top snapped shut, causing Pete to withdraw his hand at speed to avoid injury. He looked hard at his father-in-law, who smiled. "No, you're right. Keep it under lock and key. I'm sure when some thirty-foot anaconda, or a jaguar, or," he pointed in the direction of the brooding forest, "whatever other prehistoric hybrid is lurking in there attacks, we can appeal to its better nature. Maybe offer it a fucking cappuccino." He stalked to the water's edge and stood looking at the plane as it faded to a dot in the sky.

As the drone of the engine became so faint that no-one could pinpoint the exact moment they stopped hearing it, Professor Edward Sutch experienced a frisson of fearful self-doubt. He hoped he had done the right thing in agreeing to Dirk's decision not to stay, and wondered whether he had given the Aussie the perfect excuse when he made known his paranoia about the plane being spotted.

He could not know that it had already been picked out on his first visit a few weeks before.

CHAPTER FOURTEEN

Robbie, Cobus and Catalina had started emptying the boxes, finding the tension between the Professor and his son-in-law a bit uncomfortable, but also feeling exposed, which made setting up camp a priority. Without mentioning it to each other, they felt like a thousand pairs of eyes were watching them from the forest.

Once Pete realised that there was no supportive wife standing by his side, he turned and came back to the boats. Picking up his kit bag he started rummaging in a side-pocket for a cigarette. "Okay to light up?" he asked of nobody in particular. "The flame of my lighter won't act as a beacon, attracting spy planes from all points of the compass?" Then he noticed that Catalina had produced a mobile phone from her bag and was in the process of trying to obtain a signal. Fuckable, but stupid, he thought. "Keep trying." Pete's acidic tone was accompanied by snorted smoke through his nostrils as he walked by. "I think the mast is on the far side of the island."

Catalina looked up, did a double-take, then blushed and popped the mobile back into her bag before anyone else noticed. She looked in embarrassment at Pete's departing figure, hoping he would turn again and see that she got it; in some measure repair his opinion of her, which was not the greatest, judging by his acerbic comment. But she knew, she *had* been stupid. Did technology do that to you; cause atrophy of the most important muscle in the body – the brain? She prided herself on being self-reliant; well, in most things. She had trekked for weeks in the Outback with maps and no radio; not a GPS unit in sight. Yet she might as well have been draped across a car bonnet in a bikini for all the impression of intelligence she had just given. Now she saw Jane staring at her and her blush deepened. "I know, it was stupid. I guess we all get conditioned to... being..." Her voice trailed off as she realised that Jane wasn't staring at her, but past her. "What is it?" She looked over her shoulder.

Sutch had been waiting for someone to see it and wondered if Jane's skin now had goose-bumps, as had his when he'd first spied it through his zoom lens on that preliminary flight with Dirk.

Jane dropped everything she was holding and walked across with her mouth open to stand in front of the object, her head now tilted to one side, reminding Sutch of the first time his little girl had observed a butterfly close up.

It stood just inside the edge of the forest, half-hidden by ferns, the tangle of low-hanging branches, and camouflaged by a coating of lichens; a printer's obelisk, telling the reader that the book they were opening might seem obscure, but here was one footnote, at least, to guide the reader.

The Professor had followed Jane across, and was likewise awestruck. Time, wind, rain and moss had all but obliterated what might have been a face near the top of the pillar, which stood about twice the height of a man. Jane moved closer, took a handkerchief and wiped it on part of the surface to remove the mould, though not without difficulty.

"My God!" I recognise some of these symbols." She looked round at her father, who nodded and returned her knowing look.

"The amphora."

The entire company had joined them now and stood amazed. Jane turned to Sutch and gave him an almighty hug. "You were right, father; to believe." He saw realisation dawn on her and she gave him a playful thump on the arm. "You knew this wasn't a wasted trip, didn't you? Just wanted us all to sweat a bit. So that's why we're making base camp here. Boy, it must have been hard to keep this a secret."

You have no idea, my girl, he thought, *what I'm keeping from you still.*

"Yes," he responded. "So at least we know that civilisation, however primitive, has visited this place. And that in itself is enough. But now, who's to say that we won't discover the secret of which the fisherman spoke?"

Jane hugged him close again, though not before he caught the doubt in her eyes. What and whom she doubted did not bear too much scrutiny at that moment, and if he was frank with himself, he preferred to leave it like that for now. Then she turned back to the totem-like structure. "What do you think it is? A drum-idol? I've seen them on Pacific islands, supposedly containing ancient spirits? But they're normally in groups."

Now she tutted at herself in exasperation. "Am I stupid or what? It's made of stone; how could it be a drum-idol?"

Jim spoke up. "No, look. There seem to be some sort of metal rings halfway up. Could be a mooring post," he suggested. Perhaps the sea came up higher once upon a time."

"Maybe." Sutch shrugged his shoulders. "A major geological event could have affected the tide line."

"A totem pole?" ventured Robbie.

"Or a whipping post," added Pete. "Or worse?"

"What do you mean worse?" Jane turned on him. Sutch could tell straight away that she regretted her display of disdain. Any time Pete got under someone's skin, it was a little victory for him.

Pete took a long drag on his cigarette. He may have been excited by the find – who could tell – but he was not going to allow any cracks in his veneer of studied nonchalance. Sutch knew he was the target and so, by inference, was Jane. "Look, even the most advanced of ancient civilisations worshipped gods who demanded human sacrifice. Maybe the unlucky ones were left chained here till the tide covered them, or the rats got 'em. That was still a method of execution centuries later, along the Thames in London." Nobody said anything, not even Sutch. If his son-in-law was making a point of needling them, his tactics were spot-on; making observations that might well be correct.

It hit them now, to a man and woman – the oppressive silence of the forest before them. It had given them one tantalising glimpse of the secrets it might hold; that was all they were getting for free.

Jim returned to the boxes that held his camera equipment and stood now taking shots of this ancient artefact. As he did so, he spoke. "So what made you come to this particular island, Professor, or did you just get lucky?"

"No, when I did a recce with Dirk it struck me that this bay didn't look to be naturally formed. For me the tidal currents wouldn't have eroded it this way – wouldn't you agree, Cobus? You're a geologist."

The Afrikaner flushed, flattered to have been asked something by the renowned academic. "Ja" was all he could come up with.

Pete couldn't resist: "Ah," so you really *are* a rock-spider." The colloquial, perhaps a touch derogatory, term for a Boer needled Cobus when coming from Pete, so Sutch moved on.

"And as we flew past a second time I got lucky and found our friend here. I think once we look at the arms of the bay more closely we'll find that, whoever these people were, they decided this channel..." here he pointed out to sea, to the way they had come in, "... was one of the few safe routes in and hewed the rock accordingly to build a harbour. This pillar could be a mooring post, but if we don't find any others I'd doubt it."

The sea breeze beat in their ears like myriad bats.

"Okay." Jane had organised countless camps in the past, and knew it was time to focus on the tangible. "Let's check the equipment and make this place feel a bit more like home."

"Ah, maybe now I'll find out what I've been missing all these years." Pete looked up from opening his rucksack to find one pair of glistening eyes glaring at him and all others focussed with excessive zeal on what they were doing.

"A bit more like the nerve centre of the operation." Jane did her best to push on. "Where do you stand on fires, father?"

"In a scout camp in the morning." Cobus' quip brought a burst of much-needed laughter. Jane pursed her lips in mock-annoyance and gave him a light cuff on the head.

Robbie chipped in: "You planning a career as an after-dinner speaker when your rugby days are over, are you?" Then he ducked the pair of rolled-up socks aimed at his head.

Sutch, contemplating the original question amongst the banter, knew that a fire would be essential to buoying up spirits. This was a forbidding place – unwelcoming. In his desire for secrecy he had contemplated banning a campfire proper and just using the stoves, but reality had kicked in some time ago. They were in a remote part of the Southern Ocean with no regular shipping lanes or flight paths to concern them. Paranoia really was a guest who would not stop eating; Sutch, as the host, needed to show him the door. Besides, he'd proved already that people had once been here and one of the most respected photographers had captured the evidence. That alone warranted the return trip that he would lead. His was the discovery, his the achievement. That could not now be taken from him. It was important not to lose sight of that. His other hopes for this trip might, after all, turn out to be nothing more than a pipe dream. It was why, on the plane, he had withheld, for the time being, the huge element – in all senses – of water. The secret of eternal youth – not something to discuss, he felt, if one wished to continue living at home and wearing jackets with sleeves that weren't tied about one's waist!

"Father?" Jane must have seen the distance in his eyes.

Sutch blinked and remembered the question. "Fire's good."

Jane nodded at the three students.

81

"Okay, you guys," Catalina slapped her palms together, "see if you can find some wood."

Cobus and Robbie looked at her, and then saw that she was grinning, so saved themselves the embarrassment of pointing out the forest.

The others checked through the kit. Catalina, who was a veteran of trekking, started pulling items out of one of the yellow boxes and nodded her approval of each in turn:

"Harrier Softie sleeping bag – Mountain Equipment breathable waterproof – North Face light fleece – Duofold base layers – hot and cold climate Berghaus hiking gear – heavy duty Scapa walking boots. No expense spared here. Campingaz stove – various cans of food. How much water do we have, Professor?"

"Sixty-three litres."

Catalina did a quick calculation. "Nine litres each." She was too respectful to say anything, but Sutch saw the look of concern:

"Enough for three days. Dirk and I had to think of the weight in the plane and decided that either we'd find a spring or have to ration. You'll find water purifiers and iodine droplets for stream water."

Now Catalina produced a rolled up piece of leather and opened it to reveal a carefully packed machete and ice-axe.

The Professor pointed at the other rucksacks. "Each one contains one of those."

"Hmm, that would have been interesting at Heathrow." Jim smiled. His personal specialised equipment consisted of a Canon EOS 50 camera with a 70-200mm lens and a bag full of Fujichrome film. He looked across at Jane as he saw her take a battered Nikon from her rucksack and she pulled a face of mock shame. "Looks well-travelled."

Jane grimaced. "Well mishandled and mislaid as well."

"What are those?"

Jane had produced her precious notebooks. They contained her on-hand observations from twenty years of archaeological digs and bore the scars to prove it.

"Never go on a dig without them. I've got this old-fashioned, pseudo-Victorian approach; sketching and noting the things I see. I hope one day they'll find a place in the archives of the Royal Geographical Society. I love delving into the records."

"Me too."

"It's a kind of hobby for me." She stopped for a moment and looked into the distance. "Something about the sepia prints and pen-and-ink drawings appeals to the..." she hesitated "... romantic in me."

"Perhaps they encapsulate a time when there was still a world to explore; when it seemed a brave thing to do and was, above all, subject to chance."

Jane gave a rueful smile. "Perhaps it's because I'm better known for my dealings with the past and the dead that I envy those who've unearthed the mysteries of life."

"Like I said at dinner the other night, you have an ability to bring the past to life. Your work under modern-day Alexandria is fantastic."

Sutch sat smiling at them, wondering whether this trip might bring him at least one unexpected reward – a new son-in-law. Then he shook his head and turned to his goods and chattels. He had come with minimal equipment, relying more on the others. The one thing he had ensured accompanied him, which was in some ways a mistake as he was loathe to let it out of his sight, was the amphora, packed with loving care – indestructibly, he hoped – in a small flight case. But he knew he was not the lightest equipped – that was Pete, who had brought cigarettes and a Zippo lighter, as well as a hip flask. He was, in Sutch's eyes, the very definition of someone along for the ride.

Unbeknown to the Professor, Pete was carrying a bit more baggage than he might have been prepared to admit.

CHAPTER FIFTEEN

They were all delighted to find the Coleman tents. "They're just like me, man," Cobus lowered his voice as he addressed Robbie and Catalina, "erect with one quick flick of the wrist."

"I'd have thought you're more like the Softie sleeping bags." Catalina winked.

"Ja, I'd keep you warm at night for sure."

Last, but not least was the safety equipment. In addition to the arsenal of rifles there were flares, whistles, lanterns, GPS tracking systems, brightly coloured, heavy-duty survival bags, ropes and another sort of lifeline, which the Professor produced like a rabbit from a hat.

"Is that what I think it is?" Jim looked taken aback.

"That depends on what you think it is." Sutch was looking a little smug.

"A satellite telephone."

"Correct." He could almost feel the ripple of relief pass through the camp. "Well, you didn't think I was going to leave us completely cut off, did you?"

Jim took the equipment from the Professor's hand. "Light and compact." He looked at Sutch with raised eyebrows. "That means expensive in my experience. I had one similar to this in Rwanda. I was glad I was only renting it for a short period."

"You're right." Sutch grinned. "That's why I pulled a few strings and, shall we say, borrowed this from my team in the western Indian Ocean. Otherwise, it would have blown most of the budget." He looked at the others, who had gathered round. "This means we have worldwide voice communication through a network of satellites. But I warn you now, this is not meant for you to impersonate ET. Emergencies only, okay? So hopefully we never have to use it."

"Good old Dirk," whispered Sutch to himself. Having supported many an expedition or exploratory team, the Aussie had known pretty well what to provide to cater for most needs within the budget, even down to the tin of cigarillos that Sutch had just discovered at the bottom of one of the cases; he liked to puff on one from time to time. With the tents pitched, a fire lit and Jane in the process of organising the stoves, he lit one now and stood looking at the pillar. For a moment he half expected to find a symbol at the top of it, like the acorn on the West Highland Way-markers, showing him that he was on the right track.

Well, stranger things have happened!

The thought brought him up sharp. In fact, such strange things *had* happened, perhaps there were indeed more pillars. He turned and looked towards the sea. This might indeed have been a way-marker. Perhaps there had once been an iron basket or brazier of some sort at the top, which contained a fire or lamp to guide boats through the narrow channel... maybe...

Maybe.

Standing facing the sea, Sutch relished his first moment of supreme contentment. It was hard to believe that, just a few weeks before, he had been preparing a lecture on the impact of overfishing on coral reefs. The mystery kingdom beneath his feet had occupied a recess labelled 'pending' in the very back of his mind. Unbeknown to him, heading his way, courtesy of FedEx, had been a big boot that would kick him out of his comfort zone onto this narrow strip of shingle at latitude 50 in the Southern Ocean.

Despite his vast experience on the world's oceans, the last two words generated a sudden chill and the moment of contentment passed. He headed to his tent to get a fleece.

Cobus approached Sutch, now that he didn't feel he would be disturbing him. "Excuse me, Professor."

"Please, call me Edward."

"If it's all the same with you, I'll keep it as 'Professor'. I feel more comfortable that way; must be down to my time in the army. And I haven't earned the right to be on first name terms yet."

"You've earned the right, as you call it, by being here on this beach with us."

"That's just a stroke of fortune. If it's all the same with you..."

"As you wish, young Cobus. Anyway, what were you going to say?"

"I was just wondering what the plan of action is?"

"Good question, Cobus, good question. The truth is there isn't one. We're at the bottom of page one. We have to write page two ourselves. Tell me something; as a geologist, what did you make of the cliffs? Describe them to me."

"You mean apart from sheer and bloody frightening... excuse my language... and a bit more than a grade one scramble?" That drew a laugh from Sutch, before Cobus continued: "Well, they were granite."

"And the weathering?"

"Smooth as a baby's bottom. Must have taken..." Cobus paused, and then gave up bothering to wonder, "... God knows how many years, even allowing for the power of the wind and the sea down in these latitudes."

"That would be a challenging climb, don't you agree?"

"You kidding me? No handholds, and then that overhang for the last hundred feet. Amazing, man... sorry, Professor," he looked embarrassed. "Those are some waves coming in there."

"How do you think the cliffs were formed?"

"Who knows? We're not far from Antarctica. Maybe the ice-cap once stretched out to here and the glaciers wore them down. In fact, thinking about it, the cliff-face is smooth, but there are some marks that could be striations from a glacier."

"But whether by glacial or other means, you think we're talking erosion here over a long time."

"Ja, absolutely."

"You don't think the land fell away in a recent volcanic eruption; I mean in the last three hundred years." Tariq's tale of his and the fisherman's flight from that place was reverberating in Sutch's mind.

Cobus rubbed his chin. "The beach looks like volcanic sand, but that could have been carried a long way in the air. If there was volcanic activity here, it was a long time ago."

Sutch nodded. "Yes, I agree. I mean, the way those waves come in is a bit like Hawaii, isn't it, as if they're in full flow, unbroken by any continental shelf that reduces their height or impact, so while there's a chance the land has fallen away, or this archipelago has risen from the sea as a result of volcanic activity, even three hundred years ago, mankind would have known of something of that magnitude – even then. The forces that shaped this island are far, far older than that."

Comprehension lit Cobus' face. Jane and Jim had both picked up on this conversation and now moved closer to listen. "Are you saying...?"

"Yes, the land here may have fallen away millennia before," continued the Professor, "yet I was told about a wave of some sort hitting this island much more recently, and streams of lava. But from what you're saying, and what I believe, I can't help feeling something else is at play here. Nothing quite fits." Sutch stopped and frowned, and then he tried to sound positive. "So, if this is a harbour, there's every chance that between here and the far side of the island we'll find something of the original settlement. Even if there were a giant wave, it would have to have been incredibly powerful to surge up these mountains and drive everyone and everything over the cliffs."

"This could just be an unfinished tourist resort." It was Pete chipping in from his place by the fire. "I've seen modern Greek towns in a worse state."

Sutch ignored the attempted witticism and looked at Jane. She returned his troubled gaze with one of her own. He could guess why; always concerned for her father's reputation, she might have been concerned that, if Tariq had bent the truth, just what was her father to believe? If those were her concerns, they mirrored his own. The thing Jane didn't know – that none of them knew – was just how much his mission depended on belief.

Sutch moved on: "Anyway, thank you for your valued input, Cobus. For now, I guess the question of what destroyed this civilisation is less important than what was destroyed. That's what will occupy us during our time here."

"So, Professor," Cobus was still glowing from the compliment, "going back to our original conversation, I assume," here he pointed to the darkening fringe of the forest, "we just take our *pangas* and hack our way in."

"I'm afraid you're right." He turned to the others. "So, as the summer down here will be granting us a long day tomorrow, I suggest we all garner our reserves of energy with a good night's sleep; and before that we grab something to eat. What have we got, Jane?"

"How would I—" She stopped, having caught the wink from her father. "You had me going there." He knew she was a hunter-gatherer, not a domestic goddess. Years in a male-dominated field meant she had scrapped with the best of them. A homebody she was not. "A corned beef hash or equivalent is the best you'll get from me."

"My daughter could wipe out entire civilisations just by cooking them an omelette," joked Sutch. He received an appropriate glare.

"Okay, what's for dinner then, Catalina?" Robbie joined in the fun and got pursed lips beneath a narrow-eyed frown that could not quite conceal the girl's grin.

"Don't worry, Catty," said Cobus. "We all know why the Outback is so empty. Everyone's run from your tucker."

"Where are the machetes when you need one?" responded the butt of the jokes. Jane looked at her for a moment. Despite seeming to cope with the abuse, there was some sadness or discomfort rippling below the surface still. Jane made a mental note to talk to her later.

"Well, she knows it's a machete anyway." Robbie wasn't quite done. "I could've sworn I saw her trimming her nails with one." He got no response.

By now the Professor was rummaging around in the food supplies. Suddenly he burst out laughing and produced a vacuum-packed kangaroo steak. "As I said, good old Dirk."

**

They decided that one person should keep watch that night to keep the fire alive, in case any wildlife was attracted to the smell of food. Yet the forest seemed devoid of any sound and was all the more menacing for it, as if its dead eyes were watching them. Its presence weighed on Cobus as he took the first watch. In his experience, night-time was when jungles and forests came alive – for better or worse – but there was nothing; not the scurrying of a mammal, the chirp of an insect or the croak of a frog. What he could hear was that his heart was racing, and not through fear. When you had already represented your province at 1st XV level in South Africa, and been at the bottom of a ruck on the wrong side of the ball, not much scared you. No, it was as if he had an excess of adrenaline. It appeared Catalina felt the same, because after an hour's fruitless search for sleep she joined him.

"Can't sleep, man, eh?" It was more of a rhetorical question from the Afrikaner.

"Nah, I'm fidgeting a lot. Feeling a bit restless. Plus, I don't like the silence." She gestured with her head towards the trees. "Even the sea can't seem to suppress it."

"Doesn't feel right, does it?"

"I've spent a lot of time in the rainforest on Tas. I'm not a great lover of snakes and spiders, but I can tell you, I'd prefer the sound of slithering or scratching or crawling."

Cobus put an arm around her and she moved in against it, her need for some comfort clear. "Oh well, down here it'll soon be morning. Let's see what that brings."

CHAPTER SIXTEEN

SCORPION ARCHIPELAGO, OCTOBER 29TH 1997

What it brought was warm sunshine, and though there was not the level of humidity one would find in a jungle, still it became oppressive once they were under the blanket of the forest. Despite the early night and fresh air, most of them felt weary, their dreams having been invaded, on a subliminal level at least, by the watchful darkness.

Jane spoke to her father between hacks of the machete. "I can see... why you wanted... us to... have these." She fought her way through another obstinate thicket, then paused for breath and gestured with the blade. "When you said forest I envisaged a clear floor, but I've never seen such a twisted, gnarled, knotted place. It's like Fangorn or Mirkwood."

"Where?" Catalina looked blank.

Jane raised her eyebrows in mock exasperation. "Oh, the youth of today. Haven't you ever read Tolkien?"

Catalina moved to metaphorical safe ground. "The trees haven't grown that tall, I guess because of the wind, cold and darkness at certain times of the year. But they seem to have compensated by spreading and growing thick. And if there was any volcanic activity in this island's history it would be very fertile here with the potassium and other minerals. Look just how profuse these ferns are."

"Of course, the sixty-four thousand dollar question," for once Pete kept his voice low, "is whether we know we're heading in the right direction."

"I'm sure the Professor knows what he's doing." Jim's comment in Sutch's defence drew a look from Pete that almost said: *You would.* "Uh huh," was what came out as he hacked with feeling at a bramble.

Jim wasn't done: "Well, we've found signs of human life, plus what we think was some sort of harbour. It makes sense to head straight inland from there."

"Yes, but aren't you all overlooking one thing? If this were a harbour, surely there'd be dwellings around it. I mean, I've not yet seen a harbour that wasn't surrounded by human habitation."

"Maybe," conceded Jim, "but if there were an underwater earthquake followed by a tsunami hitting the coast, it might have swept everything before it. Buildings further up might well have survived. But also, people always build on higher ground if they can, for any number of reasons."

Jane's little glance of approval at Jim didn't go unnoticed, and that same glance took in the way his sweat-soaked shirt stretched across his back. She wondered what the hell was going on with her, having worked with any number of well-muscled teams of perspiring men before. Even her husband... she stopped that thought in its tracks. But just now she'd imagined her nails raking down Jim's back. Sure, she was attracted to him, had been from the moment she had set eyes on him., but her desires seemed to have attained some lycanthropic, feral quality that was straining to escape. Had it been a peculiar foretaste of this, a few nights before, when she stood in her bedroom assessing her figure? Was something hormonal at play here over which she had no control?

They were starting to tire and struggle as they pushed their way uphill, picking or hacking the best path they could through the tangle of tortured roots, brambles, ferns, bushes and low-hanging branches of this eclectic forest, slithering up the damp slope while the soil sucked at their walking boots. There seemed to have been plenty of rain in the recent past, which had worked its way down the mountainside. Moss was everywhere, slimy beneath their hands on tree trunks or boulders which they grasped at for support. It hung from branches and rocks like the embodiment of a green pestilence. The only flowers they saw were pitcher plants, and when Catalina looked into the first few they came across, there were no insects captured inside. "Is there no life in this pissing place?" she muttered. The lack of breeze beneath the canopy added to their general discomfort, as if even the elements had died. The aura of lifelessness was rendered all the more obscene by the contrasting abundance of undergrowth. There seemed to be an underlying sound of water running, but it might have been a trick of the sodden landscape. Otherwise, there was only silence. Jane spoke for all of them, even the Professor, when she stopped again: "Why anyone would see this land and choose to settle here is beyond me."

"Maybe it looked different then," ventured Jim.

Catalina chipped in: "No, I think we can assume a forest like this would have greeted the first settlers."

They stopped again for a drink, grateful to remove the rucksacks, which had dragged them down into the cloying mud, and using them as seats in the absence of any dry spots.

Catalina, hands resting on her knees, looked up and around. "Nothing."

"Mmm?" Cobus looked at her then followed her gaze. "Ja, man, that's what I was saying last night – there's nothing. No bird song; no insects buzzing; no nothing."

"It doesn't feel right, does it?"

Jane heard this and looked in her father's direction, to see what impact the comments might be having on him. What she saw worried her. He had been quiet all morning; said more or less nothing, rather like on the flight. In fact, since he had spent most of the morning at the back of the group, she might almost have forgotten he was there, were it not for the ever-present filial bond. Now he looked drained and did not appear to be taking part in any discussion, nor making any observations. Was time catching up with him at last? Was this one expedition too far? She moved over and sat next to him. "Are you okay, Father?"

"Not really, no."

She put her hand on his arm. "What's the matter?"

He took a deep breath. "Janey, I'm getting this peculiar feeling I shouldn't be here. None of us should."

She tried to sound reassuring, though it was tough in the face of such an abstract observation from her pragmatic father. "Oh, that's just this place." She looked up at the trees. "Do you remember what the Romans said about the Teutoburg Forest? It played with their minds."

"I remember what happened to Varus." Jane realised the slaughter of three crack legions by barbarians was the last thing her father needed to be reminded of right now. He made a tired gesture in the direction of the students. "They're right – this place does have a peculiar feel to it. It's dead, but somehow... alive at the same time. Perhaps it's alive with the dead. Who knows how many souls were lost here."

"Father—"

He talked over her. "Suddenly – no that's a lie, it's not the first time – I'm wondering why I'm here. Have I just been a foolish old man with an obsession, determined to prove myself right? Has my vanity put us all in danger?" He turned to his daughter. "Why exactly have I brought us to this God-forsaken place?"

"Oh Father." She put an arm around him. "You *are* feeling down, aren't you? We've been in more forsaken places than this."

"Maybe you have, my girl, but I'm used to the ocean, which is alive, and moving, and breathing."

"And pitiless," she countered. "What about those shipwrecks you've encountered?"

He smiled, his mind's eye moving beneath the waves. "Full of fish, barnacles, anemones; life."

"And death on occasion, Father... and death."

"At least there I can see the dead."

"Well, I am feeling very much alive." She spared her father the details of her disinterred libido, which had been buried deeper and for longer than King Tut.

"And I, for the first time, am feeling very much my age." *She'd known it.* "This forest feels suffocating, like one of your tombs. Jane." He looked at her with a frankness that brooked no flippant response. "Am I just an old fool who's brought us to the edge of the abyss?"

"No. Look, to return your analogy, you found the needle down in the bay. We're just following the thread."

"As long as it doesn't lead us into the labyrinth instead of out of it."

She took his hand and smiled. "Well, the Minotaur is something I *don't* believe in. But if there's something to find here, we'll find it."

CHAPTER SEVENTEEN

But not that day. They strained, sweated, hacked and scrambled their way through an untold area of forest and returned to the camp late afternoon when fatigue overtook them, despite the energy bars.

Before hitting camp again, however, there was one moment of rare pleasure and relief when, believing they could hear water moving freely on a surface, they cleared a path through the trees and discovered a delightful pool into which tumbled a sparkling cascade. The beauty of the scene was enhanced by a more practical consideration. They had been wondering where they were going to find more drinking water, and somewhere to wash away the sweat and dirt of the day's labours, before stale body odour became an addition to the pleasures of the trip. This al fresco shower, just a quarter of a mile or so from the camp, was the one blessing the island had granted them that day.

They were standing near the base of the little waterfall. Everyone dipped their hats in the stream before putting them on again and gasping at the cold that gripped their veins.

"It'll take a brave person to jump in there." Cobus shook his body in mock shivers.

"Och, ye've not spent enough time in Scotland, ye jessie." Robbie puckered up his features. "Ye should try a dip in the North Sea."

Jane stooped to take a handful of water and in doing so she slipped on one of the moss-covered rocks. Jim was a couple of feet ahead of her, having moved in closer to take some pictures, and caught her as she stumbled towards the water. As he helped her straighten up his face registered momentary surprise and puzzlement.

"Thank you, I'm such a klutz." She retreated to the safety of the flatter ground.

Despite that discovery, it was a subdued party that set about its various tasks in the camp in the early evening light. Jane was pleased to see that the three students sat by the Professor. They had a thousand questions for the man who had mapped most of the world's oceans during his life. Pete had wandered off and stood with his feet cooling in the surf, enjoying a cigarette and, Jane noticed, taking nips from the hipflask he had brought with him.

Jim seemed restless. "Hey, so no-one wonders where I've gone, I'm just going to wander along the shoreline a bit; see if there's any good photo opportunities. And who knows, there might be another totem, or an easier route up onto the tops. If I'm not back in a couple of hours feel free to come and look for me. I'll certainly be back for dinner." He smiled. There was a general acknowledgement and he headed off along the edge of the bay.

Jane came and stood by Pete. "Not quite what you're used to, is it?"

He took a long draw on his cigarette and looked sidelong at her. "Nor you, I wouldn't have thought."

"Oh, you'd be surprised. People think that 'x' marks the spot in archaeology, but it rarely does. Swap thick, impenetrable forest for endless square miles of sand. And deserts shift over the course of time. There's a lot of monotonous, back-breaking toil. It's not all doorways with curses above them – just a lot of cursing – nor Howard Carter's wonderful things glittering in your lamplight for the first time in millennia."

Pete glanced back over his shoulder and drew on his cigarette again. "Old man seems a bit down. Do you think he's realised how fruitless this might be?"

Jane sighed in irritation. "You know, everyone seems to have forgotten – and I include my father in this – that we've already made the most fantastic discovery, that obelisk there. No one knew there was life here. That's an absolute sign of it. It's wonderfully exciting."

"Yes," the ennui in Pete's voice conveyed the absolute opposite, "I'm sure it is."

"Okay, it's not sky-diving from twenty thousand feet or free-form climbing, but if something had been a puzzle to you for forty years you'd be thrilled at a glimpse of the solution."

"Sounds like my life, old girl. That's been longer than forty years and it's certainly been a puzzle." He grinned and despite herself, Jane did too; his dry wit, when not being directed with sarcasm, could still make her laugh. Then he looked at her. "Maybe I'll find some answers while I'm here." He pitched his dog-end away. "Look, all I'm saying is he doesn't look very excited. Perhaps it's dawned on him that, whatever's happened here, this is a place of death. The only puzzle or secret as far as I'm concerned," he looked around, "is what the hell made anyone want to live here?" There was a brief silence. "Anyway, he's not as excited to be here as some people."

"What do you mean?"

He looked long at her. Jane knew her sunburnt skin wouldn't hide the blush she felt rising. "You ask me that a lot. But this time you know damn well what I mean. You've been like a hormonal teenager ever since Jim and his amazing zoom lens turned up."

"Well, I'm... it's exciting to meet somebody so famous in his field."

"And in his barn and his hayloft, I imagine."

"You're impossible." She tried to fake some jollity. "Judging people by your own standards."

"Maybe." There was a peremptory note to the word. He looked at her and held her gaze. "Anyway, I'm dog tired." He tapped his hipflask. "I think the old Glenfiddich has mellowed me out a bit." He leaned forward before she could prepare and kissed her on the lips, his mouth hard against hers, like he meant it. "We must do this again sometime – talk. And if there's anything else you want to do again..." he pointed to his tent, "... just come and open my fastening." He flicked the brim of his walking hat and went on his way; an urban cowboy in a wild place.

Jane looked around and saw the students watching her. Catalina, in particular, looked intrigued. Doubtless she was watching with a woman's eyes and knew exactly what was going on. That was something Jane would have to deal with.

It wasn't long before she could hear Pete snoring from the tent he had chosen to pitch a short distance away from everyone.

A few minutes later she addressed the others: "I'm going back to that pool to wash and freshen up."

"You be safe," warned the Professor. "Do you want someone to come with you?"

"No, that's the last thing I want," she laughed at the thought, "as I'm going to strip off."

She could tell Cobus wanted to make a crude comment but held back. He was still in awe of these people. Jane grabbed her field toiletry bag, which was pink and frilly as a deliberate concession to her femininity during all those times when she was surrounded by colleagues and circumstances that led her to doubt it. Also, she took a change of clothes:

a red plaid shirt and Levis. She had purchased them during the stopover in Singapore and worn them for the flight to Sydney to try to – *appeal to Jim?* – feel civilised.

It took her about fifteen minutes along the now comparatively clear path they had hacked. When she reached the pool, with its collection of strange weathered rock attendants, she was quick to strip and dive in. The icy water shocked her to the core, but she persevered, washed in a hurry and then – an unnecessary, perhaps ingrained action, given the isolation in which she found herself – tied a towel around her.

Her timing could not have been better. Moments later, Jim stepped into the clearing. She turned to face him.

"Ah, you came." Her voice quivered with the force of the pulse in her throat.

"Yes. What's going on, Jane?" From his pocket he produced the folded-up piece of paper that she had pressed into his hand when she'd stumbled earlier in that very spot. He read: "*I must see you. Be at the lake an hour after we return to camp.*" What's it all about?"

"This." She stepped forward and kissed him with pure hunger. Then she backed away, breathing hard. "I'm sorry, I don't know what's come over me."

His breathing was also heavy now. "There's a very crude joke there."

"Hah!" With that she pressed herself against him again. He pulled the towel from her and his hands moved up, finding her breasts.

They found the rest of each other pretty soon after that, with no questioning of whether they should. The intensity of the sex astonished them both. Afterwards, Jane stood with her head resting on his chest. "I don't know what's happened to me since I met you."

"You archaeologists, always unearthing things you don't fully understand."

She laughed. "What I do know is that I've wanted you from the moment I met you, but the feeling has grown every hour since, till it's almost out of my control."

"You're a very attractive woman, Jane, but you're married, so I never really thought much more about it. But when you kissed me just now, it seemed absolutely right to seize the moment. I can't explain it any better than that. And it's taken my breath away to discover how much I must have been suppressing my desire for you." He looked around. "Perhaps it's an affirmation of life in a lifeless place."

"For this island, read my marriage. Perhaps that's why I did what I did a couple of nights back."

"What was that?"

She looked down. "I'm ashamed to admit I had sex with Pete." Now she looked up at him again. "But I imagined it was you. You'd filled me with such desire that I had to have you then, even when I couldn't." She circled her nails playfully on his chest and looked him in the eyes. "So, does all that mean you wouldn't want me as much if we were back in England?"

"Probably."

His eyes gave the lie to his words and she slapped him playfully on the chest. Then her lips curled in a lop-sided, arch smile. "Well then, we don't have much time to experience everything there is; and what might have been." She kissed his chest, and then he felt the tip of her nose moving lower.

They arrived back at camp from their separate directions. Not everyone was fooled.

CHAPTER EIGHTEEN

SCORPION ARCHIPELAGO, 5AM OCTOBER 30TH 1997

"Robbie! Robbie!"

Cobus had risen early, a habit he had acquired during his national service. The others stirred. Catalina jumped up at the urgency of his voice. She looked towards Robbie's tent and saw through the open flap that it was unoccupied.

"Oh my God! Where's Robbie?" Now they were all up. "Perhaps he's gone to the pool for a wash."

"If he's up early, man, I think that'll go against the habits of a lifetime, from what I know of him at uni, but let's go look." The soldier in Cobus surfaced. "Professor, with all respect, you save your energy and stay here. I sense something funny and don't want to leave the camp unguarded."

With that, Cobus, Jane, Catalina and Jim set off at a brisk pace. When they reached the lake, despite the urgency of the situation, Jane could not help feel a moment's guilty thrill as she looked at the rock over which Jim had bent her the previous evening. She could almost feel the moss on her hands – and other things besides. She didn't dare look at him. But more pressing matters soon pushed her lewd thoughts to one side. Robbie wasn't there.

"Stupid bastard's gone walkabout."

Catalina's angry words were pure concern, and Jane, despite her own disquiet, decided calmness was required first off. "Look, he might just have gone along the coast a ways out of curiosity. Perhaps he couldn't sleep."

"Ja." Cobus backed her. "Jim, you got back okay yesterday, so I'm assuming you didn't see any place that he might have got into trouble today?"

"Ah... um, no. But actually, I didn't go very far."

That's certainly not true, thought Jane, who had to stifle a smile that would have been as inappropriate as her behaviour last night. Again, she wondered what demons were driving her now. Was this what happened when the cork had been in too tight for too long? That image directed her thoughts to the amphora. As one of the least superstitious of archaeologists, which made her a tough cookie indeed, she was shocked to find herself wondering whether that jug had contained some sort of djinni which she had released by translating the inscription.

"I got a bit distracted by the sunset on the water," continued Jim.

"Okay look," Cobus pushed on, "it's early. I might have woken everybody for no good reason." He gestured towards Jane. "This place does indeed make it difficult to sleep. Maybe he got up and has gone for a wander. But he knows what sort of time we would get up, so I would say, if he's not back in an hour or so, then we start to worry. There's no point trying to find him if he's in this forest somewhere, though why he would be here is beyond me. We made about four miles yesterday in six hours."

"We can't just ignore it if he doesn't come back," said Jane.

"And I'm not saying we should. Of course we'll look for him. I just meant we should wait a little longer and try to eat some breakfast; we'll need our strength." He looked around him then shouted in anger: "Robbie, you poes!" Jane knew it was the strongest oath an Afrikaner could utter.

They returned to camp and waited, forcing down some food.

As ever, it fell to Pete to say something no-one wanted to hear: "Gonna have to face it folks; he's not coming back."

"Ja, he is." Cobus was bristling. "He's just being a bloody idiot."

Pete lit a cigarette and stuffed his other hand into his pocket. "C'mon, he's not popped down to the local off-licence, he's not gone for an early morning swim – he's not gone anywhere. He's been taken."

The combined intakes of breath from the others had an almost theatrical effect.

Now Jane's anger surfaced. "What are you talking about? If you can't say something sensible, don't say anything." She looked at her father, but his silence to that point, along with the downcast eyes, showed that the onus of responsibility, the guilt, was a weight on his shoulders already – as she had known it would be. Her irritation with Pete was as much to do with his insensitivity towards the old man as it was with her worries for Robbie.

"Oh, come on, sweetheart, if he got up before our rock-spider here," Pete gestured towards Cobus, who smouldered, but said nothing, "he got up before the crack of dawn." Now he pointed towards the forest. "In there it would've still been as black as Newgate's knocker; hardly the place for a little constitutional. And that..." his thumb jerked over his shoulder towards the sea, "... is as cold as hell, if hell is cold. I can vouch for that, having bathed my feet in it yesterday. I've checked, and none of the inflatables are missing, so he hasn't gone island-hopping. If he's buried in the sand I trust you'll find him, Jane."

"There's one little flaw in your argument – who took him?" Jane's retort prompted a general murmur, but not of pure agreement; there was an undertone of curiosity, as if they all hoped the dissenter had an answer; something they could reach for.

Pete took a long, deliberate draw on his cigarette. Jane felt her jaw muscles clench; somehow, he had manoeuvred himself into the spotlight.

He shrugged. "Ghosts. Whoever built that?" He pointed to the totem. "I don't know. I'm just pointing out the obvious conclusion, which I think the intellectuals among you are trying to avoid. At least one of you was voicing this very concern yesterday." He didn't bother to look at the Professor, but everyone knew who he meant.

Sutch seemed to feel the pressure of eyes avoiding looking at him. "He may be right. We don't know who or what is, or isn't, here."

The others all glanced at each other and once more Jane felt deep concern for her father. He had been quiet since yesterday, by his own standards. If this was what happened when you followed a dream, she would just keep on digging. She threw him a lifeline back to his old self. "What do you suggest we do, Father?"

He sighed. "Well, I think it's pointless racing off on some erratic search and rescue mission."

"We could radio for help," ventured Jim.

"I'm not sure how much that would achieve. From the air these islands... well, you've seen for yourself. They just look like giant pieces of broccoli. You'd never find one man in that forest, not without a very large team, which would take some time to assemble and get out here. You saw how Dirk had to strip the plane to get both us and the kit on board. And yes, planes could fly over the sea and search, but if you were out there in those temperatures, you'd be dead by now."

Jane saw Catalina screw her eyes shut. So, it seemed, did her father, because he raised an apologetic hand: "Sorry, I'm so..." He searched for the right word; found it. "... sorry." With that, he wandered away from the group, perhaps another lost soul on the island.

"I'll tell you something else." Pete hadn't finished but had shown enough *savoir faire* to hold back till the Professor was out of earshot. "If a plane arrived here now, I, for one, would be wanting to hop on and head back." Jane looked hard at him, but instead of ignoring it, which he did most times to wind her up, he turned on her. "What? Don't give me the evil eye. I'm just voicing what everybody else is thinking. Let's face it, nobody wants to be here..." he looked across at the Professor's distant figure, "including your father now, I suspect. His stubbornness brought us in pursuit of some fairy tale, which doesn't appear to be ending with everyone living happily ever after – or even just living."

Cobus was unable contain himself any longer. "Show some fucking respect, man, which is how we treat our betters where I come from. Why don't you shut the fuck up, man? Whatever's happened to Robbie is not the Professor's fault."

Jane tensed, but Pete appeared to take the insults in his stride. "Well, who else is to blame then? Who's in charge?"

Jane heard grudging acknowledgement in the ensuing silence. This was bad.

It might have ended there for the moment, but Pete flicked his cigarette ash in the general direction of Cobus. "And anyway, why don't you make me shut the fuck up... Cobie?"

Cobus took a step forward. "I've packed against prop forwards, man, who'd have your skinny arse for breakfast."

"Yes, I've heard about Afrikaners and your liking for arse."

Cobus took another pace and Jim stepped up. "Guys, what are we doing here?"

"That's what I was just asking." Pete took another nonchalant drag on his cigarette.

"You know what I mean."

Cobus pointed a finger past Jim at his tormentor. "I've faced up to fuckin' guerrillas, man. Don't think you scare me."

"Whadya do – offer them your banana?" It seemed Pete was on a roll and not backing down. A dark corner of Jane felt some shocked admiration for that.

Cobus tried to step past Jim, who blocked his way. "Okay, Cobus, okay. Let's leave it."

Jane could see the anger in those green eyes and wondered for a moment why he didn't back the student, but at that moment he cast her a look of apology that said: *"I'm sorry, but I'm suffering some atavistic guilt for having fucked the other guy's wife."* She decided to take some heat out of the situation: "Look, let's just all take five minutes to absorb this and think about what to do."

Cobus and Jim wandered off in one direction, the photographer's arm round the South African's shoulders. Jane took Catalina another way, while Pete took a drag and pitched away his cigarette butt. Catalina turned to her: "I'm sorry, Jane, I'm a plain-speaking Aussie and I've gotta ask you; is that what life with him is like? How did you end up with him?"

"A combination of hormones and naivety, I guess."

"Ah yeah, I mean, he's good looking..." Jane saw the girl blush; she had reddened often enough of late herself to identify with that uncontrollable feminine blight. It would have been quite sweet if anyone other than Pete had been the cause – and had it not brought back such regrets. "But provoking your dad like that when he must be feeling bad enough about what's going on..."

"I guess he was just telling the truth – as he saw it anyway. Perhaps he did utter one or two things that the rest of us didn't dare to."

"I suppose. But there's telling the truth and then there's rubbing it in. What about a little respect for his father-in-law?"

Jane put a hand on the girl's shoulder and stopped her. "Look, there's no good pretending. It's pretty obvious to you all that our marriage isn't the happiest. And my father? – well, if I'm honest, he's never hidden the fact that he doesn't have much time for Pete." Inside, Jane applauded Catalina's attempt to act surprised at the non-revelation.

"Jim should've let Cobus teach him a lesson."

"Catalina, firstly that would have achieved nothing. Secondly, it wouldn't have worked out that way."

"What d'you mean?"

"Pete was reeling Cobus in. Not all his words are empty. He's a bit of an adrenaline junkie. Extreme sports are where he spends a lot of his time – and money! There, and in casinos. But he also gets his kicks, in all senses, from martial arts, jujitsu, tae kwon-do you name it. And he's good. Possibly the last thing Cobus would have remembered would have been taking his first and only swing. I guess that was among the reasons I married him. A woman likes to feel her man can protect her."

Catalina seemed impressed. "Yeah, that's always good – till you tire of each other and he gets jealous. Who's going to take him on then?"

Jane just nodded.

Sutch made his way back to the camp. Though he had wandered off, he'd still been able to hear the exchanges.

"Okay everybody." The words of Jane and others had galvanised him. He knew he had to make something happen; hoped his tome carried some weight. They grouped together again, though the tension was as tangible as the silence of the forest. "This is what I think we should do. We know that trying to find Robbie here will be like looking for... actually I'm growing tired of having to use the needle and haystack simile. I think we have to at least cover this island, while Jim, I would like you to take one of the boats and make a sweep around the other islands, just to see if there's any obvious sign of activity, past or present.

"I know we don't have lots of fuel, but I don't want to think we didn't try. If you see something, don't attempt anything alone. Report back and we'll go suitably... prepared." He looked in the direction of the gun case. "The rest of us will continue from yesterday, except our main hope as we go will be to find our friend." He paused. "I'm now going to say something that you may think callous, but that is so far from my intention." He looked at each of them in turn. "We came here to achieve something. Now we have a double challenge – find the lost kingdom and find Robbie. He would not want us to give up on the former, and no way will we give up on the latter." He swallowed hard before continuing – but some things had to be said. "If we do not find the young man, I will ensure that his name lives on. This will be renamed McCulloch Island. But first, let me just ask, does anyone have a better idea, or think that we should simply go home?"

There was silence – not even any sarcasm from Pete. It did not seem an obvious signal of consent; indeed, perhaps it meant they disagreed, but not vehemently; had ideas, but not better ones; wanted to go home, but wanted to be able to look in the mirror. Maybe Tariq's universal truth applied – wondering was sometimes better than knowing.

It was time to inject some positivity, perhaps even a little humour – God knew, they all needed it. "I'm sure the possibility of having an island named after the young Scotsman will make some of you even more determined to find him... eh, Cobus?" There was laughter – a genuine sound. "In that case, we have work to do; a kingdom and a colleague – a friend – to find."

He saw Jane smiling through her tears; her pride shone through. Was he worthy of it? Finding the truthful answer to that question would have needed an even larger team, to hack through the twisting creepers of hypocrisy that he felt were hiding the ruins of his soul.

"I think we should have someone guarding the camp," said Jim. "Just in case." He saw them look at him with concern and added: "You know, in case Robbie returns and wonders where the hell we've all gone."

CHAPTER NINETEEN

Rather like the moment when he'd found the key that had opened the door to the world of dreams, Sutch was struck by the suspension of time that followed their second discovery. They had been pushing forward for perhaps an hour. Jim had left to make a circuit of the archipelago and Catalina was watching the camp. For the briefest of instances after the machete clanged against stone, there was a vacuum, then excitement and disbelief followed, like litter dancing in the slipstream of a car. They all turned their head towards the sound. It was Jane's machete, the irony being that it had been hanging loose in one hand as she had used the other to push aside a branch. "Oh my God!" She was staring down at something.

The Professor came stumbling over to stand by her. Jane hacked at the shrubs and there it was, a tiny section of wall. No more than seven or eight blocks of stone; not the most imposing piece of architecture, but wondrous in the eyes of the team. Sutch took the bandana he'd been wearing beneath his hat and started a feverish wiping of the lichens and moss. "Look, look how they're slotted together, like those... oh, what are they Jane, those Mayan sites in South America?!"

"You mean Tikal and Naachtun – or Masuul, to give it its correct ancient name."

"Yes. You were involved in excavation work there for a time."

"I see what you mean." She frowned. "But at Naachtun the walls were defensive. The Mayan city states, like Tikal and Calakmul were always attacking each other and Naachtun sat right in the middle of them, so they built walls to protect themselves. But why would they need to do that here, miles from anyone or anywhere? Yet these blocks do look typical of the large-cut blocks they would have used," she ran a hand deferentially over the stone, "fitting perfectly, without any need for cement."

Pete had stepped up. "What did I say – a series of small walls." In his moment of triumph Sutch could have happily swung his machete at Pete, but before he had the chance his son-in-law seemed to see just how he had needled him and, for whatever reason, changed his tone. "Actually, I'd have thought you've just answered your own question. If the Mayan people were always attacking each other, perhaps the separate islands formed their own kingdoms and built their defences accordingly." He reached for a cigarette. "And does it strike anyone else as strange that the Mayan civilisation also famously just disappeared?"

Father and daughter looked at Pete and found themselves in the pretty unique position of thinking that he might just have made a very valid point. Then the daughter withdrew her notebook from her rucksack and started to sketch, while the father addressed Cobus:

"Have you got the tape?" Cobus threw down his pack and withdrew a large reel of yellow and black tape, along with some metal tent pegs. "Mark this out. Then I think we'll need two small teams. Jane, you and I will continue upwards." He thought back to the recent argument at the camp. "Pete, you come with us. Cobus, when you've finished head back to camp and wait for Jim. He must be due back very soon if he's not back already. Then send him and Catalina up and you take a break. Tell them to follow along the line of these stones and see whether there are other fragments, as if it were indeed a city wall." Cobus looked disappointed, so Sutch went up to him and kept his voice low: "I'm letting you go back because I trust you to get it right and also look after the camp properly. Plus, if Robbie has returned, what better welcoming party than his favourite rock-spider?" He saw the young man's face brighten a little. Also, the implied criticism of Pete had probably helped. "There'll be plenty of work this afternoon."

There was a sudden spring in action and step; everyone had needed something concrete – or in this case stone – on which to focus all energies.

When Cobus had gone, Jane looked up from her sketchbook and towards her father: "I think this must be a defensive wall, you know. Assuming there is a link with the Mayans, a lot of them still lived in thatched farms. I've not dug up too many dwellings with walls as thick as this."

"Okay, c'mon Jane – Pete."

"Hang on, I'm still drawing."

"Haven't you finished yet? It's just a few stones."

She snapped her notebook shut. "Yes, Father." She smiled and he returned the gesture. It struck the Professor that, for a short while at least, Robbie's disappearance had been washed over by the waves of discovery. Though it would resurface when that tide retreated again, even a moment's respite was welcome.

And it was as if scales had fallen from their eyes; tired eyes that had been seeing only the dripping, sodden green of the forest. Now everywhere they looked, bricks and pieces of masonry peeped from their hiding places on the ground.

"There must have been some track or road, long since overgrown, that led up from the harbour," said Sutch, "and, now that we've entered the city limits, what treasures we're finding. Look!"

Jane stood open-mouthed. Repossessed by nature, but still visible, was the spectre of an arch. Even Pete let out a long whistle. "Congratulations, father-in-law. If I'm not mistaken, this looks very much like the culmination of forty years' research."

They went to it and all put their hands on the stonework.

"Unbelievable," whispered Sutch in awe.

"It's almost Byzantine in style," Jane's words came out in a gasp. "That's amazing; not at all like Mayan architecture. Look at the detail on the keystone. Is that one of those... oh, what the heck were they called?"

"Chupacabra?"

"Yes, those things people claimed were aliens; the goat-sucker – sucked the blood out of farm animals."

"It could be." The Professor nodded.

"These people may have come across from the west coast of South America originally. The forest appears to have done us a favour. It's protected a lot of the detail from the salt air and the wind. This is magnificently preserved."

"Oh my word, just look!"

As if they had adjusted the focus on a camera lens, their eyes were able to pick out all manner of half-collapsed structures beyond the arch. The forest was littered with the ruins of houses, both plain dwellings and more extravagant villas, and much grander structures that might have been municipal buildings. There were isolated arches, devoid of the stonework they had been supporting; the ribcages of a dead civilisation picked clean by the vultures of time. Those arches were in a variety of styles; rounded, square, Gothic, as if this were an architect's workshop.

"It's eclectic in the extreme." Jane spoke in awestruck whispers as they wandered amongst the ruins of temples and markets in the diffused light beneath the forest canopy, "such a confluence of styles and influences." She put her hand to her forehead in puzzlement. "This is so weird. Naachtun is known for its varied architecture, but that was a reflection of changing political allegiances and the impact of regional styles. But here, we're looking at a right old hotchpotch of influences in a kingdom that kept the outside world at bay."

"Perhaps that's what happens," suggested Pete, "when your merchants sail to various distant ports and return with tales of what they've seen. Nothing develops organically."

Not for the first time Jane and her father looked at him in surprise.

"Fair point, darling." The term of endearment slipped out before she could prevent it – and how she wished she could. She was shocked – she could not remember the last time she had called him that – and she could see from his face that he couldn't either.

"No need for tape here." Sutch laughed, oblivious to the moment's awkwardness.

The three of them moved on, amazed, through a huge, moss-covered plaza. Then Jane pointed to three stone pillars at the far end. "Aren't they—"

"The same as the one down by the camp." Sutch completed her thought. As they got closer, they could see there were hieroglyphics on these too.

"These are almost certainly stelae," responded Jane. "The Mayans used to record their history on them. My God, it's all pointing to this island as having been peopled by them. If that's the case, then Pete's earlier comment is... well, no-one *has* ever explained why such an important and advanced civilisation just collapsed. What we do know is that wherever they went they built huge cities, as big and complex as anything in the known civilised world, and they seemed able to adapt to and exploit whatever environment they chose to live in. But then they just seemed to... I don't know... up and go."

"Kinda spooky, huh?" Pete lit another cigarette, which to Jane felt like an affront to the majesty of the ruins, but with yesterday's adultery still tingling in her loins, she bit her tongue. She was still trying to recover from what she assumed was her guilt-induced use of 'darling' moments before.

Typical – just when she had hoped Pete would act like a Philistine that morning, as if that would have somehow justified what she had done, he chose instead to make sensible, salient comments. It seemed for a moment that the disrespectful cigarette might help to redress the balance, but when he spoke again he seemed determined to frustrate her. "I wonder what these people worshipped."

"The Mayans had any number of gods, most of them worshipped by pretty bloodthirsty rituals. As you mentioned the other day, the cult of human sacrifice was strong."

"I'm betting that image of Cobus back there," he gave an oblique jerk of the thumb in the direction of the first arch, "that Chipolata, or whatever you called it, wasn't content with goat's blood. Its image seems to be everywhere." He pointed around them. "It's like a day out in Natal."

It had been too good to be true after all, thought Jane.

"I suggest," the Professor exchanged furtive raised eyebrows with his daughter, "that we uncover the full extent of this site before we start analysing the detail. I think we're a bit overcome by all this – I know I am – and it's a lot to take in. Also, let's not forget that we're the vanguard of a much larger expedition that I'll now have to organise." He sighed. "And let's not forget, there is something – someone – much more important we need to find." He turned to his son-in-law. "Pete, I think I'd like you to take next shift of guarding the camp. Send Cobus and Catalina up here and also Jim, assuming he's back," Pete's narrow-eyed look through the cigarette smoke was a pointed response. "If you wouldn't mind."

"Not at all." The way he pitched his cigarette to the floor gave away the lie. "I need another bloody coffee anyway." He turned and started to make his way back.

Jane watched him go and, despite everything, felt uncomfortable. Who the hell had she been when she married him? Part of that was answered as he swaggered away. Looking at his open, sweat-stained shirt clinging to his bulky pectorals and latissimus dorsi, she could forgive, as well as regret, her youthful indiscretion. Still, she winced at the less-than-subtle dismissal by her father. It smacked of being sent to the back of the class, especially as Cobus had only just been sent down to rest. She wished her father had left things alone for the time being. The only people to have done actual wrong in the last twenty-four hours were Jane Sutch, the adulteress, and Jim Bolton, her lover.

"Oh, Pete!" Pete stopped at the sound of the Professor's call, but kept his back turned. "We'll make the next change after four hours. Otherwise, we're not allowing ourselves enough time here."

There was the merest turn of the head, a curt nod and Pete wandered on – then stopped again. "To find Robbie McCulloch? You're absolutely right." He headed off.

As parting shots went, it was a ripper. Jane watched it hit home, and there was nothing she could say.

CHAPTER TWENTY

Just over an hour later, Jim and Cobus arrived at the ruined citadel.

"Any luck?" Sutch tried to sound positive as he questioned Jim, though the impact of Pete's last comment still stung.

"'Fraid not. I saw nothing worth investigating."

"Where's Catalina?"

Jim looked down. "She said she's going to stay at the camp. I think Robbie's disappearance has unnerved her."

"Ja," Cobus chipped in, "she wasn't ready yet to spend more time in the 'forest of the dead', as she called it."

Sutch shifted, awkward, and then turned back towards the ruins.

"Nice one," whispered Jim to the South African.

"Ah shit!" The response was hissed. "Me and my big mouth."

Jim was in a profuse sweat because of the climb and the heavy bag of equipment. "You guys got any water? I only brought photographic stuff."

Then, despite the circumstances, Jane saw Jim's eyes widen and keep widening at the sight before him. He pushed his hat back off his forehead and whistled. "This is incredible! National Geographic, Royal Geographical Society, start putting the zeroes on your cheques now." Yet even in the excitement of the moment, he seemed to notice the cool clasp of Jane's fingers lingering against his as he took the bottle of water from her. As he looked into her eyes, she gave a loaded glance towards her father. Jim turned to him, looking businesslike. "I want to thank you, Professor, for giving me this opportunity."

He'd misread her eyes – how she hoped, to her shame, that was a passing occurrence – and it was left to the Professor to clarify. "The thanks are all from me, dear Jim, for agreeing to come on this hare-brained, ill-planned expedition..." Sutch paused and looked around, "... which I so wish I could say had turned out so wonderful." He paused, then called over Cobus, who was also staring open-mouthed at the frayed majesty all around them. "We must never forget our priority is Robbie. I will be brutal here – there is a limit to what we can do, where we can go, our resources – all of it. I will not risk any more lives. What we must do is keep our eyes peeled. In all honesty, I fear the worst." He fell silent for a moment; a space filled with echoes of everyone's thoughts. "I would have called for Dirk to return but could not bear the thought of Robbie somehow getting back from wherever to find us gone. Or, of him calling us from somewhere we are about to discover in the coming hours, but us not hearing him because we turned back. Please believe me, I am not just saying this, but we should carry on for now, for his sake. I will share this with the others once we are back in camp."

With that, the four of them embraced, although the shadow of their missing colleague flitted amongst the ancient ghosts around them.

Jim seemed to be the first to come to terms with the practicalities of the situation; in all probability to help them move forward, but Jane wondered if it was also to assuage the guilt from his first comments. He slipped into professional photographer mode, pulling out a telescopic tripod and a clutter of lenses, from which he selected a 200mm for starters.

Jane was ready to settle down with her notebook, when her father spoke again: "No you don't. You and I are going to wander on a bit, my girl." Sutch seemed so focussed, he failed to notice the disappointed undertone to Jane's protest, but duty called, so she left Jim behind and followed him as they nudged, pushed and hacked their way forward for what seemed like another half mile.

They had moved away from the grander central area of the plaza and the imposing temples and palaces.

"I think we're entering what might have been the residential areas of the city," said Jane, "though that may be too grand a term! These buildings seem increasingly humble. I reckon they're dwellings – or the shells of them anyway."

"An interesting word – shell; very apt." Sutch looked around with a hint of sadness.

They passed yet another home. Like so many of them, it contained numerous artefacts of pottery and fungus-encrusted wood, all of them pointing to lives put on hold with an immediacy that spoke of some sudden and dreadful event. "Shells they are; things of beauty that tell a substantive tale of their former occupants, who either abandoned them or were ripped from them." He paused, emotion visible on his face, and then whispered in awe: "I never thought I'd find the Marie Celeste on dry land."

Now Sutch felt obliged to enter the house and straighten a toppled stool. "Astonishing," he looked at the wood beneath his fingers, "even the woodworm has fled."

In building after building lay the flotsam of a sunken civilisation; more pottery and mouldy wooden furniture, jewellery, combs, bottles, goblets; all manner of things that revealed a people whose love of trade and material possessions was at odds with their apparent sociophobic desire for secrecy.

All of this was veiled, to a greater or lesser extent, by a forest that had swallowed its prey, but only partially digested it. At length the buildings and detritus became less frequent and the land started to rise more sharply. They could hear a dull pounding and sighing that they knew must have emanated from the waves at the base of the cliffs.

"There were always one or two, even back then." Jane's words seemed to go unheard for a moment. The Professor, who appeared to be mulling something over, followed her gaze in a distracted way and then saw, perched further up the mountainside, what appeared to be the remains of two houses of lavish proportions, peeping out from the trees.

"Oh, you mean those who want to live at the top of the hill looking down on the plebs?"

Then Jane noticed his face revert to a frown. "What is it, Father? I recognise that look."

"Well, at the risk of sounding gruesome, I'm missing bodies here."

"Surely they'd have decomposed centuries ago..." she stopped, "... no, you're right, there'd still be bones. Or are you talking about cemeteries, tombs? I take your point."

"No, they wouldn't have had any—" He stopped.

"What do you mean?" She saw an evasive flicker in his eye but did not pursue that line for the moment. He was old enough to have earned the right to deal with things in his own time, and the time clearly wasn't now.

"Even assuming everyone fled from some cataclysm – even if everyone somehow scrambled up this precipitous slope and then threw themselves from the cliffs in despair – there's no sign of a wall of water having passed through the city, even if it were capable of getting this far. And that would be one hell of a wave, I can tell you. Rather like the terminal moraine of a glacier, you'd expect the debris of human life to have been pushed along and deposited as the water receded. Yet it looks like everyone just went out for a stroll at the same time. We've seen pottery and other artefacts lying where they belong. And as for the buildings, well-built though they are, there's no mortar holding the stones together. Hit by a force as powerful as a tidal wave or an earthquake, there should be more damage."

"You've said this before, Father. So, what do you think happened?"

He looked at her and smiled. "I have no idea. And maybe I'm completely wrong for doubting. Anyway, I think we've come as far as we need to. Let's head back to Jim and Cobus."

They turned and Jane gave a cry of alarm. Though she had seen such things more times than she could count, the unexpectedness of its discovery in this place shook her.

"What is it, Jane?"

She pointed.

Behind a small, isolated section of wall, curled in a foetal position, with desiccated fragments of skin on the back of the head and neck, lay a body. It looked like nothing so much as an unwrapped mummy, clad in a dirty brown djellaba that camouflaged it beneath the overgrowing vegetation.

When their legs felt capable of supporting them again, Jane and Sutch made their way over to the find.

"Perhaps I wasn't missing bodies so much after all." Sutch shook his head.

Jane's soft voice quivered. "You sure have a habit of making things happen, Father. Look for ancient, undiscovered civilisation – find one. Wonder about absence of bodies – find one. Please don't think ill of me ever."

"That what you call graveyard humour?"

It seemed the same thought struck both of them. They fell silent and Jane watched her father look to the heavens, close his eyes and whisper: "Robbie." She put an arm around him, gave a loving smile, and then they moved nearer to the corpse. "Strange."

"Um, technically I think that's what's known as an understatement." Jane held back, frustrated by her weakness, but unable as yet to overcome it. The body had spooked her, but not as much as her own had recently, as if every suppressed, distaff nerve was being pulled taut. She looked up and around, and the irony was not lost on her – ever since they had discussed coming to this place of death, and in particular since they had been here, she had never felt more alive or aware.

"I meant the clothing. It looks in perfectly good condition."

They squatted and Sutch reached out a tentative hand to pull at the corner of the garment where the shoulder would have been. The body collapsed with a horrible, bony rattle onto its back.

113

Now Sutch gasped in reflex, then reached over and took something from the clawed hand. "Seems to be a parchment of some sort." Then he spotted something on the ground by the body. As he picked it up, he appeared to fight the urge to drop it in horror, before holding it in shaking fingers towards Jane. "And this, if I'm not mistaken, is a very obviously twentieth century pen with 'Marriott Hotels' written down the side."

Jane backed away and felt the onset of hysteria as an incongruous mixture of bile and laughter fought its way up through her chest. She put her hands on her knees for support.

The sound of running feet caused her body to jerk, as if all her taut nerves had contracted further. To her intense relief she saw Jim, who had heard her previous scream. She collapsed against his chest.

"Jane, are you okay? Where's the Professor?"

"I'm here." Sutch rose from behind the wall, seeming to reflect in the movements of his old, creaking limbs a certain consanguinity with the lone corpse. He had the rolled parchment in his hand. "I thought this was not mine to take, but I believe this dead stranger would grant me leave." As he unrolled the document, something caused him to stagger. "I was wrong on two counts! The parchment *is* mine to take – it's addressed to me!" Jane and the others gasped. He looked at them, his face pale, and pointed to the body. "And this was no stranger."

Cobus arrived now, having been a little way behind Jim when he had heard Jane's scream. He was just in time to see Sutch's distress and hear Jim's question: "Professor, are you alright?" The Afrikaner had some first aid knowledge, acquired during his time in the army, and seeing Sutch turn white he wondered whether it might now be needed in administering CPR.

"Father!"

"It's..." the Professor hesitated, "... from Tariq."

CHAPTER TWENTY-ONE

SCORPION ARCHIPELAGO, 2PM OCTOBER 30TH 1997

He was cold now. Nothing seemed to warm him; not the campfire, the blanket, the tot of whisky or the afternoon sun. An hour before, the thought of a letter from his old acquaintance, the sound of his voice on parchment from beyond the grave, would have made him glow inside.

The others were also in a state of shock, the letter having chilled each of them in different ways. All sat in silence, but in four of the six minds one image must have been common; that of an emaciated dead body hiding in the ruins of a city in a stagnant forest, issuing a warning none of them understood. In some ways the written words were superfluous; the very discovery was enough of an ill omen, like waking to find a dead magpie on your doorstep. There was the added, unavoidable thought – would that horror be a reflection of Robbie's fate?

The youthful eighty-year-old that had been Professor Sutch just hours before seemed to have gone the way of his friend, Tariq, as if a blanketing doom had smothered him. In the silence he stared into the fire, and then unrolled the parchment again and read in silence:

'My dear Professor Sutch, Edward, forgive the rolled-up parchment – old habits die hard, as do old men of the island kingdom. The latter I have discovered to my cost. I am much further along the road to death than I was when I sent you the amphora, a gift that has turned into a curse. How I wish now you were not coming here, but even though I have spent only a brief time with you, I know you will. That was why I entrusted the amphora to you – and why I am writing this letter, which I hope you will find. I knew I had whetted an appetite that was hungry for knowledge, so you would seek out this place and keep it alive, if only in the history books. I needed someone to be the keeper of the secret, so that it did not die with me; a secret I kept for two hundred and fifty years.

When I talked to you forty years ago of the place that had been my home, I felt a sudden longing to see it again before I died. I took a chance, hoping they were dead – the priests. Believing they must have simply lost the will to live in this remote and blasted place. But they are still alive and it seems they have heard my boat. So, in an attempt to deceive them, I set it on a course to the west of here and left the engine running while I slipped overboard and made my way to the shore. But they have followed me. Evil minds are suspicious and not so easily fooled.'

Here the script became ragged, almost illegible.

'Oh, I am wracked with pain. It is as bad as I feared. If you have come so far as to discover my body, a man of your intelligence will know by now that it was not some natural disaster from which I fled all those years ago. If you are reading this, I warn you now to leave and I beg your forgiveness for my lies. You may ask why I never came back to my home before. I could not. There would have been no forgiveness for me here, only slow death. Besides, there was a world to discover – is it not a strange irony that you have explored most of the world, but what has fascinated you most is my part of it?

It is hard to explain why the melancholy of the Southern Ocean lived on in my blood, enough that I should want to die here.

Do not go to Temple Island – it is alive; alive with death. You must flee. Nothing can prepare you for that place. I thank whichever god looks over me that I am about to die and pray that he will protect you.

Your Tariq'

Pete broke the silence, his words cold but succinct. "This Tariq's not just a linguist, he is a good story-teller, 'cos he's sure spooked me, whether I believe him or not."

The story would have amazed them all the more, had Sutch not chosen to keep certain details to himself. Luckily no-one had asked to see the letter, or they would have discovered just how much he had held back.

Now Jim spoke up: "So, let me get this straight – there was no cataclysm, no tidal wave, no volcanic eruption."

"No," said Sutch. "Just before we found Tariq I expressed my doubts to Jane."

"Well then, what do you think happened to this kingdom?"

"It would be pure speculation, without being able to explore all the other islands. And that's too big a job for this little party. Too dangerous as well, by the sound of it."

"I tell you what," Catalina spoke up, "whatever happened here, you can count on this 'Temple Island' playing a part." She shuddered and looked around. "Perhaps we're on Temple Island now." She was voicing everyone else's fears. "God, I wonder whether Robbie's disappearance is tied in with this?"

The day's various finds had conspired, at times, to overshadow the fate of the young Scotsman, but now the mention of his name was like a rumble of thunder, reminding them of the storm clouds overhead.

Sutch had been staring out to sea, taking in some of the other islands, but his gaze returned to the team. "My dream has become a nightmare; one I've dragged you all into." There were some half-hearted denials. "How often do we warn to 'be careful what you wish for, because it might come true'?" Suddenly, he made a decisive move and stood up. "I'm going to call for Dirk. We'll spend this one last night here together and he can come and pick you all up tomorrow." He could almost feel the relief flooding from the others.

Except Jane: "Meaning what, as far as you're concerned?"

"I'll stay and continue to search for Robbie on this island, or in case he comes back, while you can organise to return as soon as possible with a bigger team. I won't rest until we know what became of him and what Temple Island is all about."

"Father, don't be—"

"Enough! I've decided. Would you have him return to the camp to find we've deserted him?" He stalked away to his tent and Jane knew better than to follow at that moment.

***

"When we were out on night manoeuvres," Cobus gave the fire an absent-minded prod, "we used to say a campfire is a contradiction; bright and warm, with a comforting circle of light, but making the darkness beyond that much deeper. It's like you're seeing the back of the cave but filling it with dancing shadows."

Catalina puffed out her cheeks. "Thanks for that – I didn't believe I'd be able to eat or sleep before you said that, now I know I won't."

Jane started to hand out mugs she'd been brewing. "Well, here's the famous British panacea for all ills, a cup of tea."

Indeed, that seemed to calm them, to the point where they realised both how ready for food and how exhausted they were. But still, the image of Tariq hovered in the shadows at the margin of the firelight, like Banquo's ghost, waiting to be offered the spare place where Robbie would have sat. After dinner Cobus took the forward position:

"We'll take it in turns to sit watch, in pairs. We've got a positive arsenal in that gun-box there. Anybody thinks they're gonna come wandering in and helping themselves to... anything tonight, is in for an attack of lead poisoning. I've been here before – in Zimbabwe, when their army decided they could use a few recruits from their friendly neighbour South Africa – so I'll be on all night. Who's gonna take the first watch with me?"

"I will." Jim raised a hand.

"After two hours I'll wake you, Pete." Cobus looked at the others with a wry grin, but his comments were still directed at the playboy. "I'm guessing you're a bit of a night owl."

"But why should you have to sit up all night?" No-one had heard Sutch return from his tent, having had a chance to get things straight in his head.

As if a senior officer had spoken, Cobus stood, years of training kicking in. "Sir, I'm the only one who's shot a gun here. I mean to kill... people." There was no shame in his voice; it was the reality of a bush war and though the words struck a chill in everyone, the whole team recognised a stark truth – better to have that experience on your side in the silent darkness.

"Sounds like you're perfectly qualified to me, then." The confession seemed to resonate with Pete. "Boy, I bet that's the ultimate adrenaline fix."

The firelight only emphasised the contempt on the faces of the others.

Cobus looked at his chronometer. "So, Professor, you gonna try Dirk again in the morning?"

"Yes." Sutch's words reflected his resignation. "I guess I couldn't really expect him to be sitting by the phone." The unanswered ringing tone had been one of the loneliest sounds the Professor had heard in a long time, which was really saying something!

"Okay, all of you try to grab some sleep." Cobus gestured towards Jim. "We're armed; we've got a fire. The biggest difference of all to last night is that this time," he brandished the gun, "we're ready for any trouble."

"Yes," Jim spoke under his breath as the others headed to their tents, "but from what?"

CHAPTER TWENTY-TWO

It was unfortunate that the possibility of danger had not proved enough to keep Jim awake, and he felt himself being shaken.

"Jim?" An urgent whisper from Cobus.

"What?" A sleepy response accompanied by a sudden, guilty jolt into a sitting position. "Shit, sorry."

"Never mind that now. Look." He tried focussing his bleary eyes. "You see them?"

He did.

Out on the water, towards the eastern arm of the bay, were two faint lights.

"Is that a ship in the distance?" A rhetorical question perhaps, but Jim provided the answer himself. "Can't be, eh? The movement isn't right."

"Ja, the lights must be much closer to bob like that – it's not that rough a sea tonight." The lights were moving south and would soon be hidden by the arm of the bay. There was no sound that they could pick out above the rush of the tide, and the speed of approach suggested wind or manpower was driving the vessel. "C'mon, let's not lose them."

"Let's wake the others."

"Nah, let 'em sleep for the moment." Jim picked up a frisson of excitement in the young South African's response. "We need to move and also, we might scare everyone unnecessarily. Besides, this way we've got an element of surprise. If this is trouble coming, it might be scared off if the camp comes to life, with six people stumbling and blundering around. We'll move faster if we're just two. No offence mate, but I'm the only one who's used to this sort of thing, so trust me. Bring your rifle. C'mon."

"I'll bet you our friend Pete has done some hunting in his time."

Cobus looked at Jim. "Ja, but he's also a prick."

That was that settled then. They moved with caution across the shingle towards the softer, quieter ground around the margin of the forest.

"They're probably wanting to land in the forest and creep up on us through the trees." Cobus gave Jim a knowing look. "I'm guessing we know what happened to Robbie."

"Yes... we just don't know why – or who the fuck they are."

The lights, which they had to assume were on a boat, were about to disappear from view. The pair's way was hindered by roots and low-hanging branches.

"C'mon man, we've got to hurry." Cobus was breathing hard every two words or so. "If we get to them before they land we can take 'em out. If they beat us and disappear into this forest, which we've got to assume they know well, we've got a problem."

"I'm doing my... best!" Jim slipped on a wet root even as he uttered the last word.

The lights were gone. Cobus and Jim were struggling, their faces and hands covered with cuts from lashing branches. Jim, less sure-footed than his friend, was bleeding and bruised on his knees and shins from countless stumbles. Now they rounded the promontory that marked the end of the bay and ran through the surf.

They were just in time to see the lights reach the shingle by the forest edge a couple of hundred yards or so ahead of them – it might have been much further, but the swaying lights, which seemed to be attached to some sort of mast, hypnotised and confused their eyes. Cobus raised his hand to stop Jim. "Can you see anything?"

"To be honest, Cobus, I can't even see the boat yet."

Suddenly Cobus punched his thigh in anger. "Poes!"

Though he didn't understand the word, its anger was clear enough to Jim. "What's wrong?"

"There are night vision goggles in the inflatables. I'm such a fuckin' idiot." Now the Afrikaner turned his attention back to the lights. "There's something not right here. Let's go. Keep low, and don't look at the lights; try to see beyond them."

They ran forward hunched. When they had covered about three quarters of the distance, Cobus raised his hand again. "Stay here and cover my back. I'm gonna see what this is all about."

Jim watched Cobus' shape grow indistinct in the starlight, and then, faint but audible, he heard the word "SHIT!" and the Afrikaner was sprinting back across the shingle. "Get back to the camp man, quick! It's a fuckin' decoy!"

"What?!"

Cobus bolted past him. Jim turned and followed.

"Man, they're clever, but I'm stupid. It's a tiny boat with two storm lanterns fixed to it."

"How the hell...?"

"They must know the tides here, man. But there's no way that would have floated all the way across from one of the other islands." He held his rifle in both hands as he ran and gestured with it now towards the blackness of the sea. "They must have been out there all along. Fuck, I've been a *doos*."

They had lost all track of just how far away from the camp they were. They shouted as they ran, slipped, stumbled, but the surf and the distance killed their words. As they got closer it looked as if nothing was wrong, but so it had the previous morning.

"Let's get everybody up and armed." Jim pointed back the way they had come. "We need to be on our guard."

Cobus didn't answer, but he didn't need to. They both knew that their enemy was skilled and if their intention was to kidnap someone they would already be finished and away.

They were nearly there now and could see that their shouts had, at last, stirred the sleepers. Catalina was the first up. "What's going on?"

"We saw some lights on the water," panted Cobus, "but they were a fuckin' decoy."

"Lights?!"

"We thought a boat was coming and went over to where it landed, but it was just a trap. Get the guns." Sutch and Pete were also up, looking confused.

"What's happening?" The Professor sounded as dazed as his eyes.

"We'll tell you in a minute. Open the gun-box first... sir, please."

"Where's Jane?" They all looked at Jim, who was holding open the flap to her tent.

"She wouldn't just have wandered off!" Catalina's shaking transmitted through her voice. "Not tonight."

The Professor looked ashen faced. "You're right. She might have defied a thousand curses in her career, but this place – it's different. It's got us all scared." He turned towards the trees. "JANE!"

Cobus threw his head back, eyes squeezed tight. "Oh my God, this is all my fault! If I'd woken all of you as Jim suggested before we went after those lights..."

They peered out across the water towards where they knew the nearest island stood but could barely make out its bulk.

Jim put a hand on Cobus' shoulder. "Listen, none of us could guess we'd be up against something like this. Whatever it..." His voice trailed off and he raised his hand. "Hey, I'm not sure, but is that something out there?"

"Where?" asked several voices.

"Wait a minute." It was Cobus, who ran across to one of the flight boxes and rummaged inside, before returning with a pair of what looked like bulky, hi-tech field glasses. "Night vision glasses," was his response to the puzzled looks from the others. Then he looked shamefaced. "If I'd remembered the bloody things before, we wouldn't be in this mess."

"Spilt milk." Pete's words threw Cobus a little. He had learnt the maxim during his time in England and was taken aback by the apparent magnanimity. He held the Professor in such high regard, and had so little for the quintessential arrogant English rake, that he had forgotten the man must be worried about his wife, no matter what domestic issues they might have. He looked at Pete in expectation of sarcasm, but none came. "You tried to do what was best. Now let's just find my wife and bring her back."

Cobus nodded with new-found respect, and then trained the goggles out across the waves, screwing up his face as he tried to locate his target. Then his features dropped and he tensed. "There is something out there. It's a boat." There was a murmur of fearful anticipation from the others. "Looks like two people in it. Don't think either of them's Jane, but it's hard to tell. They seem to be heading towards that other island."

"They must have her." Part of Jim regretted his statement, but the time for treading on eggshells was past. "To have got her away from the camp like that without a sound... how'd they do it? Might have drugged her."

"Yes, Rohypnol." It seemed eggshells were never part of Pete's surroundings. "Very popular in ancient civilisations."

Sutch looked at him. "I hardly think this is the time for your cynical wit. My daughter's missing and—"

Pete turned on him. "My wife, too! Isn't that a coincidence?" Sutch said nothing, perhaps the wisest move for a number of reasons, amongst them being the fact that he might have questioned his son-in-law's sudden concern for Jane. Pete held out a hand towards his father-in-law. "The keys to the gun-box, as Cobus asked – please. I'm not sure why we're all standing around unarmed."

Cobus looked in apology at Sutch. "Sorry, Professor, but I think he's right. While you're sorting that out, I'll get the boat ready"

"I am right. But hold on – we can't just jump into a powered dinghy and chase after these guys. We know nothing about them." He looked at the Professor and said with less-than-subtle sarcasm: "If they've got drugs they may have guns. One hole in the side of our mobile paddling pool and we'll all be stuffed. And that's if they decide not to pick us off through a telescopic sight." He pointed to the shadowy hump of the other island. "And yes, I know we've also got guns, but there might be five hundred of them over there. I say we follow, but carefully."

"By which time my daughter may be dead." Even in that charged atmosphere, Sutch's words brought a chilled pause. "Or is that your alternative plan?"

Nothing was dulling Pete's anger now. His eyes blazed, even in the lambent glow of the dying campfire. "Maybe it's yours, so you don't have to have me as a son-in-law." There was a nervous gasp from the others at those harshest of words, but Pete was not going to hold back now. "We don't know they have Jane – and old man or not, I'll take you apart if you ever—"

"For God's sake, stop it!" It was Catalina, whose nerves seemed stretched to the limit by all that was happening.

"Hey, everyone." As on the previous occasion when things were overheating, Jim raised his hands, "let's calm down. Let's not do their job for them."

"So, are we just going to sit here and let them – whoever they are – pick us off one by one?" Sutch's gaze was still fixed on his son-in-law.

"That's not what I'm saying, Professor Branestawm, and you know it." It seemed Pete was past all respect now.

Cobus had stopped in his tracks when the row kicked off, but continued now on his way to the boat, speaking over his shoulder as he went. "I still think we should go now, and we may even have an element of surprise helping us. They'll be expecting us to be confused, scared; they certainly won't be expecting pursuit, as they can't be sure we've seen them." He pulled the cord that powered the pump on the inflatable. "Also, though I hate to admit it, Pete may be right. If there's five hundred, or even fifty of them, six of us with rifles are not going to overpower them. So, we'll go carefully, not gung-ho. Do a recce, then decide. Also, I don't think we should all leave the camp." Now he came back across to the others, who said nothing, just waited to hear; needing a leader; needing direction. "Who's to say that isn't another decoy boat out there – though I don't think it is." With what still took him a great effort, Cobus put his hand on Pete's shoulder – he needed him onside right now. "I must say I admire how you're managing to think straight under the circumstances."

Pete looked down and stayed quiet. Another silence ensued. It spoke volumes, but nobody was too sure what it was saying. "Like I said," continued Cobus, "we do have to act now. Jim and I will go."

"It's my wife, for fuck's sake," spat Pete.

"Ja, sorry man, you're right. I just meant that we are responsible for this – me in particular. You come with then. Jim, you stay back and guard the camp. Apart from anything else, two men in the boat is enough. We'll be faster."

"We won't be if we don't get moving." Pete cast what seemed like a loaded look at Jim. "She's my wife, and none of you know what she means to me." With that he grabbed a rifle and started pushing the boat out into the surf.

"She's my daughter, too." They turned and looked at the Professor. "So, you go and bring her back." The three younger men might have been butting horns like male mountain goats, but amid the huffing, puffing, flying stones and dust they had all overlooked the fact that he was the only man who commanded Jane's unequivocal love. But he was old. In his voice, everyone heard how close he was to being broken. Still, he found it in himself to say one last thing: "And be careful. We don't know what we're up against. This is a place where mankind does not belong."

Quickly, Cobus grabbed his pack – something he had always done from instinct when setting out into the unknown, ever since it had taken a bullet from a rebel sniper and saved his life – and leapt into the boat to start the engine. "Let's get Jane."

CHAPTER TWENTY-THREE

"I don't think we could catch them even if we tried." Pete looked out through the night vision goggles. "If they're rowing or paddling, they must be incredibly strong; they've nearly reached the island. Maybe they're on some other sort of drugs." The last sentence was muttered under his breath.

Cobus risked a quick glance at him, and then, almost despite himself, grinned as they shared a rare, indeed unique, moment of complicity. It had been a risqué thing to say, but Cobus could tell the guy was using that very British defence, the combination of stiff upper lip and graveyard humour, to keep himself strong. He couldn't help but admire that. "Just think, we might be in pursuit of the last survivors of an ancient civilisation."

"You don't believe that crap, do you?" was the terse response.

Cobus pursed his lips. "I didn't, but then who the hell are these guys?" There was an embarrassed pause. "You're right. I dunno why I said that. Who gives a shit, right? The only important thing now is your wife's safety. Lucky the sea's become a little rougher; it's got to have slowed them a bit and hopefully they won't hear us until we're quite a bit closer to them. In rifle range at least!"

Pete looked ahead again through the goggles. "The sea might be rough, but it also means we're not gaining on them."

There was about a mile and a half between the two islands and they could see that the mystery boat would reach its apparent destination very soon. The two men were aware they didn't have a firm plan.

Cobus spoke. "You do realise, if we lose these guys—"

"This is not necessarily a search and rescue mission? Yes, I'm aware."

"I'm sorry man. I know we don't see eye to eye, but I wouldn't wish this on anyone."

"Thanks." Cobus heard Pete exhale. "Look, I'm not pretending Jane and I had – sorry, *have* – a perfect marriage, but I want to get the old girl back. At the same time, I know I can't risk everybody's life to do it."

"Ja, I've a feeling these guys don't take any prisoners."

"Perhaps not the best phrase under the circumstances."

"Ah shit, man, sorry. You know what I mean."

"Won't this FUCKING boat go any faster?!"

"It's not us, man, it's them. This is effectively an inshore lifeboat, so it's not slow, but we wasted too much time arguing on the beach and underestimated how fast these guys can paddle."

The boat was being thrown around on the rollers despite the relative power of the motor. In the starlight of that southern sky they could just about see the sleek lines of other boat cutting through the water and heading towards a large area of exposed shingle. Seeing that the quarry had nearly reached its destination, Pete looked yet again through the goggles. Only a few seconds passed. "They've just landed."

Although they had both known it was coming, there was an ominous ring to that bald statement of fact.

"And can you see her?" Cobus cursed himself in silence for not having brought another pair of goggles with him; frustrated once again with the speed at which the basics of military training seemed to have deserted him.

"It's difficult to keep these things trained on them, but... there's only two of them walking. Wait – they're carrying something. Fuck, these guys must be strong. If that is a... if that's Jane they're carrying, one of them has just slung her over his shoulders like a sack of potatoes, even though they've just paddled at that speed. Now they've disappeared into the trees." Cobus gave Pete a concerned look. "I'll try to keep an eye on exactly where they've entered the forest."

"Shit, man, if I hadn't been so stupid." Cobus slapped his hand against the dinghy.

"Don't beat yourself up so much. Any of us would have done what you did."

Unexpected as it was from a man whom he had thought was a prick, Cobus found Pete's conciliatory approach only made him feel worse. It had happened on his watch; that was the bottom line. He tried to focus now on the job in hand. It was the only way he knew. He had witnessed friends blown into pieces by mortars and landmines, and if he had allowed himself to think about it at the time, he would never have made it back home.

About a hundred yards out from the beach, he spoke again: "If we're going in, then we're at the point—"

"I know," Pete interrupted, "we're going to have to cut the motor; run black and silent. Let's do it. We can't help her if we're caught. As we said before, we don't know how many of them there are or whether they're watching us even now. They certainly seem big strong boys."

They killed the motor and picked up the two emergency paddles from the loops on the sides of the boat.

The stretch of shingle looked horribly exposed in contrast to the furtive shadows of the forest beyond it, which were alive with the suspicion of possibility. They beached their craft and picked up the rifles.

Pete slung the goggles back in the boat. "I'm just going to let my eyes adjust to the darkness. Besides, I need both hands on my gun." They peered into the shadows. "Doesn't feel fantastic, does it?" As understatements went, it was right down there.

"Na, man. Look, I'll leave it up to you. You wanna turn round?"

"Would you?"

"I guess not."

"In that case, let's go."

They removed the safety from their rifles.

"Do you still have an idea where they went?" asked Cobus.

"They disappeared with such ease, I'm sure there must be a track. Yup, I think I know roughly where it was."

They touched fists and moved off. Both of them could think of people they would rather have been with when moving into the slow jaws of death, but only suicide victims really get to choose their end, and even they do not always know the finer details.

After a few paces, Cobus whispered: "You know, I thought we might meet a reception committee of blowpipes, spears or AK47s, but the reality – the absence of any sign of life – is worse."

The sound of blackness and the colour of silence, extreme paradoxes, were encapsulated here, at the end of the earth. Both men were wondering how much of that they could take, when Pete raised a hand: "Is that a break in the tree-line, over there?"

They crossed over and found not so much a path as a tunnel, where undergrowth and overhanging branches had been cut away. With just a brief glance at each other they set off, walking at pace, even running once their eyes had adjusted, fearing to stop, lest their flow of adrenaline stopped with them. But then Cobus did come grinding to a halt: "Am I imagining it, or is there some kind of light – a flickering – up ahead?"

"No, I think you're right. At first, I thought it was just the result of my own blood pressure."

Both of them lifted their guns in readiness and went forward, though much slower now. They seemed to be approaching a clearing in the trees. Then both men stopped again; likewise their breathing for a moment.

"You're kidding me, man," hissed Cobus.

"What the fucking hell...?" was Pete's equally prosaic response.

"I think we might have found Temple Island."

CHAPTER TWENTY-FOUR

Ahead of them, incongruous in the middle of the forest, was a rock-face forty to fifty feet high, in the base of which was an opening. It appeared to be the entrance to a cave but had been hewn into a square portal. Someone had even gone to the trouble of carving faux pillars around it. There was also a riveting but gruesome adornment to the tympanum, where someone with great skill had hewn myriad skulls, which looked on like an audience at the devil's own cabaret. All were flanked by flaming torches, creating the glow on which they had commented. Pete stared at that gaping maw. "I think we've also found where Jane is."

Cobus nodded. "And Robbie."

They looked around. There were no guards; no signs of the people who had kindled those torches.

"It may seem a superfluous thing to say under the circumstances, but I don't like this."

"Ja, feels like walking into a trap, or the lion's den." Cobus agreed and turned to Pete. "Listen, man, I say again; your decision – on or back?"

"Has to be on. D'you know, even if they didn't have my wife," he paused, "and Robbie, of course, it would feel wrong to turn back here."

Cobus just nodded, less convinced perhaps. They moved with cautious speed across to the dark opening, peered through from opposite sides...

... and jerked their heads back.

"Did you see what I just saw," Cobus mouth hung open now in disbelief, "or are we back to those drugs again?"

"I'm not one hundred per cent sure what I *did* see."

"Didn't look to be anyone around."

They steeled themselves and ducked inside.

What they found astounded them and was rendered all the more surreal by the flickering light from more torches, which confused their eyes, giving the illusion of movement to the stonework. Cobus nodded, remembering his comments of only hours before. "The ghosts in the caves." It was a whisper.

They were in a huge natural space, doubtless a cave, which had been worked into some regularity of shape so that it resembled a rough-hewn cathedral. Cobus reached out and touched the nearest wall. He put his fingertips to his tongue. "Rock salt."

On either side of them, huge staircases, carved from the very rock itself, led down into the main body of the hall. Along the walls, seeming also to be fashioned from rock salt, were statues of naked figures, most of them appearing either to be in agony or supplication. Were they saints or sinners? In a moment of peculiar detachment, which freaked him out, Cobus thought how much certain of them resembled a member of the old glam-rock band Slade, with their square fringes and long hair. Inappropriate though it was, he felt laughter trying to force itself through and decided that, perhaps, he might be nearing hysteria. However, one look at the far end of the hall killed any laughter, as he saw the *piece de resistance*: an enormous statue of some indeterminate, snarling beast that exuded malice, emphasised by the interplay of light and shade on its features.

Pete had been looking at all corners. "Where the fuck is everybody?" He paused; puffed out his cheeks. "And if I didn't know the answer already, I'd be tempted to ask what the hell we're doing here."

"Ja, doesn't score high on the feelgood factor here. C'mon, you take the far steps and let's go down. A split target is tougher to hit. There must be some way through at the back. I don't sense anyone here. Guess they don't expect too many tourists round these parts."

It was soon evident that Cobus was right and they were alone in that vast place with its hostile statuary and the conspiratorial whispers of the torches. They looped round to meet in the middle of the hall.

Pete shuddered. "This is giving me the creeps, to put it mildly – and we don't even know they came in here."

Splitting again, they looped around the back of the huge, sneering beast-god.

Both of them saw the opening at the same time.

"Aha! What've we got here?" said Cobus.

Pete peered into the darkness of what seemed to be a tunnel entrance, about eight feet across. "I don't know, but it makes the rest of the temple feel like a sanctuary of peace and light." It was as if the blackness came at them in waves; the flickering torchlight barely touched it. "Don't think even the night-vision goggles would be a lot of good in there."

"Nah, but I know what will be." The Afrikaner removed his rucksack, dug around inside and pulled out some head-torches.

"You're not Batman are you? Is that your utility belt?"

Cobus grinned and shook his pack. "Absolutely. I always have a couple of these torches with me, for whichever date is foolish enough to come out into the bush with me." He peered at the tunnel. "Looks pitch black. No point going for secrecy at the expense of safety."

They fitted the torches around their heads, switched them on and then, the very definition of reluctance, stepped into the tunnel; into a world devoid even of shadows.

"This looks like part of some original tunnel at the back of the cave," Pete stopped and looked around, "except this has clearly been hewn by man."

They were at an intersection. Again, Cobus touched the stone. "Part of the mines, d'ya think? The ones the Professor mentioned on the plane."

"Don't much care. I know I shouldn't admit it when my wife's life is at risk, but I'm fighting a very strong urge to retreat." Pete looked left and right. "The question is, which way do we go? I don't much fancy getting lost in here."

Given he was a man of action, Cobus' silence spoke volumes. The darkness was almost tangible against their skin and fear leached out to meet it through their pores. At length he spoke: "Shit, I should have brought a compass. I just haven't been thinking straight. These islands have completely fucked my thought-processes."

"That makes two of us." Pete's tone was grim, but then he added with irony: "I just can't understand why we're a bit shaken up, standing in some primeval, shadowy temple, having just pursued a boat that might contain my wife, kidnapped during a night-time raid by an unseen enemy."

Cobus put a hand on his shoulder. "You wanna go on, man?"

"Okay, let's give it a go." He looked at the crossroads again. "Let's just go straight; ignore any diversions."

But soon, they came to a fork in the tunnel where *straight on* just couldn't be defined.

Then Pete had a thought. "Hey, you got any of that marker tape in your utility belt?"

"Ja, I have!" Cobus pulled off his pack again with a winning enthusiasm. "Good thinking, man. I had this pack on when we found the old city."

"Let's stick a piece every ten paces. I know it'll slow us up, but we're no good to anyone wandering in these tunnels forever."

Of course, Cobus did not voice it, but it seemed to him the adrenaline junkie might have met his match. "We'll put the tape where, hopefully, no-one else will see it. If we're... not alone, or whatever, we don't want anyone seeing twentieth century tape and knowing we're in here."

"You really think they don't know already?"

There was no response.

The roof of the tunnel was about two feet above their heads. Having taken an arbitrary left fork at the previous junction, they leapt up after every ten paces and stuck a small piece of tape that would reflect their lights.

Progress ceased at a three-way intersection. They stood, hopeless and bewildered. Pete raised his hand. "Just a minute – you hear that?"

They stood motionless. Above the rushing of blood in their ears, there might have been faint noise akin to the distant thrumming of an engine. They moved to the head of each tunnel in turn.

"I think it's coming from here." Cobus pointed down the left-hand tunnel. Pete joined him. They looked at each other and felt the chill of fear brush past them; a spirit, raising goose-bumps on their skin.

"You're right. C'mon." They marked the entrance and moved on.

Silent now, as if words might shatter their fragile courage rather than bolster it, they lost track of time and, despite the tape, had no real sense of place. Their world, for now, consisted of the resonating sound somewhere ahead and the cones of light they threw before them as they moved at an increasing pace.

Despite their need to push on, they stopped to peer with caution into the black fissures that split the smoothness of the walls from time to time. They looked like nothing more than crawl-holes, but someone could have been lurking in the shadows. The sound was a thread they had grasped at in their blindness, preferring the devil's guiding hand to their own clutching at nothingness. It could have been a hundred yards or a thousand they travelled, but then Cobus hissed: "Shit!" and they found themselves at a marked intersection. Both men stared at the mocking piece of tape. "It's led us round in a fuckin' circle. How can that be happening if we're following a sound?"

"It could be echoing. Or maybe this place is just playing with our minds. I suggest we mark the entrance with a double piece of tape."

"What good'll that do, man? We've still got to go down the same tunnel. It might be further ahead that we went wrong."

"Well, if we end up here again we'll know which way not to go...
oh, I see what you mean. FUCK!" Pete butted the air in frustration and
shouted, not caring whether he was heard or not – if someone was toying
with them, then it made no difference anyway. Then he frowned. "Wait
a minute, there was one intersection where we really weren't sure which
fork to take. The sound hasn't grown any louder since then. We'll take
the other fork. We've got nothing to lose except our way." They looked at
each other yet again. Pete scratched his chin. "Did that make any sense?"

"Fucked if I know."

"As long as we're both confused then."

They burst into sudden laughter; more hysteria than anything else,
but somehow, they had needed it to happen if they were to carry on.

"I don't think..." Cobus had to stop while he wiped his eyes, "... it made
any sense at all." He smacked Pete on the arm. "Man, if you'd told me
yesterday that we'd be pissing ourselves laughing together I'd have shot
myself."

They calmed down and followed Pete's hunch. Sure enough, the
sound seemed to grow in intensity. It felt now like any laughter had been
well and truly left behind in the tunnels.

"Man, I hope we don't come across any more of our tape now." Cobus
looked up at the roof of the tunnel. "If we do, I think we're fucked."

"I believe that is the technical term for it."

They moved on, with nervous looks into any tunnels that joined their
own, hoping not to experience the desperation of seeing a little piece of
reflective yellow.

And their luck held, till they found themselves confronted by a
different intersection of three tunnels.

The hairs stood up on the backs of their necks; not because of the
choice that confronted them, but because the sound had started to take
on definition. In the confusion that was their sensory world right then,
it was like being able to see pitch and tone. And they knew, this was no
devilish engine thrumming in the heart of a mine, but voices chanting in
unison.

"Fuckin' hell, man." No other words were needed from Cobus – he
was speaking for both of them. They tested all three entrances.

"It's coming from here." Pete stood a few paces into the middle
entrance. "I think." The sound still seemed to echo around them.

They moved along. Perhaps a hundred paces down the tunnel, Cobus
gestured downwards with the palm of his hand. "Kill your light a
moment." Once they had both done so, it seemed the Stygian darkness

was no longer so intense. There was a glow ahead. As they edged forward again, the voices grew louder. There was another sound too, unless their ears were playing tricks; the faint babbling of water.

"The outside world?" Pete's suggestion was made more in hope than expectation.

"Nah, man. I reckon we're right in the heart of the shit."

They crept forward and could see the end of the tunnel ahead, beyond which was an as yet indefinable space filled with flickering. Getting as close as they could on foot, they crawled the rest on elbows and knees. They could tell there was a drop ahead and soon it was apparent that this was the top of a set of steps.

"No sentries posted," whispered Cobus.

"You've said it yourself; I don't think they've been expecting anyone to drop by."

Flattening themselves against the floor of the tunnel, both men slid forward. Cobus peered over the edge, then jerked his head back. "Shit, man, shit, shit, shit!" He buried his forehead in the crook of his arm.

Pete had not seen anything yet and stretched his neck further forward. "My God!"

CHAPTER TWENTY-FIVE

As Cobus had put it so succinctly, it was the heart of the shit. There were perhaps fifty men, wiry yet muscular, bare-chested, their lower bodies clothed in ragged kilts that might once have been magnificent. They were in kneeling in ranks, facing what appeared to be an altar or other object of worship; a pedestal studded with stones or gems that caught the firelight from the torches held by the supplicants. On the pedestal was an object, perhaps a hand span across, too far away to see in detail. It seemed to give off sporadic pulses of light, though it was made of something that might have been brass, or perhaps gold. It stood in a stream of water that rose from the top of the pedestal, flowed down its side and drained away through the base. All strange and wonderful in its own right, but what had caused Cobus' reaction was the object standing next to the pedestal; a rough stake of wood about ten feet high on which was skewered the body of Robbie McCulloch, or at least what was left of it.

Cobus had seen enough sights during his time in the army not to release the contents of his guts onto the floor of the tunnel, but it had been close. Sudden anger blazed in his eyes. "The bastards!"

He made to get up, but Pete held him down. "Cobus!" he hissed, "get a grip."

"But that's my friend down there."

"These," Pete shook his gun, "are not machine guns, they're rifles. And those guys down there look big and mean enough to me. You might get a few of them, but they could rush us, maybe even surround us, in the tunnels. It's too late for Robbie."

"But not for your wife, man. She might be next."

Pete looked at him and clenched his jaws. "I know. God knows I know. But we said at the start we might not be able to launch a rescue this time round. What use are we to her if we're dead?"

"I don't get it. How can you say this?"

Pete pushed with anger at the Afrikaner's shoulder. "You think it's easy for me? But we don't know for sure they've got her."

"Oh yeah, man, she just went walkabout, like Robbie."

"And she might have done just that. You've been a soldier; think like one. We've done a recce, we know what we're up against. Now we get reinforcements. We'll fetch Jim, and we'll come back with automatic weapons. Plus some of that plastic explosive the Professor tried to hide. We'll give these mother-fuckers something to pray for. We'll threaten to blow up that precious object of theirs, whatever it is."

"So, we're coming back in broad daylight?" Cobus was not happy about this at all.

"Don't be stupid." Pete glanced at his watch in the firelight. "It's only one o'clock in the morning. Even at this time of year we still have a bit of night-time left. We'll get back to the camp, grab Jim and the guns and head straight back here. With any luck these bastards will still be at worship and we'll have the higher ground – take them all out if they don't hand Jane over. Anyway, we haven't got enough ammo. Neither of us was thinking straight, and we didn't grab any spare clips."

Cobus smashed his fist on the ground in desperation. Then he managed to get a grip on himself. "Ja, man, you're right." He put a hand on Pete's shoulder and looked at him with great intensity. "Sorry I lost it there. I tell you, I see you in a whole new light. Your wife could be in there, but you're thinking straight. Not like me; I haven't used my brain all night. I dunno what this fuckin' archipelago had done to my head."

They headed back, switching on their torches once they were away from the grisly chamber to seek out their pieces of tape in the light.

Then something stopped them in their tracks. They looked at each other; questioning; afraid.

"You feel that?" Cobus switched off his light.

Pete followed suit and gave a slow nod: "Like you, suddenly I don't want to be seen."

They looked around them as best they could in the darkness. No way out.

"What you reckon, man? Back to the chamber of horrors?" Cobus' question needed no answering and, though it went against every warning sign, they flicked on one torch, hand-held by Pete, who was leading the way, and moved on towards the source of their growing unease – a presence somewhere ahead of them, which felt like it was drawing nearer.

Then to the left of them they spotted what they were hoping for, one of the niches in the tunnel wall. By now, a disturbing mixture of cold and heat was oozing down the tunnel towards them.

"Quick, in here!" Pete flicked off the light and squeezed in sideways, unsure at first how far he could go, but managing to push his way twelve to fifteen feet in. "C'mon!" he urged Cobus, whose backpack had prevented him from getting into the crevice. The Afrikaner removed it with a clumsy, anxious fumble, and then forced his way in; a tougher operation for him, as he was perhaps twenty-five pounds heavier than Pete. Still, he made it in, dragging his pack.

Now both of them stood silent, motionless. Waiting.

At first it was only a feeling, but then they fancied they heard a soft tread of feet. Whatever it was, its approach was marked by an aura of malevolence that was all the more sinister for the gentle footfall.

Now they couldn't be sure, but the presence seemed to pause at the mouth of the crevice. Both men tried to hold their breath, then realised that they had already stopped breathing. Cobus turned his head – a slow, terrified twist. He fancied he saw eyes straining through the darkness towards him, and he shut his own, telling himself it was to avoid the remotest possibility of any glistening reflection. The reality was he had gone the way of the child that hides under the blanket in the hope the monster can't harm him. He was sure the thundering of his heart would give him away, like some bizarre twist of the Edgar Allan Poe story.

At last, the spectral presence moved on.

Only when the feeling of menace had faded at last – when they sensed that the deeper darkness within that lightless place had gone – did they dare to move.

On leaving the crevice, they stood and looked down the tunnel in the direction of the departing shade.

"I think our decisions to hide and to leave have just been vindicated," Pete's morbid dry wit was a shield against the terror. "I'm not so sure about the one where we said we'd come back. What the hell was that?"

"Fuck knows – but I felt its dark soul, whatever it was. Got to admit, for the first time in my life I'd be happy just to run from something."

As if Fate was playing games, Pete shot across the tunnel with a cry, fumbling for his light, while Cobus, in a confusion of reflexes, raised his gun and pointed it blind into the darkness.

"What is it, man?"

"Something grabbed at my ankle." Pete found his lamp switch at last and turned it on – which was when they discovered they were nowhere near done with the horrors of the labyrinth.

Lying in the opening of the crevice, looking up at them in desperation, was a figure straight from the liberation of Auschwitz. It – they assumed it was human – pleaded with hollow eyes, which had seen the Day of Judgement and been found unworthy. One skeletal arm lay extended into the tunnel while the other attempted to reach in their direction. As this husk of a human being, weighed down by savage, crushing weakness, tried to crawl towards them, Cobus could hear his bones scraping on the stone floor and the sound almost put hair on his teeth. Pete's unusual silence was testament to the horror. To describe the cobweb of rags on the body as clothes would have been stretching imagination. Cobus and Pete looked at each other. It was clear, despite the revulsion, that both of them felt the profoundest pity for the obvious, prolonged suffering of this human being, on whom that epithet had as tenuous a hold as his rags.

Now he was trying to say something, in a grating whisper that told of one who had lived a comparative eternity in silence.

Cobus shook his head. "I don't know what the hell he's saying, man, but I think I can translate it anyway."

"Yes." The single word caught in Pete's dry throat, as if it was coming out in sympathy. "Let's get this poor bastard out of here."

The man was incapable of standing and they helped him to a position where they could lead him out supported on their shoulders. The feel of the non-physique beneath their fingertips made them wince. Cobus rummaged in his rucksack and produced a lightweight fleece, which afforded him protection against direct contact with bone as much as it eased the man's pain. "Three hundred grammes – his body should just about be able to bear this."

They continued on their way, staying slow, despite their desperation to get away, as they sought not to harm their burden. Although sharing an unspoken acknowledgement that they wanted their own carcasses away from the place that had spawned this being, they knew his suffering had to be off the scale and took care not to hurry him.

Cobus glanced over his shoulder as they neared the tunnel exit. "I think our luck's holding; we don't seem to have been followed."

At last, they were out; first into the twilight of the temple and then into the outside world.

"Thank God!" Pete raised his face to the night air.

Cobus looked at the stars. "Never seen them looking so bright."

It was a moment's respite only, and they moved on till the black fingers from the temple entrance no longer brushed against their necks.

"C'mon fella." Cobus adjusted his shoulders under the armpit of their gaunt companion and Pete followed suit. Now they carried him through the forest over the worst of the shingle, though he groaned with pain at the pressure of their hands. They placed him with gentle care into the boat, pushed out into the surf and started the motor. Neither Cobus nor Pete looked back; there were a number of reasons, chief amongst them being the fear that one glance might have been enough to convince them not to return. The skeletal figure did, however, turn his fragile neck and a peculiar expression crossed his bony features. He muttered something, recognisable only as being the same two or three phrases repeated.

"Sorry, old chap," Pete shrugged his shoulders, "haven't got a bloody clue what you're saying."

They rounded the headland that hid their camp from view and in the distance saw the campfire was now blazing. Their passenger was something of a paradox, becoming both more agitated and weaker. He was slumped against the side of the boat and his mutterings were growing in intensity. Meanwhile his breathing had become as ragged as the rest of him.

Cobus shook his head. "This might be stating the bleedin' obvious, but I don't think he's got long left."

"His voice doesn't seem to be getting any weaker." Pete spoke with evident irony and some irritation. It was as if the man was investing the last of his strength in his message.

"It's no good, buddy, we don't understand a freakin' word." Then a light clicked on in Cobus' head. "But Catalina might."

"Oh yeah?"

Pete's comment had a dismissive ring and Cobus bridled a little. "Hey, I know she looks good in her dry suit, man, but she's also bright – one of the best in her field. And what might help us is the fact that she's studied botany, so she has an interest in the life and work of Schomburgk—"

"Yeah, I was just thinking that – good old Schomburgk."

Cobus allowed Pete his sarcasm. "He was a German botanist. No, I hadn't heard of him either, but Catty was going on about him. Anyway, her interest meant she spent a lot of time in South America. Along the way, a bit like..." Cobus hesitated, but was too far along, "... your wife, she's become pretty good with ancient languages. It's one of the things they shared... sorry man – share. Look, I may be clutching at straws, but back at the ruins, wasn't it you who mentioned something about the Mayan civilisation?"

"'Twas I, though God knows where that came from." Pete's self-deprecation seemed genuine.

"Ja, you did. So did the others – when we found that section of wall. So, perhaps Catalina may be able to make out what he's saying. And if there is some South American connection there, remember – Cat's family was originally from Argentina."

There was no response from Pete. Cobus looked at him. Perhaps mention of Jane had affected him. He seemed lost in thought. The Afrikaner had to acknowledge once more how tough it must have been for the guy to walk away, knowing his wife was being held in that monstrous place.

Indeed, Pete's dark thoughts were with his wife, but even more so now with that strange artefact they had seen in the temple. Some power had been emanating from it. In the shock of seeing his dead and mutilated friend, Cobus had perhaps not felt it, but Pete had. And with an inherent certainty he knew it would be a prize worth having. That black force in the tunnel knew it too; was part of it, because the air around it had throbbed with the same pulse, beyond the hearing of those whose hearts were not alive to its darkness. They had to be linked, as inextricable as light and shade. The others could have their piles of bricks; he sensed something greater was waiting for him.

CHAPTER TWENTY-SIX

SCORPION ARCHIPELAGO — BASE CAMP, 12.20AM OCTOBER 31ST 1997

Once again, as the inflatable had whined off in pursuit of the other boat, looking as fragile as their hopes when it bounced on the waves, the Professor had been close to giving in to despair. He saw now that the loss of his daughter would succeed where all other setbacks in his life had failed; it would destroy him. No amphora was as precious as her life, returned safe and sound to him, and nothing was more ridiculous than ambition in an old, tired heart. Jim had placed a hand on his shoulder: "That Cobus is a tough nut. I'm sure he and Pete between them can bring her back, if indeed she has been taken."

Then Jim had wandered off towards the box of guns. *A wise idea*, thought Sutch; *keep yourself busy*. At least one of them was thinking straight. Jim had an old head on young shoulders, or better put, a practical one, since an old head had got them all into this mess. Had he taken the same liking to her as she had to the young photographer? Was the feeling mutual? Was Jim now going through his own private agonies, albeit nothing compared with Sutch's?

Now he watched Catalina go to sit with Jim. The girl had been very quiet during most of this trip. She might have thought of herself as intrepid prior to this, but once the proverbial had hit the fan she had discovered otherwise. She had lost a newly made friend in Robbie and might lose another. There was every chance she was rethinking her ambitions for the expedition and they panned down to one stark aim – stay alive. Sutch wished he could give her absolute reassurance and security, but he was having a tough time just keeping himself together. So, it was no surprise that she sought strength instead in the company of the younger man, who was loading a gun; who lived in the present, not the past.

With that, Sutch returned to his tent to continue with something he had started earlier but abandoned, perhaps unwisely. Why had his mind refused to accept that myths and legends had an inevitable core of truth? Had that not been the basic tenet of this expedition? He knew, now, he had been acting like the three wise monkeys rolled into one. So, he pulled out Tariq's letter and started to read it again in detail, or at least the first part, which he had concealed from the others after skimming through its contents.

This account was not so much a letter as a brief history written during the merchant's final voyage. Sutch saw now, too late, that keeping these details from the team had been unwise, even though they might have been dismissed as some dark fairy tale. He saw, also, that the amphora brought with it a legacy of lies. From the moment he had set eyes on it, he had withheld information from people – Candice, Dirk, Sir Arthur at the RGS, the team. Did the amphora turn you from the path of truth? Tariq had lied, or at least bent the truth, on more than one occasion. As he considered the consequences of his own actions, while reading again the details in the letter, Professor Edward Sutch regretted that he had proved a worthy heir.

'In the anticipatory excitement of reaching my journey's end, floating towards my Valhalla, and in the hope that you will find my body, here is the true story of how I came to be who I was on the day you met me. My people fled, not for the first time in our history, from persecution in the fourth century after your Christ was born, led by a mighty king and his powerful shaman, who promised that for us there would be, somewhere, a promised land. We preferred to take our chances with the sea than try to withstand the forces of evil. We left what is now called South America and perhaps half of us were lost before our ships beached upon the archipelago, on which you now stand if you are reading this. It did not look welcoming, but freedom, and land beneath your feet, count for so much.

Most scratched a living together, but man being man, some things cannot change. The priests chose to inhabit a separate island, the largest one at the end of the chain that is now named Escorpion Archiepelago. Here they discovered a perfect place to conceal their secret, both wonderful and terrible, like so many hidden treasures. They wandered deep into the network of mountain caves and found a spring of fresh, clear water; a suitable place to build their altar and continue with their dark practices. Once more they could channel and corrupt the power of the Earth goddess.

You see, throughout history the priests moved from tribe to tribe, race to race, holding the people in thrall by dint of their immortality, and one, the high priest, whose name, even now, I cannot utter, seemed to have existed since the beginning of time. It was rumoured that he was the oldest man alive and had fled civilisations from the earliest of times when fear had led men to revolt against his power. For, *unbeknown to commoners or kings, he possessed an object for which secular men would kill had they ever learned of its existence. Though his strength was beyond that of other men, he was still mortal and would not have withstood the onslaught of an army raised to seize his prize. The artefact, called a k'ib in my native tongue – meaning water jug, but not to be confused with your amphora – throbbed with some mystical energy. It seemed able to imbue the universal structures, truths and life-giving forces that are inherent in water with unimaginably greater power, endowing all who drank from it with these gifts. And more; the k'ib took that innate power and charged the very air one breathed with its eldritch energies, though there was a limit to its reach – only those on Temple Island would have felt that strange effect – and it relied on water to awaken it, just like a vampire needs blood.*

The k'ib enabled the priests to perpetuate the myth of their holy powers as they continued with their claim of being able to bless water with life-giving forces. The high priest himself said this grail – I use the word advisedly, if technically it is incorrect – was a gift from the gods. None of us knew enough to disagree.'

"More half-truths, Tariq, more lies." Sutch shook his head. "You said the spring itself imparted the powers." Even as he muttered to himself, the Professor grew more desperate, feeling like he had been lured by the beauty of a web, only to discover its deceit – every way he turned now he was held by more strands. And Tariq, though it pained Sutch to admit it, had spun the threads. Perhaps he had been powerless to do otherwise. Perhaps it had been inherent to his nature, just as a spider is driven by instinct to lay its trap and perform its gruesome rituals. It was clear now to the Professor that Tariq must have been a priest, since he told here of things 'unbeknown to commoners or kings'. It seemed to Sutch that the water of life, rather than the amphora, was the breeding ground of lies. So, having drunk of it for more than a thousand years, was Tariq powerless to do other than deceive? Because despite everything, the Professor still believed the old merchant had been, in essence, a good man.

'Now the high priest forbade all settlers other than his acolytes to live on the sacred island. The ordinary people feared the ageless priests and did their bidding without questioning, so that the high priest grew more powerful than the king. At first there was an uneasy truce. The people of the archipelago, while quarrying for stones, stumbled upon caves full of rock salt. Except on Temple Island, where certain slaves were employed in carving an edifice fit for the priests, the people mined it in vast quantities. The king sent them forth to trade, building great ships from the plentiful timber around us. I believe that time and legend has transmuted the rock salt into precious stones, but as you know, salt was of enormous value back then and rock salt was one source of it. As a result, we wanted for nothing. Here, too, the myth of the priests was perpetuated, for they supplied water for the departing

ships, knowing their crews would always return; eternal life is a delicious, addictive poison. Also, a priest would travel on every ship to ensure no man dared betray our kingdom.

Likewise, the inhabitants of the citadel were granted a small ration of blessed water that kept them young and healthy, but not as strong as the priests. Still, as with all ancient kingdoms that grow rich, there was a striving for overall power between the religious leaders and the king. Ambition attacked; a cancer thriving on the healthy cells. Certain ancient religious practices were resumed, notably human sacrifice. It was a terrible darkness that hung over us, and one of the reasons the king commanded the building of the walled citadel; so that his people could choose to raise a family and the priests could not simply go among the people and claim the young. But still, they would come to the wall of the citadel and demand one life for each full moon.

The unfortunate volunteer – or terrified victim – would be chained at the appropriate time to a pillar down at the harbour, on top of which a fire would be lit to signal to the priests to collect their booty.'

Sutch shuddered as he recognised the marker he had found. There had been no fire, no victim held in chains, but he had been summoned just as surely to claim his prize.

'The high priest himself had almost passed into mythology during the course of a thousand years. Some said he had become dark and terrible to behold; others that he would not leave the object that gave him his power and stalked the tunnels of the temple. Yet more believed that his heart and the k'ib now pulsed in unison. Whatever the truth, the cave beyond the magnificent temple they had built was turned by the priests into a labyrinth; some said it was to prevent the theft of the k'ib, others that it was to keep the dark lord contained.

At last, it came to the ears of the king that the high priest was planning to come forth and take both the citadel and the kingdom from him. One priest, sickened by the reawakening of the sacrificial cult, broke ranks, betrayed the high priest's plans and the secret of the source of his power. So, the king, an enlightened leader and a brave warrior in his time, led an army across to Temple Island. The priests bade him enter the temple and take the k'ib for his own. He was never seen again.

Then the priests, numbering but fifty, took on the king's force of five hundred men and slaughtered them. At once they boarded boats and headed for the citadel. I was lucky. Along with my friend the fisherman, we were amongst the few who escaped. From the ocean we watched powerless as the priests scaled the walls with ladders they had prepared and the citizens fled, some choosing to hurl themselves from the cliffs, rather than face the wrath of the holy men. Others we saw captured and led back to the boats. Their fate I know not, but I can guess. With the power of the k'ib keeping them alive, they would have fulfilled the requirements of many a full moon. I care not to dwell on it.

I return now to honour the dead by dying among them; because I escaped while they died; because this wild place was my home for a thousand years; because I have wandered too much since, for any other place truly to be called home. And I return in the hope that, with four thousand full moons having passed, the gruesome banquet of the priests might be over and they will have died at last.'

Sutch knew in his gut that Tariq was the one who fled the priesthood, driven by the shame of human sacrifice; that he had brought the corruption of the cult to the attention of the king. How the Professor wanted... needed to believe that.

And then, any sadness about Tariq, or his lies, or his fate, was pushed aside with a jolt that might have stopped his ageing heart. Had the horrors of this dreadful manuscript blinded him to the obvious during his first reading?

Temple Island is alive!

Oh God, let it not be so!

Had two more lives been sacrificed, as surely as if Sutch himself had dragged them down to the harbour by a full moon?

He read the last words on the parchment that shook in his hands.

'Please believe me, my dear Professor, when I say that I agonised over whether to allow you to find this place. But every man must find his dream and the dead must be allowed to speak again.'

Now Sutch was shivering. He was beyond redemption. What had he let those boys head off into? He had been even more of an arrogant fool than he thought.

No – he would not allow himself to believe it! Hobgoblins, dark lords and waters of eternal youth. He tapped the paper, needing to feel something real. There, Tariq himself summed it up; all the precious stones of legend were nothing more than good old prosaic rock salt. So what if the king was never seen again? Small wonder, when he walked into a network of cave tunnels. Probably got lost and fell to his death somewhere. Human sacrifice – for sure, that was real enough in South American culture and elsewhere. The rest were bedtime stories; that was all.

There were other anomalies too. If indeed those shamans had survived, how the hell had they managed it, trapped in the anachronism of their ancient ways? Had they kept some of their prisoners alive as slaves; sent them out to fish; made them till the soil; held them in unending bondage?

Or had modern civilisation somehow drifted onto Temple Island and left enough of a footprint to enable the inhabitants to stand up to time?

But, as his finger continued to tap on the paper, his fears, like ancient priests, would not go away. This document was found in the hand of a dead man who had been writing with a twentieth century biro; a man with no guarantee his words would ever be read. Why would he have continued to lie?

Where the hell was Jane?

He shook his head, angry with himself for allowing his thought to wander from her plight.

The occasions when he had been around to read her to sleep were too few, yet there had always been a strong bond between them. It might have been forged in the fires deep beneath the earth's crust but had found its ultimate expression in a shared love of discovery and a shared perspective – that everything about humankind was transient. Jane would have acknowledged that, every time she dug up ruins which had once represented the magnificence of man; had found another crumbling example of the Ozymandias principle. Just as he recognised it whenever he sat on, or sank below, the vastness of the ocean. Perhaps their love had been strengthened by absence; the privilege of the father who comes home to the clean and well-behaved child. But Candice never complained.

Darling Candice, so far from here.

A hand tapped on the flap of his tent and he heard Catalina's voice. "Professor? They're coming back."

He looked at his watch and saw that he must have slipped into some kind of reverie. And now he could hear the distant, mosquito-like whine of the inflatable.

CHAPTER TWENTY-SEVEN

Sutch came out in time to see the boat scrape to a halt in the surf. At least the two men were alive and appeared unharmed. Then his stomach lurched as he saw them reach in to lift out a third figure. But he knew with horrible certainty that it wasn't Jane. Something was wrong. He heard Cobus shouting:

"Get one of the spare sleeping bags, quick!" They carried the figure across towards the camp. "Put it by the fire. I don't think this poor bastard's got long left. Let's make him comfortable."

Pete looked across at the Professor approaching: "I think we found your Temple Island."

"And my daughter?"

Like a Hydra seized by remorse, all heads looked down.

"No sign." Pete glanced at Cobus. "Nor of Robbie. But that's better than—"

"Yes." The light and shade flitted across Sutch's features; feigned optimism in a windblown sky, "yes, of course. No news is good news." He reached the group, looked around, distracted, before turning to the figure they had brought ashore and winced. "Who is this poor creature?"

Cobus took up the dialogue: "Got absolutely no idea. Like Pete said, we found what we assume was a temple. At the back of it was a network of tunnels, like a labyrinth. He seemed to be hiding there. We'll fill you in on everything in a minute. First, while we're trying to save his life – though I think we've passed the point of no return – let's see if we can make out what he's trying to say." Cobus looked at Catalina, whose face bore the exhausted lines of utter mental defeat. She was staring in horror at the dying man. "Catalina." No reaction. "Catalina!" She dragged her eyes away from the horror towards her friend. "You're a bit of a linguist. He's saying a couple of things over and over. Can you make them out?" She hesitated. "C'mon sweetheart."

Gathering her scattered wits and slippery courage with visible effort, the girl stepped forward. They had eased their guest's body onto the sleeping bag – getting him into it seemed a task too far. His eyes kept rolling upwards. Catalina knelt by him and listened. She bent her head closer, seeming caught between pity and revulsion, but academic curiosity won out, as she struggled to interpret his dry whispers. "There are sounds similar to some Central American languages, but the inflexions are different."

The man's gaunt skull was turning from side to side, his skeletal fingers resting on his chest but picking at the air.

"I suspect he's gone quite mad." For once, there was no hint of dark humour in Pete's words. "If he's been where we've just been for any length of time I'm not surprised."

Catalina raised her hand to silence him as she strove to hear what the man was saying, her ear almost pressed to his mouth.

"He's not just gone mad." It was Jim. He had been standing silent; the Professor noticed how his eyes had been scanning the forest. But now he was looking at the figure and they all gasped as they saw how his condition was worsening, impossible though that seemed. "He's dying before our eyes." The remaining skin was desiccating and creasing even as they watched. Sutch could see Tariq's description of the old fisherman's death brought to substantive reality – *to life* seemed an inappropriate phrase under the circumstances – and knew at once that this man before him had lived for centuries. In God's name, or the devil's, how much of that life had been spent lost in the labyrinth of which the others had spoken? Could he be...? Of course!

Catalina backed away in revulsion. "What's happening to him?"

"Time is catching up with him." The Professor looked at the fading figure with sadness.

"What do you mean?"

Sutch gave no answer, though he felt questioning eyes turn towards him. "Did you catch what he's saying?"

Catalina shivered. "It's hard to say, but I might have got lucky."

"How so?"

"Well, the Maya spoke any number of languages. There wasn't a Mayan language as such. But one of the languages I do recognise is a variation of Tzotzil, and I'm almost sure that's what he's using; as sure as I can be, anyway." She looked at the others. "I thought I heard 'king' or 'kingdom', 'darkness'," she shrugged, "'kingdom of darkness' perhaps. And 'lost'. 'The lost kingdom'? I'm really not sure."

Now a smile seemed to form on the skeletal face. Perhaps it was just the approach of the death rictus, but there was the faintest hint of serenity on the tortured features.

Sutch was moved: "It's as if, after all he's been through, he welcomes death, here, under the stars, by a campfire, surrounded by concerned faces." The Professor bowed his head, thinking of Tariq.

Jim shuffled his feet and then hefted his rifle. "Why are we wasting time here? We haven't found Jane... or Robbie." The latter name seemed to have been added as an afterthought.

The Professor felt an unusual flush of anger rising in his cheeks. "If I, as her father, can take a moment to show respect for what I fear this man may have gone through, so can everyone else."

"Absolutely." Pete gave Jim a pointed glare.

Sutch felt Cobus watching him and heard him say: "And what do you believe he's been through, Professor?"

Sutch held up a rolled parchment. "Despite everything, I'll allow myself the time now to tell you. I couldn't bring myself to believe it, but faced with this, I think I have no choice. Furthermore, I think it's important that everyone understands what we might be up against. My sincerest apologies to all of you for having withheld this." He unrolled the parchment and started to read.

**

"Let me get this straight – you believe this dying man here was that king? You, the world-renowned scientist, believe that out there, on that piece of rock, is the secret to eternal youth?"

Sutch could not be sure whether Pete was settling old debts by ridicule but decided he couldn't blame him. So, he tried to give an objective answer: "I don't know that for sure, but based on the words we think he might have been saying, it could be true." He looked at Pete, then Cobus. "You haven't told us what you saw."

Pete stayed silent, but Cobus spoke up. "Hard to say for sure, but we did see a group of men. They were chanting in front of some sort of altar. I... didn't look for long."

Pete interjected. "We kept our heads down. Didn't want to risk being seen."

Sutch almost bristled with vindication. "So, we have a labyrinth, and we have a group of men who appear to be worshipping something. I'd say there's a fair to middling chance Tariq's wild story might well be true.

149

Then we have a seemingly ancient man who is wasting away before our eyes and – possibly – whispering something about a king. Is this him? Was he lost in that labyrinth for more than a thousand years? Did the priests who invited him to enter and search for their grail post guards to prevent him ever leaving? Imagine eternity in the darkness; the power of that grail keeping you alive; no food; no water; unable to do anything but run and hide – eventually too weak, except to crawl – and hope that you might find your way out." Sutch exhaled shakily. "Surely death would have been preferable." He saw the glance exchanged by Cobus and Pete.

"It could be worse than you think." Cobus shuddered visibly as he thought of the labyrinth.

Catalina was shaking. "Worse than that?" She was close to tears. "When death already seems better?"

"We felt something when we were in there." Cobus looked down, as if he did not want to face it again, or let others see its impact in his eyes.

"Some*thing*?"

"Ja." He groped for the right words but settled on the simplest. "Darkness; evil. They might sound dramatic, but the words fit. We felt it approaching in one of the tunnels, and I'm not ashamed to admit we also hid. I can't be sure, but it seemed to stop at the entrance of our crawl-hole, and then moved on." He pointed. "And in there was where we found our friend here."

Catalina sank to her knees. "Oh God, how awful." She was weeping. Pete reached down and placed a hand on her shoulder, then lifted her to her feet. She buried her face in his chest and wept. Her response seemed to make him uncomfortable, distracted even, but he put his arms around her. He whispered in her ear. The gesture made Sutch feel ashamed. He might well have been guilty of not giving his son-in-law enough of a chance; not seeing through the brashness.

"Well, old girl," Pete rested his chin on top of Catalina's head, "it's not going to get easier in a hurry." He gave a slight nod in Cobus' direction for him to continue.

"Ja, we came back to get armed. We need the semi-automatic rifles and pistols, lots of ammo and the explosives."

The Professor felt a moment of atavistic regret, but he suppressed it. Some things just had to be. It would be another sad episode in modern man's response to the ancient and unknown, but on this occasion the time for understanding was short. One way or the other, he needed to know if they had his daughter and Robbie. He saw Cobus looking at him. "I'm sorry, Professor." *As if the young man had read his mind.* "But I'm sure you'll agree – saving a good life now is worth a thousand bad ones. And if we are looking at a race that possesses the sort of gift, or curse, you're describing, we might need one hell of a lot of weaponry to kill them."

"Absolutely." Sutch nodded his agreement. "How many did you say there were?" In all that had happened, and with time short, there had been only a disjointed exchange of information so far.

"About fifty, but we can't swear there weren't others – maybe in some other part of the labyrinth. Who knows? But somehow I don't think so, especially having heard Tariq's letter now. Perhaps there were more priests, but they ran out of sacrifices and started eating each other."

"Tariq didn't say they ate each other."

"Nah, you're right. I meant it as... never mind, it was inappropriate."

Sutch felt for the young man, who looked like he wanted to find the nearest and quickest route to the earth's core. "That's okay, Cobus. I know you were just trying for some comic relief. Sorry I picked you up on it. This is all too heavy for words, isn't it?"

Indeed, the Afrikaner had touched on a fundamental question; one they were all avoiding answering. If Jane and Robbie had been taken, then why? What was the *raison d'être* of the priests? They had once been shamans to a civilisation, but what were priests without worshippers?

Cobus made a swift move onto safer ground. "Anyway, we go over there and we take the bastards out. And we blow up their fuckin' temple... sorry Professor..." even now the apology was for swearing, "... and their grail with it." He hesitated. "After we find our friends, of course. Jim, Pete, c'mon. Let's load up."

"I'm coming with you." Catalina started to head for her tent. "Let me get my fleece."

"No." Pete's single word was accompanied by a glare. "You stay here."

"No way."

"Way. With due respect to the Professor here, we can't take him with us and we're not leaving him on his own here."

"I've backpacked in the Outback; I can fire a gun."

"Catalina, sweetheart," Cobus joined in, "you're not coming. Some of us have shot more than dingoes." Seeing the look she gave him, he followed up with as much encouragement as he could: "But as you say you can handle a gun, guard the camp and the Professor."

The three men headed towards the boxes of weapons, but then Pete hesitated long enough to stroke Catalina's hair. "I know you've been through a lot and I'm sorry for being abrupt, but you know it makes sense. And make no mistake, you have a responsibility here." Then he pointed. "Oh, and by the way, I think he's just died."

They turned as one and looked at the figure on the sleeping bag. "Think it sums up the seriousness of our predicament, when we failed to witness the death of one of the oldest men on earth." Cobus, Catalina, the Professor and Jim all crossed themselves. "But unfortunately, it's possible he's not *the* oldest, so we still have a problem."

"Peace at last." As Sutch bent forward he realised there were no eyes to close. They had already fallen through. He took his bandanna and placed it over the skull of the king, whose reign of perhaps sixteen hundred years on this archipelago had just ended. "What have we come to," his voice full of reproach, "when we argue while a man dies a few feet from us?"

"We'll give him a decent burial when we return." Cobus turned back towards gun-boxes.

"No." Jim raised a hand of apology for the abruptness as the others looked at him. "This may sound strange under the circumstances, but we should take him back to civilisation with us. In the meantime, let's put him into that sleeping bag and let his old bones at least rest."

Sutch nodded his agreement. "He's right. I know my daughter would want there to be something positive and ground-breaking to come from this expedition. This man's bones may yet have an extraordinary tale to tell."

CHAPTER TWENTY-EIGHT

SCORPION ARCHIPELAGO - TEMPLE ISLAND, 31ST OCTOBER 1997

He had forgotten many things over the course of several millennia. Memory had become a soup; a sludge into which everything was stirred. From time to time, the odd thing bubbled to the surface. All that really mattered in the dark brew of his life was the k'ib.

Until recent events, he had long forgotten how he came to stalk this labyrinth, drawn to the torchlight only by the beating of the drums or the chanting of the acolytes offering obeisance and sacrifice. They looked so different from him. He had little memory of the man he was – until the brew had been stirred again, he had even forgotten his original name of Kaz'khar – but at some distant point in his past he had become known as `Ak'ubal`, because, like the night, men knew he was coming and most dreaded his arrival. For him, the darkness in the tunnels was preferable to the horror in men's eyes. He knew they feared him now as one might fear a loathsome, bloated spider that crawls forth to kill while others watch in morbid fascination. And despite his fearsome power, no one hated him more than he had come to hate himself.

Yet it had not always been so, and he had been reminded of that just hours ago – was it hours? – time had no meaning for him anymore. Something in the tunnel, as he responded to the calls of his acolytes; a feeling – perhaps a barely perceptible scent, so fleeting it might have been imagination – had taken his thoughts back into the light; and he had known the simultaneous joy and dismay of remembering; the danger of looking back.

It was almost too much to bear, though nothing could compare to the fire which had flared from the ashes of his soul just days ago as the acolytes had called him to the outer temple. He had stood blinking, weak like a child, in the daylight. For the first time since he abandoned the world outside, he was standing on the shore again. The smells and sounds had coursed through him with a power bordering on destructive. And the memories were starting to live again, shaking off the dust of centuries. There he had stood, confronting an army; facing them down; challenging a king who had addressed them in an imperious tone.

***

SCORPION ARCHIPELAGO - TEMPLE ISLAND, COUNTLESS YEARS BEFORE

"I stand before you as your ruler and demand your obedience. The cult of the priests has grown too powerful and corrupt. I am here to set that right."

He heard this address to the other priests as he stood in the shadows of the temple entrance, the gravitas of the words enhanced rather than diminished by the powerful, background surge of the eternal tide on which this army had arrived. He felt the hesitation of the acolytes in the shuffling of their feet. Strong though they were in arm, they were weak in mind, relying on his leadership. None of his followers could boast his physical and spiritual strength. He had not allowed it. And now they were confronted by an army, four or five hundred strong as far as he could see, though for all their swords and finery he knew that they had not fought a serious battle in living memory – which to the people of those islands meant a long time!

`Ak'ubal was merely waiting for his moment, like an actor wishing to make an impact by his entrance. He knew his appearance was baleful – some whispered he was already dead and such was his bond with the k'ib now, it was hard to tell whose heartbeat was the stronger. If a man cannot tell whether he is alive, then either he is no longer a man or he is dead.

"Where is Kaz'khar?" The name, uttered by the king, was alien to the high priest's ears, but brought with it such a tsunami of memories and emotions that it threatened to overwhelm him. "Where is the man who would take my place?"

Word did get around. It followed in the footsteps of traitors.

"Here I am." As he stepped out from the temple, he seemed to bring its darkness with him; a black wake. Deep in the shadows of his cowl his face remained hidden, except for a cruel, thin-lipped mouth. His followers parted before him like corn before the wind, and the opposing army rippled in expectation. He felt their uncertainty; smelt their fear

– a scent all too familiar to him. But the king, nobility itself, stood his ground. The priest saw how his fingers flexed, sending ripples along his forearms, as though grasping already the hilt of his sword. They might have been equals in strength, for now, but there was no doubt that the k'ib gave with one hand and took with the other. Sometimes `Aku'bal's body struggled to contain the dark strength he had absorbed from the presence of the grail. The king, on the other hand, seemed in rude health, though of course he owed that to the gift of blessed water bestowed by the priesthood. Perhaps it was true what they said about the water; that it did not give but drew on what was already there. However, though the man before him might be dangerous, `Ak'ubal knew only he would win the day. Where was the sport in that?

For a time they stood in silence, just the whistling wind and whipping waves as backdrop to the challenge. A guttering flame, which might have been Kaz'khar's soul, kindled at the sound. Then, to the astonishment of all, the high priest bent a little at the waist and made obeisance, before saying:

"Our lord is most welcome. Too long has he stayed away from the holy ground."

"Ground stained by too much sacrificial blood," growled the king. "And were that not enough, word reaches me of insurrection and ambition, combined with a secret so powerful that it makes a mockery of your so-called divinity."

The high priest had straightened during this pronouncement. "Ah yes, where is the maggot they call Ta'rhik?"

"A maggot, as you call him, that tired of feasting on human flesh, rejected the corruption of the priesthood and remained loyal to his king."

"The very same." The contempt in 'Ak'ubal's voice was almost slime-coated, so thickly did it issue from his throat. "But a maggot nonetheless, as you concede." He saw the king's jaw muscles clench at this deliberate and disrespectful misinterpretation.

"This can still end peacefully."

The priest pointed with a bony but powerful hand towards the king's men. "Easy to say, with an advantage of ten men to one priest. But we do not stand here seeking a fight. We are unarmed."

"You lie. I would wager your swords have newly seen the whetstone and, were we to look below that grey-cowled robe of yours, we would find armour. Indeed, were we to search this island, we would find the accoutrements of war." The king allowed the scowl to fall from his features for a moment. "But, put that all to one side and we can still exist alongside each other. Give me the k'ib."

The man once called Kaz'khar did not waste time with denials. "I see Ta'rhik has advised you well, and doubtless he has told you where the k'ib is kept." He turned his body, gave another slight bow and gestured towards the temple with one arm. "Go seek."

The king's face betrayed indecision for the first time. "Bring it to me."

"I will not, for the lack of trust shown in me."

It had been a clever move by the priest, for his king, so confident and strong to this point, could not allow himself to appear in any way unmanned. He squared his shoulders. "Then stand aside. I fear not the ghosts and demons with which you seek to terrify our people."

"They are not to be feared," was the ambiguous response.

The king beckoned to his captain. "Ready the men. Bring half and leave half here to prevent anyone escaping."

Now `Ak'ubal raised both his voice and his head. He observed the impact of those actions on all who heard and watched. He had chosen not to look at any reflection of his own features for what seemed like an eternity – the looks on the faces of the soldiers now as they saw him confirmed his own fears, but likewise his power. They were afraid. "No man save the king may enter our temple. Death to all that do so." The soldiers hesitated. Their beliefs and dark superstitions ran too deep. `Ak'ubal could see the cornered look in the king's eyes and took the advantage that he thought he still had.

"Very well. Captain," the soldier straightened at the sound of the king's voice, "ensure no man..." – here he looked at the priest – "... or creature follows me."

"My lord." The soldier nodded his obedience.

With that, the king drew his sword, and with a set jaw that could not mask his trepidation, strode into the temple. The soldiers watched till the last glints of daylight from off his crown disappeared.

Morning turned to afternoon and then to dusk. With the failure of their king to reappear, the soldiers' courage started to fail them, though they did not desert their posts. `Ak'ubal knew this and waited, watching unease go rotten and turn to fear. He knew their resolution was straining against its leash and pulled the fraying rope tighter, by instructing the priests to strike up the peculiar, skin-crawling ululation that was the preparatory chant for sacrifice. No man dared bid them be quiet. It grew colder. At last, as the sun started kissing the ocean, the high priest turned to the soldiers. "Your king has entered a labyrinth in which he is doomed to wander forever, unless I deem it otherwise. You know by now, in your hearts, that he will not return." He pointed past them. "I bid you look your last upon your home and the sun, for you will see neither of them again."

With that he threw off his cowl and every man fell back, even his acolytes. He knew what he had revealed by throwing open the curtain. "As I guessed," he whispered to himself and sent forth a laugh that all present wished he had not; a sound that, in itself, would render an island uninhabitable for centuries. Had there still been birds in the trees on Temple Island, they would doubtless have fled in a flurry of cries and beating wings. Though he wore no armour – the king's guess had been wrong, unaware that the high priest knew no fear – he carried a sword, which he drew now. It seemed to blaze red in the sunset. He looked across at the other priests and nodded once. They too threw off their robes to reveal shining breastplates, vambraces and swords. At another signal from `Ak'ubal they set upon the cowering army, who fell back. Such blows as they tried to land were in self-defence – terror had their hearts. The surf boiled red as the priests hacked, slew and hacked again. One of them turned to the high priest, though he averted his eyes as he spoke.

"Shall we capture some for sacrifice, my lord?"

`Ak'ubal stared ahead. "No. Kill all. We shall reap the harvest elsewhere."

Not a single soldier was spared – a blessing, had they but known it. Those bodies that did not float out to sea were hurled into some of the boats in which they had sailed across. Now the high priest addressed his acolytes, who stood blood-stained and proud, full of energy despite being fifty men who had slain five hundred. "Load the ladders and yourselves into the other boats. How perfectly has that traitor Ta'rhik done our bidding for us, ensuring we now have a fleet in which to make our crossing? As soon as you are in deep water, hole the boats with the bodies and let them sink." He raised a finger, to take pause for a moment. "Except the captain. Keep his head to display to the people. Show them the price of disobedience. Let it be the last lesson they learn as free citizens. Then round up every man, woman and child you can. Load them in the boats and bring them here. Those for whom there is no room, let them live in their doomed city... for the moment. Bring all provisions you find; we will feast well." He gave that chilling laugh again, before his expression changed and he looked over his shoulder. "Oh, and post two men at the door of the temple, lest our former ruler should, by some chance in a million, ever find his way out again." He smiled. "And now, I have hunting of my own to do."

With that, the high priest returned to the temple and plunged into the darkness of the labyrinth. First, he had returned to the inner sanctum to reassure himself that the k'ib had not been taken, though he suspected he would have felt that, even in his obsidian heart. Then he stalked the tunnels.

CHAPTER TWENTY-NINE

That had marked the start of a timeless hunt.

A part of him had grown almost to pity his adversary. There had come a time when he found his quarry's armour, discarded like a snake's skin, no longer of any use, just a noisy hindrance. `Ak'ubal had called into the darkness:

"Why do you still run; still hide? You are trapped in this lightless world, with no torch to offer hope, no food to sustain you and no hope of dying as long as the power of the k'ib chooses to keep you alive – if this can be called a life."

That was when, almost on a whim, he had discarded his own torch. Had he wanted to even the odds? Perhaps his life would have ceased to have meaning if he no longer had a prey to stalk. Whether the irony of those final words occurred to him now – could this be called a life? – he did not know. His thoughts wandered in a mind every bit as twisted and dark as the labyrinth.

His eyes had grown accustomed to the dark; as did, he assumed, the king's. At last, the high priest himself had become lost in the ways of the labyrinth, or rather, became one with its shadowy confusion, as his obsession cast a veil across what remained of the dim light of his humanity. Now even his priests avoided him, but they too were lost souls, knowing no other way than to obey him. He had replaced their gods. So, they summoned him ritually, like some demon of the underworld, their chanting his only guide through the tunnels; their obedience so blind that, knowing his hunger now was only for human flesh, they sacrificed their own.

The harvest of citizens had long ago dwindled to nothing, and they could not kill those who had been kept in perpetual slavery to work the land or fish the sea. *Fish* had developed a nuanced meaning. Sometimes, the sailors, accompanied by priests as of old, would lure boats from distant ports to the archipelago with tales of magic and promises of eternal life. Those mortal seamen who made it to Temple Island discovered too late *whose* desperate, decaying relic of an eternal life was being described. The flesh and blood from the new world gave him some strength, and `Ak'ubal became aware of the part of him that might be mortal as he feasted.

The first sighting of the huge, roaring bird some moons ago had thrown the priests into a state of terror, and he had demanded to be told if it ever came again. When it did, two days before, he was not scared. He had witnessed man's progress through the eons; knew that an unfathomable length of time had passed since his people reached these islands and that man would have moved on in his thirst for knowledge, whereas the priesthood had stood still, trapped by its old ways and an ancient, vast ocean. `Ak'ubal had long ago become one with the shadows – dark with knowledge. He was not afraid; as he watched through the distant-eye that one priest had brought back from a trading trip, he saw men and women disembarking from the bird – clearly some sort of flying ship. Astounding! Man had grown greater than the gods. Then, as he had watched them reach the shore in their strange boats, he had at last felt a frisson of fear. Who were these people? One thing he knew; where man goes, man follows. Part of him longed to join them, but this new age of magic would hold no place for the likes of his priesthood. His only chance – their only chance – was to kill the new invaders, keeping safe the secret of the lost kingdom, and the k'ib.

That very night he had sent two scouts in one of the few remaining ancient boats – the fleet they had acquired after the defeat of the king was in the process of rotting, despite the primeval knowledge of those who worked with dwindling raw materials on their upkeep.

To his dismay, the scouts returned to the temple with one of the new settlers as captive.

"This will betray our presence," he had rasped in the whisper that he knew filled the other priests with fear.

"We had no choice, my lord," they had quivered in response. "He woke even as we entered the camp and would have roused the others."

He had gestured for them to drag forward the prisoner, who'd already regained consciousness and was struggling, though his puny body was no match for the acolytes. There had been such terror in his eyes as `Ak'ubal leaned towards him. "Who are you?" No response. "Why are you here?"

A helpless, horrified shaking met both questions.

"Should we use him, my lord, as bait to bring in the other fish?" asked one of the other priests.

"No." `Ak'ubal considered something. "Did the others see you?"

"No, my lord."

"Then they will not know where he has gone. We will take them one by one."

"They may post guards now."

"There are six of them; two of them women, one an old man, but I do not doubt, as they have mastered the art of flight, that they will have weapons of great power beyond our understanding, so we should be cautious. Let us hope, when they discover this one missing, that they think their enemy is around them on the island of the citadel. Let them turn their backs to the sea." `Ak'ubal had stared at the prisoner and seen him quail, before looking back at his brotherhood. "For now, the fate of this man shall be that of all first captives in our history of combat. The gods demand it."

He had seen the wolfish grins spread across all the faces in the flickering torchlight as they remembered what this meant, and then a chilling ululation had issued from their throats.

Two more of them had come forward, stripped the prisoner, and then seized his legs so he was held spread-eagled on the ground, while another acolyte had come forward with a stake the length of two men. In reality, `Ak'ubal did not know whether this part was indeed demanded by the gods, but it had become his preferred method of sacrifice. He seemed to draw strength from the victims' prolonged agony; the slow death that ensued as a mighty hammer drove home the stake, impaling the unlucky captive upwards between the legs. Done skilfully, it had been known for the wretch still to be alive when the first limb was ripped away. This captive had not been made of strong stuff and had died early in the act. As for the other priests, he suspected they watched with a mixture of relief and despair. The priesthood had once been one hundred strong. The full moon still required a sacrifice and not every sailing expedition had brought back victims for the dungeons! This sacrifice was a reminder to the watchers of the fate they had escaped for the moment, but that might be theirs in the fullness of time.

And then a remarkable thing had happened. The high priest had felt new life and power surge through his ancient body as he had ripped off the victim's arm and consumed this foreign flesh. He had seen the truth; the error of his belief that these new settlers should be killed. Fresh blood was needed to save the priesthood from extinction. And not just in their stomachs; more important – in their veins. New flesh was needed to yield; not to the knife or impaling stake, but to his body and will, so that he could cease to be `Ak'ubal and become Kaz'khar, high priest of a proud movement once more. Otherwise, there was no escaping the fact that the priesthood was dying, even were it to abandon its ancient, cannibalistic practices, which the bloodstained mouths around him had suggested would not be imminent.

He had risen from his throne, after they had made their lengthy obeisance to the altar, and addressed them: "Hear me my priests; this—" here he had gestured towards the half-eaten corpse, "has tasted good. The gods are pleased. Can you not feel the new power inside us?" There had been a murmur of consent. "This race is strong. We must breed with them. Let us think on how best to bring them, impregnate the women, and make the priesthood strong again."

An old, long-forgotten beast had risen within him as he pictured the women spread-eagled and being impaled, but not by some sacrificial stake.

**

However, at this moment it was his anger that needed appeasing, having discovered that two priests, seeking to satisfy their own desires, had returned to the island of the citadel without his knowledge to capture one of the women. Another of the acolytes, doubtless wishing for favour in `Ak'ubal's eyes, or hoping to postpone his own death, had informed him, and for the second time in two nights, the high priest found himself summoned from the labyrinth. His bitterness – he knew no other state of mind now, only degrees of rage – deepened with the late arrival of the two guilty men, whose tardiness merely confirmed their shame. They quailed before him now.

"Fools, why did you float a decoy?" he demanded, still hiding the full extent of his rage, after the priests had sought to explain their actions, claiming, of course, that they had tried to capture the woman for him.

"They had posted guards, my lord." The two men shook.

"Now they know the threat lies across the water from them, not on their own island. You have betrayed us. They may come with their weapons."

"But we would have succeeded, my lord, had we not been disturbed by another of them emerging from the trees. But he did not see us; their weak eyes cannot pierce the darkness. Are they truly to be feared, mighty one? Would a master race still sleep in tents? Nor did we see boats, my lord. They cannot follow us."

`Ak'ubal rose from his throne and descended the steps. "I bade you only to think on how best to seize the women. Clearly your minds have grown weak and are no longer capable of thought. And I have seen their boats. You would call me a liar in this gathering? Do you truly believe that they are not to be feared; that I am wrong?"

Both priests shook their heads in vehement denial and their eyes flickered around, not daring to look at his fearsome face, while doubtless also seeking in vain for an escape route. "No, my lord," they whimpered in unison, "we beseech you."

"But I know your plots. You took one of the women for yourselves and would fill her with your seed in the hope of supplanting me with your own line. Where have you hidden her? Why were you late when all were summoned here?"

"Please believe us," one of the priests sank to his knees, "we only... we were ashamed of our failure and feared to show ourselves."

`Ak'ubal placed his hands on the first priest's shoulders. He moved them inwards, almost caressing the man's neck as he raised him to his feet again. "Calm yourself." He continued to raise his hands and, with a sickening, tearing sound, pulled upwards, removing the head. He looked at it. "Do not lose your head."

The other priest started jabbering and backing away, but he found no escape through the acolytes, who pushed him forward again to his fate. When `Ak'ubal had finished, he placed the two gruesome trophies on either side of the k'ib on the altar. The eyes of the two victims continued to move and the mouths to speak, such was the power of the grail. This gruesome show could last for an hour or more and never failed to amuse `Ak'ubal, but its primary purpose was to serve as a warning against disobedience.

However, this night he wanted more than amusement and he addressed the others: "In the belief that you are all equal fools I will go with you tonight and seek the woman these traitors have hidden here on Temple Island. If we do not find her then..." he put out a hand and touched the k'ib, in which the pulsing appeared to strengthen, "... our beating hearts will, at next moonrise, make their first journey across water since the day of our arrival on this shore. Once again, it will signal a new beginning."

The priests turned at his signal, filing from the inner temple through the lower tunnels that led to their cells and onwards to the cliffs on the opposite side of the island. This had been built as an escape route should the population of the citadel have ever realised that five thousand people could end the reign of one hundred ageing priests. But `Ak'ubal waited behind, looking at the k'ib pulsing beneath his fingers. It sharpened vague memories already awakened by the taste of new flesh.

Then he looked up. There it was again; the presence he had felt earlier in the tunnel when he had been summoned; smells he could not recognise, in an alluring mix with some that he could. It disturbed him. He would be alert tonight, watching, waiting – more Kaz'khar than `Ak'ubal – strengthened by fresh blood and new purpose, for the first time in... he cocked his head, but time betrayed his memory once more.

CHAPTER THIRTY

PERTH – WESTERN AUSTRALIA, 6AM OCTOBER 31ST 1997

"Oh, you've no idea... comfort it is... a voice from civilisation... crackling one."

The signal was dreadful. "Who's that? Is that you, Catalina?"

"Dirk, oh thank God – yes... Catalina... people in countries... overrun by the Nazis... they tuned... free world on their hidden crystal sets."

"What's the matter girl? I lost most of that."

"It's... Dirk, it's bad!"

"Shit, what's wrong?"

"Some... are dead."

The signal was coming through like someone was standing at the top of a mountain in a high wind. So much for sat-phones, thought Dirk; a good old-fashioned radio would have been no worse. But the disjointed content had already made the Aussie's blood run cold. "Repeat. Did you say somebody's dead?"

"... obbie... Ja... issing."

It was getting worse, but he had heard enough. "Sit tight. I'm coming to get you." He cut the link; it was playing havoc with his nerves and tricks with his ears.

Fuck! What the hell had gone wrong? He'd been planning to check over the plane tomorrow, but he'd have to get over there now, even though it was early morning. That way he might be able to get to them in ten hours or so. He shook his head. If he had heard correctly someone was dead and... *no, stop*, he told himself. Deal with the facts. He was Australian, for Chrissakes!

But then again, there was no point denying the intuition, the creeping coldness that had touched his skin when he had first set eyes on those forsaken islands. It had been more than the fear of boredom, which had made him fly home again – he squeezed his eyes shut – to his shame. Overall, he liked to think that he had bottle, but some places just felt wrong and Mother Nature, for whom he had the utmost respect, had her reasons for letting certain things lie hidden. No, he would stick with what he knew, which was checking over his plane and conducting this rescue mission.

***

SCORPION ARCHIPELAGO, 1.45AM OCTOBER 31ST 1997

From a distance the boat might have appeared to be skimming from wave-top to wave-top like a giant orange pebble, but in reality, the impact of each crest jolted through the passengers and threatened to hurl them into the choppy waters. They each hooked an arm through the safety rope.

"So, what's the plan?" Jim had to shout above the crashing waves.

"Fuck knows." Cobus allowed his eyes to stray from the target ahead long enough to glance at Pete.

"Actually, I have one," was the response.

Cobus was again impressed by the man's ability to stay focussed under such trying circumstances. Perhaps that calmness was what adrenaline sports gave you. "Shoot."

"Well, yes, that's part of it." Pete gave a wry smile. "Of course, we may get there and find the temple's now guarded. But, making a big assumption here, which is that we can get in there and still follow our trail through the labyrinth, I suggest the following: everything we've heard indicates that strange artefact we saw on the altar is the key to the lives and the worship of these bastards. So, we get in there, plant some of the explosive on the altar. Then we show them a bit of what we're capable of – a touch of firepower; take a few of them down. They're like the bloody Jocks, still wearing kilts and waving swords. They'll be terrified of the sound and the effect of guns. When we have their full attention, we make them bring us Jane. I'm sure we can make ourselves understood." He looked at Jim. "You've also got a smattering of some Central American languages, if I'm not mistaken."

"Yes." Jim looked a touch confused. "But going back to what you just said, what about Robbie?"

"I'm afraid it's too late for him."

"What?" Jim looked at Cobus for clarification.

166

"Ja, sorry mate – we didn't want to say anything in front of Catalina or the Professor, but if you're unlucky you'll see what's become of Robbie."

"Yes, that's one Jock who's not going to be waving a sword anymore." Pete seemed unable to curb his dark wit.

"Oh, for fuck's sake, Pete." Jim shook his head with anger and stared out across the sea.

"Sorry, old man, but I'm all out of compassion. My fears are now just for my wife."

"Okay, look, I can understand that... hey, why don't we just take all these freaks out and then hunt through the tunnels ourselves; search the rest of the island if need be?"

"With respect, we've been in that labyrinth. You start wandering round in there, you're likely to be doing it for a very long time."

"So, what do we do if they refuse to bring us Jane?"

"Exactly what we do if they hand her over – kill everyone and blow the fucking place to pieces."

"And if we don't find her?" Having to shout above the engine and the sea gave their conversation an added air of desperation.

Pete said nothing for a while, just looked into the distance. At length, he responded: "That's something I'll have to live with." Now his gaze refocussed and he gave an intense, rather telling look at Jim. "You won't." Despite the tumult around them, there was an awkward silence. "But if you want my honest opinion, I suspect she's dead already. If she's not..." Pete appeared to have mastered the pregnant pause, "... let's just say, it might be better if she were." There was nothing the others could say.

If Cobus had considered disagreeing, the image of Robbie's fate, tattooed forever in his limbic brain, made him realise Pete's words held such truth. He tried to instil some more positive vibes: "We'll still look for her of course. At least we'll know, if we take the destructive road, the horror of that priesthood has ended."

They were silent again in the roaring darkness, then Jim spoke: "God knows how the Professor must feel. This place has been a dream of his for half his life; how he must be wishing it had turned out to be a chimera. Instead of which it's a reality that might have cost him his daughter and another young life."

"And his credibility." Pete's cold words carried a touch of vindication.

"How can you say that, man?" Cobus turned his head. "Look, I know that you're upset, and that's totally understandable, but wasn't that a bit harsh?"

"No. The man's a scientist, but he treated this thing, this endeavour, like his own little secret; brought an ill-prepared team to an uncharted part of the world—"

"It's called exploring; the spirit of adventure," interrupted Jim. "With all your activities I thought you'd appreciate that."

"Yeah, well my *activities* didn't risk the lives of those I hold dearest. Or anyone else's loved ones, come to that."

Something about Pete's protestations of love for his wife was grating on Jim, but there was nothing he could say. Part of him wanted to scream, *"She didn't love you! If fate hadn't taken her, I would've,"* but a combination of guilt and decency prevailed. Besides, what did he know? One lust-fuelled hump by a waterfall did not a romance make.

What was it he was experiencing now? A frisson of frustrated sexual jealousy, exacerbated by the fact that, though she might have grown to love him, he would never have proof of that, not even the memory of the words from her own lips? Was he being consumed by the knowledge that, like a secret lover at the funeral of a mistress, he could inflict eternal damage with one damning word, but would be the more damned for doing so?

There was something discordant in Pete's grieving avowal of revenge, but until Jim could be sure that his own judgement was not impaired, he would have to stay silent.

It was gone two o'clock in the morning and dawn was already starting to lift a tired eyelid as the boat scraped onto the shingle. Cobus led the way, less cautious now, through the trees towards the temple. A few yards back from the clearing they dropped down and the Afrikaner crawled forward to take a look.

"Still no guards. Still at worship. And I thought the Dutch Reformed Church was devout."

He came back, removed his pack for a moment and unstrapped one piece, an automatic rifle, clunking the magazine into place and stroking the barrel with satisfaction verging on recidivism. "Ja, that's what I'm talking about." He loaded a semi-automatic pistol and slid it into his belt. Then he grinned at the others and turned to Pete: "Ill-prepared, were we? C'mon, tool up."

They followed his example, caught up a little in his energy field. Cobus then checked that the PE4 plastic explosive was in the rucksack before pulling it on again. "I suggest we make our way to the tunnels and have a listen. I'm not totally happy with what we're doing here; we don't really have that good a plan – it's all a bit haphazard – but we can't wait. But I tell you what," he patted the semi-automatic again, "I'm happier than I was."

"What happens if we meet any of them in the tunnel?" The impact of that possibility was etched into Jim's features.

Pete gestured with his gun. "Then that's the decision made for us. We kill the bastards, and then we carry on killing."

"As Cobus said, we haven't really thought this through, have we? We've just come rushing over here like Rambo, armed to the teeth..."

"Well, what would you suggest?" Pete was out of patience. "Wait for them to have their second course, which happens to be my wife! Well I, for one, can't just sit around. What we do have here, at least, is the element of surprise. After all, we haven't got a fucking clue what we're doing, so *they're* never going to guess." He gave a perfunctory grin and added: "Anyway, Rambo usually does alright."

Cobus observed the impact of those words on Jim, in particular the meal analogy. It had hit home. "He's right. The last thing they'll be expecting is for us to come over here; come into their labyrinth. It doesn't look like they've even realised we're onto them. We are literally taking the war into the enemy camp. Plus, we've got twentieth century technology on our side." They all looked at each other. "Okay, whatever we're doing, let's do it."

They left the cover of the trees and crossed the clearing towards the looming temple entrance at a trot. As they looked up at the glowering architrave, Cobus and Pete exchanged glances, realising that what they had taken for carvings of skulls before were the real thing! Then, as they stepped inside, Jim stopped in amazement, unable it seemed, despite the circumstances, to keep the lens cap on the photographer in him. But the magnificent statues held no fascination for the other two, with the claustrophobia of the labyrinth and its grim secrets still fresh in their minds.

They hurried Jim along, though he, like them an hour or so earlier, stood in shuddering awe before the colossal, malign edifice that guarded the entrance to the labyrinth. Again they nudged him, till they stood once more at the greedy mouth of the tunnel that they knew had consumed one, possibly two, of their party.

Jim swallowed hard. "Looks grim." Then a graveyard grin twisted his lips. "You can lead."

"I found another of these in the equipment boxes." Cobus handed Jim a head-torch.

Then Pete beckoned Cobus over. "Hey, is this mother of a statue also made of rock salt?"

The Afrikaner went over to the carved monster and, taking a knife from his pocket, cut its surface. "Ja, like all the others."

Pete looked up the colossus. "That's a hell of a lot of salt. If that came down, it would block this entrance, wouldn't it?"

Cobus gave a nod of complicity. He then removed his rucksack and pulled out some of the PE4, which he placed at various points around the base. When he was done, he ran the wire and detonator round to a few yards in front of the statue, before coming back and slapping his palm on its bulk. "Let's hope they don't follow us out. It would be a shame to destroy something so old."

Pete shook his head. "Followed or not, we're bringing that bastard down. Let 'em live on in their tunnels if they want, but they'll have to mine this salt all over again if they want to come out to pray."

With that, they switched on their lights. Cobus moved to the head of the tunnel and listened. "Nothing yet. Let's go."

Moving forward, they were relieved to see that the pieces of black and yellow tape were still in place. They stopped every few paces to listen. Cobus heard Jim's whispered words: "What if we meet this thing you say you encountered?"

Cobus tapped his rifle. "I reckon this will take care of it. I think we were probably a bit spooked by everything. In fact, the tunnels don't feel so bad the second time round."

Again, Pete dug into his seemingly enormous ammunition belt of dark humour: "You're right, they're only terrifying." He cocked his head, listening. "I think we've come further this time without hearing anything, though I couldn't swear to it. I wonder if they've dispersed, and if so, where?"

They looked in slight panic behind them in the tunnel. "Well, I think I hear something now. Voices."

"Yes," Pete strained to listen. "But that's no incantation."

They continued forward, till they came to what they believed was the crawl-hole in which they had hidden. Cobus suppressed a shudder and then gathered himself together. "Let's count how many paces from here to the hall. If we need to duck down here again, we'll know where it is in the dark."

They switched off their lights and saw, somewhere ahead in the darkness, the glow that they knew emanated from the torches of that horrific inner sanctum. Cobus moved forward on foot, counting, then dropping from the potential sight of enemy eyes. The others followed suit.

They were about to crawl to the edge when they froze, as one, at the sound of a voice that crawled under their skin and emulsified their blood. When they could force themselves forward again, they lay flat and peered into the chamber – they had given up thinking of it as a sanctum – in time to see two dripping heads, which, it was clear, had only recently taken time off from their bodies, being placed on either side of a pulsing object by a tall, powerful man of immense and frightening presence.

"Jesus!" Cobus and Jim uttered the same hushed exclamation as they recoiled. The former crossed himself. His voice was shaking as he tried to bolster his wits with some irony. "I tell you, man, I'm going to give up looking over that ledge. Not that I'm planning to make this a regular trip." He tried to smile but was brought up short. Two heads!

Pete's words helped him realise Jane's wasn't one of them. "Incredible," Pete was the only one still looking, "the heads are still talking! And that thing – what did Tariq call it, a k'ib – seems to be getting brighter." The others crawled forward again; their faces now not much healthier-looking than the two on the altar. "Hard though it is to swallow, the story must be true. That thing must be keeping them alive, just like it did the old man."

Now Jim noticed the other horror on the impaling stake and put a closed fist to his mouth before managing to talk. "I saw some shit in Rwanda, but this... who is this freak?"

That was when something occurred to Cobus. "Hey, we forgot to mention this k'ib thing to the Professor. I guess with everything else going on—"

"I didn't forget *about* it though." The pulsing light was bright enough now to throw alternate light and shade on Pete's features as he spoke – a touch of Hitchcock in a real horror story. Then he broke away from looking, though a gleam, reflecting more than the k'ib, still shone in his eyes. "That thing means fortune and fame, guys. But you're right; it hardly seemed the right time to mention it in camp earlier. Anyway, to answer your question, Jim, I think Cobus and I have a feeling we know who this is."

"Ja," Cobus nodded, "or at least what it feels like to be stalked by him." He shuddered. "And I bet our recently deceased friend, the king, knew only too well how it felt. Man, what a nightmare."

Jim put his palm to his forehead. "Of course! Tariq's letter mentioned him. Yes, from the way the others are grovelling before him, he's the high priest all right."

Pete turned to Jim and pointed his thumb towards the monster below. "Do you understand what he's saying?"

"No idea. Like a lot of ancient languages, we can only guess at how they were spoken."

But now they were alert and focussed again, as the priests turned in silence and headed towards the two tunnel entrances on the opposite side of the chamber.

"Where do you think those lead?" Pete's question was directed to no-one in particular.

Jim shrugged. "Maybe to some sort of monastic cells. Let's hope it's not a short-cut back to the temple, otherwise we'll be outflanked. Let's also hope this is some sort of idiorrhythmic set-up – when they're not all kidnapping and sacrificing." He gritted his teeth. "Poor Robbie, dying in this god-forsaken darkness at the hands of these bastards. I just hope—" He stopped himself.

Cobus saw Jim's look at the back of Pete's head – relieved he had shut up in time – and decided to move away from that subject. "What's idio—whatever that thing was you said?"

"It was the way of life for certain ascetic monks from centuries ago. They would live in their separate cells, then gather once a week, or just live alone in the desert. I'm hoping these bastards are—"

"Hey, you two." Pete's urgent whisper drew their attention and they ducked down just as the hooded figure below lifted its head to look around. They could almost feel his gaze probing the darkness like a searchlight. When they dared to look again, he was still standing in that pose. Then, as if he had made up his mind about something, he strode away and followed the other priests down one of the tunnels.

"This is our chance." Pete got to his feet.

"Those fuckin' heads are still talking." Cobus shuddered.

"I've got a couple of their CDs." The other two gave Pete a blank look. "Talking Heads."

Jim turned away, his features a very readable reflection of his thoughts.

"You're a fuckin' enigma, man." There was utter disbelief in Cobus' voice.

"Not one you want to solve."

"I dunno. We're surrounded by blood and gore, looking for your missing wife and you crack a shit joke like that. I put it down to a defence mechanism, but I tell you what, if that's the famous British stiff upper lip, I'll just let mine quiver."

Pete looked down. "I... maybe you're right. I hope I didn't offend you." There was silence for a moment. "Anyway, I want my wife back more than you can know. It just doesn't feel like she's here. That might sound strange." There was no response. "But let's find out for sure." He started to move towards the head of the steps.

Jim returned from wherever his anger had taken him. "Does this smell like a trap to anyone else?"

"Maybe," Pete shrugged, "but what choice do we have? C'mon." The last word was impatient and he made his way with extreme caution down the steps. Then he stopped and looked at the tunnel entrance behind him. "Hey, it looks like they've had to put some wooden supports there. Perhaps the rock's not that stable. Let's make sure we put some explosive here. And these steps are wooden. Obviously this chamber was carved naturally and the tunnel simply dropped into it."

Cobus looked where Pete was pointing and nodded. "You're right, man. I'll put enough PE to blow the steps as well, and then our arses are covered if they try to chase us."

"Good man." Pete helped the Afrikaner off with his rucksack as if to show Jim that the two of them were still in tune.

They waited till Cobus was finished, not wanting to split their strength, before coming down to the altar, all the time looking both at the tunnel they had just exited and the ones to their left. They approached the k'ib, with its gruesome sentinels.

"Wish I knew what you guys were saying," Pete drew nearer to the heads, fascinated. He turned to the others. "More PE4 I think."

Cobus cut further strips of lard-like plastic explosive, and they placed two narrow strips of it either side of the k'ib. Now, after discussion with Pete, he led wires back to the foot of the steps and placed the detonator there.

Jim had been distracted; his attention drawn like a fly to the tattered, ripped remains of what had once been Robbie McCulloch. When the image of the processed meat in a doner kebab shop came to him unbidden, he knew his mind was starting to claw its way towards the edge of reason. The incessant murmuring of the two severed heads only strengthened the impression of lurking insanity. With their vocal cords torn, their words were the sibilant ranting of lunatics. Jim tore his gaze away towards what the others were doing with the detonator. "Shouldn't we put that right at the top of the steps? Don't want to bring the roof or the steps down on ourselves before we have a chance to get out."

Pete shook his head. "No, here is good. There's a ten second delay once we've pressed it," he looked at Cobus, who confirmed this fact with a nod as he finished with the wiring, "so we've got time to get away. They won't understand what we've done and they'll chase us. By the time they get to the steps, they'll walk into the explosion and the blast from the altar will take them out as well. With luck the force of it won't get to us up there."

"With luck?" Jim shrugged – he was not a munitions man. "Okay, but what if the blast doesn't get them or destroy the steps?"

Pete showed the two rifles he was carrying; his and Cobus'. "That's where these babies come in. Even if the blast doesn't kill them, they won't know what the hell's going on. They'll be terrified and confused and we can pick them off. In the meantime, we hit the other detonator at the top of the steps and leg it."

"Won't that blast follow us down the tunnel?"

Cobus chipped in. "Nah, man, I've put the PE4 so it'll bring down some rocks from above the tunnel, but the blast will go out into the chamber." He fingers opened like an anemone to illustrate the path of the explosion, then he grinned.

"And Jane?"

Cobus grin faltered and he looked at the floor in atonement.

"Look around you, Jim." It was Pete. "We can't exactly go wandering around looking for her. If they don't bring her, it's for one of two reasons; either she's not here, or she's already dead. I have to accept that as her husband. Why can't you? Whatever we do, even if we come back when the dust has settled, even if she is being held in some dungeon in a drug-induced trance, we have to get rid of these monsters first."

Jim wanted to say so much, but it was not his right and he just gave a curt nod.

"Okay," Cobus looked at the lower tunnels, wanting to move on, "let's do something to get their attention."

"Agreed." With that single word, Pete set the wheels in motion. He launched a tae kwon-do kick at the front of Jim's right kneecap, shattering it. "That should do it."

CHAPTER THIRTY-ONE

Jim collapsed screaming. With a swift movement, Pete grabbed the rifle that fell from his grasp.

"What the fuck...?!" Cobus started to advance on Pete.

"Uh uh." Pete sounded to his own ears like he was admonishing a naughty child, though the gun he raised in Cobus' direction would have been considered a bit over the top as child-care went.

"Oh God!" In a horrific, slow-motion moment of clarity, the Afrikaner reached for his rifle and rucksack only to find them both still in Pete's possession. Pete saw in Cobus' eyes that the myriad pieces of the puzzle, meaningless on their own, were linking, too late, into the semblance of a picture.

"Yes," Pete's gun was still pointing at Cobus, but his words were directed at Jim, "you didn't really think I was going to let you get away with fucking my wife?"

Jim was groaning, words still impossible through the blaring pain.

"What's he talking about, man?" Pete saw confusion in the big Afrikaner's eyes, but something else too; the shame that came with an undeniable frisson of hope – that one's own life might yet be spared at the expense of another's.

"I saw them, yesterday evening, up at the waterfall." He looked at Jim for a moment. "Good, isn't she?" He was met by another groan that might have been an oath. "Well, I hope it was fun while it lasted." He caught a movement out of the corner of his eye and brought the gun around again towards Cobus. "Believe me, I'll kill you."

"Hey listen, man, it takes two to tango." When Pete nodded in agreement with Cobus' statement, he saw further enlightenment dawning on the big South African. "But you already know that, don't you? That's why you're not bothered about saving her."

Pete pursed his lips as if considering. "Partly. And partly because I've already killed her."

Even Jim seemed to rise for a moment from his sea of crashing pain. "What did you say?" For just a few seconds, the psychological trauma seemed to outweigh the physical agony.

"Yes, she's a lovely, permanent addition to the island now."

"You're sick." Jim's words were for Pete but addressed towards his own knee – the pain could not be ignored.

"And you're dying. You know that now, don't you? You're not leaving this chamber alive."

"For fuck's sake, man, is it worth that?" Cobus raised and lowered his arms, fighting the urge to step forward.

"Oh absolutely," Pete assured him with almost surreal sincerity and politeness.

"How did you do it, man? We were on guard last night."

"Ever the opportunist, I guess." Pete broke off to look across at the lower tunnels, but there was no movement, so he continued. "I happened to be awake, contemplating exactly what I was going to do about the star-crossed lovers, when I heard some noise and looked out to see the two of you run off." He considered something for a moment. "You know, tai chi may look gentle, but it teaches you how to kill very swiftly and silently, and it's one of many martial arts I've studied. Once I'd done with her, I just carried her off, dumped her deep in the woods and returned; funnily enough, just in time, I think, to frighten off our two other would-be kidnappers. By the time you guys came back I'd got my breath back and... Bob's your uncle." Again, he paused to check the tunnels. "Well, for some reason your screams don't seem to have attracted much attention."

"Why do you still want their attention? You've done what you set out to do."

Pete ignored Cobus. "Time we made a bigger noise – although on second thoughts, I've got a feeling this might do it."

He stepped across to the altar and picked up the k'ib. There was an immediate horrible, ominous roar from one of the lower tunnels; it seemed to freeze the very marrow in their bones.

"Yup, that did it." Pete stuffed the grail into his rucksack, though not without feeling the peculiar pulsing. "Time we weren't here." Cobus stepped towards Pete with intent. "No, Cobus, don't do that. Instead, please press the detonator." Cobus looked shocked. "Do it for your old friend Jim's sake. You wouldn't want them to find him alive."

"You fuckin' cold-hearted bastard, I'm not doing it!"

"Simple then, I just kill you and do it myself. There's your choice." He relished the Afrikaner's dilemma. "I thought so." Then Pete's face set into a snarl. "Do it."

The initial preternatural roar from the tunnel had been reinforced by others.

"I really would advise you do it now, Cobus." Pete's words were dry; he had thought things through and seemed calm. "There's only a ten-second delay, don't forget."

Cobus looked at Jim in utter helplessness. "I'm so sorry, man." Then he turned to Pete. "Oh, for God's sake, shoot him! There's no guarantee the explosion will kill him."

Pete pointed the gun at Cobus' head. "You've got two seconds."

"Shiiit!"

He pressed the two red buttons together and the two men tore up the steps towards the tunnel, throwing themselves flat just before a blast wave hit them, as the altar and steps were blown apart. Behind them, like a freakish hailstorm, shattered rocks clattered to the ground.

Pete got to his feet in a flash. "Get up, Afrikaner." Cobus rose, looked back to see dust and stones filling the space of the chamber, and then stumbled on down the tunnel. Pete pressed the second detonator. "Move!" Both men raced on, hoping Cobus had done his work well and that the blast from explosive at the tunnel entrance would not follow them. There was a boom, followed by a wave of hot air, but it seemed their plan had been successful. Only one of them took any satisfaction from that.

Then, despite the ringing in their ears, they became aware of voices ahead of them somewhere down the labyrinth.

"Somehow I don't think we killed all of them." Pete's dry irony could not mask the chill inside him.

"Give me my gun, man. At least I can help fight them."

"Oh yes, of course, what a ridiculous oversight." He pointed his rifle at Cobus. "Just get fucking running."

They switched on their head-torches and ran past several junctions where they heard voices, but knew they had got past their pursuers for the moment. Of course, the priests might have known ways through the network of tunnels – short-cuts leading from the lower levels – but it seemed for a moment that the two men had got away. Then a group of figures emerged from a side exit just as they ran past it. Grasping fingertips brushed them; they heard the slap of bare feet on rock as the hunters chased. Pete stopped, turned and levelled his gun. Before he fired, he saw cruel, grim faces from another time, with dark eyes framed by straight black hair; living versions of the statues in the temple – six or seven of them. He fired a burst, which sent chunks of flesh and gouts of blood flying into the darkness. Bodies staggered and fell. He fired at those coming through from behind, but even as they, too, collapsed, the ones who had been hit first started to haul themselves to their feet. He opened fire on them again. They jerked and juddered once more. Yet the others were recovering now!

It's the k'ib, thought Pete. *If it can help two severed heads to have a conversation, what are a few bullet wounds?*

He sent one last merciless burst of fire into the pack. He turned to see Cobus standing watching the horrific spectacle open-mouthed. The two of them ran for their lives.

"They're never gonna stop, man," panted Cobus over his shoulder with still some element of satisfaction in his voice. "You want the k'ib, you've got them as appendages."

"Not if I can get far enough away from them. They'll die without it. Look at our friend the king."

The sound of feet behind them was growing louder. The way ahead seemed clear, but they had lost track of how far they had still to go. Added to that, they were slowed by the need to watch for the coloured tape way-markers. The pursuers were catching them, no doubt about it – driven, Pete assumed, by their absolute need for the k'ib. Without it, they were going to die. He guessed that focussed one's attention!

In a fleeting moment of distraction, he wondered what made these men – *were they men?* – want to continue living. But he felt strong. Hadn't everything he'd done tonight been the adrenaline fix to end them all? For a moment, he wondered what that said about him, given fates the two star-crossed lovers had suffered at his hands – but only for a moment. The adulterer and adulteress had reaped what they'd sown. Fear always gave the ultimate turbo boost. Plus, he had touched the k'ib; stood in its aura.

He dared another glance round – it was not a pleasant sight; not only were the priests still in hot pursuit and gaining, they bore the violent marks of where he had shot them, like bodies which had risen from a battlefield after being strafed. Set against the darkness behind them, they were the stuff of nightmares, gaping wounds which struggled to conceal their insides. He had to slow them down, if just for a few seconds, though he wasn't sure how many bullets were left in the first magazine. He pictured stopping to fire again; the hollow click of an empty chamber being the last sound he heard before they fell on him, ripping the k'ib away and carrying him off to heaven knew what grim fate. He had listened to the Professor's reading of Tariq's tale with more attention than he let on, having already seen and set his heart on taking the prize. He knew, without water to unleash its mysterious powers, the k'ib was just a bauble that could not help him right now. The pursuers must have built up reserves of strength through centuries of exposure to it, and that was what kept them coming on, as if their batteries were still charged.

Pete still had Cobus' gun, of course, but he didn't know what lay ahead in the temple, so would not waste those bullets here. He had also been picturing different scenarios during the boat crossing, so had a contingency plan. What was it they said about successful people? They were good at visualising their achievements in advance. At a tangent, he remembered the old joke about the two wildlife photographers about to be chased by a lion. One stopped to pull on running shoes. When his companion said: "You'll never outrun a lion," he'd replied: "I'm okay as long as I can outrun you." So now he fired three shots, two of which hit their target, ripping into the back of Cobus' legs, causing the Afrikaner to collapse with a startled shriek of pain. Another figurative photographer to add to the one he'd already left behind.

Pete's momentum carried him past the stricken South African. He looked back at him for a moment, then beyond him to the group of blood and gore spattered priests, who had stopped in respectful fear of the death stick; they had felt its venom and could feel it still. "Test your scrummaging skills now, you fucking rock-spider."

"You're gonna rot in hell, man. That's three deaths you'll be carrying on Judgement Day."

"Actually two. Jane's not dead. I just wanted Jim to believe she was before he died; wanted him to despair, and to recognise that I had the power; over her; over him. Anyway, I'll take my chances with my judges. Meanwhile, I'll get my skinny arse out of here as yours appears to belong to someone else."

Before Pete turned, he saw the grim faces of the priests as they started to advance again and fired his remaining bullets down the tunnel in their general direction. Then he ran, having bought himself perhaps a few valuable seconds, courtesy of the flesh of a doomed Afrikaner.

CHAPTER THIRTY-TWO

He had no idea how much further he ran – judging distance was an impossibility – but at last he saw a less dense darkness ahead. There was now cooler air against his skin as he burst out into the temple, heart thumping, eyes bulging both with the effort of running for his life and of peering down the dichromatic kaleidoscope of the tunnels. He looked back towards them and raised the second gun. His pursuers were nowhere to be seen.

Now, for the first time, he experienced a more primal level of fear. These... priests, acolytes, whatever they were, had been following the k'ib. Why would they stop? They would know by now that Cobus did not have it. Had they fallen back to make way for something worse than themselves? Did they perhaps give up, knowing what lurked in the temple? He uttered a hysterical laugh at the way he was developing an imagination, but still, he could not shake the feeling something worse – and there was only one thing it could be – was very much alive. Adrenaline junkie though he was, Pete had no desire whatsoever to meet the Grim Reaper.

And even as he thought about it, the temperature in the temple dropped. He looked around at this cavern of the grotesque, the features on the statues sliding and dancing in the uneven torchlight; was the Reaper already here? Had he escaped through some other secret passage to lie in wait? One thing was for sure – standing and thinking about it was bottom of the useful list right now.

It was getting colder – was he cooling down after the sprint through the tunnels, or was something else at play? And had it become darker? After all, his eyes should have been adjusting to the half-light. But this was not imagination, because now he noticed that the torches around the walls of the temple had started to go out, beginning with those closest to him.

At the same time a sound reached his ears; it was indescribable and getting closer – it appeared to be coming from the tunnel, but he could not be sure. The guttering and then extinguishing of each torch continued and Pete decided to combat his growing fear by firing a few rounds into the tunnel; the deadly familiarity of the repeated explosions almost melodic compared with the soundtrack of that awful place. When the report died down there was silence again – until another torch went out with a soft pop.

A voice screamed, but this one emanated from Pete's mind, telling him to move or die. That was when he remembered the detonator and the plastic explosive they had left at the base of the huge statue. He ran round to it, pressed the two buttons, and then fled, yelling at the top of his voice, firing bullets around him, half expecting figures to emerge from their hiding places in the shadows of the other statues. Behind him, the torches continued to die. At any moment he expected a cowled shape to step out and block his path.

So, he was shocked to a standstill when he emerged unopposed into the nascent daylight beyond the temple entrance.

Boom!

The delayed explosion roared, and he could just make out, in the darkness at the back of the temple, the first tottering steps of the monolithic statue as it started to collapse.

There was no time for feeling relieved; he knew something was following him and could almost have believed it was the vengeful soul of the beast-god, released from the prison of its statue. On fatigued legs he ran, knowing the dark man was coming; feeling his fingers of shadow reaching out towards him; the ancient, stinking breath, putrid from gorging on human flesh, making the hairs on the back of Pete's neck stand in expectation of being touched. He knew that if he stumbled even once, over a root or rock, it would be all over for him. Not until he had scrambled down to the beach and across the shingle to the inflatable did he dare to stop and look around. He could see nothing, and nothing suited him fine.

He looked up and down the beach – no sign of life. Had any of them got away? He hoped his theft had drawn them all back into the temple or tunnels and their doom. Part of him wanted to go back and look through the temple portal, but what if some of them had survived and were watching him now from the trees, scared of his firepower, and waiting to destroy the boat so they could keep him here while they thought of a way to disarm him? There was no point in going back. All that mattered was that Jim and Cobus were dead. If some of those freaks had survived, they would not last long without the k'ib.

Now he remembered his prize, opened the rucksack and removed it. What the hell was it, lying inert in his hands, made of some unidentifiable metal or element? When he had picked it up from the altar it had been pulsing, proving that water did indeed power it somehow. Maybe it also performed some complex ionisation of the air, affecting the oxygen you breathed. Pete shook his head; if that were the case, who the hell were these guys who, when they weren't ripping each other's heads off or eating each other, invented a machine capable of something he could not begin to understand? What a sucker punch – perhaps the most incredible invention in the history of mankind and you were too scared to let anyone find out, or unable to get off your piece of rock long enough to make it worthwhile.

He looked up, imagining several pairs of vengeful eyes watching him from the tree line. Nothing. He held the artefact up above his head and showed it to the island. "Your secret's safe with me!" he shouted in mockery.

There had been no time to think over the financial benefits it might bring, but it was possible he would have an eternity in which to work it out. The only problem he could foresee was if he ended up looking like the Caped Crusader back there; it seemed eternity had a price. But he would cross that bridge when he came to it.

Pete looked up at the lightening sky. A pall of smoke and dust had issued from the mouth of the temple and was rising against the dawn. The last of their merry band, old Sutch and Catalina – assuming Jane was in no state to feel merry – might have noticed it by now and be wondering what the hell was going on. Time to get away from this place of death.

He saw the wooden boat sitting where the two would-be kidnappers had left it on their return, took aim and fired several holes into it. With the rifle-butt he smashed the holes wider before getting into the inflatable. He knew it had to be low on fuel and for a moment regretted his rash decision to smash the other boat, which would have been easier to row back than his own, but to his relief the motor started up. With a last look over his shoulder at the scene of his greatest triumph so far – a strange accolade to a life! – he set off back towards base camp.

The short trip seemed surreal, as if he was travelling forward through time from a forgotten, dangerous place into a world full of opportunity.

The daylight having almost returned in this southerly latitude, he could make out the figures of the Professor and Catalina on the beach. He saw the old man sink to his knees. Had he realised that, not only was there no sign of Jane on the boat, there was just the lone figure of his erstwhile nemesis. Pete knew his return would be of no consolation to Sutch at all.

"Just the two of them." His tone would have puzzled anyone listening.

CHAPTER THIRTY-THREE

SCORPION ARCHIPELAGO BASE CAMP, 4AM OCTOBER 31ST 1997

For a moment he had drawn strength from the rising column of black smoke above Temple Island. Had they done it; stormed the enemy stronghold and rescued his daughter? The return of his Jane was all that mattered. And if it meant that Cobus and Jim, and yes, Pete too, had blown to pieces a building or a citadel of astounding historical interest, so be it. But when at last the orange boat had appeared around the headland of the other island and through the binoculars, he had seen there was only one person on board, the one about whom he had to admit he cared the least, all strength had left his legs and he had collapsed onto the shingle.

At last, he remembered the gentleman within and turned to Catalina. The poor girl, who had come with very high recommendations from Jane, seemed to have withdrawn into herself pretty early on during the expedition. He had expected different from a seasoned trekker with, according to Jane, an unquenchable thirst for knowledge. But as with everyone else, this place had proved too much for her and after Robbie's disappearance, she had pretty much gone to pieces, her nerves fraying. He found himself feeling a duty of care towards her. After all, choosing to survive in the Outback for a finite period with no responsibilities was one thing, but he had brought her to a place upon which God appeared to have turned his back. She and Jane – he swallowed hard – seemed to have been getting along despite the age difference. Perhaps his beloved daughter had spotted some of her own spirit in the girl. For that reason alone, he had to get her back and ensure that seed had a chance to grow; nurture it from afar. Jane had picked her out and that was good enough for him.

Now he thought of who was approaching in the boat and realised the grim irony of that last thought; she'd also picked Pete. But there, too, he would now have to adjust his mind-set. Pete appeared to be in genuine distress about his wife's disappearance and had not hesitated in taking instant action to try to rescue her, heading into the lion's den with no thought of the dangers ahead. All past disputes and misgivings to one side, Sutch had to try to be fair.

He heard the engine being cut; saw Pete pull the inflatable ashore as far as the rounded pebbles weathered by the sea, avoiding the more jagged volcanic stones, then stagger towards them and into the waiting arms of Catalina. The bleakness of Temple Island was already mirrored in his eyes. He seemed exhausted. Sutch did not dare to ask, wanting and fearing the knowledge. "We've kept the fire going. You'd better come over and warm up."

Wordless, they moved across to the flames. Catalina threw a sleeping bag across Pete's shoulders; a mug of coffee was placed in his hands.

"They ambushed us in the temple. We followed the route we'd marked before. They were still at worship, but then they left. We crept in, meaning to search." He stared into the fire. "There was no point searching for Robbie." He put a hand on Catalina's. "We found what was left of him." The girl folded her arms across her chest and shuddered. "I'm sorry." Now he looked at the Professor. "But there was no sign of Jane." Sutch looked at him with intensity. "Surely that must be a sign of hope there."

"Yes... there... but where?"

"Do we *know* they took her?"

"You and Cobus followed them."

"But it was dark. We can't... couldn't be sure. Anyway, we searched some of the tunnels, but in the meantime they doubled back behind us. Somehow, they knew we were there. We returned to the inner sanctum to find ourselves confronted by ranks of angry, evil faces and more of them were coming down the tunnel behind us to cut us off. We opened fire, but they were onto us too quickly. It was then that we saw the effect of *this*." He reached into his rucksack, pulling out the prize, the booty, Number 42, the time machine, a treasure not yet understood.

Despite everything – the loss of Jane and the deaths of young men helping him chase his fading dream – despite all of that, Pete saw that Sutch was transfixed for a moment; a moment in which Pete's contempt for academics, which had festered within him since his expulsion from Harrow, reached its zenith; or nadir, depending on one's point of view. He preferred being who he was; someone celebrating life, rather than legends – those repositories of the dead, waiting for new members!

The old man held out a hand and, not without a momentary twinge of possessiveness, Pete handed him the k'ib. As he saw the piece turning over and over in Sutch's hands, it re-emphasised for Pete that often, in the history of archaeological discovery, so many lives, deaths and dreams distilled to a tiny piece of matter; so small it might be a pebble on the shore of time. This did not stop him reaching across after a few moments and taking back the k'ib. He noticed the slight resistance of the Professor's fingertips; it was like pulling a mussel from a shell.

He continued, taking some resentful pleasure from dragging his father-in-law back to the harshness of this pressing world after the brief escape of a moment's blissful reverie. "We ploughed bullets into them, but soon it was clear that wouldn't be enough to stop them. There were too many of them, and they refused to die. As for their leader... well, let's just say that when I realised our only chance was to steal this and I lifted it from its altar, he turned his gaze on me." Pete felt a chill; his shiver was genuine enough. "I'd be more than happy never to see him again. By now some of them were dragging Cobus and Jim away down tunnels. I have to say that rock-spider was a hero – never thought I'd hear myself say that." He broke off. "Sorry, have either of you got my cigarettes anywhere?"

"Um, yes, they're here." Sutch handed them across. Pete lit one with shaking hands and inhaled deeply, an evident quiver in this throat.

"Yes, both of them were heroes. I knew I only had a few shots left and would have followed them, though God knows I'd have been lost in that labyrinth, but Cobus shouted 'Blow the place!' We'd planted plastic explosive by the altar and in the entrance to the tunnels by an enormous statue. If they saw us doing it they can't have understood what we were doing.

"Now I noticed the remaining ones were looking at me. I had their precious brass god and without it they would die. Unfortunately for them, they didn't realise the other object in my hands held the same fate. They began to chase me as I ran. I pressed the detonator first, which brought them right into the path of the delayed explosion. I'm not sure if any of them escaped. I didn't see what became of their leader, but I could still feel his presence – that's not something I can explain. When I emerged from the tunnels into the ante-chamber of the temple I detonated a second explosive, which brought down an enormous statue across the tunnel entrance. I'm pretty sure it would have blocked it completely.

"I have no idea whether the others made it out – Cobus, Jim or the priests, but I have a feeling some of the tunnels wouldn't have taken too kindly to the blast." He took a long drag on his cigarette and exhaled a steady stream of smoke; he was feeling calmer. "It looked like they'd had to shore up some of them with timber when they dug extra passages to turn the caves into a labyrinth. By the way, the statues were made of rock salt." He looked sidelong at the Professor. "That, I suspect, was the source of the precious cargoes your merchants were trading. Looks like your pirate captain got that bit wrong."

Sutch gave an equivocal nod: "Yes, but rock salt was a valuable commodity in itself in those days." That the Professor bothered to argue that point only increased Pete's contempt for him and spoke volumes about the old man's state of mind.

"Anyway, I'm not scared to admit it; I kept on running. You know what; I could still feel him, His Royal Darkness, the high priest, king of the castle. I could feel shadows reaching out from the tips of his fingers, seeking his little yellow idol." Again, Pete did not need to call on RADA level skills. There was a chill in his bones, and he pulled the sleeping bag closer around him. He stared into the fire. "If there is anything to this story of eternal life, I wonder if someone can live too long?"

"You mean, can you transgress so far against the laws of nature that you affect them, becoming a part of them, and they of you?"

Pete looked across and saw that the Professor, too, was staring into the fire. "I don't know what I mean." He pitched the cigarette into the flames. "I'm so sorry about Jane. Like I say, there was no sign of her. But I just can't imagine where she could be. I mean..." he hesitated, "... look, I'm sorry to say it, but they'd wasted no time with Robbie." He looked at Sutch and Catalina in turn. "No sign of her here then, I guess." The girl shook her head in silence, turned and walked away towards the water's edge.

Sutch tapped Pete on the shoulder. "I have been a fool, and in my folly I am become Death." He stopped to reflect on that statement – an echo of earlier times. "A destroyer of futures and families." Pete tapped out another cigarette and stayed silent. *You might have destroyed your family's future, old man,* he thought, *but I've got mine planned.* "Do me a favour will you, Pete?"

"If I can." The familiarity from his father-in-law rather took him aback.

The Professor gestured with his head towards the troubled beauty by the sea. "Look after her. Make sure she gets back in one piece. This has been traumatic for her. I just don't think she was ready, or as strong as she believed."

"Were any of us?"

"I brought her to this place of death; I want her now to have a life."

"You're talking like you're reading your will."

"Well maybe I am."

"Meaning?" Pete frowned, but could not look the Professor in the eye. It was not just that past indifferences, as he liked to think of them, might still be revealed. He was scared of what Sutch would see in his eyes. Stranger still, he was scared that in the old man's eyes he might see someone he didn't recognise.

"I can't leave here without knowing Jane's fate. Perhaps she has wandered off into the forest; got disorientated; lost. She might be lying injured somewhere. This is a peculiar place. We've all felt it. I can't help believing there's more to this; that the story – her story – isn't over. Maybe she is alive on Temple Island. Maybe the others are. I'll paddle across in one of the boats and search. There will be no place that I will not look, on any of these hellish pieces of rock."

Pete was looking at him now, in amazement laced with a little foreboding. He noticed Catalina was also looking; it seemed she had picked up on the Professor's ominous behaviour, as if the calmness disguised the unravelling of his mind. "You can't be serious. You're going to stay here?"

"Yes. When Dirk arrives in a few hours – we managed to get hold of him on the sat-phone, didn't we Catalina? – I won't be going with you."

"Pardon me saying so, Edward, but that's crazy. What about Candice? You've got her to think of. Okay, you've lost Jane..." The Professor shot him a look, "... well, it's the truth, isn't it?"

"I won't believe that!" Sutch's face reddened before he calmed down. "Can't allow myself to believe it. My daughter is resilient. She may have escaped and be hiding on Temple Island. I couldn't bear to think of her hoping and praying for someone to come and help her, and that person never coming. I'll search every inch of this blasted kingdom, which met the fate it deserved if it was destroyed."

Pete stood. "You're a scientist; think like one."

Sutch rose to meet his gaze. "That's always been my burden."

Pete paced away from the fire, then turned and walked back to stand almost eyeball to eyeball with Sutch. "Do you want to hear some facts? Like Robbie was a rugby player, ex Royal Navy, a tough lad. And he ended up in the archipelago's equivalent of a fast-food joint; skewered, like some antediluvian kebab." Pete looked across at Catalina, who went pale. He was not in the mood to spare her feelings; took pleasure, in fact, from what he saw as her distaff weakness. "I mean that in all senses, since they were eating him bit by bit." Though the Professor had gone pale, Pete fixed him with his eyes and did not spare him. "If he couldn't get away, what chance Jane?"

Sutch tried his best to gather his wits, rescue them from the wind that was trying to scatter them to the furthest reaches of the Southern Ocean. "Then I owe it to him as well as her not to give up." He turned and surveyed the rest of the camp. "We're only three days into a five-day expedition. There are provisions enough now to see me through much longer than that."

Catalina came over. Only her Argentinean complexion saved her from looking paler than the old man. "Professor, this would be madness."

"It's my daughter, dammit!" She flinched as if he had slapped her face and Sutch raised his hand in apology before rubbing his eyes. "I'm sorry. I'm not... myself."

She moved forward and put hesitant arms around him. "It's okay Professor, you're in shock; hardly surprising. That's what's caused you to make this irrational decision." She expected a reaction; instead, all she felt was the collar of her shirt becoming damp.

CHAPTER THIRTY-FOUR

It seemed the old man had lost the will to move. Perhaps if he did not, he might even be able to believe he was in the arms of his darling Jane. He wondered if he had lost his mind, knew the very act of wondering proved he hadn't, but still, he felt how close he was to the edge. He needed a rope to haul himself back, and searching for his daughter would give him that. Besides, he could not return home, could he? Could not stand in front of Candice and explain how his hare-brained pursuit of a mirage had cost them their daughter, as well as the lives of three other fine, intelligent young people. In his grief he recognised that this was where he belonged. He was the rightful heir to this blighted kingdom. This place was also the fitting home for the amphora, the exotic whore to whom he and Tariq proved worthy sons. So now the circle would be complete; for he did not doubt that he might well join his blood-brother in ending his days here. Perhaps that was why Tariq had returned.

Candice would understand why he could not come back to her, at least not until he had overturned every stone, including those in the destroyed temple, or had died in the attempt. He had nothing now but time – and ironically not much of that.

He released himself from Catalina's embrace. "Well, there's no time like the present."

She craned her neck back in disbelief. "You're not serious?"

Pete's Zippo clicked and hissed, and then he turned back to the Professor. "When did you get through to Dirk?"

Catalina answered. "Shortly after you left; a couple of hours ago? It was a poor connection. He recognised me, and I think he got the gist. So, what does that give us – ten, maybe twelve hours, assuming he gets fuelled pretty quickly?"

"Look, I'll tell you what, Edward – I'll come with you and help you search this island as best we can in the time available, but *then* we leave with Dirk."

Sutch looked him in the eye. "Pete, I appreciate all you've done and acknowledge that, in a lot of ways, I've misjudged you. I always thought you'd be the author of Jane's misery, not me, and for that I apologise. But I'm staying. In a way, it's where I belong. Hopefully Dirk can send over reinforcements. I'm going to comb these islands till I know, for better or worse, the fate of my daughter."

Pete pressed his lips together. He looked up into the trees for a long time, seemed to come to a decision, and then nodded curtly. "Okay, we'll come with you; at least until Dirk arrives."

"Uh uh." The sound of denial came from Catalina. She folded her arms across her chest. "I'm sorry, but I'm going nowhere in this terrible place. I'll stay here and wait for you."

Sutch pursed his lips as he responded. "We should stay together. After all—" Then he noticed that she was shaking. "Okay, you wait here. Try to reach Dirk again. Pete and I will start at the one place we know we can get to quickly."

Pete nodded. "The citadel."

"Yes. If you were going to kidnap someone in camp that would be your quickest route out other than the sea – or the best place to hide someone."

Pete nodded. "You could be right. The guys in the boat fled because of Cobus and Jim returning, but there might have been others involved who also ran off. And they'd be likely to have used the easiest route – the one we hacked clear to the citadel. I know the words straws and clutching spring to mind, but we might as well start somewhere."

With that Sutch turned on his heels and marched towards the track leading to the citadel. Pete gave a long, hard look at Catalina, to which the adjective loving could never have been applied. He slung on his rucksack, though not before remembering to pack the k'ib, and followed the old man.

The gradient was steep and immediate – Pete was soon sweating and panting. He slapped his palm on his rucksack; his words were parenthesised by deep breaths: "So much for mystical powers; right now this thing - just feels like a small dumbbell on my back"

The Professor gasped as he replied, but pushed on in dogged fashion: "I don't care anymore." His tone told of a man walking in the shadows of failure and so tired, he was ambivalent about the fitful, fading light of redemption.

"It's not what I expected either. I thought it might be made of gold or studded with diamonds. Isn't that what hidden treasure is all about? Been watching too many action-adventure movies, I guess."

"Where was it when you took it?" Sutch could not suppress the inquisitiveness intrinsic to the man he had been.

"Standing on an altar, or some sort of plinth, in the middle of a stream of water. It looked like either the plinth had been built there deliberately or the stream diverted."

"And how did the... thing look when you first saw it?"

Pete could tell Sutch was remembering Tariq's exposition about the priests and the power that water gave to the k'ib. Undeniably it gave Pete a certain sadistic pleasure to drip-feed the facts. He had found the k'ib. He had seen the k'ib. He *had* the k'ib. He had the power. "It seemed to pulse with a sporadic light and there was a kind of..." he sought the right word, "... thrumming in the air, and when I picked it up it seemed to be vibrating beneath my fingertips. Maybe the water *was* powering it somehow. Maybe they have a sort of symbiotic relationship, just like Tariq said."

Sutch stopped and looked at him – scanned his face in fact – before saying: "Maybe." Then he looked past Pete's shoulder, and through a gap in the trees saw Catalina back at the camp. Even at this distance she looked scared. Then she moved away out of his line of sight, just as he was lifting his arm to acknowledge her. "As I said at the camp, I want you to look after her. She's been through a lot. She wasn't ready for this."

"Which of us was?" Pete looked round and saw no-one. "I give you my word – for what that's worth."

They had gone another couple of hundred yards when Sutch shouted: "Look!" He pointed to the right. It was the path to the waterfall, but that wasn't what had caught the Professor's eye. Rather, it was a piece of red cloth hanging almost motionless in the still air beneath the trees. He hurried towards it, took it from the branch where it had snagged and played it between his fingertips. "It's not one of the base-layer shirts we've been wearing during the day. It's cotton. Jane changed into this last night, didn't she?"

"Um, I think so." Pete knew so; knew she hadn't been wearing it while Jim fucked her – *why did the image still hit him hard, right between the legs, in the middle of the male universe?* It had been lying with her other clothes by the side of the lake, but he wasn't about to admit to having witnessed that deed. He had more than one reason; to his surprise, he wanted to show some curious, belated respect for the feelings of an old man who did not need that information about his lost daughter. Lost indeed; a mystery to all of them. "But didn't she come up here for a wash? This doesn't really tell us anything."

The Professor's face reflected the hard truth of that, but he appeared determined to clutch at every one of those straws Pete had mentioned. "I remember now; she bought it in Singapore because we left Portsmouth so early the morning after our dinner. This was her new shirt. And you know women – if she'd torn it, I'm sure even my uncomplaining daughter would have mentioned it when she came back to camp. Let's go and take a look. She may have been brought here by force." His voice shook with nervous energy.

Pete looked at the ground. "There's no sign of any—" He frowned. "No wait, you're right. There are drag marks here in the mud." He led the way as they hurried as best they could through the tangle of roots towards the little lake; the sound of water babbling over the rocks by the falls growing louder, but also more ominous. Despite his age the Professor overtook Pete. He rushed to the water's edge, then let out a moan and sank to his knees.

Pete approached with caution. He looked past the old man's heaving shoulders. An image shimmered beneath the surface of the lake, its shape transmogrifying in the disturbed waters, but offering an occasional tantalising, split-second image of its identity. "Oh my God!" It was no feigned surprise.

She was not wearing red. He had wanted to tell the old man that his daughter would hardly have slept in her new shirt, but it seemed such an irrelevance in the overall scheme of things. Likewise, he had wanted to say that Jane would not have drawn any sort of attention to herself, ripped shirt or not, on returning to camp the previous evening, as she would have believed her shame was written all over her face. So, it seemed that Fate, coincidence or the vengeful spirit of this island had taken a hand and led them to this spot by means of a tiny, blood-red flag.

His stomach churned, and not for all the right reasons. There was a double-edged sword being held out towards him by this lady of the lake and one sweep of its blade could end his problems or multiply them. He stood transfixed. There was something disconcerting about a dead face staring open-eyed at you from beneath water, the ripples causing expressions to flit across it. Pete felt it might have been better, if no less gruesome, if fish or crabs had attacked the eyes, taking away part of the humanity.

Now he looked at the back of the Professor's head. The old man was silent for a moment longer, but then he turned and stretched out his hand towards Pete, making a grabbing gesture with his fingers.

"Give it to me."

Pete frowned. "What?"

"The k'ib. Give it to me."

Pete just stared at him. "What good will that do? She's dead. Can't you see that?"

Sutch got to his feet and snapped impatient fingers. "But who knows how long she's been here? It might not be too late. Give it to me!"

Pete felt himself drawing back. "It doesn't work like that." He knew there could be no harm in handing over his prize, but he was reluctant nonetheless. Was this how it started – standing outside oneself, watching the beginning of one's enslavement to this ancient vessel?

"What do we know?"

"Remember Tariq's document. It won't bring her back to life; it prolongs life. But let's get her out of there; at least show some respect instead of arguing." Pete removed his rucksack and bent to untie his boots in preparation for entering the water.

"Respect? You never showed her any while she was alive."

Pete stood up again. "Hey, now wait a fucking minute. That was a two-way street."

"Maybe, but you did nothing to earn *her* respect. You never loved her, did you, from the beginning? Just enjoyed the kudos of being married to someone of worth and reputation."

As far as Pete was concerned, this was just typical of the contempt with which the old bastard had treated him from the beginning. Just because he hadn't chosen to live his life with his nose buried in books and his arse in sand. "Much good your worth has done you. Here." He picked up the rucksack and hurled it at the Professor. "I hate to say it, but I want to see you fail. But at least let me get her out of there." Sutch fumbled in the bag and felt the metallic surface beneath his fingers, inert and heavy. He pulled out the k'ib. "I risked my life twice to try to find her," continued Pete. "I loved her well enough. But things change. Life moves on."

There were two loud cracks.

"Or not," said the voice from behind them. The Professor pitched forward, with the cold *giver* of life still clutched in his hand, while the barrel of the *taker* smoked in Catalina's. "We didn't have time for all that."

194

CHAPTER THIRTY-FIVE

As Pete spun round, Catalina met his astonished gaze with one of icy pragmatism. He stood open mouthed, doing his impression of a spectator at a tennis match as he looked backwards and forwards between the assassin and the victim, on whose side two red stains were spreading. "What have you done?" It might have ranked as the least incisive question of that whole sorry expedition and got the answer it deserved.

"I thought it was pretty obvious. I didn't want to stand here listening to whether you did or didn't love her."

Pete pointed towards the lake. "I meant why did you kill her? Why? Why!? You knew the plan." He sounded desperate. "What did you do? Give her a 'goodnight sweetheart' dose of adama; just a tiny bit too much? I just wanted her out of the way for a while; long enough for everyone to go a bit nuts and give me the opportunity to kill that fucking photographer. She was still alive when I took her up to the citadel."

"Yes, leaving her alive was the bit of your plan that didn't appeal to me."

He nodded in recognition of something. "I thought your behaviour was a bit strange today. You seemed distracted; edgy. I put it down to your nerves at having to get involved in something like this at all, but now I see you were just like a cat on a hot tin roof." He heard the pun on her name – strange how the perverse mind grasped at irrelevant minutiae in moments of stress – but for once he was not in the mood to be flippant. "No wonder you didn't want me coming up here just now. But what did you think – I wouldn't find out? The Professor wasn't the only one keen to take another look up here. When I saw that she hadn't returned to the camp by the time I got back, I had a feeling something had changed."

She came and stood in front of him, green eyes blazing. God she was beautiful, but he had failed to recognise just how deep her passions ran. "Did you think I was going to let the two of you kiss and make up?

195

You're mine," – she hissed the words – "and you told me I was yours. Why should I have let her live? I call it a win-win scenario – for me; I might have lost you to her, but now I can't, even if you hate me forever.

"After we'd reached Dirk on the radio, I came up here and broke her neck. She told me you were a bit of an expert in tae kwon-do. In that case you'd have been proud of the side kick I used – the arrival of Koreans in Argentina in the 1980s sparked something in us." Her eyes seemed lost in the past for a moment.

"Did any relatives of Lee Harvey Oswald move there as well?"

She ignored him and refocussed. "Then I thought, where could she have slipped? She'd already done it here once in front of everyone, so it seemed perfect."

"Remind me never to piss you off."

"Exactly."

"I thought you seemed less distraught when I told you about Robbie's death than you were when he first went missing. You'd killed by then. Must have toughened you up."

"No, I just didn't need to try making you jealous anymore. Besides, I have killed before." Pete was aware his mouth had fallen open. "Nothing the bastard didn't deserve. There's nothing like having a tag-along hiker try to rape you in the Outback to focus your mind. I don't know to this day whether they ever found him – that's the risk you take when you choose a remote spot to try to sexually assault someone."

Pete looked at her, quite lost in another netherworld for a few moments, and she looked him straight back in the eye, then put her hand up and placed it on his chest. "But isn't this what we wanted? And am I any worse than you? You killed them – I killed her." She squeezed her fingers like claws against his chest and her eyes smouldered. "The jealousy you felt when she fucked Jim – multiply it by a hundred and you'll know how I felt when I saw you were jealous."

He took her hand from his chest and saw the hurt register in her eyes. "But it was all falling into our laps. Yes, I felt a twinge of jealousy, but only in a selfish way. There is..." he looked into the lake, "... was no love there. It was who she chose to fuck that did my head in, and the way she threw herself at him."

"Then what's the problem?!" He felt her strength as she tried to pull her hand from his, but he was going to show her who was in charge now.

"I'd photographed them. I could have used that to get a very favourable divorce settlement. She's a wealthy woman. Now the investigation into her death and potentially the lack of remains will take years, and there'll be no inheritance. She didn't know you'd drugged her food. I just wanted her out of the way. It was all falling into place so well. Fate had even dealt me a couple of kind hands – finding the k'ib and getting the chance to turn the Afrikaner prick into a piece of collateral damage. All it needed now was for her to wander out of the forest, or for us to find her. She wouldn't have been any the wiser; would probably have thought she'd been kidnapped by some of our shaman friends. Now there's every chance a search party would come and find the bodies."

"Well, nobody knows to find them here, thanks to the Professor."

Pete noticed that her eyes didn't even flicker as she mentioned the man she'd just shot in cold blood, whose body lay no more than ten feet from where they now stood. Then he frowned as he mulled over her comment. "No, the best form of defence is attack; if we try denying things and it turns out we lied, how'll that make us look? Besides, Candice knows something – I'm not sure how much, but I can't take any chances. I'm sure there's enough evidence in Sutch's study to lead someone here eventually. Then there's Dirk."

Catalina gave an abstract smile, devoid of humour and warmth. "You can fly a plane."

Pete actually blinked in surprise. "Like I said, remind me never to piss you off."

"Hey, have you forgotten? We've killed already. The way to Hell beckons. What's one more?"

"The blood-lust's getting to you. Don't forget, the airfield will know where Dirk's heading."

"But it's a huge ocean. He could've ditched anywhere."

"He'll have given his route. They'll know what direction he was taking, and they won't assume it was Antarctica."

"You're being very cautious. It's not like you."

"I wasn't a murderer before. Nor sleeping with one."

She grinned again at his comment. How could cruelty look so fair? The twitch in his loins caught Pete off guard, as did her next suggestion. "We could fly off somewhere, till it all dies down."

"We'd have to refuel and they'd want some I.D. It's not so easy to just disappear in this day and age."

"I know some people in Oz. They like bypassing the law whenever possible. They could help us."

"We might get back to Oz without refuelling, or we might not. But even if we could, I don't want to involve anyone else. Our strength lies in the secrecy of the original expedition. No, I'm going to stick with the idea that's forming."

"Pete?" He'd turned his back on her and walked off.

"Just let me think for a minute."

It was clear from her voice that she was stung. "Hey, I'm sorry if I spoiled your plan to play happy families again."

He spun round. "I told you not to come when you phoned me that night at the dinner party."

"She'd asked me. I didn't plan to kill her. Besides, when I called I didn't know you'd be on the expedition; didn't even know what it was all about. I just wanted to get closer to the enemy; find out about her, and through her find out what really made you tick. Seems I was harbouring the false hope that you might want me forever."

Now she seemed struck by a thought, crossed to the Professor's body and took the k'ib from his hand. It might have been a trick of the light, but Pete could have sworn it pulsed for a moment. Perhaps deadly passion drew something from it! She held it up: "And forever is what we have in our grasp. I heard your conversation with the old fool. You believe in this, don't you?"

Pete's eyes narrowed and he came forward. "Give me that."

She pulled it away from his reach, held it in teasing manner behind her back. "I see you do." She smiled and then handed over the k'ib. "You never really had a plan, did you? You came here seeking... what, another adrenaline rush?"

He looked down – she was wiser than he had imagined. "Yes, I came in curiosity, I'll be honest; I also needed a bit of time away from the hurricane of our affair just to think – work out where you and I went from there. We couldn't have carried on like that; we'd have burnt each other out. That's why I was so pissed off when you disobeyed me and showed up. But then things just started to fall into place. Her unfaithfulness gave me the chance I needed to be rid of her and that prick the photographer at the same time. The rock-spider was collateral damage; whether he had insulted me or not, he had to go. And fortune and glory showed up as well." He brandished the k'ib to emphasise his point, then retrieved his rucksack, dug into a side pocket and, pulling out his cigarettes, offered her one. She took it. He saw her hands were steady – they must have been, to shoot the old man with such clinical accuracy. As they stood there, Pete wondered just for a moment whether this was a dream conjured by the island; two hedonists drawing deep on cigarettes amidst carnage of their own making in a forest in the kingdom of the dead. If Dali had nightmares, this might have been the stuff of which they were made.

"So, I didn't really figure in your plans." Catalina broke the thought-pause. "You didn't really need me... until you did. Till I happened to mention that one of the plants flourishing in this dead place was adama. Only then did I have a use, other than as your fuck-buddy."

He stepped up to her and saw sadness flit across her eyes. No way was she a child of Australia. Her face reflected the moodiness of Tierra del Fuego, not the constant heat of the desert. She had said on the plane over that she was Latin American by blood. There was sweat on her top lip and in the hollow of her neck. "How can we trust each other?"

"Look around you." She made an almost casual gesture with the cigarette. "How can we not?"

"How do you know I won't just kill you?"

"Ditto." She threw down the cigarette and ground it with her shoe. Then a lascivious look gleamed in her eyes and she started to unbutton her shirt. "But I know you won't harm me – you prefer fucking me. And if your fuck-buddy for life is what I must settle for, that's cool." Her cleavage appeared in the opening of the shirt and she gestured with a disdainful toss of the head towards the pool. "Why did you want her kept alive? Did you enjoy betraying her?"

He was aroused despite everything around them, and her eyes took in that arousal. She dropped the open shirt over her shoulders. She looked magnificent. He grabbed the front of the shirt to pinion her arms and they kissed each other as if it was an act of brutality. Then they pulled apart, breathless.

She looked across at the lake. "Did it turn you on to fuck me and then go home to her? Well now let's do it in front of her."

Pete was teetering on the edge of a black gorge that might have been the rest of his life. He had free-fallen into deep caves in Mexico where the bottom was hidden in shadow hundreds of feet below. Being the lover of Catalina, he could see, was like doing it without the parachute.

He could not have guessed, right then, at the irony of that image.

For now, he was left to wonder whether she had him drugged with some other plant known only to her. How else could he explain enjoying the fuck of his life with the woman who killed his wife and father-in-law, while they lay dead just a few feet away?

CHAPTER THIRTY-SIX

After the unreasoning madness of sex had passed, he waited for the shame to kick in, but it did not. Then he looked at the k'ib and wondered whether it would decide his fate from this moment forth.

He watched Catalina smoking a post-coital cigarette. He guessed they belonged to each other now, but if greed and lust were the twin pillars of the temple at which he worshipped, then this raven-haired, green-eyed, uninhibited killer might as well be the goddess. And neither of them could risk leaving the other; whatever the nature of the prize he had stolen from the universe, it would not keep either of them out of jail, so he guessed they had an understanding there.

As fatigue started to hit him, the pendulum of his thoughts swung from the future to the past; to the day he had first set eyes on her, at that university Freshers' Ball, which he had attended under duress at Jane's bidding.

They had caught each other's eye too many times not to speak at the bar afterwards. Her brazenness had thrown him; a combustible mix of her South American fire and Australian forthrightness.

***

KING'S COLLEGE, CAMBRIDGE, SEPTEMBER 1997

"So, what are you studying?" he asks.

She raises one eyebrow. "You. And Botany."

She has caught him off balance. For one absurd moment he is tempted to come back with a stupid rhyme about being lost for a riposte but regains his senses. They look at each other for an eternity of slow seconds, and then he places his drink on the bar and says: "Well, I'm not very good at this sort of thing, so I'm gonna shoot." But he does not move.

"Eats, shoots and leaves," she says.

"Something like that."

"We could change that paradigm."

"Meaning?"

She leans up on tiptoes. He smells smoke and shampoo from her hair. "Meaning you could fuck me."

The ball is being held in the debating chamber on the campus. They leave separately and meet up in the darkness of the Arts Faculty building. From the first lecture theatre they are about to enter comes the throaty, rhythmic grunting of somebody already part-way along the path they themselves are intending to take. They look at each other and stifle drunken laughter; then head along the corridor to another room. Once inside, he has his first taste of her; the hunger in her kiss is almost cannibalistic. Then she breaks off, urging him to: "Wait, wait." As if he's going anywhere. She delves into her clutch bag and produces a mirror, though it soon becomes clear how she intends to powder her nose.

He grabs her wrist. "What are you doing?"

"Don't worry, I only use it during sex. Boy, does it make me come!"

He feels unexpected rage; an irrational jealousy, as if he's having to share her. "Somehow, I get the feeling you restrict sex to days that have a 'Y' in them. But if you want me, you do it without that shit. I don't sleep with coke-heads." He stuffs the items back into her bag and tosses it across the room.

"Who the fuck...?" She raises a hand to strike him.

He grabs her wrist. "You wanna come, I'll make you come."

He is as good as his word. But not once, even when it has become almost unbearable for her and the sensitivity of her nerve-endings has her thrashing like a speared fish in its death throes, does she plead for him to stop.

His is not the only seed sown that night. A pattern is set; the need for danger. Jane's frequent absences make life easy for the lovers, but it takes away the thrill of deception. They find, like countless generations before them, that the chance of discovery gives their physical relationship an edge. So, for those times when his wife is back from her travels, his addiction to gambling is born. It's the perfect excuse; back in the early hours and always short of money. But what gives him the biggest kick of all as he slips into bed beside his wife is the knowledge that he has deceived both her and her patronising prick of a father. On those rare occasions when she welcomes him back with more than just open arms, he savours the knowledge that she is, literally, up against stiff competition.

Though there is no denying that sex with Catalina registers on the Richter Scale, she develops a worrying trend; an increasing need to be told that he loves her. When he discovers that she switched from Botany to Archaeology to get closer to him via Jane, he starts to hear the sound of bunnies boiling. So, when she calls him at the Professor's dinner party on the eve of their departure, to tell him that she has been asked to join the expedition, he instructs her not to accept and determines that he will go – it's the perfect opportunity for a few days' break from her. Besides, the stab of possessiveness he feels at his wife's ill-concealed flirtation with the photographer has surprised him. However, it does not blind him to opportunity. He can kill two birds with one stone.

Except Catalina arrives at Heathrow Airport after all. He punishes her in the only way he knows, by freezing her out. She tries hard to conceal her dismay, but he knows her eyes well enough by now.

Then things start to happen, which he guesses are typical of a man. Like a dog in the manger, he grows jealous of the burgeoning friendship between Catalina and the other two students. They won't be tasting that honey pot if he can help it. And when he catches her furtive glances in his direction, his confidence grows. There had been a time during their... he guessed 'relationship' was the only word that fitted... when he'd felt he was losing control, but now he has it back. At one point during the flight, he makes a discreet gesture towards her neck, reminding her of her love of being choked during sex. She blushes uncontrollably. He has the power.

Then such jealousy as he feels for Jane turns to contempt when she surrenders her cunt to that photographer cunt no more than half a mile from the camp. A plan forms. The rest – of the team at least – is history.

***

THE PRESENT

"What's the matter?" She said it with such insouciance – almost a weariness beyond her years as she exhaled smoke – that he was taken aback. She had known he was watching her. That scared him. As did her apparent ability to read his mind: "You wondering what an eternity with me will be like?"

He watched with envy as she took another calm drag on her cigarette. How could she be so at peace when minutes before her cries had threatened to wake the dead?

202

"I knew the answer to that from the very first time you whispered your dark longings in my ear."

She turned and looked at him. "Meaning?"

"Meaning you're a mirror in which I see my own soul."

The reply seemed to appeal to her and she turned away, smiling. But for Pete, there was no pleasure in what he saw – his reflection revealed damaged goods, and she was the price.

Despite, or perhaps because of everything that had happened, he found himself struggling to keep his eyes open. Maybe Morpheus was being merciful.

***

Sleep must indeed have taken him, because he felt himself being shaken awake.

"Pete... Pete! I think we need to move."

"What?" Lumpy concrete poured from the mixer in his throat. "How long have I been asleep?"

"Six or seven hours, I think. Me too. But—"

"Shit!" He rubbed his eyes, sat up and looked at his watch. "We've got to get..." he hesitated, "... things sorted out before Dirk arrives."

Catalina was looking pale. "That's not really my concern right now. Look. Can you see it?"

She seemed to be pointing into the trees and his eyes were still gritty. "I can't see anything."

"There," she wiggled her finger for emphasis, "through the gap."

He could just make out the sea if he peered at a certain angle between the branches. The waves were not as choppy as before. At last, he saw what she was pointing to and though he could not make out the detail, his heart froze. It looked like there might be a boat coming round the headland of Temple Island.

He sprang to his feet and rummaged in his rucksack, pulling out a pair of field glasses. At first all he could see were the swooping blurs of the furthest branches moving in the sea breeze, but then into focus came a very bad dream.

"Shit!" He fired out the word several more times in rapid succession, like a rocket launcher, while still looking through the glasses. "We have to move."

"That's what I just said." Catalina's response was testy.

"Yeah, but you didn't know why."

"Well, what is it then?" She'd guessed it was a boat but hadn't thought to use the binoculars. "Cobus? Jim? Are they still alive?"

Pete lowered the glasses and looked at her; for the first time since she had known him, Catalina saw fear in his eyes. "It's worse than that. Better get a coin ready; it's the fucking ferryman."

He handed her the glasses and she saw what he meant. "Oh my God! Is that him?" Catalina knew the answer to her own question already. Pete had spoken of the high priest as if he were the very embodiment of ancient evil; that seemed like a good description of what was making its way towards them now. Even from this distance his sense of dark purpose was palpable.

"I thought... he must have had another boat."

The cowled figure stood in the boat, propelling it forward with long, easy strokes of a single paddle. Then he looked up and Catalina caught sight of a hard mouth and a wicked contortion of the jaw that might have been a grin, a grimace or a death rictus, set in a dark face both young and of immeasurable age. It was a mercy that the eyes remained hidden, but there was no doubting his intention.

"There's not much time." Pete looked around in with urgency. "C'mon, back to the camp. He found the k'ib and placed it back into his rucksack, almost unable to believe that lust had caused it to slip his mind with such ease. That was a salutary lesson if ever.

"What about the bodies?" asked Catalina.

"No time for that now, and no need."

"You have a plan?"

"Hey – it's me." He looked up at the sky. "Let's hope your fellow countryman's on time."

She was too scared to find his self-confidence reassuring.

CHAPTER THIRTY-SEVEN

OFF THE COAST OF TEMPLE ISLAND, OCTOBER 31ST 1997

He knew that the k'ib was still there on the other island, and his strength had not yet failed him. After millennia taking the water of life, its effect would not fade so soon. Now, the nearer he drew, the more he could feel the dust in his veins stirring.

He had used his ancient wits, where the others had not. Though they might not yet be dead, they were trapped, and their strength would leave them. They were doomed. Perhaps it was best so. They were nothing now but decadent parasites, following him in blind faith without once questioning their purpose, while their traditions and beliefs neared extinction.

But he was the keeper of the k'ib. He needed no other purpose. It was as if the k'ib knew and that was why he was the only one who had escaped from the labyrinth. Why only he could reclaim the prize. He had been so close to his prey, but once the thief had used some more of this new world's powerful magic to block the tunnel, `Ak'ubal had used his knowledge of the labyrinth to find his way back to the far side of the island.

In water lay memory, and though he had not left Temple Island since that day of arrival long, long ago, some instinct in him seemed to remember that he had once been but a humble fisherman, before destiny had chosen him. It seemed the innate skill with the boat had never left him and he paddled with ease.

He could feel the call of his heart from the other island. For an instant, during his escape from the destruction in the temple, he had felt a faint pulsing, just a fluttering, and knew for certain where he must head, though he could have guessed. But it was as if the k'ib called him. Strange – it would survive without him, find a new master, but their fates had been intertwined for so long now, it was as if history would have to start all over again if they were torn apart.

And yet despite that, his senses were almost overcome by a powerful surge of memories reawakening in the daylight. For how long had he denied himself this air, this sea, as he guarded the darkness, scared of the light from a changing world? Once he had reclaimed the k'ib, he would think on the question: what next for Kaz'khar, the last survivor, the final living remnant of prehistory?

***

Once they were back down in the camp, as both of them cast anxious glances out towards the still-distant but menacing figure, Pete gave his instructions: "Kick some things around; make it look like there was a scuffle. I'm going to inflate the other boat."

"Why?"

"Just do it."

As the boat exploded into life, he watched Catalina knock over a few pots and throw some items around. "That'll do. Now help me put some stones into the spare boat – big ones; enough to sink it properly when we're at sea. We'll put the guns in there as well."

That being done, he instructed her to grab something warm and the sat-phone.

Out at sea, the hunter had closed about a quarter of the distance.

Catalina stopped and looked puzzled. "Surely we—"

"Just do what I say. It's not just His Supreme Blackness we're racing against here." Pete searched for and found a first-aid kit and a couple of bottles of water, as well as a GPS tracker. He showed it to Catalina. "Dirk'll pick us up on this if nothing else."

"But we have the sat-phone?"

"We're ditching that."

"Why?" She sounded confused and a bit panicky. "I'm not happy at the thought of bobbing around in a dinghy on the Southern Ocean with no means of communication."

"He took it with him – Jim – along with the guns."

"Can't we at least take the dry suits?"

"Nope. We managed to escape but didn't have time or the chance to kit up properly."

A faint light of comprehension started to flicker in the girl's eyes. "Okay, I get your drift... I think. Jim saw what you would call fortune and glory."

Pete nodded: "Remember, it was all down to the outlandish powers of this place – he could not resist. Jim has travelled the world and not succumbed to greed before, so we have to emphasise that it was as if a spell had been cast."

Catalina picked up the thread: "He returned to camp – told us Robbie and Cobus were still doing a recce, but it was dangerous and he needed guns, explosives, the whole shebang, as he wanted no part of it, and they would do the same to us." She looked at the mess she had made in the camp. "There was a fight; we all ran, but Jim or Cobus shot the Professor. Jane will have died by accident when she slipped or something. You and I got away, hid, then made our escape."

"Correct, my girl. There's just one factor I didn't allow for." He pointed across the sea towards the immediate problem. "We probably don't have all that much juice on the boats, and he won't stop coming after us if we just try to outrun him. In fact, he can probably outrace us if it comes to paddling. So, we let him come to us a bit and then we sink him."

"Why don't we just kill him?"

"I'm not sure there are enough bullets left in this." He shook the rifle and looked out to sea yet again. It was not an encouraging sight to see a centuries-old, vengeful shaman coming to take back the holy relic that you had stolen from him, and just for a moment Pete was unnerved. "If the other priests were anything to go by, this one won't die easy. He'd be like your worst nightmare, refusing to lie down." He looked across at the approaching boat. "But I'm willing to bet he can drown."

He turned back to their camp and saw Catalina looking at him. He could tell she was pinning all her hopes on him keeping calm. That threw him a little, given the iciness of her recent actions. Perhaps there was a still a place for the muscular, sexist male in the universe after all! With that in mind, he moved on: "Okay, it's time to move, while he's still far enough out." He had attached the inflatables together with a length of rope. "Let's get these into the water."

Once out into the shallows, they clambered into one boat. Pete fired the motor, and they skittered out into deeper waters. Soon they were within a hundred yards of the spectre.

The cowled figure stopped paddling.

Fifty yards.

Forty.

Pete killed the motor, and they bobbed perhaps thirty yards from that vision of Hell.

With a sudden pseudo-theatrical sweep of the hand, the dark man threw back his hood. Catalina gasped and buried her face in her hands, while Pete felt his body shudder. The high priest reached a hand towards them, the gesture looking like nothing so much as the Phantom of the Opera when he was unmasked in the old Lon Chaney movie. Pete felt the darkness of that ancient soul touch him as it had in the temple a few hours before.

Now the cruel mouth was moving, and guttural sounds crossed the void of water and time.

Pete's skin crawled. "Catalina." Her face remained hidden and he nudged her with his foot. "Catalina!" She managed to drag her eyes upwards, but he saw she had put her fingers in her ears. "What's he saying?" She ignored him and dropped her gaze again, shaking her head.

Pete took a deep breath, raised his rifle and, not without a moment's hesitation, or perhaps even unexpected regret, fired. The semi-automatic splintered the side of the wooden boat below the waterline and it started to sink. For a moment something seemed to drag at their own boat. Pete looked at his rucksack, wondering. Then he watched as the high priest looked around him in panic. His mouth opened, the bottom jaw falling away at an impossible angle, and a cry issued from it, which had no place on their Earth. Pete copied Catalina, putting his fingers in his ears. With that, the corvine figure leapt into the water and started to swim towards them.

"Fuck!" Pete gave a hurried pull of the cord engine. "C'mon; c'mon!" It misfired. Was it out of juice? Twice, three times – still nothing. And the priest, though weighed down by his sodden robe, was closing the gap. There was a keening sound, which seemed to be emanating from Catalina. Pete almost laughed; felt as if he was standing outside himself for a moment looking at a ludicrous B-movie, where the director was using every cinematographic cliché to crank up the tension – and in keeping with that, as if on cue, the engine coughed into life. Pete took off towards Temple Island. When he turned again, the bowsprit of the little boat was disappearing below the water and their attacker was nowhere to be seen in the choppy waves. He nudged Catalina, who surfaced from the world into which she had been trying to retreat. Pete pointed towards the wooden boat's death throes, then sank down and started to laugh. He recognised the note of hysteria in the sound, and it infected the girl, who sobbed with relief.

Now Pete remembered something and looked up at the sky to the north and east. Still clear. Still time!

"Catalina." She looked at him through tear-stained eyelashes and he saw in that look his complete mastery of her. *Better make the most of it,* he thought, *she'll want to start pulling the strings soon enough.* For a distracted split-second he was almost tempted to pitch her over the side, but decided he stood a better chance of avoiding suspicion if he wasn't the sole survivor of this expedition. "We've still got plenty to do. First, let's sink the other boat. We're out over deep water now."

She untied the rope. "Are you sure we should be doing this? What if anything happens to *our* boat?"

"C'mon old girl, engage brain. Jim and Cobus would have taken one boat for themselves. I can see we're going to have to work on getting our story straight." He looked over at Temple Island; the pall of smoke and dust has cleared. "Remember, we don't know where they ended up. It doesn't have to be Temple Island they went to. No-one need ever know what they found, or where. They certainly wouldn't have told us."

Then Pete fired four shots into the spare inflatable and it was soon pulled down into the depths. "Time to lose these as well." He pitched the rifle and sat-phone after it. At least Catalina saw the sense of that – after all, the others would have just grabbed a boat and fled. She was about to throw her pistol away when Pete stopped her. "You're a good shot. Shoot me."

"What!"

"When we ran away, Jim shot at us and hit me. Shoot me in the arm – from behind. I'll get over it."

"I knew shooting the heads off snakes would come in useful sometime." The slight, sardonic smile that twitched at her mouth showed the old Catalina might be starting to resurface. She raised the pistol and took aim. They looked at each other. Something passed between them. An awareness, perhaps, of the fine thread that tied the twin eternities of life and damnation. By aiming to the right, she could sever it with more ease than she had untied the spare boat, and one of them would have been drawn down into the void. The question was, who?

Pete turned and waited.

"Perfect!" The word was little more than a gravelly expulsion of breath, such was the pain as she hit him in the exact spot he had indicated and the bullet exited, leaving a clean wound. He let it bleed for a while, soaking his shirt sleeve for some visual impact before asking Catalina to fasten his belt like a tourniquet while he swallowed some pain killers. Next, he took the pistol and threw it overboard. "It's the same gun that shot the Professor. The bullet wounds should look the same, but we don't need to make it any easier for the authorities." He puffed out his cheeks. "Okay, old girl, now let's head further out to sea." He used his good arm to start the motor. "We'll keep going till the fuel's out, then we'll just have to wait."

"Can't we go back to the camp and wait?"

"Either we'd have buried the bodies of the Professor and Jane out of respect, or we'd still be hiding, fearing the return of gun-totin' Jesse James."

"You're right, of course." She sank back against the side of the boat but then sat up again. "But there's one flaw in your plan; why would Jim have left a boat behind for us to steal?"

Pete scratched his chin. "Because he got complacent. He took the sat-phone so we'd have no means of communication, not knowing you'd already got through to Dirk while he was off on his own selfish mission. Are you sure Dirk's coming, by the way?"

"It was a crap connection, but yup, he knows we're in trouble."

"I'm guessing that elliptical message works in our favour now – Dirk won't really know what was going on."

"So, what will happen if anyone comes back to try to find Jim, but finds nothing?"

"Who knows? Perhaps he took his chance with the lack of fuel. Faced with the Devil or the deep blue sea, he chose the latter and sank. Who cares? Just relax, Catty. As long as you and I stick to our story, we'll be fine. After all, there's nothing to link you and me prior to this. We're just two members of an ill-fated, ill-prepared expedition. If our shared adventure brings us closer together after this, who'd be surprised."

Catalina leaned back again against the side of the boat and there was a certain admiration in her voice: "Well, I have to admit, you seem to have all the bases covered. You thought hard and fast there." Pete saw her smile become arch. She pushed herself towards him and her hand rested at the top of his thigh. "Talking of hard and fast, have you got any plans for when the motor dies?"

Later, Pete enjoyed the unique experience of indulging in a little plane-spotting rather than sex. Otherwise, even his quick mind would have had difficulty explaining that particular scenario to Dirk.

CHAPTER THIRTY-EIGHT

"Look, we've gotta get him away from here; he's lost a lot of blood!" She had to shout above the noise of the engines and the pounding of the sea, which had grown quite a bit rougher in the last hour.

"But the Professor, Jane, the others—"

"They're gone, Dirk, they're all gone. The Professor and Jane are dead! I don't know where the others are." She decided their story could wait until they were away from here. A surge caught the inflatable and nearly threw it against the floats of the plane. "Look, for God's sake, get us on board!" They had brought the boat a few miles north of the archipelago. Once the fuel had run out, and the sea had grown wilder, their anxiety had gone up several notches. The edge of hysteria in Catalina's voice was real enough.

Dirk threw them a rope and reeled the boat in. Catalina saw just how clever Pete had been. He had lost enough blood to look pale and his stained, gory shirt meant the sight of him would prompt Dirk to take action. Nevertheless, she knew his apparent state of semi-consciousness was an act. There was no love lost between the pilot and his injured passenger; Dirk was probably tempted to go look for the Professor's body, but he could not deny a sick man a flight back to civilisation – he was too professional for that.

When they had managed between them to haul Pete aboard the plane, followed by the deflated boat, Dirk eyed them both up. "What the hell's happened? How did Jane and the Professor die?"

Catalina saw now that Dirk himself was pale. "Jim killed them."

"What?!"

"It's a long story, Dirk," Catalina started to wipe her eyes with the back of her hand, "and I don't feel ready to tell it right now."

211

"And Robbie?"

"Please Dirk," she sobbed.

"Where are their bodies?"

"On the island – the Professor and Jane at least."

"Well, I'm going back for them."

"Dirk, for God's sake, we've gotta get Pete to a hospital. And that fucking maniac could be back at the camp by now. I wouldn't rate your chances of getting away alive – they'd want your plane for sure."

"But I can't just leave my friends there." The Aussie was looking through the door towards the horizon. There was a mixture of emotions on his face, none of them winning the battle to form an expression.

Catalina saw her chance. "I know Pete's not your friend..."

He gave her a sharp look. "Hey, I wasn't saying—"

She pushed on through: "... but you strike me as a guy who lives in the here-and-now. Well here and now, we're alive, one of us is wounded, and we're both possibly just the tiniest bit traumatised," her tone had taken on a suitably sarcastic edge, "so I, for one, would like to get the hell away from here."

"I know, but—"

Catalina put a hand on Dirk's arm. The coldness that sometimes extinguished the fire in her heart wondered how he would feel if he knew, that same hand had fired the gun that killed his friend, and helped her balance while she delivered the blow that broke Jane's neck. It would have been happy enough to shoot the big Aussie too, if she'd had her way. "Dirk." She turned her tearful, jungle-green eyes towards him. "They're dead. If you must come back, come armed, and bring the relevant authorities."

"Okay sweetheart, I guess you're right." He looked at Pete. "There's some brandy in the first-aid box; better bring him some." Dirk puffed out his cheeks. "To be honest, I don't think I'd have the fuel to make another landing. Let's get away from this hell-hole for now."

***

PERTH, WESTERN AUSTRALIA, AFTERNOON NOVEMBER 1ST 1997

"So, he just turned?" queried Dirk.

Catalina looked to Pete for support. Dirk had brought a field doctor he knew to his place that morning, rather than go to a hospital. He thought it best to avoid the publicity for the moment.

"There was something about that place." Pete swallowed hard. "The forest kind of... played with everyone's heads. It was silent as the grave. There wasn't a trace of life in there. I don't know whether it got to Jim a bit. Also to the Professor; he seemed to withdraw into himself. Everyone seemed on edge somehow. But things weren't helped by Jim going around telling everyone that he didn't believe in fairy tales; that he'd seen enough of the brutal realities of life to ignore make-believe, which I guess was a reference to the Professor's story of the lost kingdom and its secret."

"Secret?"

Pete winced as he leaned across to pick up the glass of water by his chair. He washed down the second pain killer. It bought him important time to gather his lies into a presentable package, wrapped in half-truths. He knew Dirk would return to the archipelago, possibly find certain things that would incriminate the two of them if the story wasn't watertight – there was always a chance they hadn't covered all bases. Also, experience had taught him that the thing a liar needed above all was a good memory. The closer he could stick to events, the less he would need to rely on recall. "After a day of hacking and sweating our way through dense forest, everyone was in low spirits. On the second day, there were two discoveries: we found the ruins of an ancient city and the Professor found a body, which turned out to be the old merchant, Tariq. He had documents on him claiming that there was still human life on the islands and implying that those people were some of the original settlers."

"You're shitting me."

"I shit you not. He said that water from one of the islands could give the gift of eternal life."

Dirk said nothing, but Pete could see it was only deference to his old friend Sutch that stopped him from snorting in derision.

"It was around then that Jim told the Professor he wanted to do his own thing; take one of the boats and scout around the other islands. Sutch suggested they had already made an important find and should record everything in detail before wasting valuable time and resources elsewhere. After all, it was a preliminary expedition. But I guess Jim had other ideas. He saw fortune and glory.

"He also seemed to have quite some influence on Cobus and Robbie, who wanted to go with him. It's not surprising really; they're young and impressionable, he's a Pulitzer Prize winner—"

Dirk frowned. "I don't get it. The students all held the Professor in the highest regard. Why would they go against him?"

"Like I said, you had to be in that place to know how it felt. It played with your mind. Perhaps they wanted to see if any of the other islands were less... suffocating.

"Whatever the reason, perhaps to avoid a scene, the Professor allowed them to take one of the boats. But he made sure the guns and explosives stayed where they were, under lock and key. Jim tried getting the rest of us to go with him, but my wife's loyalties were to her father, and my loyalties were to my wife."

"My loyalties were with Jane as well." Catalina seemed to feel it was safe to chip in. She had left all the talking to Pete, fearing to say anything that might tangle the roots of his nascent story. "After all, she picked me for this trip. Plus, I thought we females should show solidarity."

Pete continued: "Anyway, they didn't come back that night. That was why, at first light, we contacted you. As a split party we were never going to achieve anything. But the Professor was also worried about the welfare of Robbie and Cobus – Jim perhaps less so, given his insurrection."

"This is crazy. I can't quite believe it. Why would Jim do this? He seemed a level-headed guy."

"Dirk, how many times do we have to say, the island had a peculiar effect on you." Catalina struggled to conceal her growing irritation. "The Outback messes with your head, but this place hung all around you like a black curtain, as if bad things were just waiting to happen on the other side."

"Who knows." Again, Pete took over, still feeling some slight concern that the girl's feisty spirit might lead to a misplaced step on their path of lies. "Maybe it messed with Jim's mind. He'd seen a lot of bad shit in his time. Who knows what he'd been bottling up, just needing some catalyst to spark a reaction. Really, I can hardly believe it myself. But the worst is to come."

Dirk raised a hand. "Sorry, I interrupted. Carry on."

"Not long after we called you, Jim did show up again... on his own. We were up by a waterfall we'd found, washing ourselves and he came marching up, not making a hell of a lot of sense, with a strange look in his eye. He said that he'd discovered something amazing. He was going to need more guns, ammunition, explosives, and he also wanted to take some kit away to set up another camp. Only thing was, he didn't seem inclined to share why, or where. But I think he underestimated the Professor. My father-in-law didn't get to lead teams around the world and be who he is... was... without having a backbone. He told Jim that – how did he put it? – this wasn't a pick'n'mix expedition. He'd organised it, paid for it, was more than happy to invite input, but he was in charge. He certainly wasn't about to hand over the keys to the gun-box or the explosives.

"You know yourself, Dirk, there wasn't a hope in hell of breaking open those boxes and Jim knew it too. So, this was where our photographer friend showed his true colours. He claimed to have left Cobus and Robbie doing a further recce on the other island and that if the Professor didn't hand over the keys, he'd leave them there. The Prof was shocked, but he wasn't simply going to back down. Things got a bit ugly, and Jim's posturing got more and more aggressive. Now Jane stepped forward and told him to back off. He was behaving like a lunatic at this point. He shoved Jane to one side." Pete looked down in his best approximation of grief; an emotion he'd only truly experienced when totalling a Lotus a few years before. "She slipped on the rocks." Catalina placed a reassuring hand on his shoulder. They were working well together, though it would not have surprised Pete if the hand of comfort was also a reminder not to grieve too deeply. It was the hand of a murderess; was she reminding him of that, or was he simply reminding himself? "Her neck must have snapped. The next thing we know, she's lying under the water. I rushed forward to see if she was okay, to pull her out of the pool. I didn't see what happened next."

"But I did," Catalina interjected. "Both the Professor and Jim stood there shocked – I don't think Jim meant to kill her. In fact, Pete didn't notice it, but he seemed to have taken quite a shine to her."

Pete glanced at her. It was a look that could have been interpreted as surprise, but he was wondering what the hell she was doing. This was dangerous. It meant he could have had a motive for killing his wife. Was she sending him a message? She continued before he could react further. "But even as Pete was struggling down the rocks to try to get to the pool, the Professor turned on Jim. He might have been an old man, but he came forward full of rage. The next thing I heard was two shots..." She buried her head in her hands and her next words came muffled through her fingers. "... he – Jim – shot that poor man."

There was silence in the room. Dirk squeezed his thumb and forefinger against his eyes. It must all have seemed unbelievable – but hopefully not too much so. He would be questioning just how wrong something could go. How could one old man's dream turn into this mayhem and murder? What had gone on down there on the island? He looked at the two survivors. "How did Jim have a gun if the Professor wouldn't allow him access to the gun-box?"

Pete thought on his feet, though he was annoyed with himself for not having covered that ground. "We posted guards each night. It had been Jim's turn the first night with Cobus. He must have already been hatching his plans, so made sure he didn't return the gun in the morning."

"How did you two get away?"

Pete wasn't sure he liked the tone of the question but decided to keep that to himself. There was no point giving anyone a glimpse of your cards when you held the aces. "I saw this was only going one way. For a moment after he'd shot the Professor, Jim seemed almost catatonic, as if he, too, couldn't quite believe what had happened. I saw that was our only chance. I grabbed Catalina and ran. The next thing I know it felt like someone's hit me on the arm with a rock. I kept running – I think I'm more aware than some of the staying-power you get from chemicals in your body. When I was in Miami once, I remember seeing this guy being chased by the cops; he was so full of barbiturates they literally had to pump fifteen bullets into him to bring him down. Anyway, I heard a couple more shots rip into the trees around us, but for some reason he didn't follow us. Maybe he thought it'd be a waste of energy, or bullets. Or maybe he just realised we had nowhere to go. He had access to the keys for the guns and explosives now. Perhaps whatever he'd discovered was consuming him, and he couldn't wait to get back.

"We hid in the forest for hours, but didn't hear the boat leave, so assumed he was still around. We knew we'd have to come out; find some way of letting you know where we were. Also, my wound had bled a lot and I was feeling weak. That was when we had a change of fortune. We crept back towards the camp. It seemed deserted. The guns and the sat-phone had gone, as had some of the food. Either we just hadn't heard the motor, or he'd decided to save fuel by paddling back. But we couldn't believe it when we saw he'd left the other boat."

"Why do you think that was?" Again, Pete imagined – *was it imagination?* – an undertone of suspicion in Dirk's voice. But wasn't that only to be expected? People he cared about were dead, and someone he held in ill-concealed contempt had survived. Perhaps it was just despair, not doubt. But there was no denying; Dirk looked like someone who'd been left with a pan full of dirt when he'd been prospecting for gold.

Pete shrugged and then grimaced as the movement sent pain through his shoulder. "Perhaps he just wasn't thinking straight."

"D'ya think?"

Pete reached for his cigarettes and chose not to take the bait. "I'll give you that one." He pushed himself up, wobbled a bit and started to make his way outside for a smoke. He turned at the door. "Whatever the reason, we got out of there, and that was our next bit of luck. So, here we are." He stepped outside and lit up.

Dirk rubbed his chin. "What about the bodies – I mean the Professor and Jane?" He directed the question at Catalina, but Pete answered from the porch. "They're still where they fell – or at least that's where we last saw them. We didn't get a chance to return to them, and bringing them with us was impossible. Of course, Jim may have moved them by now. I mean, he's got to be expecting that someone's going to come back. In fact, he'll probably be calling you as planned. He won't know what's happened to us. And he won't know we had already called you."

"Yeah, but he'll see the boat's gone. He'll know there's a GPS unit in it. I just don't figure how he thought he could get away with this."

"He has the sat-phone. What use is a GPS tracker unit when you're hundreds of miles from anywhere and no-one's expecting you to be there? We're not expected to call in for at least another day. As far as he's concerned we took our chances with the sea. And if somehow we survived, he'll just turn the tables on us." Pete threw down his cigarette, twisted his foot on it angrily and stalked in. "After all, who are you and the rest of the world likely to believe?" He glared at Dirk. "The reputable Mr Jim Bolton, or the playboy Pete Prince? You don't like me; I know that. But Catalina and I have just come through a hell of an ordeal and quite frankly, I'm fed up with questions for now. For Chrissakes, I haven't even been able to bury my dead wife."

With that Pete slumped back down into his chair, then put a hand to his shoulder in pain.

Catalina looked at Dirk. "So, what happens now?"

"One thing's for sure, there's gonna be hell to pay... for someone; Jim by the sounds of it, if we ever catch him. But until we get to the bottom of why this happened, I suggest we keep it quiet."

"We can't just hush this up." Pete winced again as he went to raise his arms in protest. "There are families to tell. Candice."

"Yeah, but nobody's expecting to hear anything for a couple more days. That gives me time to get my head around this; get myself organised so that, at the very least, I can get back out there with a couple of well-armed buddies, bring the Prof and Jane home and... take it from there I guess." Dirk looked out of the window, as if he couldn't quite believe his dead friends weren't standing there, relieving him of the burden of grief. "I'm truly shocked; not just by the deaths, but by how it's happened. If you'd asked me to name three people who struck me as being steady as a rock I'd have said Jim Bolton, Cobus Smuts and Robbie McCulloch. Didn't know any of them well, but that was just first impressions, which I've learnt to rely on." He looked at Pete and Catalina, but said nothing.

Pete felt himself tense. "Meaning?"

Dirk looked long at them, weighing up what to say. "That your – our – confidence and trust was misplaced. Then again, had the Professor got it all wrong? Were they right to try to search elsewhere on the islands and my old friend was too stuck in his ways. Did they just want to make the most of the limited time?" He paused.

Pete realised he couldn't just let that observation go. Was Dirk laying man-traps? "And you think that justifies killing my wife and my father-in-law?" He congratulated himself in silence. They weren't just names; they weren't just people; they were family.

Dirk looked long at him. "No, of course not. Nothing justifies that. Nothing. My apologies – my thoughts are confused and all over the place." He leaned back in his chair. "Anyway, you two've been through a lot. I suggest you rest up here for a couple of days while I get things sorted." He shook his head again. "What a fucking mess. And to tell you the truth, the moment I saw that place I just knew something bad would happen."

Dirk got up and made to leave the living room in which they were sitting. At the door he turned. "I'm sorry if I gave you guys a hard time."

CHAPTER THIRTY-NINE

"It's so tempting."

"Mmm?" She didn't even break off from kissing his stomach.

"I just want to test it."

"Me too." Her mouth continued its odyssey.

"Put it in water and see if this arm heals any quicker." Now Catalina did stop and looked up in frustration. "Not to stop the pain. I need to be sure it's not just a worthless piece of junk now that it's away from the island. I mean, it's not helping me as things stand and it didn't do the old man much good as he lay—" He broke off. It wasn't an image he was comfortable with yet.

Catalina propped herself on her elbow. "Well, you daren't risk it. Dirk doesn't know you've got it and I can imagine his response if he comes back to find your wound healed – or rather, I can't."

Pete looked at the bandage. "Certainly feels better more quickly than I would have expected. I wonder if that's simply because I've handled the k'ib."

"Well, just keep it to yourself. It gives you a motive for killing the team – that's what men do for such a prize."

"Men?" He looked down the bed at her and then reached across and picked up the k'ib. Both of them looked at it, transfixed for the moment. "There's something about it, isn't there?" He weighed it in his hand. "Y'know, I can't shake the feeling that it's not of this earth. After all we've been through these last few days, I wouldn't be surprised if travellers from some distant, dying world crossed the universe seeking a planet with water where the k'ib could live again, and they with it." He placed her hand on the cold metal. "Don't you feel it's as ancient as time."

He gave a little intake of breath. "I wonder if I have drowned the last being that understood its power."

Catalina shrugged. He knew she wanted to get her hands back onto something different and did not share his growing fascination – at least not with some inanimate object! "Well, I'm sure it'll remain an enigma."

Placing the k'ib again on the table, he sat up, not liking the mix of condescension and ennui in her voice. "Hey, I might give the impression of being a waster, but I'm not unintelligent. Jane Sutch would never have fallen for me if I was." The flash of annoyance in Catalina's eyes pleased him. "Okay, I know the attraction of opposites played a part too. And yes, my public-school education was cut short, and my father didn't hide his contempt for my lack of business nous too well, so I've developed a thick hide, but I'm not insensitive. You think I didn't see the looks of arrogant surprise when I ventured logical and sensible opinions on the island? Well, who's dead and who's alive? Who are the fuckwits now?"

As he lay back with a thump, he realised just how right he might be. If the k'ib had an intelligence, had it recognised in him a worthy successor; someone more suited for this new age than the old robed shaman, who had brought it so far, but was perhaps incapable of taking it further? He had seen things with a prescience and sensitivity which had surprised even him. And ideas had come to him *in extremis*. How else could he explain the clarity of thought that had enabled him to formulate plans with such speed and cunning in the midst of chaos and fear?

Strangest of all, where was this innate knowledge of the history of the k'ib coming from, and this peculiar certainty that he was right? For he knew that water was its memory and its blood and he remembered, where others had forgotten, that the Mayan civilisation was reputed to have died out because of drought. Had the high priest taken this treasure into hiding knowing the drought was coming?

"Hey." The hand on his cheek. "It's me, remember?" He had been staring at his prize on the bedside table, rather than at the one lying next to him. "You wanna feast your eyes on me instead?"

She peeled off the shirt she'd been wearing since they'd finished their first session of love-making – if that was the correct term for the ferocious release of tension and pent-up animal desire they had just shared. There was no doubt; whatever her flaws, the sight of this woman was also capable of triggering universal, ancient responses in man.

The two days since Dirk's absence might have been described as a chill-out period, but large chunks of if had been spent in sexual gratification. He told himself to enjoy her now. Who knew what their future held?

220

Her hands and mouth had wandered, prompting in him, at those very moments, the belief that he could never do without her, though he knew only emptiness would follow the temporary sating of his lust.

So it was again now. His body took over, driven by her demands and the intensity of her desires. In some way he welcomed the smothering of the cerebral by the carnal – a few minutes escape from the thoughts that plagued him; doubts about the way forward; mistrust of Dirk. Her body seemed to conjure endless ways to pleasure him. Was this what happened when you combined Latin American blood with an upbringing in a land that was ninety-five per cent wilderness? Or maybe he was just reading too much into it, and she was no more exotic than any cheap slut in the back of a lad's magazine, making him no less of a slave than any other porn aficionado.

He had a sudden need to control her; dominate this woman who had killed, and then demanded sex within sight of the corpses. Just for a moment, resuming his place in the driving seat mattered more than anything; perhaps because even now, he could not be sure he had ever occupied it. Or was this for Auld Lang Syne, now that he realised her intelligence and sensitivity might be subsumed by her need for sex? Was she no longer the way forward for the man he hoped he might be?

He put his healthy arm around her waist and flipped her onto her back. She gasped in a theatrical, cheap way and put up an immediate pretence of a struggle. He knew this game; fighting, but not so hard that she didn't welcome him with open legs.

And then they began; wave after wave, thrust after thrust. She clung to him, gasped and screamed and dug her nails into his back; scratching him – urging him with her words and her hips to fill her, never stopping, even if the graves threw forth their dead. Then his name was on her lips. She screamed it; shook and struggled beneath him, and he seemed to be driving her towards some volcanic eruption of a climax – except he looked at her face and saw her eyes staring in terror over his shoulder. She screamed, more than once. Pete turned.

Of the people he might have expected to see, Jim was not very high on the list. In that moment, as his guts turned to water, Pete knew everything was lost, but he could not even begin to imagine how. Was this a trick being played by the k'ib; some projection, some memory?

He must have looked as if he had seen a ghost, judging by Jim's words: "No, I'm not some figment of your fetid imagination." At the sound of the voice, Catalina started to whimper. "For God's sake, shut her up," demanded the Pulitzer Prize-winning phantom. As he spoke, there was a weary brutality in his features that did not sit easily. It had nothing to do with the newly acquired scars.

Despite his plight, Pete could not help but see the irony of it; it was how he had pictured Jim in his mind's eye as he described the psychotic who had shot the Professor. He looked like, well, someone who had done exactly what he appeared to have done, which was to escape from his own grave and come seeking vengeance.

Pete raised his hand to the girl, signalling for calm, though at that moment he understood how King Canute must have felt.

"He made me..." she cried, "... made me come with him!" She was sobbing now.

Pete looked at her in disgust, then turned away and shook his head. "Women."

"Don't worry." It was perhaps the most ineffectual statement Jim could have chosen, "You think I believe the bitch? I've observed for the last few minutes just how much you were forcing her to go down on you, ride you, etc etc."

Jim pushed himself away from the doorframe on which he was leaning, and Pete saw now how, only with difficulty could he put any weight on his left leg. Then, as he produced a pair of crutches from the hallway, he beckoned. "Come through as soon as you're... dressed. I was going to say decent, but—" Now he grinned. It was an expression devoid of humour. "There's someone in the lounge I think you should meet."

CHAPTER FORTY

A hailstorm of thoughts and images – thousands, millions of them – came at Pete, driven by the wind, and he was powerless to do anything other than weather them. Amongst them were, or course, the possibility of escape, and regret that he had thrown away his weapons. Yet, in the end, he was intrigued. Besides, he assumed they had allowed for the chance of him trying to get away and posted some sort of watch. Pulling on trousers and a top, he invited Catalina to leave her trance and do the same. He remembered to pick up the k'ib and then led the shaking girl through into the lounge.

That she collapsed into his arms was not surprising; even he felt his legs shimmy, at the sight of the Professor, sitting in a chair by the window.

Sutch pointed towards two empty armchairs. Pete carried Catalina across and, without words, they sat down. He did not bother asking any questions, knowing an explanation would follow, as surely as life, it seemed, followed death.

Jim sat near the Professor, and spoke first. "Almost a perfect crime, but let me tell you something about that thing," – here he pointed to the k'ib – "water—"

"...gives it life." Pete's interruption was laconic. He might have been on the back foot, but he was not going to let these smug bastards get one over on him. Jim's ironic smile told him that he had surprised them again. "Believe it or not, I listened along with everyone else to Tariq's journal."

"I guess we all underestimated you." The photographer matched his terse tone. "Rest assured, that won't be happening again. A pity for you, you didn't pay more attention to that." Jim's eyes turned towards the window and the past. "Your own greed outdid you. You see, if you hadn't taken it from its altar, then maybe the bogeyman might have torn me limb from limb in the temple. Instead, he retreated; lived to fight another day – to find his Precious, you might say. And I lived. Killing me took second place to his need to stay alive. Also, if you hadn't taken the k'ib from the temple, the Professor wouldn't be alive now." Pete frowned, unable to work out why, but Jim continued. "Your first explosion wrecked only part of the inner sanctum, but it extinguished the torches and I was left in blackness. I crawled blind, knowing a second explosion was coming, and put my hands on a large slab of stone that was probably the remains of the altar; it seemed the bottom of that block of stone survived. The next blast destroyed – as poor Cobus intended, unfortunately – the staircase up to the tunnel entrance and brought down some of the entrance itself, blocking it from my end. But still, I could hear." He turned back and looked directly at Pete, blank fury in his eyes. "Gunshots, as you fled. You sacrificed that young guy to save your neck."

"And you know that how?" Pete stayed cool despite how he felt. "You're fishing."

Jim ignored him. "The third explosion, the one planned to block the other end of the labyrinth, succeeded, I assume. Then I heard Cobus again. Distant, somewhere in the darkness of the tunnels. He was crying for help. Screaming. And I couldn't do anything, with my ruined knee and still dazed from the explosion. His voice was faint, but still, I could hear too much. And then, those who weren't killed in the explosions must have come back to him. Trapped in the tunnel, they vented their fury on our screaming friend. I swear I could hear his flesh being torn." Jim squeezed his eyes shut for a moment and then re-opened them. "But no, that must have just been my terrible imagination; an automatic response to hearing tortured cries once more. Some things can't ever be closed out. The sound of a machete slicing time and again into innocent flesh. The cries of hurt and betrayal." He looked at Pete. "If the Tutsis can forgive the Hutu's, I could forgive you your anger at what I did, but I'll never forgive what you did to Cobus; what you left him to."

The two men stared at each other for a long time, at opposite ends of another dark tunnel from which they had both just emerged. Pete broke the silence. "Guess you'll be sticking to photographing weddings from now on."

"And you." It was the Professor's voice, quiet lest his rage consume him. He was looking at Catalina, but she most certainly wasn't looking at him. She stared down at her hands, as she had from the moment she'd seen Sutch, sitting, accusing, like Banquo's ghost. "My daughter trusted you. Singled you out, held you in high regard, and how do you repay her?"

Catalina made to reply, but Pete lifted his hand. "Say nothing. What proof do they have? Eh?" He looked at Jim. "Oh, I know I said in the temple that I'd killed her, but it was simply to torture you; rub rock salt into the wound, as it were."

The Professor went to rise from his seat. "Monstrous!" he spat. But even before Jim's restraining hand was on him, he had collapsed again, putting his hand to the left side of his chest, his strength gone for the moment.

Jim continued: "Well, I guess I crept from your torture chamber. You see, the stream continued to run over the altar after the explosion, and as I lay there in agony, my throat closing with dust and Cobus' screams still tearing at my senses, I heard the water and followed its sound. I drank, and then, incredible to relate, felt a lessening of the pain. Then it seemed that the knee you smashed started to mend. Not perfectly – I'll need surgery – but enough that, after a few minutes, I could stagger in the general direction of the tunnels on the lower level. There was faint light from them, which turned out to be daylight – distant, but visible in the intense darkness. And it seemed the water was also helping my night vision. I could see well enough to spot my rucksack lying in the rocks. The water bottle was inside, and intact as ever. I filled it and made my way out.

"I followed the light and found the outside world. The tunnel opened out at the base of the cliffs and there was a precarious, narrow path just above the pounding waves. Incredibly, I saw the dark man, miles ahead of me on the path, but unmistakably him. I forget how many hours I spent on that narrow ledge, battered by the wind, just one slip away from being smashed against the cliff-face; my legs healing, but still with a mind of their own.

"At last, I made it round the headland, away from the path, too exhausted to care about the dark man or anything else. I assume I collapsed and slept like the dead.

"But my worst moment was waking. In the distance I could just about hear a plane. I looked for it, thought I could make out a dot in the distance. I guess it was Dirk homing in on your signal. After I'd waved frantically, shouted, and the plane had disappeared, I felt like the only man at the bottom of the world." He looked across at the Professor. "I didn't know that a mile and a half away was another man burying his daughter and feeling exactly the same.

"I think I spent most of the next two days in a state of delirium – hungry, weak, in pain still and unsure whether any of the priests were still alive. I thought the sound of the plane returning was part of a feverish dream. That was when I remembered the waterproof matches in my rucksack and managed to build a fire. I thank God the Professor and Dirk saw the smoke."

Jim lapsed into silence.

"You were dead, I know you were." Pete addressed the Professor, as if Jim's words hadn't registered with him.

Sutch had recovered and spoke again, first to himself. "Witness to my own death." He looked up. "The ironic part is, as Jim pointed out, the same fact you discovered for yourself is what kept both Jim and me alive. You see, when you shot me, I was still clutching the k'ib, and my other hand must have rested in the very edge of the pool. I can only think that I acted as a conductor between it and the water, just before the last of my life could drain from me." He paused. "In so many ways I wish it had... just drained away."

The Professor pointed at the k'ib before pushing on: "That thing may derive its power from water, but it seems to return it tenfold – a hundredfold – and the touch of that power on my hand kept me alive after you departed – just. It might be better to say it stopped me from dying. I was indeed on the point of death, and my recovery was slow. At last strength returned, and my wounds started some sort of healing process, that continues now, albeit at its own pace because I am old." He put his hand to his head. "It was too late, of course, for my darling Jane."

"Yes, how come she's still dead?" Pete knew the answer well enough but took pleasure in the brutal phrasing and intonation of his comment. Nothing good could possibly come from this situation, so he figured he might as well go down with guns blazing. These men who had treated him with disdain were at last getting what was coming to them.

"You bastard!" Jim was in the process of getting out of his chair and it was his turn to grimace in pain; the Professor's turn to raise a restraining hand. The latter spoke, addressing his comments to Pete.

"You know well enough it cannot restore life where there is none, and I know enough about dead bodies to know that Jane died from a broken neck. I also know enough about people to recognise genuine surprise when I see it. You didn't expect to find her dead." Now Sutch glared at Catalina. "But you... what hellhole did you spring from?"

The girl just sat, ashen-faced and withdrawn. All fight, all passion, seemed to have drained from her at the sight of the Professor.

"Nice. Well, thanks for sharing that," said Pete, "but I'm afraid I've got to be going now."

Jim looked at him and shook his head. "You're something else. And you're going nowhere. What you will be doing is facing up to what you did."

Pete perched on the edge of his seat and rested his elbows on his knees. "And what exactly did I do? A woman's dead; there's no witness to any crime. Another man claims a young female student shot him; again, there's no witness to any crime. Nor is there a victim, if your rapidly healing wound is anything to go by. A young Afrikaner with an attitude goes trying to steal some artefact from its rightful owners and gets ripped apart. Was he shot? There's no body to check. Again, no witness. And you? You fuck my wife, so I bust your kneecap. Again, no witness, but possibly it's an understandable reaction – a *crime passionnel.* How's all of this going to stand up in a court of law? They'd be more likely to believe that you're still alive because you've discovered the secret to eternal youth." They just looked at Pete, who pointed to Catalina. "Even if she pleads guilty to anything, that's up to her. She's not seen me do anything that she can swear to on oath. Sorry guys, I'm outta here."

He got up, turned, and stopped in his tracks when he saw the barrel of a gun pointing at him. Ah, that was one little item he had overlooked in all the excitement of seeing dead people – where was Dirk?

Jim smiled. "You see, it wasn't just you we were 'sharing' with. We've not had a chance till now to tell Dirk everything that transpired. To be honest – though I doubt if you know what that word means – he never really believed you. He tells me your explanation of what happened was all a bit too slick for him. That and the she-devil's transformation from the strong, persuasive woman he picked up from the ocean to the little mouse who let you do all the talking, as if by pre-arrangement."

The Aussie, who'd been standing out of sight in the kitchen behind Pete, motioned with the gun. "Siddown again, mate. Who said anything about a court of law?"

CHAPTER FORTY-ONE

OVER THE SOUTHERN OCEAN, LATE AFTERNOON – ONE DAY LATER

Dirk had pulled a few strings, and the plane, with its brace of unwilling passengers, plus a couple of steroid-enhanced cabin crew to ensure their in-flight comfort, had been able to take off in the early hours of the morning, avoiding any prying eyes.

Jim's mood wasn't helped by the Professor's decision just before boarding:

"I've decided I'm not coming."

"I understand."

"With all respect, I don't think you do. I want justice for my daughter," he squeezed the bridge of his nose in despair, "but can I be sure that this act wouldn't be more about revenge? I'm afraid I don't have the necessary heart of stone for dispensing Old Testament retribution; an eye for an eye."

"And that's not what we're doing. I thought we agreed this was a suitable compromise."

Sutch put a hand on Jim's shoulder. "Nevertheless, I'll stay away. Some wounds still ache; some will never heal."

Jim could understand though. The old man had been through enough and he doubted he ever wanted to see the Scorpion Archipelago again. Nor did Jim.

Now he looked at their two passengers. No ropes or other restraints had been necessary. When Dirk had explained that their choice was to come quietly or in body bags, they had believed him. Besides, the girl could have changed her name from Catalina to Catatonic now. Jim almost felt pity for her. Her love for Pete – or was it purely desire? – had drawn her too close to the flame. But still, cold-blooded murder – twice – could not be dismissed as a crime of passion. He looked at her beauty, corrupted beyond repair in his eyes; such a waste.

"I can guess where we're going." It was Pete. "And why. You're going to execute us on the spot of our alleged crimes."

One of the heavies looked at Jim. The latter just shook his head and the man settled back in his seat.

Then Dirk spoke from the front: "Think of it as a magical mystery tour. My bet would be, you wouldn't guess in a million years what's happening. Having said that, when I tell yah you might *have* a million years, it's probably a big enough clue." He looked out of the window. "Won't be long now."

They all followed his eyes and saw the two fangs of rock that marked the mariner's gateway to the archipelago.

"So, you're just going to leave us there?" At last, there was a touch of fear in Pete's voice; even he could not hide it. This departure from his hitherto defiant tone seemed to penetrate the subconscious world into which Catalina had retreated, as if his confidence was her shell, now breached.

"No!" She looked around in desperation. "No!"

Pete grabbed her arms before she started to scream and Jim recognised in that action that he didn't need her panicking now. None of them did. It was never easy when a beautiful woman was involved, not even one who was as guilty as hell. Then the former son-in-law of Professor Edward Sutch turned to him. "So, you've set yourselves up as judge and jury, and you're prepared to condemn us to this."

"Look at it this way," Jim tried not to show the discomfort the words had caused, "once we've done this, we're done with you. If you manage to escape, that's your business. We're giving you life where maybe you don't deserve it. And don't you talk about dispensing justice. You set yourself up as executioners. I think you're getting off pretty lightly, compared with what you did to Cobus; the death you condemned him to. But as I said, for what it's worth, I forgive you for what you did to me. I wasn't blameless."

Dirk interjected: "Yeah, and who knows, in a couple of years' time maybe there'll be some polar expedition that chugs past and sees your signal fire – if you survive the darkness of the winter." He looked at Jim, who in turn looked away.

Catalina was shaking; on the verge of hysteria. Pete could not blame her. He held her, as much for his own comfort as hers. The full impact of their terrible sentence was starting to hit home and though he refused to show it, he was panicking. Surviving alone in that place, on the island of the dead, with only an insane woman for company, was ordeal enough, but he hadn't thought about the permanent night of the winters that far south. There was a further, appalling, ironic twist. Would he be able to allow himself simply to die? Man clings to life. Would he be able to resist the urge to drink from the pool by the waterfall? It was the only supply of fresh water he knew of on the island, so he would have no choice. With the chances of escape more or less zero, he saw now what had been meant by Dirk's comment about the million years.

When Catalina pushed away from Pete with force, it came as a surprise to him. But her words came as a shock to them all.

"Men." She paused, allowing the full contempt with which she uttered that word to sink home, though she seemed to be talking to herself. "Young or old – they promise you dreams you'll never have; worlds you'll never visit. But such is their dominant hold on the one we have that you end up believing theirs is the way, and violence is the path." She looked now straight at Pete. "God knows what journey I thought you were taking me on, but only the devil knows why I wanted to go and where it's leading me. But know this, all of you; the Scorpion Archipelago is not where my story will end. There'll be a sting in the scorpion's tail, I swear it." She looked at the floor now, finished. Her star had flared before it died.

As one, the men shivered, though whether through some atavistic, primeval fear of witches and vengeful she-goddesses, or because they were witnessing the breakdown of a once intelligent mind, they could not be sure.

Pete was the first to break the spell. "Nice try, Catty. Blame the men and shed a few crocodile tears. But you're wasting your time. Rather appropriately, we're in a kangaroo court with only one outcome. Let's get one thing straight. I didn't want you to kill Jane, and I didn't need you to kill the Professor. My crime was reaching for you when I had no right to. I lit the match, but you lit the fuse. I did what I did out of frustration and anger, but it was wrong, I guess, in the greater scheme of things. You, on the other hand, killed cold-bloodedly; two people who'd never harmed you in any way."

Catalina brushed a strand of hair from her face and said nothing. But Jim saw the look she gave Pete from under her hooded eyes. It was one he neither wanted to interpret nor remember. He, too, felt the need to speak:

"So that would be cold-blooded as opposed to what; the way you left me to die; the way you shot Cobus and did the same to him?" He received no answer.

"Hate to interrupt the philosophising back there," Dirk's dry Aussie tone called them from the cockpit, "but you two'd better put on those parachutes."

Pete's brow furrowed. "What do you mean?"

"I mean I'm certainly not landing to drop you off. You've got ten minutes, I reckon, if you want to hit land."

Catalina pushed back in her seat: "I'm not putting on a parachute – you'll have to throw me out, you heartless bastards!"

"We're bastards?" Dirk glanced back over his shoulder at the girl. "That's rich."

"What right do you have?"

"Hah! You tried to kill a man who was helping you to make something of your life."

"His daughter wasn't exactly without blemish, was she?"

"Nothing punishable by death as far as I'm aware." Dirk gave a look and turned back to the front. His face had been an open book and its story brooked no ambiguity. "Now shut the fuck up and put on your parachute, because believe me, if I have to throw you out without it, I will."

Pete got out of his seat and looked at Catalina. "C'mon, the bastards mean business. It's better we take our chances together; live to fight another day, even if it's only with each other." He took one of the parachutes and held it towards her despite her disengaged state. At last she looked at him and took the 'chute from his hand.

Jim had been shifting uncomfortably in his seat as the argument he'd started raged on either side of him. Casting the first vengeful stone did not sit well with him, despite all that had happened, because he was not without sin. And now Catalina, whose behaviour was having an unnerving effect, seemed to read his mind. She pointed to him. "You – you've seen the horrors of the genocide in Rwanda." Her voice started to tremble. "And you've seen how, even there, people extend the hand of forgiveness and reconciliation. They can forgive; why can't you?"

He was at a loss for an answer. She had thrown him now. He couldn't argue with her logic. The bright, if benighted mind was still there after all, an unexpected vein of that most precious metal – wisdom – running through it. Still, it might have been fool's gold.

Perhaps sensing his discomfort, a weakening of resolve, Dirk looked round from the cockpit and signalled to the two heavies. "Guys."

Jim turned away as they moved in and stared ahead towards the archipelago. All was not well in his world. There was nothing from Pete.

Jim had noticed how he had, if not accepted his fate, at least registered the futility of resistance. But the girl, whether her intention or not, had made this more complex than he had expected. He wanted it over soon.

The door at the back of the plane was opened. Catalina started to scream and it went through Jim like the sound of nails down a blackboard, despite the roar of the engines. He could not watch but heard the changing timbre of the pleas as she struggled. At one point it sounded like she had been forced down on the floor, face first. The screams lost their strength and became sobs. For a moment he was indeed back in Rwanda, watching from a hiding place as militiamen brutalised... no, he had to stop punishing himself. This was very different.

Wasn't it?

He put his head in his hands.

Then, as the plane filled with the roaring chill, as the void raced past the open door, the sobs turned to screams again. It reached the point where Jim could take no more, and just as he was about to turn and call an end to the madness... silence. He sank back in his seat and took a cautious sidelong glance at Dirk. Neither man spoke for some time, both understanding during those moments why the Professor had chosen not to come.

CHAPTER FORTY-TWO

PERTH, WESTERN AUSTRALIA

He sat in the wicker chair by the bay window, a ghost of steam rising from the coffee mug at his side, and looked out towards the harbour, where his spiritual home, the sea, flickered in a million places. A long way over the horizon lay a kingdom that he, alone of men, had discovered after years of seeking and dreaming. He should have been so happy – instead he was numb through a combination of painkillers and the mind's own anodyne. It would kick in soon enough – despair hovered above him like a guillotine blade. Already he could hear the first creaking of its imminent descent and the sound of the executioner's approaching footsteps as he allowed himself the first dangerous thoughts – the what-ifs.

They were almost as many as the glass shard reflections of the sun on the sea and he squeezed his eyes tight to repel them. In doing so he returned himself to the darkness, where the *what-actually-is* thoughts lived; the reality that he would have to face; the one in which his naivety had brought so much destruction; the one that would find its true mirror in the face of his darling Candice when she landed today as planned in Hobart, to be told the dreadful news.

He had decided to leave Jane's body on the island, at least for now. It was not a symbolic gesture. There would have to be an official investigation. Also, he had not been able to face the thought of disinterring her so soon after the trauma of putting her in the ground. Nor could he stomach the image of Candice standing by the stark wooden coffin just yet. He hoped she would understand. They could decide together what would be most fitting for their daughter; would she have wanted to come back to Britain, or would the thought of being buried at the scene of one of her greatest discoveries have appealed to her?

He would hope for a sign.

Unable, even at the end – and to his utter disgust – to let go of his dream, a part of him had been tempted to fill the amphora from the pool before he had left. He looked across at it, still sitting in the bespoke crate he had made for it. The jug reminded him of the early days, when its image in his memory was all he had to hold onto. For a few moments before Dirk had come to rescue him, he had clung to something else; to the hope that, if he and Candice drank of the water and lived long enough, then time would heal the wounds and they could live again; start another life. But who had he been fooling? He would always be an old man, bereft of a daughter. And she had not even lived a full life. Why should he be granted more than one? Besides, how much more destruction would he wreak if he lived forever? He had failed with the life he was given. That was why he decided not to bring back any of the water with him after all, and for once his judgement had been correct. Better to leave things alone.

It soon became clear, his memories would not grant him the same mercy. He heard his heartbeat and remembered.

***

THE SCORPION ARCHIPELAGO, JUST DAYS BEFORE

He feels it trembling in his fingertips. Something has penetrated his subconscious – some sound – but he has no recollection of it. Now there's the muffled murmur of waves and the warmth of sunlight; just one shaft that's fought its way through the canopy of trees and beats on the back of his neck. Slowly, he comes round. His body is awakening bit by ageing bit to the purity of sensation. He feels like he could stay this way forever, though he does not yet appreciate the irony of that thought.

Something's nagging at him, urging him to stand. Now he becomes aware that his hand is wet and he twists his head to see his outstretched fingers partially submerged in the very edge of a pool. It all starts to come back to him, and it is as if the water level has risen suddenly to fill his lungs with a cold, choking sadness. Yet he cannot dismiss the wonder of still being alive, despite the growing sense of horror that makes him resist looking into the pool for now.

He tries to push himself up and a band of pain crushes his chest. Looking down he can see his blood-soaked shirt. At last, he is able to stand. The terrible sight in the pool is unavoidable now and drives him to his knees again. Then he forces himself up, out of duty to her, and begins the task no parent should have to undertake; retrieving the body of his child. He wades into the water, hooks his arms under her, and the deadweight, combined with the heaviness of his heart, drags him down at first. Yet there is no denying, as he stands in the water, a sudden surge of strength that seems to permeate his body. The wounds also seem to ache less. He finds himself able to lift her and carries her out in his arms, his darling girl, before placing her with tenderness on the ground. He looks at his hands and the water in turn. Something has happened here. Water is memory, and he remembers that he was clutching the k'ib when he was shot. Has it fallen into the pool? For a second he harbours the absurd idea of looking for it, but then thinks of the evil that his dreams and wishes have unleashed. Who knows if that mystery of antiquity has been at the centre of everything? Best to do what he should have done from the beginning and leave it alone. Besides, its hold on Pete and his desire for it had already been evident, so he is not likely to have left it behind.

More important – he has to take care of his beloved Jane.

He hears sudden gunshots, but who is left alive to kill? He knows now with certainty that Cobus and Jim must be dead, killed by Pete over on Temple Island – Robbie too, probably. So, who is shooting at whom? He contemplates hiding but then realises that he would rather be dead too. Besides, they must assume he is; that latter-day Bonnie and Clyde.

His thoughts turn to Candice but that brings no consolation. After all, he would have to break to her the news of where his folly has brought them. He wonders if she will ever find out what happened to him and if he will ever see her again.

He sits for a while, cradling Jane's body. The water did not save her. Water is memory. He remembers her sitting on his lap in his study, but then struggles to recall the previous time she had sat there. Yet he cannot afford to start questioning now the way they had led their lives. He had been proud of her, and she of him – what does pride come before? At last, helped by his new-found strength, he manages to put her over his shoulder and carry her down to the remains of the camp. He is not prepared to bury her here, in the forest of the dead, more food for the roots of that fecund yet sick place. He will lay her to rest down by the waterfront, somewhere he can watch over her and where the sea can come to pay its respects.

He has no idea whether they will ever leave this place.

He finds a pickaxe in the equipment boxes and starts to dig what will be a shallow grave. Though he cannot know it for sure, he feels positive that he will be left alone now and that the killers have gone.

He has looked around and can see no-one. They must have a plan for returning to civilisation, and that plan must involve Dirk. The missing satellite telephone would appear to confirm that. Despite the nihilism that suffuses his emotions at this moment, he cannot avoid the chill that the thought of isolation and abandonment brings as it comes ashore with the breeze. As soon as he has buried his daughter he will try to light a fire, for warmth and as a signal. He may be dreading speaking to Candice, he may rather wish that he were dead, but man still clings to life and light.

And then, as he starts to dig, something catches the corner of his eye and he turns. Astonishing! A bedraggled figure is dragging itself exhausted through the surf. He races forward and then stops, horrified and fascinated in equal measures, as the figure pushes itself to its knees. His mind is taken back to the dying man whom Jim and the others brought back from Temple Island. Not that this man is as emaciated and gaunt, but he bears a similar haunted look in his eyes. There the similarity ends. He does not exude the same air of desperation, or if he does there is a ferocity underlying it – a determination in his sharp, cruel features. The face is truly terrible to behold. It does indeed bear the look of someone who has lived forever in the darkness and forgotten how not to hate. He believes he understands who this man might be and why he is here. It seems the nightmare will never end.

Nevertheless, he feels a certain pity for this creature. Perhaps he should fear him, but he is beyond that. He moves forward and extends a hand to the enervated man, who manages to both look ashamed and exude immense pride, retaining something haughty in his demeanour as he gets to his feet unassisted. The socketed orbs that are his eyes look beyond Sutch towards the forest. That one glance speaks volumes.

The Professor gives a slight bow and gestures to the priest to follow him. For possibly the first time in thousands of years, the priest does as he is bidden.

As they pass Jane's body the priest stops. What he is thinking can only be guessed at, but at last they move on.

Their progress up through the forest is slow. The priest seems ill at ease. If, as Sutch's team had surmised, the cult of human sacrifice had been strong amongst these people, it may be that he fears the vengeance of the spirits. As they near the pool and the sound of the little waterfall reaches their ears, the priest's pace quickens and his dreadful face appears to be contorting itself into something approximating a smile – another old man lost in the wonder of desperation. At the water's edge he scoops several greedy handfuls and drinks. It is like some warped experiment in osmosis, watching him recover, and the rehydration of his spirits is almost visible. The dust of ages is washed away like a flash flood in a desert. However, nothing can make the priest's features more agreeable; centuries of corrupt thoughts have shaped them and only the winds of time could ever erode their cruelty. He wipes water on his face and neck, on his arms, and makes gestures that appear to be the observance of some ancient ritual. When he turns and looks at Sutch, the Professor is surprised to see that although the despotic malice he expected is still there, some vestigial light of humanity seems to be flickering in the priest's eyes. Sutch stoops and draws in the earth with his finger; it is the shape of the k'ib as best he can remember it. He points to it and then out to sea. The priest nods and walks past him, heading back towards the camp.

Sutch is about to follow him when he stops and stares amazed at the ground. Despite everything that has passed, the scientist in him is not completely interred, and he experiences a 'Eureka!' moment. The shape he has drawn is more or less the same as the one symbol on the amphora that rebuffed all of Jane's attempts at translation. It was clearly this people's written representation of home; yet the commoners never knew of the k'ib. It is a conundrum that will never be solved. Even as he makes a mental note to tell Jane, the reality of now rises from his stomach and fills his throat with despair.

At this point a distant humming reaches the Professor's ears and he hurries past the priest, running the quarter mile or so back to the shore. He reaches for a pair of field glasses and looks into the distance. At last, he spots it – Dirk's plane, but it appears to be heading west, away from the archipelago. In despair he realises that he has not lit a fire, nor does he have time to light a flare, and the noise of the plane is fading. He is desolate. Whatever plan those two hatched for their escape appears to have succeeded.

Then a bony but powerful hand rests on his shoulder. As he looks at it, it turns and beckons him. He follows the priest, who leads him to Jane's body. Sutch looks on in amazement as the ancient, tyrannical shaman lifts the pickaxe and starts to attack the soil at the margin of the beach.

Together they set about the task of burying his daughter.

The day has advanced. Although it is early summer, in the Southern Ocean that does not herald the start of balmy days. With Jane interred, they build a fire. The presence of each other means that they are not quite, yet, the loneliest people in that vast, unforgiving sea. Despite the circumstances, it affords Sutch some pleasure to observe the priest, whose name, as a result of their limited communication, he believes to be Kazkar, as he encounters for the first time the wonders of camping stoves and tinned food. It is perhaps one of the starkest ironies of the Professor's life to be sitting with this fearsome man and welcome his company. He notices how the priest looks at the stars, as if it is the first time in centuries. A wave of pity washes over Sutch. He knows what it means to have been enslaved, but his sentence had lasted only forty years. He also knows how it feels to lose something precious. They break bread together that evening, like fugitives yet to come to terms with the agoraphobia of their freedom, and like partners in grief.

It is late afternoon two days later when the humming returns. The two men stand. They seem to have settled into an agreeable silence, though the Professor senses that, if either of them chose to speak it would be the priest.

Such is the enormity of the emptiness in these parts, a vastness that dwarfs the hardy dust of humanity that has settled this far south, that he knows this plane must be coming for him, and he presumes the priest knows it too. Something has happened. The plans of those miserable wretches have gone wrong somehow. As the plane draws nearer, and he recognises it as Dirk's Cessna, he turns towards the priest. With as appropriate a gesture as he can make, he invites Kazkar to make a trip with him into the twentieth century. Even as he does so, he ponders the magnitude of that step, both for the priest and for the scientific community of the modern era. That plane would hold a unique place in history, the first time-machine, if it brought this old shaman into the future.

Sutch suspects that fear has always been an alien emotion for Kazkar till this point. Now he sees it register on those harsh features. The plane draws nearer, grows louder, the sound of its engines...

***

... dragged him back from his memories and caused his mind to pitch forward hundreds of miles to a desolate place he knew for a brief time: to what would be happening there now. A part of him – a part of which he was ashamed – believed there had to be punishment for the sins and crimes committed, but that did not sit comfortably with him. After all, a lot depended on one's definition of sin. He had led an expedition, which had stolen an artefact from a people who, right or wrong, followed the cult of human sacrifice. The high priest of that people had spared his life. Who was he, Edward Sutch, to decree that someone should die? For it did not matter how much they dressed it up; death was what lay ahead for Catalina and Pete. If not from exposure or starvation then... He squeezed his eyes shut for a moment, before rising from his chair and taking shaky steps across to the windows, allowing a summer's warmth, containing the sounds of that day, to dominate his senses.

CHAPTER FORTY-THREE

OVER THE SCORPION ARCHIPELAGO, NOVEMBER 5TH, LATE AFTERNOON

When Dirk bellowed his instructions about the parachutes down the plane, revealing the determination of the judge to pass sentence, Pete decided to weigh up his options. It appeared to be a rather lop-sided set of scales. The two heavies stepped forward to enforce the instructions. One of them made a point of discouraging any resistance by pulling back his jacket to reveal a Walther PPK. At the same time, Jim turned away to protect his troubled conscience, which made it obvious that they weren't bluffing. Pete wasn't used to that taste of fear so, at first, did not recognise the metallic tang in the back of his throat for what it was. They were going to be forced out of this plane. The bastards, Jim and Dirk, were turning their backs on it all; didn't even have the guts to face up to what they were doing. Just a quick push, and somewhere down below two people would be left with a catch-22 situation involving living or dying. At least he'd had the guts to enforce his own vengeance, and the devil took the hindmost.

Pete started to slip on the parachute, whereas Catalina sat frozen in hers, having made her last play. She looked terrified, so he could not help but admire the strength she had found to display and voice her fatalistic defiance. When she had taken the 'chute from him, she'd looked at him and something had passed between them, but he couldn't define it. It might have been a vestige of their old feelings for each other, but whatever it was, it had flitted away.

Now Pete's arm became entangled in the 'chute. He swore and tried to free it. One of the heavies went to draw his pistol. Pete had just known they would resort to weapons; they were the sort of muscle-bound numb-nuts who would rely on intimidation rather than any agility; who could bench-press three-fifty in the gym – a figure about ten times higher than their IQ. It was why he knew he could kill them if opportunity presented itself, which it had the moment Jim turned his back.

The first one came forward impatiently, still reaching for his gun, maybe with the intention of breaking Pete's arm as he forced it into the harness. He had been so easy to lure in, and the chop to his Adam's apple left him choking in relative silence on the floor. The time needed by the second gorilla to process this information was more than enough for Pete to knock him out too, with a kick to the temple.

Now he had to act fast. He opened the door, grabbed the man who was still struggling to breathe and, with the roar of the outside world drowning the noise, dragged him to the door and pitched him out. The other unconscious man soon followed, once Pete had helped himself to his gun. He glanced at the cockpit – they were still facing front, protecting their finer feelings and waiting for the dirty work to be finished. He knew they would not expect the door to be open for long.

Catalina, whose nerves were stretched to snapping point, had muffled a scream as each of the heavies took their impromptu sky-dive. Pete signalled for her to come forward, putting a finger to his lips and gesturing towards the cockpit. The comforting arm he placed around her shoulders coiled with the sudden swiftness of an anaconda, constricting her cries. He could have killed her, perhaps should have done for her disloyalty, but hell, she had been wonderful in the sack. With the speed and dexterity of someone quite used to operating in extreme conditions, plus knowing her martial arts skills might fight their way back through her terror, he hooked her parachute to the static line. His lips pressed against her thick black hair, the scent of which still inveigled in his loins. He kissed her head. "I'm sorry." She tried to twist round to look at him, but he resisted, not wanting to see into her eyes. *Who's salving their conscience now, Pete old boy?* As he threw her from the plane, it was about as emphatic as the ending of a relationship can be. He could see her 'chute was heading straight for the island. It seemed a suitable wild kingdom for that tempestuous princess.

Though she might not yet have been a lost soul, still there was something horrible and symbolic about her descent towards Hell; a slow drift down to the scene of her crimes, to a place devoid of humanity, peopled only by the souls of those she had killed and the memories of the sins she had committed; in possession of just enough remnants of her sanity for her to suffer. No amount of returning to nature in the vast wilderness of the Outback could have prepared her for the ordeal ahead.

And her mind was too young to withstand everything to which it had been subjected.

Then Pete shut the door and turned his attention to the cockpit. He had spent more than enough time in the company of Death. Although he could fly the plane himself, if he could avoid any more killing, he would.

***

Unbeknown to Catalina, she was echoing Pete's thoughts – would she have the strength to let herself die? She doubted it, and hoped that her mind would prove fragile, granting her the release of oblivion.

The ground drew nearer.

Oh God, oh God, what was she going to do? Would she be forever cursed with hope, burdened by the will to survive; the same will that prevented her from just shrugging off her parachute and falling to her death. Except what if she didn't die, but suffered some awful injury?

Was this thought the trigger for her screams, or had she been screaming from the moment she was thrown from the plane, discarded by the very man, the pursuit of whom had brought her to this terrible, desolate harbour, where she was doomed to wait for a ship that would never come?

The survival instinct had already taken over. She had jumped with a parachute before and used those skills now to bring herself down in the bay where she had taken her first real steps towards damnation.

However, it was still more luck than judgement that she landed in the surf just a skimmed stone away from the abandoned camp. She stood shivering and then turned to watch the Cessna disappear with teasing slowness – she wondered whether this was additional torture and they would circle back – against a blue sky inappropriate to the mood and circumstances. Again, she cursed hope, knowing that it would be sometime before she would stop looking to the horizon. But she had killed – not once, but twice. Irrespective of the powers of magic, she had broken the laws of the universe they all knew, which had broken again to defy her; reverse what she had done. Besides, it was Pete who had thrown her from the plane. He would kill the others, pitch them into the sea and fly to freedom. It would take more than wishful thinking to save her now; he wasn't coming back.

She wiped salt water from her face, uncertain where tears ended and sea began. At last, she turned and, looking like a drenched crane-fly, dragged her parachute out of the waves; she would need it to make some sort of tent. The last thing she wanted was to shelter within the ruins in the dead forest. She would set up camp here on the beach, light a fire, try to take some comfort from it and hope that she might be seen.

The curse of hope.

She shuffled through the remains of the camp, remembering how she had disturbed certain things at... his instructions. A motley selection of items remained – Dirk must have retrieved most of it when he rescued the Professor – but it was a reflection of how far her world had shrunk that she was almost overjoyed to find a sleeping bag, a stove, most of the tinned food, matches. As she moved near the ashes of the campfire, she thought the sea breeze carried with it some faint warmth and, putting her hands above the ashes, she could tell the fire had not been standing untended for long. Something tickled the back of her neck; perhaps the tip of a dagger of fear and suspicion.

She turned and saw him standing in the shade at the edge of the trees; His Grey Majesty, frightening to behold. He lifted an arm towards her, as he had done on the water when they had sunk his boat, and she felt the soft, irresistible touch of darkness against her cheek. Then he uttered something. The words did not pour into her ears, like the honeyed deceptions of a seducing devil; rather they were guttural, as if the very act of uttering them must have raked his throat. But his meaning was all too clear, as was the primal gleam in his eyes.

Catalina's last screams as a sane woman issued now from her, followed by her first as the deranged queen of a lost kingdom.

***

He had felt his fading strength building again the nearer he had come to his ancient prize, but then they had used their weapons of the future to sink his boat. For a few moments it had seemed he might still make it, but they had departed in their strange boat and, losing hope and strength, down into the water he had sunk. Above him on the surface he saw them leaving for their world.

But Kaz'khar had forgotten how to die, and long-buried instincts drove him to the surface again, where he had headed for the nearest shore, dragging himself through the waves. Without the gift he was doomed, and dreaded the avenging pains of two thousand years. The longer you lived beneath the wing of eternity, the higher you rose with it, but the fall would be deep and fearful.

And that was when he had seen the old man, the Elder of these people who had overcome his ancient might. As the old man had drawn near,

Kaz'khar could tell that he, too, had the gift surging through his veins, and there was no mistaking it in the power of the hand that extended towards him. The scent of the water had suffused the air. Kaz'khar had stared into the trees for its source; for his salvation. As if he had understood, the Elder had gestured for him to follow, and the scent had grown stronger; the ancient scent of memory of the life that was in the water.

And the old man had shared his gift, allowing Kaz'khar to slake a thirst that could never be denied except at the very end of all things. Strength had come to him again, but different from before. It had been strange and wondrous to feel how the water responded to the manner in which it was given. In centuries gone by, it had been a means of holding a civilisation captive, but that had meant the priesthood became a slave to it too, and to their way of life. Time had passed them by. Here, it was given as a beneficence.

That had marked a fresh start and the onset of an emotion for which the priest had no name, or at least had long forgotten. It flickered as the old man heard the distant sound of the metal bird, the flying ship. He had run down to the water's edge in time to see his people – for it was them – and with them his only hope of rescue, disappear into the distant sky. The night-time which held sway in Kaz'khar's soul and earned him the epithet of `Ak'ubal had given way for a moment to the glimmering of a feeble dawn. As one who had known the curse of isolation for longer than recorded history, he had recognised the old man's despair, though he could no longer feel it.

The days that followed had opened the high priest's eyes, which had grown accustomed only to the darkness of his kingdom, his thoughts and his deeds. It was not just the wonders of the new age – strange metal eggs containing food; meat with a thin, tough skin you could see through but had to cut away; fire that came from nothing – but also those of antiquity and eternity – stars; air, the ancient need to communicate, the smell of cooked meat. That and the burial of the old man's concubine had moved him enough to spare the invader's life. He gave a life where it was given.

Then, two moons later, the metal bird had returned and he could tell by the gesture that the old man – a strange term from one who was ancient beyond his own recall – was inviting him to step forward into this new time. But it would have been a step too far for all concerned – Kaz'khar and the world – so he had made a gesture of his own. He had swept his arm towards the sea and sky, towards the forest that contained the pool of life, all the things that he had rediscovered; his new-found kingdom. And the old man had nodded his understanding. He had signalled that Kaz'khar should retreat out of sight into the forest. There would be too much to explain.

Through the trees he had seen a man come ashore in a boat, reclaiming the camp and his Elder. When they had gone, Kaz'khar had re-emerged, carrying in his powerful arms the things the old man had insisted on leaving; the egg-food, meat, fire, the strange blanket like a warm shell. He had made it clear he did not want the tent. Kaz'khar would never again sleep without the sky above his head.

He had watched the bird disappear, his heart both heavy and alive...

... and it reappeared two moons later. He hid in the trees and watched in amazement as something floated down. Not something; someone. Could it be? Whatever gods he had once worshipped were to be thanked. It was a woman.

And what a specimen, with her black hair and olive skin! He observed her as she wandered into his camp. Surely this was a gift from the old man; a queen fit for Kaz'khar, High Priest. A woman able to bear a new line as he had pronounced just days before. Despite her strange garb, he saw the beauty of her voluptuous body. It was just as it had been when he had first defied the gods, taking the gift that was not his to take, to become as powerful in knowledge, as eternal as them. Here was his Eve, and she would bear men who would be gods. He felt the gift flowing – his body being aroused as it had not been in millennia. He stepped forward, saw the terror in her eyes – which was as it should be. "Welcome, I have been waiting."

CHAPTER FORTY-FOUR

OVER THE SCORPION ARCHIPELAGO, NOVEMBER 5TH, LATE AFTERNOON

"Just keep flying. I'll tell you when to land."

It had been worth, well, everything really, all the aggravation, just to see their faces. Jim had reached on reflex for his gun at the sound of the voice behind him, but had seen sense and handed it over.

"Do you really think you're going to get away with this?" Dirk's tight lips suggested he knew the answer.

"Um," Pete rubbed his chin in faux contemplation of the question, "yes – I think the odds have swung in my favour in the last few minutes. Considering I was up against two muscle-mutts, one deranged ex-lover, a guy I'd knee-capped and left for dead, who was armed and a bit pissed off with me, and a typical whinging convict with a chip on his shoulder against all things Pommie – me in particular – I think I've turned things around quite nicely."

"For God's sake!" The despair in Jim's tone told of how close to the edge he stood. "Okay, the two heavies I can understand. But to pitch her out?"

Pete's smile faded. "And what precisely were you about to do to her? Don't forget, it was my wife she killed. Not that it bothers me now. After all, Jane was soiled goods." He enjoyed watching Jim fight to control his anger. "Bet you wish you didn't have such a prissy conscience now; hadn't turned your back on me."

"Told yer we should have just killed him and pitched him out the door." Dirk's words contained no vindication.

"And you were right." Now Pete addressed Jim. "But I guess you, like me, had had enough of death. And because of that, I'm not going to kill you – *if* you do what I say." He turned the barrel of the gun towards Dirk. "Just bear this in mind; killing the two of you would be my easiest option. I can fly a plane. I could make you bring this down right now, dump your bodies and fly to a new life. But I'm only going to do two of the three."

"Meaning?" The hostages spoke together.

"You see that little island?" He pointed ahead towards the horizon. "You're going to take a short holiday there. Start taking her down."

"Fuck you," was the pilot's pithy response.

"If you're not careful, you'll be left with only *each other* to fuck... for a long time. And I doubt there are any doctors or hospitals down there, so don't make me shoot you in the arm or anything like that. Now I understand you're a wee bit annoyed, so I'm going to allow you that one moment of bravado." He pressed the barrel into Dirk's neck. "Take her down, dirt bag."

There were calm waters around the island at that moment and no rocks, a far cry from the Scorpion Archipelago. The plane taxied to a halt. Then Pete backed down the plane and beckoned the others to follow. He kept his gun trained on them at all times as he addressed them: "You're going to get the chance you never gave me. Pick up those supplies." The remnants of the expedition camp were still on the plane. "Go on, don't be shy; help yourselves. Tents, sleeping bags, food, stove, whatever." They did as they were instructed. "Now inflate that boat and load the stuff." Pete saw where his blood still stained the side of the inflatable.

When they were done, and Jim and Dirk sat in the boat, Pete stood in the doorway. "I think this makes us quits." Dirk opened his mouth to speak, but Jim raised his hand to stop him. "In a couple of days, or however long it takes me to feel confident that the dust has settled after my departure, I'll call the authorities and tell them where you are."

"Why would you let us live?" Jim's question appeared to have no angle to it.

Pete opened his arms and shrugged his shoulders. "That's the kind of guy I am. But maybe it appeals to the thrill-seeker in me to know that you might come a-hunting for me."

"Whaddya mean *might*?" Dirk's eyes were still blazing.

"Tell you what though, I'd keep a nice fire going if I were you – that hot anger of yours will be subdued by the cold soon enough. Also, just in case I can't one hundred per cent remember where this place is. I'm not sure it's got a name. Now enjoy your holiday. Better get paddling; I don't think I left any juice in it. As for me, the flying doctor has one more house-call to make."

"You leave the Professor alone."

"I hope you'll return me the same courtesy, though I doubt it. But don't worry, I'm just going to reclaim what's mine, and then hopefully move on to live a long, healthy life – a long, long, long healthy life. Toodle-oo."

With that he closed the door and hurried to the cockpit before they had any chance to try something clever with the wing flaps.

∗∗∗

As a door opens somewhere in Perth, a piece of paper flaps in the breeze. It stands on a table by a bay window, next to a half-finished cup of coffee, and weighted down with an object that looks like it is made of brass. A thick skin has formed on the coffee.

A hand reaches for and lifts the metal object, which almost glows as it reflects the early, oblique rays of the sun. The fingers curl around it, caress it, before replacing it and picking up the piece of paper. It seems to be a note, but turns out to be a poem, written in a shaky hand and with a name beneath. A voice whispers the words:

> *Take this kiss upon the brow!*
> *And, in parting from you now,*
> *Thus much let me avow —*
> *You are not wrong, who deem*
> *That my days have been a dream;*
> *Yet if hope has flown away*
> *In a night, or in a day,*
> *In a vision, or in none,*
> *Is it therefore the less gone?*
> *All that we see or seem*
> *Is but a dream within a dream.*
>
> *I stand amid the roar*
> *Of a surf-tormented shore,*
> *And I hold within my hand*
> *Grains of the golden sand —*
> *How few! yet how they creep*
> *Through my fingers to the deep,*
> *While I weep – while I weep!*
> *O God! Can I not grasp*

248

Them with a tighter clasp?
O God! can I not save
One from the pitiless wave?
Is all that we see or seem
But a dream within a dream?

Edgar Allen Poe

THE END

ABOUT THE AUTHOR

David Palin has an appetite for the dark and mysterious. Born in West London but now residing in Berkshire, he is intrigued by the things that hide, often in plain sight, in the shadows beyond the light of our everyday lives. From studying both English and German literature, he believes we are drawn to darker tales and imaginings.

David is always keen to encourage and support creativity in others. As well as editing and co-writing for various authors, he has run writers' workshops in as diverse places as Berkshire literary festivals, Winchester and the far north-west of Scotland!

All of this manifests in his work. Away from writing David enjoys sports, music, and the theatre — all of which have seemed like elements of a fantasy tale in our recent tough times.

Also from David Palin...

The Wife Before Last

As the world celebrates the fall of the Berlin wall three men, all ex-Stasi operatives, exploit the chaos and escape Germany. Thick as thieves the trio stick together; quietly reinventing themselves in the shadows of the British criminal underworld. Michael and Richard still live and breathe the violence that got them where they are, but Marcus is different.

Crafting a sinister double life, Marcus uses the internet to target wealthy and vulnerable women for his own financial gain. However when one of his scores goes wrong and the gang's money is on the line, Marcus goes into hiding knowing that his partners are out to get him.

From the hidden corners of the dark web to the vibrant cityscapes of Europe, *The Wife Before Last* is a high-stakes game of deception. Revenge may be best served cold, but survival demands staying off the menu.

LET THE GAME COMMENCE

Arthur Du Fuss, bitter, alone, and ignored by his neighbours, has two secrets: one dies with him when he commits suicide; the other is the vast wealth he amassed through the creation of a cult board game.

Now his erstwhile neighbours receive a post-mortem invitation to the offices of a charismatic City lawyer to play a final version of the game; the prize – Arthur's fortune. As they dice with the devil, the game first exposes the fragility of their relationships, and then tears them apart, with tragic and horrifying consequences. But Arthur, too, must pay for his revenge. The old man learns that outstanding debts can still be called in, even when you are dead.